The Johnson Family Chronicles

Changing Currents ~ Changing Tides

A Novel About A Small Town Family's Journey During World War II

Stan Cromlish

DEDICATION

This book has been a labor of love for the author and it is dedicated to every citizen of Belmont, North Carolina who ever served in the Armed Forces of the United States. The author thanks you for your service and sacrifice.

Table of Contents

Foreword

The United States was a divided nation in the years leading up to December, 1941. One side, led by Franklin Roosevelt, wanted the nation further involved in the war in Europe; and the other side, led by the America First movement (and some of the country's greatest heroes of the time Charles Lindbergh and Eddie Rickenbacker), believed the US should do everything in its power to stay out of Europe's troubles.

The Great War, and consequently The Treaty of Versailles, had left the European Continent reeling and destabilized. There was no Army of Occupation or Marshall plan to allow the devastated areas to slowly recover and they did not have the means to do so. The seeds of discontent were sown, and Adolf Hitler used those seeds to grow his Nazi Party.

Across the globe, Japan was using their "Greater East Asia Co-Prosperity Sphere" to promulgate a "self-sufficient bloc of Asian nations led by Japan, of course, to be free of Western powers". All of this grandiose wording meant imperialism. The island nation of Japan needed raw materials which other Asian nations had; and Japan was going to take them by force, if necessary. The United States was the only road block in this drive for an imperial Japanese empire.

December 7th changed everything. Once the sneak attack on Pearl Harbor occurred, all Americans were resolved to fight and win. Young men immediately began lining up at recruiting stations. Women ran blood drives and planted victory gardens. Children began collecting scrap metal for recycling. Everyone pulled together.

In this first book of the Johnson Family Chronicles series, Stan Cromlish has done a magnificent job of taking his readers into the lives of one American family which could resemble a million other American families. The series tells the story of the Johnson family from Montcross, North Carolina; but it could be the Smiths from Eureka, Missouri, or the Taylors from Augusta, Georgia. You are taken into the lives of this middle class family to see their struggles, because war changes everything. How do they get to work; how will they find manpower to accomplish tasks at work; what to do about school; and how do they cope with the separation from family members who enlisted to fight the long war ahead? I hope you will enjoy this book as much as I did.

John Bailey
Blowing Rock, North Carolina
February 25, 2017

Acknowledgments

The author would like to thank many people for their help and support during the writing of this book. First and Foremost, for all the help they give me on a daily basis, I would like to thank my parents, Dick and Sandra Cromlish. Without their support and love, this book would have just been an idea without voice. Thanks, Mom, for your editing and help getting the "story" just right. Dad, thank you for helping me out with the pilot training scenes and the airplane part questions I had. Even though we both have a pilot's license, you seem to remember more than I do about what it took to become a pilot back before GPS and easy navigation. Thanks for everything, I love you both very much.

Bobby Brown, the world's greatest cheerleader, you have helped keep me going when I despaired that this book was locked in some place on my internal hard drive that I could not access. Your words of wisdom and support have meant the world to me and I want to thank you for your undying loyalty and support of this project. Mrs. Gail Brown, your advice on the customs, ideals, and mores of the 1940's have helped me more than you realize. Thank you for your support and for keeping me on track. Thanks to both of you for all your help.

Rich Hoggren, my mentor and friend, your support and daily advice has helped me tremendously not only at work but in my daily life. Thank you for loaning me your last name for a character in this book and I hope you know how much I appreciate all you have done to help me move forward in my career. Thank you for your friendship.

A special thank you to Allen Millican for allowing me to use pictures from your collection. They have made my cover special and I appreciate your help with this project.

To everyone who has supported this project, thank you for your tidbits, words of wisdom, and other anecdotes that have helped in the writing of this book. I hope you the reader enjoy this book as much as I have enjoyed writing it. Thank you for your support.

Prologue

As I sit here trying to compile all of the World War II oral histories that I have accumulated over the years from the wonderful families of my hometown, Montcross, North Carolina, I am reminded of the fact that these families suffered and sacrificed just like those from other parts of the country. The oral history of the Johnson family is not unique, but it is a microcosm sample of what other families went through during the four years that America was engaged in the bloody conflict of World War II. I have promised Lillie Johnson, who so eloquently told me her family's story, that I would tell it honestly and completely. This is their story.

A Date Which Will Live in Infamy

● ● ● ● ● ● ● ● ● ● ● ● ● ● ● ● ● ● ●

It was a bright and sunny Sunday afternoon and the Johnson family had just returned home from the First Baptist Church where they had heard a sermon on the parable of the loaves and fishes by Reverend Kelton. Sunday lunch was always a formal affair with Mrs. Elva McCann, the family's negro cook and housekeeper, preparing a meal of fried chicken, mashed potatoes and gravy, green beans, and a family favorite, banana pudding, for dessert. Gathered around the large, formal dining room table for lunch are Raymond, Bessie, Jimmy, Elizabeth, Myra, and Lillie. The only family member missing this Sunday was Raymond's namesake and oldest son, Ray, Jr. He was away at school in Raleigh, North Carolina.

Raymond, Sr., patriarch of the Johnson family and the manager of the Montcross Rail Yard, said to his youngest son, Jimmy, "Ray should be home from State College next weekend. What are your plans?"

Jimmy replied, "Our Model-A needs some repairs and I was hoping Ray and I could pool our summer job money to make them. The hardest part will be to replace the radiator which leaks like a sieve. Can you help us with that?"

"Sure, Jimmy. That won't be a problem at all. Please, pass the mashed potatoes, Bessie."

As Bessie passed the mashed potatoes, she noticed ten-year-old Myra dawdling over her green beans, "Myra, if you don't eat your green beans, you won't get any dessert."

"Mommy! I don't like green beans!" Myra yelped.

"No green beans. No dessert." Bessie replied.

Myra, knowing it was fruitless to argue, ate her green beans because she did not want to miss the smooth and succulent banana pudding that Elva had made.

Sixteen-year-old Elizabeth asked, "Will Sara be coming home with Ray next weekend? I sure would like to see her again."

As the platter of chicken was passed around the table, Bessie served Lillie a chicken leg and said, "Yes, Sara will be accompanying Ray home on Saturday and will stay here for the entire week. I am looking forward to seeing her again."

"Do you think they will get married soon, Mom? After all they have been going together for over a year now." Elizabeth asked between bites of mashed potatoes.

"I would hope that Ray would finish school first before contemplating marriage. They need to establish themselves before embarking on anything like that. Your Dad had a good job at the Montcross Rail Yard and we went together for more than five years before we got married. I hope Ray and Sara will wait."

"Mommy, may I be excused?" Lillie, the youngest daughter and light-hearted comic of the family, asked before dessert had been served.

"Don't you want any banana pudding, Lillie? What are you going to go do?" Bessie asked, a little perplexed, since Lillie always loved banana pudding.

"I don't want any dessert, Mommy. My tummy doesn't feel good and I need to go to the bathroom."

"You may be excused. I'll be right up to check on you. Do you need any help?"

"No thanks, Mommy." Lillie left the table and went upstairs to the bedroom she shared with her older sister, Myra.

Bessie was concerned and said to no one in particular, "I sure hope Lillie hasn't caught the stomach bug that has been making the rounds this winter. Raymond, did you think she looked a little pale?"

"Yes," Raymond replied, "she did look a little pale to me and I certainly hope it's not the stomach bug. I think you might want to call Dr. Preslar and see if he would come check on her this afternoon."

"I think you're right. I'll call him as soon as we finish eating." Bessie replied.

After lunch, Bessie placed the call to Dr. Preslar's home and he told her that he would be by a little after two to check on Lillie. The rest of the family changed out of their church clothes and got ready to walk to their grandparents' home next door where they would listen to the Sunday afternoon CBS radio show, The Spirit of '41.

In the formal sitting room at their grandparents' home, Raymond and the rest of the family took their seats around the large console radio that sat against one wall of the small room.

Robert Johnson, Raymond's father, said, "What preparations do you think the show will share today, Jimmy?"

"I don't know, Grandpa. But, I really enjoyed last week's episode on the US Army's maneuvers that have been taking place in South Carolina." Jimmy responded.

"Where's Bessie and Lillie, Raymond?" Raymond's mother and middle daughter's namesake, Myra Johnson asked.

"Bessie has stayed home with Lillie, who was not feeling well at lunch. Dr. Preslar will be coming by at two to check on her. We hope she's not coming down with the stomach bug that's making it's rounds this winter, Mother." Raymond replied.

"Quiet, the show is about to start." Robert said.

This episode of the show painted the picture of everything that was going on in the Brooklyn Navy Yard. At two twenty-five, the show was interrupted by CBS News and John Daly announced, "The Japanese have attacked Pearl Harbor, Hawaii, by air, President Roosevelt has just announced. The attack also was made on all naval and military activities on the principal island of Oahu."

For several moments, the group sat in stunned silence until Robert said, "Oh, Lord! This is terrible."

"What's going to happen now, Grandpa?" Jimmy asked and continued, "Are we going to be all right?"

Before his grandfather could reply, Elizabeth burst into tears and said, "What does it mean, Dad?"

"Elizabeth, it looks like we are at war with Japan," Raymond replied to his oldest daughter, "and it is going to be long row to hoe."

"Will the Japanese invade California? Will Germany invade at the Outer Banks?" Raymond's mother asked.

"A Japanese invasion of California is a distinct possibility, but I don't think the Germans will come ashore at the Outer Banks because they haven't been able to conquer Great Britain," Raymond responded.

"I don't know, other than it will be a rough go for a while until the country mobilizes. What we need to do is pray for President Roosevelt. We are all going to have to pull together as one country to help the president meet the needs of the country and beat back our enemies," Jimmy's grandfather replied.

Jimmy, who had been trying to follow the radio announcements and conversation in the room about what happened in Hawaii, just about missed his grandfather's response.

"How long will that take? What do we do in the meantime?" Jimmy asked.

"If it's anything like the last war, it could take the country a year to mobilize. When President Wilson declared war on Germany in 1917, it took a full year before the American Expeditionary Forces engaged the enemy in France because it took that long to train the troops and produce all the materiel that would be required to defeat Germany." Robert replied, "Your dad can tell you what it was like training and fighting in the Great War, if he will. I know his time in the Marines was difficult and after the war and his service had ended, it took him a long time to recover from the wounds and what he saw in France."

"Dad, I was hoping that President Roosevelt would preserve the peace and I wouldn't have to tell the story of my war experiences because I've still not recovered from some of the wounds," Raymond responded, "With war upon us, it looks like I must tell the boys my story, but I am going to wait until Ray is home next weekend."

"Raymond, I know how hard that is going to be, but I also think it might help you, too. You will finally be able to tell someone about what you endured during the Great War as a member of the vaunted First Marine Division in the Battle of Belleau Wood." Robert replied.

Raymond gathered the children, "Maybe, Dad. Now, I think we need to get on home so that I can tell Bessie about what has happened in Hawaii and start figuring out what we need to do next."

Raymond, Jimmy, Elizabeth, and Myra walked back home in stunned silence after hearing more about the attack on the Hawaiian Islands on the radio.

RALEIGH, NORTH CAROLINA
DECEMBER 7, 1941

Before Ray, Jr. had left home to go to State College, he had promised his mother that he would attend church every Sunday and today was no exception. He and his girlfriend, Sara, attended the First Baptist Church of Raleigh for Sunday services. After church, Ray and Sara were guests of Mr. and Mrs. Redifer for lunch.

Mrs. Redifer asked, "What are your plans for Christmas, Sara?"

"I am going with Ray to Montcross to visit his family for the first week," Sara replied, "and then home to Edenton for Christmas and the rest of my vacation."

"Sounds like you are going to have a wonderful holiday season. I want to wish you and your family all the best for Christmas."

"Thank you, Mrs. Redifer. I hope your family also has a wonderful holiday season."

Ray and Sara thanked the Redifers for their hospitality and the great chicken and dumplings dinner then left with Mr. Redifer. He dropped them off at Johnson Hall on the campus of Meredith College.

───────

After Mr. Redifer dropped the couple off, they walked into the student commons area and found several of Sara's friends sitting around the radio and joined them.

Sara said, "Alice, are you ready for our History 21 exam?"

"I've studied, but I can't seem to remember the date of the Gettysburg Address or when the Constitution was ratified by the states," Alice replied, "what about you?"

"The dates are not so much a problem for me, but I'm concerned about the essay questions. I wonder about the specific points Mr. Riley will concentrate on for those questions." Sara replied.

As Sara finished her response to Alice, the announcer broke in on the radio and read Steve Early's statement about the attack on Pearl Harbor.

For a moment, everyone sat in stunned silence until Alice's boyfriend, John, exclaimed, "Oh Lord! What has just happened?"

Ray, understanding the bigger picture because of his father's service in the Great War and the fact that he was a Captain in the Army ROTC program at State College, replied, "Well, we are now at war with Japan. I don't know how much we can do now, but I for one am going to start making plans to enlist."

"YOU CAN'T!" Sara exclaimed, "I don't want to lose you. Don't you think you need talk to your parents about this?"

"I will talk to Mom and Dad about it, but I know that Dad enlisted almost immediately after President Wilson declared war on Germany in 1917 because he felt he must do his part. Now I feel the same way. We've been attacked and now we must go and fight. Can you understand that?" Ray responded.

"I can understand, but I don't want to lose you." Sara replied

John asked, "How did this happen? How could the Japanese have done this without the President or the military knowing anything about it?"

"I don't know how that happened, but now that it has, we need to start figuring out what we can do to help," another fellow responded.

Ray replied, "Yes, the country will need our help; especially if the Japanese invade California."

"Do you really think that's possible?" Sara asked, "The Japanese invading California?"

"I don't know," Ray responded, "but we need to be prepared if that happens. That's why I will probably enlist in the Marine Corps just like my Dad did in seventeen. I believe I should do my part to help the country."

"Don't you think we should all wait and see what happens before we rush and do anything rash," one of the guys asked.

"I know that Christmas break starts next Friday for all of us, and I am planning to finish my exams before I enlist," John replied, "What about you, Ray?"

"I'm going to wait as well; although for a different reason. I believe we should all do our part, but I want to hear what my Dad has to say about his war experiences. Every time my brother or I ask him to tell that story," Ray replied, "he always refuses. It's as if that memory is too painful to dredge up and lay bare for us. That's why I'm waiting."

The conversation lagged as more people joined the contingent in the student commons. Ray's thoughts kept turning to his family and what they were thinking at this moment. He knew he would feel better if he could talk to his dad about what had happened today in distant Hawaii.

"Sara, I think it is time that I headed back to my dorm. I want to think about this situation. I will pick you up on Wednesday at five-thirty for supper. I love you." Ray said.

"I love you too, Ray." Sara replied, "I'm scared. I don't know what I will do without you."

"Sara, it's going to be a difficult period for both of us, but our love will see us through as long as we keep our faith firmly rooted in Jesus." Ray said, "Goodbye."

Sara replied, "Goodbye, Ray. I will see you on Wednesday. Maybe by then, we will have more details of what happened and what we need to do."

Ray left the student commons and walked up the long tree-lined driveway of Meredith College until he reached the bus stop on Hillsborough Street. Ray caught the bus that was going back to the State College campus. During the short bus ride, Ray thought, *I wonder what Jimmy is going to do now that the country has been attacked. I know Dad will understand why I want to enlist in the Marines, but I hope Mom will be all right with Jimmy and me joining the fight.* Back at the dorm, there was a telegram waiting for him from his dad. It said, "Pearl Harbor attacked. Wait until you talk to us before doing anything. Love, Mom and Dad"

Montcross, North Carolina
Sunday Evening, December 7, 1941 - 6:00pm

• •

At six that evening, First Baptist Church held a community prayer service at the end of a most trying day. The community came together that evening to pray for every family who was affected by the surprise attack. With no children's services, Elva watched Myra and Lillie while Raymond, Bessie, Jimmy, and Elizabeth attended church.

Jimmy listened intently as Reverend Kelton read the words to the 23rd Psalm and preached a short sermon on the sacrifices and strength that would be required to overcome the enemy who had so treacherously attacked the country.

Reverend Kelton closed the service with this prayer, "Lord during this trying time of world conflict, please comfort us and protect us with your loving hand. Guide our hearts and minds to the winning of the peace and protect those men from this community who will fight for freedom across the globe. Please help President Roosevelt lead us to victory and keep him safe from our enemies. In Jesus name I pray. Amen."

When the family returned home, Elva and the girls greeted them at the door with the telegram from Ray which read, "Will finish exams Friday. Sara and I will take Saturday morning bus. Want to talk to Dad and Jimmy about war. Love. Ray."

Jimmy retired to his bedroom and thought, *Surely this conversation is happening in millions of homes throughout the country tonight.* He had no idea what he would do about the war, but knew he must hear his dad's story about his service before he could make his decision. *I am sure Ray is probably thinking the same thing about right now, and I can't wait for him to get home next Saturday so that we can talk about all of this*, he mused as he prepared for the new week at Montcross High School.

RALEIGH, NORTH CAROLINA
DECEMBER 8 THROUGH 13, 1941

During the week, Ray prepared for his exams as he listened to the war news on the radio. In the Student Commons, Ray arrived in time to hear President Roosevelt's speech to Congress on Monday, December 8. The President asked for a declaration of war against Japan and stated that Sunday, December 7th was a "date which will live in infamy." Ray and many of his friends agreed with that sentiment. His Military Science exam was Tuesday afternoon, and by then, many of his classmates had either already enlisted, had plans to enlist, or were seeking an appointment to Officer Candidates School. Ray finished his exam and decided to discuss his decision with his instructor who knew the cost of serving your country as a veteran of the Great War.

His instructor said, "This war will be one of the bloodiest conflicts the world has ever seen. Germany has been slaughtering the Russians on their Eastern Front for six months now. They treat Russian prisoners without respect to the Geneva Convention and Japan is more ruthless with their prisoners because they believe that surrendering is disgraceful. What have you been thinking?"

"I am planning to enlist in the Marine Corps after Christmas, because my Dad served with the First Marines during the Great War. He participated in the Battle of Belleau Wood; earning a Purple

Heart and a Silver Star during the battle. He's never told the family about his service. My brother, Jimmy, and I need to hear it before making any decisions."

"Since your father earned a Silver Star in the Battle of Belleau Wood, that means he was in the heart of the action and probably saw thousands of men slaughtered. I can understand why he might not want to tell you about it. There was nothing glamorous about being in the mud and the blood of combat with death all around you during that battle."

"Thank you, Sir. I will let you know what I decide and all the best to you and your family for Christmas."

———

His toughest exam was his Economics History exam. The exam covered a large period of time and many economics definitions. Ray carried an A average into the exam and knew this exam made up thirty percent of his final grade. Ray studied long into the night Tuesday to prepare; and on Wednesday morning, Ray awoke about nine-thirty to continue preparing for the exam. Ray sequestered himself in his dorm room to prevent being distracted by any war news on the radio. The preparation paid off because Ray knew most of the answers and finished his exam in about an hour and a half.

Ray was so engrossed in studying for his exams that he only saw Sara on Wednesday when they went to the Capitol Restaurant for a quiet dinner.

At the table, Ray gently broached the subject of his enlistment with Sara, knowing that it would cause her to worry, but his conviction that he must serve outweighed any objection that she could raise. He knew this choice to serve could lead to him losing the girl with whom he wanted to spend the rest of his life.

"Sara, I have come to a decision about the war. Depending on what Dad says, I'm enlisting in the Marine Corps after Christmas. I believe I should serve now when our country needs men the most."

Sara appeared to choke back a sob and said, "Why, Ray? You can finish this year at State College and you don't have to register for the draft until you turn twenty-one in May. I'm afraid I might lose you and I couldn't stand that."

"Sara, I love you. The Marines are volunteer only and that is the branch my Dad served in during the Great War. I want to serve in the same branch he did. I know the separation will be difficult for both of us but I am sure our love will endure."

"I love you too. I do not know how I will handle the separation but I will always be here for you."

"Now that I have told you I am going to enlist, does that change your plans for next week?"

Sara, shocked at the question, replied, "No, I am still going to Montcross with you. You are the only man I know, other than my father, who won't compromise his convictions, and I love you for that."

Through the rest of dinner, Ray noticed that Sara just picked at her food and he wondered if maybe his decision upset her more than she was letting on. Ray changed the subject to their exams and whether they would be able to maintain their high grade point averages after all the distractions this week. After dinner, Ray and Sara boarded the city bus to Meredith and arrived promptly at eight-thirty at the all women's Baptist college which had a curfew for its students to prevent the appearance of impropriety; and Ray made sure to always have Sara back on time.

─────────────

On Thursday December 11, the German dictator, Adolf Hitler, declared war and forced the United States into a two-ocean war in which it was not prepared to fight. Ray and Sara finished their exams on Friday and then they prepared for their trip to Montcross. Ray cleaned out his dorm room since he was certain he would not be returning after the break. He was very uneasy about how Sara would handle the separation of his enlistment and service in the Marines. For now his only thoughts were, *I am so lucky that Sara has chosen me and I will do everything in my power next week to show her how much I love her and how much her love means to me. I don't know what combat will bring but I hope that Sara will be waiting for me when the war is over.*

Montcross, North Carolina
December 8 through 13, 1941

••••••••••••••••••••

Jimmy sent Ray a short letter on Monday with his thoughts on the war and his plans for doing his part.

Monday, December 8, 1941

Dear Ray,

I have been talking to some of the guys at the airport and am thinking I might learn to fly while finishing up my senior year in high school. In order to fly for the Army or Navy, I need to have a high school diploma and a pilot's license since I don't have a college degree. What do you think about that? I've not talked to Dad about it yet, but I know it will ease Mother's mind a great deal to know that she will have me here at least until summer. Have you made any plans yet? I can't wait to see you this weekend.

Your Brother,

Jimmy

———

Raymond headed off to work at the rail yard on Monday morning. As manager of the Montcross Rail Yard, Raymond was met by most of his younger workers who told him they had decided to resign their positions to enlist in the military. Raymond had known these young men most of their short lives and understood they would do what their country required. He also knew he needed their help to keep the yard running smoothly. With the outbreak of hostilities, Raymond understood that the federal government would need all the locomotives and rolling stock it could muster to move the men and materiel of this war. The textile manufacturing facilities in Montcross had already started running non-stop to manufacture as much cotton yarn and cotton cloth in order to meet the needs of the federal government. Without the required trains, he knew there was little hope that the country would be able to mobilize in time to avoid defeat. *Somehow I need to keep these men here to handle the trains moving in and out of here and keep all of our rolling stock and locomotives running at peak efficiency. Without them, this community's manufacturing firms may not be able to deliver the goods required for our soldiers,* Raymond thought before he addressed the young men gathered around him.

"I know all of you are eager to revenge what happened at Pearl Harbor, but I need your expertise here. I need you to keep these trains running from our rail yard on time. Without you some of the goods that our local mills produce for the government and military will not get to their destinations. The cotton yarn that the Cronkite produces is used in everything from web belts to the gauze that covers our soldiers' wounds. Every one of you is doing what your country needs right now; otherwise, you would not have received the class II deferral designation from our local draft board during the recent selective service draft. I cannot hold you here, but I would like for you to at least consider what I'm saying. My office is open, and I will listen to each of you either individually or as a group. Now! Let's get to work!"

One by one, the employees of the Montcross Rail Yard spoke to Raymond and all but a handful pledged their support to the rail yard until such time they were drafted or determined they must serve. Three young men, friends of his son Ray growing up, told Raymond they were leaving for the Army in two weeks.

To these young men, whom Raymond respected, he said, "I wish you would stay here in the rail yard. I understand your anger and need to revenge the attack. This war will be long, bloody, and full of many hardships before it is won. I hope and pray that all of you come home safely. Good luck men."

The young men responded that they would be happy to work out the week. Raymond thanked them and put them back to work. He was sure that these young men would need all the help they could get especially after all he went through in the last war. He wished he could tell them about his service but if he could not tell his own sons, he knew he could not tell these young men.

───

Raymond came home almost every day for lunch with his wife and Monday, December 8 was no exception. He needed to hear what President Roosevelt said during his speech to Congress. Elva had prepared a lunch of cooked ham, boiled potatoes, and turnip greens which was one of Raymond's favorites, and while eating, Raymond and Bessie conversed about their boys and what the war would mean to the family. He relayed that three of Ray's friends; Johnny Poteet , Randall Cramer, and George Prater had already volunteered and were leaving the rail yard for induction in the Army.

Bessie asked her husband, "Did you tell those boys how bad war can be?"

"All I told them was that war is a terrible thing, but I could not bring myself to tell them the story I've been unable to tell Ray and Jimmy. I will tell the boys about my experience in the Great War once Ray is home. My war was terrible and I did some things that haunt me still today; although, had I not done them, I would not have made it home to you. I will tell the boys my story and let them make up their own minds."

"You should do what you think is best. I love you as much now as I did then."

At twelve-thirty, the President's speech to Congress was broadcast on the radio and President Roosevelt opened the speech with, "Yesterday, December 7, 1941, a date which will live in infamy, the United States of America was suddenly and deliberately attacked by naval and air forces of the Empire of Japan."

Raymond and Bessie looked at one another after the speech and concurred that this war was going to be long and bloody and things would get a lot worse before they got better. Bessie sat for a long time in silence thinking of her boys and how this war would affect them while Raymond returned to the rail yard.

Jimmy listened to President Roosevelt's speech during lunch and caught himself getting angrier and angrier about the Japanese attack. Jimmy talked to some of his friends about whether or not they would join the military immediately or wait until after graduation to enlist.

Jimmy's best friend, Andy Poteet said, "I'm joinin' the Navy immediately. I wanted to join the Army but my parents don't want Johnny and me in the same service to better the chances of us making it home. What about you?"

"I've not made a decision yet, but I am thinking about trying to get my pilot's license so that I can join the Air Corps as a pilot. I think that is what's best for me. Good luck in the Navy. When do you leave?"

"I'm going to Charlotte this weekend and enlist. I don't know when I will be reporting."

Jimmy was totally lost in thought about the changes that were coming with the war when the bell rang for his next class. He knew he was late and could do nothing about it. As he rushed to his next class, Jimmy thought, *The decision on where to serve is going to be tough, but I still think the best one will be to get my pilot's license and hope to fly in the Air Corps.*

With the week half over, Elva broke the news to Bessie that several families in her negro community had received telegrams from the War Department. Those telegrams announced that two men were among the wounded from the USS Oklahoma and one young man had been killed on the USS Arizona. Bessie offered Elva time off with pay if she needed to help those families. The thought ran through Bessie's mind, *This is just like the years of the Great War when the hardship of pain and loss hit the community seemingly every day. I hope our town can show the same strength and charity it showed in 1917 and 1918.*

The latest "Montcross Weekly Gazette" arrived on Wednesday and the front page story read, "The clerk of the local draft board reports that between fifteen and eighteen men have traveled to Charlotte to volunteer for service after news of the attack on Sunday."

The donations to the Red Cross increased dramatically according to another story in the paper which read, "The Red Cross drive has seen a large influx of donations since the attack, and the quota of $1,100.00 for this community has been exceeded by $250.00".

The main story in the paper was about the local textile mills. It read, "The town is gearing up for war and the mills have received a huge influx of orders for all grades of cotton yarn and cotton cloth for military use. These orders allow the mills to go from two to three shifts a day. Mill work, like rail work, is considered to be in the national interest and all men eligible to be drafted are deferred per the Selective Service Act of 1940 as long as they maintain their employment at their current establishments."

Wednesday night found the family eating dinner and worshipping at First Baptist Church. Bessie talked to many of the families who were reeling from the loss or wounding of one or more of their sons in the heinous surprise attack. She knew all too well that too soon she would be worrying about Ray and Jimmy after they decided how they were going to serve. This thought made her very nervous because she endured this hardship once before.

The week ended with more rail yard employees enlisting in the military because of Hitler's declaration of war. These losses would put the rail yard at a distinct disadvantage when it came to repairing railroad equipment, but Raymond knew that these young men were doing exactly what he would do if he were twenty years younger.

A Father's War

• • • • • • • • • • • • • • • • • • •

On Saturday, December 13, after traveling by bus from Raleigh, Ray and Sara arrived in Charlotte. They were picked up by the rest of the Johnson family at the bus station and returned to the house at the corner of Main and Todd. Ray was home for Christmas vacation and he continued to weigh his decision about what to do in the aftermath of the attack. His thoughts were, *Should I finish school? Or, should I join the Marines to fight?*

On the bus ride home, Ray and Sara had talked about his plans for answering the nation's call to join the fight against the Axis. She had plainly stated her love to him, but she also understood Ray's moral compass was pushing him to serve. Ray hoped to talk to his dad about what being a front line soldier in the Marine Corps during the Great War entailed. After he unpacked, Ray heard Sara talking to Elizabeth about going Christmas shopping downtown on Monday. Ray spoke to Jimmy about going to Charlotte to pick up parts for their 1930 Model-A Touring Sedan they had bought for $100.00 last summer. This excursion would give both men an opportunity to discuss everything that had happened in the past week and what they planned to do about it. At six, Elva called the family to supper.

Ray said to Elva, "Looks like you are happy to have me home. I get all my favorites; meatloaf, mashed potatoes, Brussels sprouts, and those wonderful crescent rolls. Thank you."

Elva replied, "You're welcome, Ray. I am glad to have you home."

Raymond asked, "How did you do on your exams last week, Ray?"

"I was holding a very high average in all of my classes before exams. I hesitate to think how I did on the exams because I was concerned more about the Japanese attack than studying for finals. Has anyone from the rail yard or in town enlisted since the attack?"

"Johnny Poteet, Randall Cramer, and George Prater enlisted in the Army last week and will be leaving after Christmas. Andy Poteet, according to Jimmy, enlisted in the Navy and will leave sometime in January. The Montcross Gazette announced that thirteen more men enlisted as well, but we don't know the names of any of those volunteers."

Bessie said, "There are several families in Elva's community who are grieving the loss and wounding of three young men on the USS Arizona and the USS Oklahoma."

"I'm so sorry, Elva. Can we do anything to help?"

"No, Ray. The families are doing well under the circumstances. Thank you."

While Bessie and Elva cleared the table, the men moved to the den to listen to the radio and talk for a while.

Ray summoned the courage to tell his father of his decision and said, "Dad, I am going to forego college right now and join the Marine Corps like you did at the onset of the Great War. I have given it a lot of thought and firmly believe I need to serve. I realize I don't have to register for the draft until my twenty-first birthday in May and even then, I could get a student deferral. I don't want a deferral. I need to serve now in order to feel like I'm doing my part."

"You know what you need to do, Ray. The path will be tough and dangerous, but you have the wherewithal to handle the tough training. I will tell you both my Great War experience after I hear what Jimmy has decided."

Jimmy cleared his throat and said, "I am going to finish high school because the Army Air Corps and Naval Aviation require a high school diploma and a pilot's license to be considered for pilot training. I want to take flying lessons from Mr. Mayerhofer at the Montcross Airport after Christmas. The lessons should cost between eight and fifteen dollars an hour which includes the airplane and fuel, unless I am accepted into the Civilian Pilot Training Program. If I qualify for CPTP, the government will pay for all training except fuel, but I must sign a contract enlisting in either the Army or Navy. I hope to complete my training and become a private pilot by the time I graduate. This should ease Mom's mind since I will be at home until I graduate."

Their father took a long pull on the Lucky Strike he was smoking before he responded, "Jimmy, I expected you to enlist at the first chance. You've always been a scrapper when someone plays dirty. I am pleased you have taken into account that you must finish high school. Your Mom and I were going to require you do that before allowing you to volunteer. I am proud of both of your choices and they show me that both of you have deliberated long and hard about what you feel you need to do."

As he weighed his sons' decisions, suddenly their dad looked very tired. Each in his own way had made their choice based on their personality. He knew he could not tell his story tonight because he needed to process the thought that one son could be in harm's way very soon, while the other son could be killed even before he faced the enemy.

"Boys, I am awfully tired now. I don't think I can tell you the entire story tonight. Can we wait until after church tomorrow?"

"Yes Dad, that will be all right. I think Jimmy and I realize war is not what Hollywood and the papers make it."

"Good night, boys. See you in the morning."

While the men talked in the den, Sara and the girls played games in the sitting room. Bessie and Sara would have plenty of time to talk once Myra and Lillie went to bed.

During a lull in the games, Sara mentioned, "I am very nervous about Ray serving, and if something happened to him, I don't know how I will handle it."

Elizabeth replied, "Hopefully, we won't have to cross that bridge; but if we do, I am sure that Mom and Dad and your parents will help you make it through. Do you really love him?"

"Yes, I do very much; and I can see spending the rest of my life with him. He is a man of such strong character and indomitable spirit. Not to mention, he's as handsome as Clark Gable."

Myra overheard just the part about Ray being handsome, chortled, and said, "Have you kissed him yet?"

Bessie instantly said, "Myra, that isn't something to ask a lady! You should be ashamed of yourself."

Bessie was puritanical in her Baptist belief that conjugal acts including kissing were only allowed after marriage. Three weeks after Bessie and Raymond had announced their engagement, her mother had caught them kissing behind the family barn in January 1916. The couple had their wedding on October 21, 1916 and exchanged their vows in the First Baptist Church of Staunton, NC. They had set up housekeeping in a Montcross Rail Yard rental house and were living there in April 1917 when President Wilson and Congress had declared war on Germany. That declaration prompted Raymond to take a leave of absence from his job and enlist in the Marine Corps. After Raymond shipped out on May 15, 1917, Bessie moved back home to Staunton while he was overseas.

Bessie said, "Myra, it's time for you and Lillie to go to bed. Give us all hugs, go tell Daddy and the boys goodnight, and get in your beds. I'll be right up to read you a story."

Six year old Lillie bawled, "Why, Mommy? It's not a school night; we only have to get ready for Sunday School in the morning. I promise to be good. Let us stay up a little longer, please."

"No, Lillie! It's bedtime and you both need your rest. Tomorrow is a busy day at church with the luncheon."

Myra and Lillie told the men good night and went up to bed. Bessie walked up to their room and read them a bedtime story, had them say their prayers, and tucked them in.

She told the girls, "Sleep tight. I love you."

When she got back to the sitting room, Bessie apologized to Sara, "I'm sorry about Myra's question. I overheard you tell Elizabeth that you might not be able to handle the separation from Ray very well. You will do just fine because you have the same support that I had in 1917. Caring family and friends will be there to support you and hopefully, you will continue your schooling while he is away."

"I wasn't bothered by Myra's question at all. I promised my parents that I would finish my education and get my teaching certificate before getting married. Ray agrees because he believes finishing school should come before thinking about marriage. With the war upon us, I don't know that I can keep my promise if Ray volunteers." Sara replied.

Bessie looked into Sara's eyes and calmly said, "You should stick with your plan to finish your education. In many of his letters, Ray has told me how much he loves you. If you are worried about Ray being faithful, don't; because I know that my son is committed to you and you alone. In his latest letter, he told me that he was thinking about asking you to marry him, but with war a reality, I will counsel both of you to wait. Raymond and I were married six months before the Great War engulfed the United States. He felt he must serve and I wasn't going to stop him from doing what he thought was right. I will tell you, waiting for news or sporadic letters is difficult. From one day to the next, you do not know if your husband is alive, wounded, or dead. My parents helped me make it through those long, lonely times. Almost a year after the war ended, Raymond finally returned home and he was a changed man. Nightmares woke him most nights; and for a brief time, he tried drinking to ease his mind. We were lucky that none of the children had arrived yet. We love you like our own daughter and are very happy to have you here with us."

"Thank you for your advice, Mrs. Johnson. You have given me a lot to think about. I will continue to talk things over with Ray and we will make the best decision we can for both of us. I'm pretty tired; thank you again and good night."

Bessie hugged Sara and said, "Good night, Sara."

As Sara went up to bed, Ray and Jimmy walked in and told their mother good night as well. In the hall outside Elizabeth's room, Ray gave Sara a hug and a kiss on the cheek.

"Good night, sweetheart. Sleep well."

"Good night, Ray. See you in the morning."

───────────────

Jimmy and Ray retired to their room to discuss their decisions before turning out the lights.

Ray said to Jimmy, "I am like Dad. I thought you'd be the first of us to volunteer. How long have you been so thoughtful?"

Jimmy looked very perplexed when he replied, "I think I've always been thoughtful, but lately it's more about figuring out what I want to do with my life. I love flying and I want to be a pilot either for the military or a commercial service. That's why I am choosing this path. Why are you thinking of joining the Marines?"

"I have always respected Dad's service with the First Marine Division. After we heard about the attack on Pearl Harbor, I immediately thought of Dad. Being a member of the Marine Corps will put me harm's way, but it might allow me to form a closer bond with Dad. Your choice to want to learn to fly is a good one because it will allow you to do something you enjoy."

"It sounds like we are making decisions that fit our consciences. Do you think Dad will tell us about his war tomorrow? Are you going to marry Sara before you leave for the military?", Jimmy asks.

"I believe Dad must have experienced some tough things when he served. It's almost like he can't bring himself to tell us what happened. I know he will tell us in his own time and before we begin our service. I would marry Sara tomorrow but it's not the right thing to do given the circumstances. We need to wait until the war has been concluded before thinking about anything else. Now, let's go to bed; we have a long day tomorrow."

"Good night, Ray. I agree."

They turned off their reading lights and it took a while before either one fell asleep. Their thoughts kept turning to the war and the paths they had set for themselves.

Johnson Family Home ~ Montcross, North Carolina
December 14, 1941

• • • • • • • • • • • • • • • • • • • •

Sunday, December 14th, dawned cloudy and cold and Ray was the first one to rise. He cleaned the chicken house, gathered eggs, and milked the cow so that he could have some time alone to ponder his decision. The little plot behind the hedge provided the family with fresh eggs and milk which Bessie and Elva still churned into butter because neither one liked the two-part margarine that had recently appeared in the markets of Montcross. For Ray, these chores always gave him time to himself to prepare for the day. Sara joined him about the time he finished cleaning the chicken house

"Your mom wants to know how many eggs you gathered? She said we could all have an omelette if there are enough."

"The chickens were very generous. They gave us twenty-four eggs. Did you sleep well?"

"I slept just fine after Elizabeth unburdened herself about her brothers and the war. She is very worried about you and Jimmy and what will happen when both of you leave. She also told me your Mom has never gotten over losing Andrew to the influenza epidemic in 1929. Elizabeth doesn't know how your Mom will handle the grief if anything happened to either one of you. I tried to comfort her and remind her that Jesus will watch over all of us during the war."

"Thanks, Sara. I love you more every day and I'm going to need your quiet strength to help me make it through this. Thank you for listening to Elizabeth. I know she is right to worry about Mom. Since that day in January of 1929, Mom thinks about little Andrew a lot during this time of year but the quiet strength she has always helps her cope with anything. I am not sure even that quiet strength could help her overcome the loss of Jimmy or me during this conflict. For now, let's trust the Lord that He will bring us through safely. Here are the eggs; tell Mom that I'll be in as soon as I milk Gertrude."

The family had a wonderful breakfast and Bessie rushed everyone out the door to First Baptist Church for the annual Christmas pageant and luncheon.

―――――――――

The Christmas pageant was performed and Elizabeth was wonderful in her part as Mary, the Mother of Jesus. She was complimented by Reverend Kelton and many congregational members during the luncheon that followed. Ray and Sara sat with some of his friends and they discussed the war, college, and Montcross current events.

Johnny Poteet said to Ray, "Andy and I enlisted on Monday morning in Charlotte to go fight the Japs. Andy joined the Navy and will report on December 27th. I report to the Army at Fort Jackson on December 29th. What are you going to do?"

Ray replied, "It is still up in the air. My plan is to forego college and enlist in the Marine Corps after Christmas. I need to iron some things out with Sara and State College before making my commitment. You know I sleep on things before making a decision."

Johnny said, "That's why you went to State College and I went to work at the rail yard. You take the time to look at things from at least three sides so you know what needs doing before starting. Another thing, there's some talk around town about guys we graduated with who weren't working before the attack seem to be scrambling to get jobs in the textile mills or rail yard in order to be deferred from service. Randy Hamstead is one of the guys trying to grab a deferred job. I think he is a coward, shirker, and worst of all, an enemy sympathizer because he didn't enlist immediately after the attack."

Very deliberative in his response, Ray said, "I don't know what to think at this point about any of those guys. I am scared how my decision will affect my family and Sara if I choose to serve. But, I will not allow you or anyone to call people shirkers, cowards, or enemy sympathizers when they may have a good reason for what they're doing. Randy's father served in the Great War and may have asked him to wait since he knows the cost. It's not an easy decision either way. This country will need all the industrial output and rail transportation it can muster to help us win the war. Give these situations a little more time before selling anyone down the river."

"There you go again Ray, giving me the big picture. I now see it is going to take everyone pulling together to win the war. I will talk to Randy and apologize. We need to be united to overcome Japan." Johnny replied as he excused himself to find Randy and the Hamstead family.

After Johnny left, Sara asked, "Can you walk me home? I promised Mom and Dad I would call this afternoon."

"Let me finish my dessert and tell some folks goodbye; then I can walk you home. I hope you don't mind having Myra and Lillie tagging along."

"Not at all."

Ray finished his dessert, then found his parents to let them know that they were walking home. As he had thought, his mother asked him to take Myra and Lillie with them.

Bessie said, "We will be home as soon as we finish cleaning up the fellowship hall. Make sure the girls lay down to take a nap before I get home."

"I will Mom. We will see you at home."

Ray, Sara, Myra, and Lillie walked home along Central Avenue past the recently completed Montcross High School building. Myra and Lillie skipped most of the way while Ray and Sara kept pace behind them. Ray enjoyed the quiet walk with Sara.

After changing clothes, Myra asked Ray, "Will you watch Lillie and me ride our bikes on the driveway?"

Ray said, "No. You know you are supposed to take a nap this afternoon. Go up and get in your beds and I will come read you a story."

Lillie blurted, "I am not tired! I don't want to take a nap! You can't make me!"

"Well Young Lady, I promised Mom that you would be in your beds when she got home from church. I can't make you go to sleep, but I can make sure both of you are in bed when she gets home. Go get in your beds. Now!" Ray scolded.

Lillie pouted, "You can't make me!"

"Either go get in bed like Mom wants or I will tell her that you wouldn't listen. You know what that means."

After Ray's admonition, Myra and Lillie went to their room and got into bed without further protest. Sara made her way into the study to call her parents while Ray went up to read the girls a story.

———

Sara picked up the phone and tapped the receiver twice to get the operator who connected her collect call to her parents home in Edenton, North Carolina.

Sara said, "Hello, Mom. How is everything?"

"Everything is good here and we can't wait to see you next weekend. Mary Wright is wondering if you would like come to her family's Christmas party on Monday night. I told them you would love the idea, but I needed to check with you since you might be tired from traveling."

"That will be fun, and I shouldn't be tired since I will get there Friday night. Everything is wonderful here. The entire family is treating me like one of their own. The funniest thing happened just a while ago. Ray and I walked home from the church luncheon with Myra and Lillie, Ray's two youngest sisters, and his mother asked him to make sure they were in bed for a nap. It was amazing to watch Ray, who handles everything with ease, deal with his six-year-old sister's stubbornness about taking a nap. Lillie had him flummoxed, but he finally got her to go to her room without protest. I about burst out laughing because he was having such difficulty and didn't know what to do."

"I can remember a time when you flummoxed your older brother in much the same way; although your ages aren't that far apart. Sounds like you are having a great time. Has Ray decided anything about the war?"

"Yes, Mom, he has decided that he will be enlisting in the Marines after Christmas. I don't know how I will handle the separation. What have Sam and Will decided?"

"You will be fine, Sara, because you have many people supporting you. I will let your Dad tell you about the boys' war plans."

Her dad took the phone and said, "I'm glad to hear you are having a good time, and as your Mom told you, we cannot wait until you get home. Sam has talked to the local draft board and the War Department advised him they need medical doctors. They would like for him to finish the last two years of medical school for which the federal government will pay, providing he serves four years in the Army Medical Corps. Sam has taken this offer from the War Department. William talked to the draft board about what he should do, and as long as he is in school, he will continue to receive a student deferral. Sam doesn't feel like a long-term, student deferral is the right thing to do; so he will finish this year at Elon then join the Navy."

"I wish I could talk Ray into waiting until the spring semester is finished before joining, but he wants to follow his father's example. Just like Sam and William, Ray feels this is his duty; but I can't help but fear the unknown. Help me understand, Dad."

"I know this has nothing to do with Ray's ego or a macho idea of being a fighter. That is not who he is. He is a highly intelligent and thoughtful young man who is making this sacrifice because it's the right thing to do. In the short time that I have known him, he has proven himself to be a highly capable young man. You are lucky to have found someone so thoughtful and caring. All you need to do is let him know that you support him in whatever he decides."

"Thanks, Dad. I love Ray very much and I will support whatever he decides. Give Mom and everyone my love. Goodbye."

"We love you too. Goodbye, Sara."

Sara had just joined Ray on the back porch when the rest of the family returned from church. Raymond and Jimmy sat down on the porch to talk with them.

Ray said, "Mom, after a little argument with Lillie about whether or not she needed to take a nap, both girls are in their beds and I think they are asleep now."

Sara excused herself to join Bessie and Elizabeth in the sitting room for afternoon tea.

Ray said to his dad, "Had a conversation with Johnny Poteet, and he had some hard words about Randy Hamstead who did not have a job until this week. He called him a coward, shirker, and enemy sympathizer. I let him know that I did not agree with any of that. Who gives us the right to judge what is in a man's heart and why he does the things he does. I let Johnny know that my plan was to join the Marine Corps while foregoing the rest of my college, but it could change. I told him that I would not appreciate it if he attached that same label to me. Johnny strikes me as someone who is too hotheaded for his own good, and I hope he does not do anything rash while in the Army that might get him or his friends killed."

"You are absolutely correct. It is not up to us to judge a man's heart. That is God's responsibility and He will judge those who do what His Word commands and those who let the teaching fly away like chaff in the wind. I have talked to Randy Hamstead and found out his family has already lost an uncle in the Philippines fighting. Because of that, his mother wants him to find a job close to home and provide for the family. Starting Monday, he will work in the rail yard and if he does a good job, I will make him a permanent employee. He told me he was torn between volunteering to serve and following the advice of his mother. For now, he will do as his mother asked. A young man cannot do any more than that for his family."

"Do you think my plan to enlist in the Marine Corps is a good one? From what I have read about the Battle of Belleau Wood, I know that it was a bloody conflict that led to many casualties for the Marines. I hope you will tell us your story because you know I don't like making decisions without all the information."

"Let's move this conversation to the den. I want your Mom and Sara to join us because they need to hear what I endured during my time in the Great War, and your Mom needs to understand why I had nightmares all those years. Sara needs to hear it because she needs to know what could happen to you. Maybe after I tell you about it, I will have some peace of mind myself."

The men left the porch and asked Bessie and Sara to join them in the den.

Raymond said to Elizabeth, "Honey, I think you are too young to hear this story, but I promise when you are a little older, I will tell it to you."

Elizabeth responded, "Thanks, Dad. I do understand and tell Mom that I will make sure Myra and Lillie do not disturb you."

Raymond walked into the den and shut the door behind him. *This will take all the inner strength I can muster. Lord give me the strength to tell my story*, he prayed.

THE STORY

. . . .

Raymond nodded to his sons, Sara, and Bessie then began his story, "This is the story of my time in the Marine Corps during the Great War. The war left me with mental scars that have taken years to overcome. I chose not to talk about my experiences because I hoped fervently that there would never be another war like the last one in my lifetime. This current conflict will dwarf the Great War in its size and scope I'm afraid."

On October 21, 1916, I married your mother at the First Baptist Church of Staunton, North Carolina and that's where my story of love and sacrifice began. I was working like I do today for the Montcross Rail Yard and we set up housekeeping in one of their small rental houses. The first six months of marriage to your mother were blissful until the fateful day that Woodrow Wilson asked Congress to declare war on Imperial Germany. On April 6, 1917, Congress declared war and like Ray and Jimmy are deciding today, I felt I had to decide whether to volunteer or not. Bessie and I talked about what I should do. I talked to my parents about whether or not to volunteer because I wanted to make sure Bessie was taken care of should I choose to volunteer. Finally, I talked to your Mom's family. I let them know how much I loved your mother and that I was thinking about volunteering for service in the war. They all told me that I should follow my heart and do what I felt I needed to do. It came down to the fact that I felt it was my duty to help the country in its time of war. That duty lead me to enlist in the Marines Corps on May 14, 1917.

On that date, I was shipped to Port Royal, South Carolina to become a Marine. For eight weeks in the summer heat and mosquitoes, I was broken down mentally and physically by the drill instructor. Thinking I couldn't take anymore of the training, I was rebuilt into a Marine by our drill instructor. After our group graduated from boot camp, we were sent to Quantico,

Virginia for pre-embarkation training where I was assigned to the third battalion in the 5th Marine Regiment of the First Marine Division. Our battalion was shipped to France in February 1918 to train with other elements of the Allied Expeditionary Force. It was in France that I got my first taste of what combat was like because our unit was bivouacked near a hospital where they brought wounded soldiers by the truck load. What I saw there made a lasting impression on me. Some soldiers were blinded by the poison gases; other soldiers were missing body parts from the heavy artillery shells that exploded in, on, and around the trenches. Everywhere there was blood and misery and I had not even fired a shot in anger yet. The close proximity to the wounded in our initial training steeled us to the fact that the war was going to be bloody and dangerous.

The German Spring offensive in May of 1918 saw the Germans break through and retake Chateau-Thierry and Vaux. They deployed their troops in a beautiful hunting preserve called Belleau Wood. That beautiful hunting preserve turned into hell on earth for me and the men in my battalion after being called up from division reserve into the battle on June 6. Major Benjamin S. Berry was called to lead our battalion in an attack on the woods. Our advance was through a wheat field in perfectly disciplined lines which were immediately decimated by the raking machine gun fire of the Germans. Two buddies and I found cover in a shallow revetment. We were ordered to dig in and hold our position. During these hellish minutes, my mind raced across the miles to Bessie and I began to wonder if I would ever see her again this side of heaven.

That first day we held our ground when a counter-attack threatened to overrun us. The Germans came in waves and we were dangerously low on ammunition. I don't know how many men I wounded or killed that day. I remember distinctly, three German boys who could not have been over sixteen that I had to kill in hand-to-hand combat. It was kill or be killed and I wanted to see your mother again so I did what I had to do to stay alive. I grow sick every time I think of those young boys attacking us. They should have been in school like you were at their age.

A sister platoon had been trapped in the open by a machine gun nest and those guys were being slaughtered. My Sergeant saw what has happening and ordered us to attempt a rescue. We moved slowly towards the nest, keeping as hidden as possible in the sparse cover. At once, another machine gun opened up on us and killed two of my squad immediately and wounded the sergeant. I was in charge of our squad now and we only had 8 men available to silence both machine guns. I chose to take three men and try to silence the machine gun that was slaughtering our sister unit. The four of us were able to move within fifty feet of the machine gun. A high revetment prevented us from assaulting the nest directly. The only option we had were grenades but, our grenades were an early model that had an issue with not arming properly especially in the heat of battle. An adept enemy could properly arm those grenades and throw them back at us. I threw two grenades in quick succession toward the machine gun nest and hunkered down to await explosions that never came. I looked up to see the German soldier standing up in the revetment and in the motion of throwing the grenade back at me. I threw a quick shot at him and he dropped the grenade. The grenade exploded and I was able to rush the position. As I dove over the edge of the revetment, I was shot in the stomach. The shock of being hit and seeing an enemy still alive gave me a hopeless feeling. I still had my rifle with its fixed bayonet when I rolled upright. I stabbed the closest soldier with my bayonet which put him out of action. The second soldier was trying to pull his pistol when another squad member came over the edge of the emplacement and shot him. With the machine gun nest put out of action, our sister platoon continued their advance. With the area secured, I was given rudimentary first aid in the machine gun position before the medics began the long process of evacuating me to the hospital.

As the long trip back home began for me that day, I had time to think about all I had lost and all that I had seen. The surgeons in the various hospitals in France, England, and back here in the United States did wonderful work, but the mental healing would take a lot longer. In a ceremony at the hospital, I was awarded the Silver Star for gallantry and the Purple Heart for wounds received. I kept asking myself, why did I survive? I think of the prayers that were prayed on my behalf by your mother and many others for my well-being, but really, it was because I was extremely lucky. I spent many years trying to forget the awful horrors that I had seen; especially the young boys who died at the end of my bayonet. I awoke many nights in a cold sweat after a nightmare *put me back on the battle field at Belleau Wood looking at those young boys' faces. I could not bear to tell your mother what happened and what I had done to stay alive over there. I buried my feelings and tried hard to move on with my life. It was extremely difficult and during my lowest point, I thought of ending my life. The strain of the nightmares and alcohol caused your Mom great pain. With a quiet resolve, she kept loving me and praying for me. Ray, when you came along, I was able to overcome the guilt of surviving. Bessie, I am sorry I kept all of this hidden from you for all these years. Boys, I want you to know that we will support you. I know from experience what you will be facing when you volunteer to fight in this war. I pray that you will come home safely to all of us.*

Raymond stood up and went to Bessie. He leaned down and said, "I love you, Bessie. Thank you for supporting me for over twenty-five years. It helped me more than you will ever realize."

Raymond grabbed his chest as he bent to kiss Bessie and collapsed to the carpet. Ray and Jimmy rushed to their father's side to check on him.

Ray yelled, "SARA, CALL DR. PRESLAR NOW!"

Sara picked up the phone, told the operator that there was an emergency at the Johnson home and that she needed to get in touch with Dr. Preslar immediately. Mrs. Preslar answered the phone and asked Sara the nature of the emergency.

Sara calmly said, "Mr. Johnson clutched his chest and collapsed to the carpet. He is unconscious. Please send Dr. Preslar quickly."

Mrs. Preslar responded, "The doctor is on his way. He should be there within five minutes."

Ray and Jimmy moved their father to the relative comfort of the couch. Ray opened the door and grabbed Elizabeth before she could rush in to the den.

"Elizabeth, Dad collapsed after he told us his story. Please keep the young girls calm until we know something."

Elizabeth screamed at Ray, "YOU CAUSED THIS! He would have been fine if you hadn't made him tell the story!"

"Jimmy and I needed to hear the story. If I had known it would have caused this, I would never have pushed him to tell us."

To the relief of the family, Dr. Preslar arrived very quickly. Raymond started coming around while the doctor checked him over.

Dr. Preslar said, "What happened, Raymond?"

"I just finished telling my wife and boys about my service in the Great War. I went to thank Bessie for 25 years of marriage. I suddenly felt a sharp pain in my chest. The next thing I know you are working me over."

"Are you still having any pain in your chest? How is your head feeling?", Dr. Preslar asked.

"I have some pressure in my chest and a mild headache right now.", Raymond replied.

"I think you had a mild stress related heart issue but I don't know for sure. There might be something else going on. I recommend that we take a trip to the hospital for further tests. If everything looks good, you might be home by Tuesday or Wednesday."

Decisions

• • • • • • • • • • • • • • • • • • • •

Ray was extremely concerned after his dad was taken to the hospital by ambulance. He called and asked Elva if she would come to the house and take care of the girls. When Elva arrived, Ray told her what happened that afternoon. At eight-thirty, Bessie called Ray and asked him to come pick her up since visiting hours had concluded. Ray asked Sara to accompany him to the hospital.

On the way to the hospital, Ray asked Sara, "Now that this has happened, do you think it was wrong of Jimmy and me to push Dad to tell us his war story?"

"Ray, you did not know that the stress of telling you his ordeal would cause your dad to have an attack. You needed to hear what happened and why he chose to fight. I don't blame you for asking your dad about it."

"I hope Mom has some good news about Dad for us. I am worried about Jimmy and Elizabeth because this is just as hard on them as it is for me."

"Your dad has kept his story bottled up for more than twenty years and the relief of sharing probably caused his attack. I am sure he will be fine in a couple of days just like Dr. Preslar said. As soon as Jimmy and Elizabeth hear from your dad, I think they will be fine too."

They arrived at the hospital and picked up Bessie.

"Mom, how is Dad doing? Is this as bad as it looked at home?"

"Dad is doing fine except for some hypertension. They are going to treat it with a small change in his diet and medication. He wants me to tell you and the rest of the children that he is relieved now that he told his story. He is scared for both you and Jimmy because he knows what you will be facing."

"Mom, Elizabeth is mad at Jimmy and me because she thinks we caused Dad's spell today by forcing him to tell his story. I don't think he would have told us the story if he didn't want to."

"I have been trying for twenty plus years to get your dad to tell me what happened over there. I had not heard his story until today. I could not make him tell his story until he decided to do so. He carried the stress and grief for all this time alone. No, you and Jimmy did not cause anything today. The stress and relief were the cause of your Dad's attack. I will help Elizabeth understand."

Elva had put Myra and Lillie to bed before the group arrived home and Jimmy and Elizabeth greeted them anxiously. Ray motioned everyone to the den so that Jimmy and Elizabeth could hear their father's prognosis and learn what caused the attack.

Bessie said, "Elizabeth, your Dad's attack today was not caused by your brothers at all. If your Dad didn't want to tell his story, nothing could have made him tell us. The doctors have determined that both stress and relief caused him to collapse today. The doctors found a little hypertension that bears watching, and before I left, the doctors gave him some medicine to help him sleep. I believe he will be just fine. He should be home at the earliest Tuesday and at the latest Wednesday. Everyone needs to go through this week as if nothing is wrong. That's what your Dad wants."

Elizabeth replied, "Thanks, Mom, I am glad that Ray and Jimmy didn't cause the attack. I admit that I was pretty angry with them when I thought they caused it. Can you forgive me?"

Ray responded to Elizabeth, "I was never upset with you about this because I thought I had caused it too. There is nothing to forgive. We are a family that loves each other enough to stick together when bad things happen. I love you, Sis, nothing you can do will change that."

Jimmy then replied, "I understand, too. You were not as hard on me as I was on myself today after Dad collapsed. I believed it was my fault until Mom told us otherwise. Sis, I love you too and we are family. That's all that matters to me. Thanks, Mom. When you see Dad tomorrow let him know how much we all love him."

"Ray, Jimmy, Elizabeth, Sara, I love you all and I am so glad we are a family. Let us say a prayer and thank God for putting his healing hand on your Dad. It's time for us all to get some rest because I need to get up early to let the rail yard know that your Dad will not be at work this week."

Bessie prayed, "Dear Lord, our family comes to you tonight to thank you for protecting Raymond. We pray that you will hold him close tonight and give him peace. Thank you Lord for sparing Raymond and for giving him the strength to tell his story. We know now what a burden it was for him and we humbly pray that you will let him know he can rest easy knowing we are here for him. In Jesus name we humbly pray, amen."

Everyone left the den for bed. Ray knew that he must be up early to take his mom to the hospital and he hugged Sara goodnight at Elizabeth's door. Once in his bedroom, Ray's thoughts turned inward and he asked himself, *What would I have done had Dad's prognosis been bad? Can I still volunteer now that I know what war is really like? Thank you Lord for taking care of Dad.* Relieved, Ray was asleep in minutes.

JOHNSON FAMILY HOME ~ MONTCROSS, NORTH CAROLINA
MONDAY, DECEMBER 15, 1941

Monday morning, December 15, dawned cold and cloudy, and Ray awoke early today to gather the eggs and to milk Gertrude. He was back in the house at seven-thirty for a breakfast of eggs, sausage, and toast which Elva had fixed while he did his chores. Elva had spent the night in the servant's quarters since Bessie did not get home from the hospital until very late. Visiting hours at the hospital were 9:00 am to 9:00 pm and nothing could keep Bessie from spending every minute of that time with Raymond. She not only lifted his spirits but also reminded him how much the family loved him. Bessie called Mr. Linkenburg at the rail yard at 8:00 am and told him that Raymond would not be able to work this week.

Mr. Linkenburg told Bessie, "We know all about it Mrs. Johnson and we hope Raymond gets well quickly. We will miss him around here this week. Your family is in our prayers and if you need anything please do not hesitate to ask. Let him know that everything will be fine while he is away and for him to concentrate on getting well."

Bessie replied, "Thank you, Mr. Linkenburg, I will let him know everything will be fine at the yard and for him to just worry about getting better."

After Ray delivered Jimmy, Elizabeth, Myra, and Lillie to school, he returned home and picked up his mom and Sara to go to the hospital.

CHARLOTTE MERCY HOSPITAL ~ CHARLOTTE, NORTH CAROLINA
MONDAY - 9:00AM

When they arrived on Raymond's floor at the hospital, the nurse took them to his room and left so they could talk quietly. Raymond was much better today and his blood pressure had returned to 120/80.

Ray said to his dad, "I'm glad you're better this morning. I want to apologize if Jimmy or I caused this in any way by asking you to tell your story."

His dad replied, "You and Jimmy did not cause any of this. The doctors said that the relief from telling the story was so great that I had a fainting spell due to the stress. They did a lot of tests yesterday and I am scheduled for more this morning. If I pass those tests and everything looks good, you could be taking me home tomorrow."

"Wonderful, Dad, that's great news. Everyone at home will be relieved to know that you are doing so well and could be home tomorrow. Now, Sara and I will leave you in Mom's care and we will go to pick up the parts needed to fix the Model-A."

"You and Sara be careful. Tell the children that I hope to see them all tomorrow. Remind Jimmy and Elizabeth that I expect them to work hard on their school work even though I am not there. As the leader, Ray, make sure you help them and do not let them get distracted by my hospitalization."

"Yes, Sir. I will make sure that they complete their work while you are here and I will tell them you're doing better. I will pick Mom up at eight-thirty tonight. Good luck, Dad, I love you."

As they left the hospital to pick up parts for the Model-A, Sara wished Raymond well.

While walking to the car, Ray broached the subject of service again with Sara, "I think I am going to join the Marine Corps and forego college; because in my heart, it is the right thing to do. While we are here in Charlotte, I would like to go by the Marine recruiting office to pick up the enlistment paperwork."

Sara choked back a tear and said, "I told you last night that I would stand with you. Yes, we can go to the recruiting office. Afterwards, I would like to go Christmas shopping to pick up presents for your Mom, Dad, Jimmy, and the girls."

"Thank you. Every day I love you more than the previous day. I will be happy to take you shopping after we get the parts and the enlistment paperwork."

Arriving at the parts store, they picked up a radiator and two tires for the Model-A, then drove to the Charlotte Naval recruiting station.

NAVAL RECRUITING STATION ~ CHARLOTTE, NORTH CAROLINA
MONDAY - 10:30 AM

• • • • • • • • • • • • • • • • • • •

The line was out the door at the Naval Recruiting office when Ray and Sara arrived. Ray found a parking space and told Sara that it would probably take some time to get the enlistment paperwork. Once Ray was in the line, he started talking to the men about their plans. He found everyone in this line was enlisting in the Navy and when he told them he wanted to enlist in the Marine Corps, they pointed him to a much shorter line. He joined the shorter line and a short while later, he met the Marine recruiter.

When Ray asked for the enlistment paperwork, the recruiting sergeant said, "Why are you picking up the paperwork instead of enlisting immediately?"

"Sir, I am picking up the paperwork so I can read through the forms, fill them out, and return them when I am ready to go. I will return the paperwork no later than next Monday."

The Sergeant almost spat back at Ray, "Here you go! Get your thinking done before you join my Marine Corps."

"Thank you, Sir!", Ray snapped and left without another word. However, as he walked back to the family car, he fumed about the Marine sergeant's unfair treatment.

On the drive back to Montcross, Ray told Sara how rude the recruiting officer had been, "It seems the sergeant was looking for immediate volunteers. I want to enlist in the Marine Corps, but I want to delay my enlistment until after Christmas because I do not want to miss the time I get to spend with your family in Edenton. Instead of waiting until after Christmas, I want to travel to Edenton with you on Friday and I will return home to Montcross for Christmas on December 23rd."

"I really think that's a good idea and I'll call my parents tonight to make sure it will work for them. You might even be able to meet the Wrights on Monday night during their annual Christmas party."

After they found a parking space in front of the Bank of Montcross, the couple began their Christmas shopping.

Downtown Montcross ~ Montcross, North Carolina
Monday - 11:45am

• •

Ray had promised Elva that they would be home for lunch by one o'clock. After they were parked, he and Sara walked immediately to Belk-Matthews so that Sara could buy gifts for her family. Sara picked out gifts for her mother which included a new quilted robe and a pair of house slippers. In the men's department, she picked out sweaters and dress shirts for her brothers and for her dad, she purchased a billfold, shaving set, and pajamas. Her bill totaled eighteen dollars which she paid and then she had the items gift-wrapped.

While Sara was shopping, Ray bought a new bathrobe, gloves, and house slippers for his dad. Mrs. Elmira thanked Ray for his purchase and gift-wrapped each item for him.

As they were walking back to the car, Ray said, "I think your family will love the gifts that you picked out for them."

"I think so too. And, your Dad will really like the bathrobe and house slippers you picked out for him."

Ray drove them back to the house at the corner of Main and Todd and they made it home just in time for lunch.

Johnson Family Home ~ Montcross, North Carolina
Monday Afternoon
. . . .

Ray picked everyone up at school and told them that their dad might come home tomorrow. He helped Elizabeth work on her report and reminded Jimmy that he needed to keep up his school work if he wanted to start his flying lessons in January. The youngest girls grabbed Sara and talked her into walking them to the Mercantile store to buy Christmas presents. Lillie and Myra had two dollars apiece to spend on gifts for their mom and dad.

While Sara, Lillie, and Myra were gone, Ray had time to talk to Jimmy about everything that had happened since the Japanese attack.

Ray said, "Jimmy, I've made my decision. I'm enlisting in the Marine Corps right after Christmas unless Dad's prognosis changes. If Dad comes home tomorrow as he expects, I will leave for Edenton with Sara on Friday to visit with her family and return home on Tuesday. After Christmas, I plan to enlist and from then on, I will be at the mercy of Marine Corps."

"That sounds pretty reasonable and it will allow the entire family to have one last Christmas together before the war scatters us. Mom will be pleased you waited until after Christmas. Visiting Sara's family is the right thing to do before you volunteer because you don't know when you will get visit her family again. After the

41

story Dad told us, I worry about you in the Marine Corps because I think the Japanese will be a tougher fight than what Dad saw in France during the Great War. My hope is that we both make it home after the war."

"One more question Jimmy, I know I said I thought would wait before asking Sara to marry me, but I don't know if I want to do that. I really think I want to ask her to marry me before I leave. I know that it is selfish on my part and I know she will wait until I come home because she told me she would. I am not scared she will find someone else but I believe if we are married that it would give me extra motivation to get back home safely."

"Ray, I don't think you should even contemplate marriage at this point. You need to complete everything in front of you before even thinking about marriage. Military service is inherently dangerous and I know Mom and Dad would tell you the same thing. Not right now. You would be doing Sara a disservice if you make her a widow before you make her a good husband. You will be leaving in less than ten days which is not enough time to plan anything much less give Sara the wedding she deserves. Plan it after you get back; that will give you something to live for as well."

―――――――――――

Sara and the girls returned home in time for a supper of chicken pot pie, green beans, and peaches. After Elva cleaned up the dishes from supper, she read to Myra and Lillie from one of the girls' Christmas story books. At eight o'clock, she tucked in the girls and told them to sleep good. While the girls were going to bed, Bessie called and said she was ready to be picked up at the hospital. She told Ray that he could visit with his dad if he got there by eight forty-five.

Ray asked Sara, "Do you want to go with me to pick Mom up?"

"No, I want to stay here and spend some time with Elizabeth."

"Sounds good. Jimmy, would you like to go?"

"Yes, I would like to go. Hopefully we'll have time to visit with Dad for a little while."

As the boys left the house, Ray told Sara and Elizabeth, "We should be back home with Mom by about ten o'clock."

● ●

Ray and Jimmy were able to make good time and they made it to the hospital in time to visit with their dad for a few minutes. Bessie met her two sons at the entrance and escorted them to their father's room.

Ray said, "Well, Dad, did the doctors give you a good report for your tests? How's everything looking for you to get out of here tomorrow?"

"The doctors poked and prodded me all day yesterday and concluded that I had a stress induced fainting spell. The doctors told me that I should be ready to leave by noon tomorrow if there aren't any complications. Knowing your Mom as well as I do, I am sure she will want to be here by nine in the morning to keep me company."

Jimmy choked up and said, "Dad, I've been worried that Ray and I caused this attack because we kept asking you to tell your story. Even though Ray told me that you said it wasn't our fault, I had my doubts but seeing you tonight makes me feel better. I love you, Dad!"

With glistening eyes, his father replied, "Neither one of you caused the attack I suffered. The doctors told me the relief of telling my story after keeping it bottled up for twenty years caused it. Your Mom and I have been discussing this and the decisions that each of you boys will have to make. Your Mom and I want you to know that we are proud of you and we support you fully in whatever decision you make. I love all of you very much!"

Just as Raymond had finished his response, the nurse told them that visiting hours were over and the group bid Raymond a good night. They were leaving the hospital in good spirits since their husband and father would come home tomorrow.

━━━━━━━━━━━

On the drive home, Ray said, "Mom, I've decided to spend the weekend in Edenton with Sara and her folks and come home on the 23rd so that I can spend Christmas with the family. After Christmas,

I will enlist in the Marines and hopefully leave after the first of the year. If Dad wasn't doing so well, I would've waited until he was better before deciding."

Bessie looked at her oldest son with a mixture of worry and pride then told him, "You've thought everything through to make sure you were making the right decision. I am very proud of you and it is my fervent prayer that you return safely. You should talk to your dad about it and you should go with Sara to Edenton on Friday. That will allow you to spend a few more days with her before you leave."

"Thanks, Mom. Please don't tell Dad anything of my plans before he gets home. I would like to talk to him myself because his story helped me understand my service in the Marines will be fraught with danger."

Jimmy was silent for most of the return trip allowing his brother and mom time to talk about what Ray had decided to do. There would be plenty of time for Jimmy to tell his mother about his plans to take flying lessons and try to qualify for military aviation training.

JOHNSON FAMILY HOME ~ MONTCROSS, NORTH CAROLINA
MONDAY - 10:00PM

• • • • • • • • • • • • • • • • • • • •

After he parked the family car in the garage, Ray walked into the house with his mom and Jimmy. He found Sara, Elizabeth, and Elva in the den playing cards and discussing today's adventures with Myra and Lillie. Sara looked up to see Ray standing in the doorway with the most perplexing facial expression, looking almost like the cat who swallowed the canary. She gave him a look that asked, "Why are you so happy?" Ray put his finger to his lip to prevent Sara from giving away his happiness. Before Ray could attempt to stifle the look that was overwhelming him, Elizabeth noticed the expression.

She blurted, "What has you so all-fired happy, Ray?"

"Well, Sis, Dad will be coming home tomorrow. He's fit as a fiddle and looks great!"

Elizabeth, overcome with emotion, jumped up, hugged her mother, and said, "That's a relief! Dad's going to be all right! That's wonderful! I hope he will be able to help me with my report before it's due on Thursday."

"Elizabeth", her mom said, "Your Dad is going to need a lot of rest when he gets home but, I am sure he will be able to help you with your report."

Ray looked at Sara and asked, "Were you able to talk to your parents tonight? Mom and I have discussed the idea of me going home with you this weekend and she thinks it's a great idea."

"Right after you left, I called Mom and Dad. They would love to have you come this weekend and they are looking forward to seeing you again. We just need to decide how we will be traveling to Edenton, bus or train."

"That's wonderful! I am looking forward to seeing your family again too! Tomorrow we will check the schedules and make our decision. I want us to find the quickest way so that we will have more time to visit with your parents."

Bessie broke in and said, "I think it's time for bed. We all have a lot to do tomorrow. When you say your prayers tonight, make sure you thank God for answering ours. Good night, I love all of you."

Ray walked upstairs with Sara and gave her hug outside Elizabeth's room.

He whispered, "I love you, Sara. My love for you grows every day. Thank you for everything. Goodnight."

Sara gave Ray a kiss on the cheek and said, "I love you too. You are a fine man and I'm the luckiest girl in the world to have found you. Goodnight."

Before Sara could see the tears glistening in his eyes, Ray turned and walked into his room thankful for her love. He thought, *I'm happy that Sara loves me and I hope I live up to the ideal that she seems to have in her mind about me.*

Decisions

Jimmy awoke before Ray on this cold and windy Tuesday morning. As he went out to do Ray's chores of gathering the eggs and milking the cow, Jimmy thought a lot about how his brother held the family together the last couple of days while their father was in the hospital. Jimmy knew Ray was exhausted from doing the chores and running back and forth to Charlotte with their mom all week so he worked it out to handle everything this morning in order to allow Ray to sleep late and recover.

Jimmy finished the chores and walked back into the house to wonderful smells of pancakes and bacon cooking. Bessie was helping Myra and Lillie get ready for school while she also got prepared to go to the hospital to keep Raymond company until he was discharged.

At seven-thirty, Ray awoke with a start. Looking at the clock, he realized that he was not just late but in trouble late. His chores had not been done and he had to take his mom to the hospital after dropping his siblings off at school. He threw on his clothes, banged down the stairs, and went storming into the kitchen.

Ray bellowed, "WHY DIDN'T SOMEONE WAKE ME? I needed to do my chores and take Mom to the hospital! Jimmy, it's all your FAULT!"

"Ray, Mom and I worked it out last night for me to take her to the hospital and the girls to school. We knew how tired you must be from taking care of everything for us while Dad's been in the hospital; and I was trying to help out a little myself. I've done the chores and I'm ready to take the girls to school. Why don't you get some rest this morning?"

"SINCE WHEN DO I NEED MY LITTLE BROTHER HELPING ME OUT? I will take everyone to school! Let's get going! I'll take a piece of sliced bread and a couple of pieces of bacon to eat while I drive."

Ray herded everyone to the car and drove them school.

• •

Ray was still seething when he got back home to pick up his mother. He helped his mom and Sara into the car and drove to the hospital where he dropped Bessie and Sara off at the front entrance and then parked the car. He walked to his father's room and found Sara and Bessie talking with him.

As Ray walked into the hospital room, Bessie said, "Your Dad says the doctor has already been in this morning and he has a clean bill of health. If you would wait, we can take him home in about an hour. They are doing his release paperwork now."

"That's great, Mom! I don't think Sara and I mind waiting. Sara, would you like to go down to the cafeteria for a cup of coffee and something to eat since I missed breakfast this morning?"

"Yes, that would be good."

"Good. Mom and Dad, we'll be back in about a half hour."

Ray and Sara walked down to the cafeteria and they ordered coffee. Ray ordered himself two eggs, sausage, and toast. After Ray paid the clerk, they sat down at a table to have their coffee.

"Were you really angry with Jimmy this morning? You've looked like you could spit nails all morning. What's wrong?"

"I'm more angry at myself that I didn't hear the alarm this morning. It's my job to do the chores and to make sure everyone was taken care of while Dad's been here. I failed this morning even though Jimmy volunteered to take my place."

"You shouldn't have been so hard on him. All he wanted to do was show you how much he loved you and I hope you will apologize when we get home."

Ray sat there dumfounded at what Sara had said about Jimmy just wanting to help him.

"I'm sorry, Sara. You're right. I'll apologize to him as soon as I see him this afternoon. Thank you for keeping me honest."

Ray finished his eggs and sausage and they walked up to his father's room and were greeted by his mom who said, "The paperwork has been completed and your Dad is ready to go home. The doctors have told him he's all right, but he must continue to rest this week. He can go back to work on Monday."

"That's wonderful! I'm sure Jimmy, Elizabeth, and the girls will be happy to have Dad home."

Raymond broke in and said, "Let's get this show on the road, I'm ready to go home."

· · · · · · · · · · · · · · · · · · · ·

Ray drove his mom, dad, and Sara home from the hospital with very little conversation. He spoke little, other than a few terse responses to the trio, when directly questioned. He was deep in thought on how to broach the subject of his enlistment and trip to Edenton with Sara to his father. Ray did not want a repeat of the episode that saw his father go into the hospital in the first place.

At home, Ray said, "Mom, is now a good time to tell Dad my plans?"

"Yes, I believe it is. Just don't do anything to upset or agitate him. What's wrong with you? You've been cross as a bear today."

"I'm mad at myself for oversleeping this morning and I've felt I've been behind and trying to catch up since the opening bell this morning. I wish someone would have awakened me so that I could've done my chores and taken care of everyone. That's my job, after all, when Dad isn't home."

"Ray, no one was upset with you this morning. Jimmy worked it out with me last night to allow you to sleep late. He wanted you to know that he could take care of things. He also wanted to show you how much he loved you by letting you rest. Don't be mad at yourself; you've done a more than admirable job since your father's been in the hospital."

"Thanks, Mom, that makes me feel a little better."

Ray walked into the den to check on his father who was resting in his favorite easy chair.

"How are you feeling, Dad?"

"Doing pretty well. I'm a little tired because those nice folks at the hospital don't allow a body to rest. I swear they woke me up seven or eight times a night to check my blood pressure, take my temperature, or do some other assorted poking and prodding. I never could quite get to sleep. It's been a rough couple of days for you as well. How are you doing?"

"Well, Dad, I was angry at myself this morning because I overslept and thought I'd failed in my duty to take care of the chores and help everyone get ready for school. Mom just told me that Jimmy had tried to step up so that I could get some rest. He did my chores and had everything ready to go by the time I skated into the kitchen at quarter of eight this morning. I made Jimmy think I was angry at him for my oversleeping. I'll apologize to him when he gets home from school."

"I know how exhausted you must be and the fact that you've not had a lot of time to spend with Sara while you've been home does not help. You need to know how proud I am of you for taking hold and keeping the family together while I've been at the hospital. Have you decided what you're going to do about serving?"

"Thanks, Dad. Yes, I've made my decision. I'm going to travel with Sara to Edenton on Friday and come home Tuesday in time to spend Christmas Eve and Christmas Day here in Montcross. After Christmas, I will take my enlistment paperwork back to the Marine Recruiting Station and enlist in Marine Corps. Your story scared me, but I still feel it is my duty to serve. Do you have any advice?"

"I will worry about you while you are gone, Ray. But, I know you will do just fine in the Corps as long as you keep one thing in mind. Always do as you're told by the drill instructor because their word is law. It will seem at times like you will not be able to go one more step or continue an exercise one more minute, but you must will yourself to take the next step or do the next repetition because the drill instructor will look for any excuse to call you names. I'm proud of you and I hope you enjoy your time at Sara's parents this weekend. I love you, Son."

"Dad, I'll admit I'm nervous. Your words of encouragement help me know that I'm doing the right thing. I promise I will listen to every instruction and do my level best to succeed in the Corps. I'll let you rest now. I love you, Dad."

Raymond was lost in thought after Ray left the den because he remembered all too vividly the conversations he had with his and Bessie's parents on the eve of his departure for the Great War.

I hope Ray knows how much his Mom and I love him and how proud we are of the man he has become. Lord, protect my son from harm and help him make it through those many lonely and terrifying events on the world's far flung battlefields. This I pray in Jesus name. Amen.

Raymond drifted off into fitful sleep, thinking about his son's uncertain future.

For the first time in three days, the house felt normal with Raymond taking his rightful place at the head of the supper table. Elva served center-cut pork chops, rice, green peas, and dinner rolls. The family table once again sang with the playful banter of the five siblings and their father.

Elizabeth got a little serious when she asked, "Daddy, are you sure Ray and Jimmy didn't cause your spell?"

"No, Sweetie, the boys needed to know my story and the doctors told me that my spell was caused by keeping it bottled up for so long."

"That's great because I was awfully mad at them, thinking they caused it."

"You do not need to be mad at them. Ray really needed to hear my story since he will be the first to make his decision about the war. How's your report coming along?"

"I have written the first draft of the report which has to be at least five hundred words. I have seven hundred and fifty words in my report which covers most of our Civil War ancestors. Can you look at it and make sure I didn't miss anyone important from the many family members who served on both sides during the war?"

"Sure, Honey. Let me finish this wonderful dessert of pecan pie and ice cream that Elva prepared for us."

Lillie piped up and asked, "Daddy, can you play with Myra and me after you fix sis's report?"

"Sure, Lil. Pick out a game and I will join you and Myra in the den once I check Elizabeth's report."

Raymond took time with Elizabeth, carefully examining her report; and he found some things she needed to correct. He left her in the study at the typewriter while he went to the den to play a game with the younger girls.

While the three were playing Go Fish, Myra asked, "What happened, Daddy? Why did you have to go to the hospital?"

"Myra and Lillie, my heart had a small problem that made me fall asleep. The doctors had to check me over like when we take the car to the service station for them to check the tires."

Myra blurted, "Oh! The doctors needed to make sure your heart was good?"

"Right, Myra. Now everything is fixed and I am home to stay."

Raymond and the girls were able to play several games of Go Fish before Bessie walked in and told the girls that it was time for bed.

Raymond said to Bessie, "With the hospital waking me up every hour to check on me, I'm a little tired and think I will retire to bed as well. Can you and Ray look over Elizabeth's report to make sure everything looks good after she makes the corrections?"

"You sure you're all right? Yes, Ray and I will look over Elizabeth's report and will help her make any other corrections she needs.", Bessie replied.

"I'm fine, Bessie. Just tired and as I told Ray, I didn't get much sleep in the hospital. It will be wonderful to sleep in my own bed and not have to worry about someone waking me every hour. I love you. Good night, Bessie"

"Good night, Raymond. I love you too."

Bessie herded the two girls off to bed and tucked them in nice and cozy. She walked into her bedroom to check on Raymond because he usually was the last one to bed on most nights and this worried her. *Was he really all right*, she thought.

———

Sara, Ray, and Jimmy were in the den talking about Ray and Sara's plans to take the train to Raleigh and the bus to Edenton on Friday.

Ray said, "Jimmy, I want to apologize for being angry with you this morning. I was actually more angry with myself that I'd overslept and I took it out on you. Thanks for trying to take care of everything this morning. It certainly meant a lot to me."

"I understood, Ray. You felt like you'd not done your part and you always get upset when you think you've let someone down.", Jimmy replied.

Sara winked approvingly at Ray as Bessie came in from putting Myra and Lillie to bed.

Bessie said, "Ray, Jimmy, your father seemed awfully tired tonight and he's gone to bed. I'm concerned that he really isn't doing well and that the doctors may have released him too early."

Ray replied, "Mom, the excitement of playing with girls and what he told me about being roused every hour during the night while at the hospital probably accounts for his being tired tonight. I'm sure he'll be his old self tomorrow."

The small group chatted a little while longer, corrected Elizabeth's report, and retired for the evening.

JOHNSON FAMILY HOME ~ MONTCROSS, NORTH CAROLINA
FRIDAY, DECEMBER 19, 1941

Before everyone realized it, Friday, December 19 arrived clear and cold and with it, Sara's visit had ended. Ray was up early to do his chores and had everyone at school on time. The tearful goodbyes had been said. Raymond drove the couple to the train station for their trip to Edenton. While neither Sara nor Ray knew where their lives would take them after this weekend, they both understood they were now making the journey together.

The Peabodys of Edenton

• •

Raymond helped Ray and Sara gather their luggage and Christmas presents from the trunk of the car and walked them to the train platform.

Raymond hugged Sara then said, "Sara, just like Bessie told you in Montcross, I too look forward to calling you my daughter-in-law. You make Ray very happy and he's lucky to have found you. I know this separation will be trying for both of you just like it was for Bessie and me. If you ever need anything, we will do whatever we can for you. Bessie and I love you like one of our own."

Sara, with tears in her eyes, responded, "I love you and Bessie as well, and I will be in touch. I know I can count on you or Bessie while Ray is away and that helps tremendously. My best wishes for a wonderful Christmas; and I am happy you recovered so quickly from the scare. Thank you for everything."

Sara started towards the train as Ray told his dad goodbye, "Dad, I am glad you came through the crisis and are feeling better. I want you to know I am happy I am making this trip. We will let you know by telegram when we arrive. Tell everyone I love them and will see them Tuesday."

"Have a safe trip and I will look for the telegram tonight. We love you and are proud of you.", Raymond replied.

Ray boarded the train just before it pulled from the station for the five-hour trip to Raleigh which thankfully passed quickly. Instead of eating lunch in the dining car, Ray and Sara ate the cold fried chicken and potato salad that Elva packed them for the trip.

In Raleigh, Sara and Ray sent telegrams to their families that they were about to board the bus to Edenton. The bus, scheduled to arrive in Edenton at ten-thirty, was delayed by several mechanical breakdowns along the route and when Ray and Sara finally arrived at eleven-thirty, they were exhausted. Sara's father met them at the station and drove them to the Peabody home where the rest of the family waited to greet them.

PEABODY FAMILY HOME ~ EDENTON, NORTH CAROLINA
FRIDAY - 11:45PM

. . . .

Sara and Ray arrived to much fanfare.

Samuel, Sara's Father, said to Ray, "We are glad to have you here with our family again and look forward to a great weekend. I think the boys want to take you hunting in the morning."

Sara's oldest brother Sam asked, "If you can get up in about four hours, we have a great duck blind staked out at the mouth of the Roanoke River. It's been providing some great duck hunts this week."

Ray, exhausted from the long trip, replied, "If someone wakes me up, I would enjoy the chance to try my luck. Thanks."

Sara hugged her mom and dad, then commented, "It's wonderful to be home again. The trip to Montcross was fantastic, but I'm exhausted and would like to go to bed."

Sara's mother, Alma, replied, "It had to be tiring. If the boys want to go hunting in the morning, it's time for bed. Glad to have you home, Sara. Ray, we hope you enjoy yourself this weekend."

Ray was shown to the opulent Nineteenth Century guest house with its Victorian furnishings. The fatigue of the trip was too much for his body and sleep overtook him instantly.

───────────

Sara retired to her own bedroom for the first time since Thanksgiving and had difficulty getting to sleep. Her thoughts returned to what would happen to Ray while he was in the Marines and if he would come home safe. As her mother prepared for bed, she noticed Sara's light was still on and knocked quietly.

Sara said, "Come in, I'm still awake."

"Why are you still awake? I thought you were ready to go to bed?"

"Mom, I can't get to sleep. I'm exhausted but I'm thinking about how Ray's decision to join the Marines is going to affect me. I know I love him, but I don't want anything to happen to him."

"Sara, the only thing you can do is support him and pray that he comes through safely. He is a young man following his conscience. His strong character shapes his desire to serve others and his country. That is one of the things I really like about him. My recommendation is that you just love and support him."

"Thanks, Mom. Talking with you has helped. I think I can fall asleep now."

"Goodnight, Sara. I love you."

"Goodnight, Mom. I love you too."

As slumber overtakes her, Sara's thoughts are of Ray and the wonderful time they will have this weekend.

PEABODY FAMILY HOME ~ EDENTON, NORTH CAROLINA
SATURDAY, DECEMBER 20, 1941 - 4:30AM
• • • • • • • • • • • • • • • • • • • •

At four-thirty Saturday morning, Sam knocked on the guest house door to awaken Ray. Ray dressed quickly in the hunting attire Sam loaned him and a breakfast of sausage and cheese sandwiches with black coffee was waiting when he walked into the kitchen. Thomas, Sara's sixteen year old brother, was joining them this morning for the hunt.

Ray asked Sam, "I've shot doves and quail before but I've never been duck hunting. Tell me, what is it like?"

Sam replied, "Mr. Jameson will take us to the blind in his trusty Harker's Island boat. William and Thomas will then set our decoys in a pattern that will attract the ducks to our blind. The ducks have been flying well this year and hopefully today will be no different."

Out of his pocket, Sam pulled a new 1941 Federal Migratory Bird Hunting stamp and handed it to Ray.

Ray asked, "What do I do with this?"

"Attach it to your hunting license and sign it. That makes it legal for you to hunt ducks. The federal wildlife officers check our area regularly and you could get a ticket without the stamp. I will tell you which birds we can shoot and how many.", Sam replied.

Ray replied, "No wonder Sara asked me if I had a hunting license before we made the trip. It makes sense now; thanks for taking care of it for me."

Sam herded the bleary-eyed hunters to the truck for the short trip to the wharf.

EDENTON WHARF AND ROANOKE RIVER BLIND ~ EDENTON, NORTH CAROLINA
5:30AM

. . . .

Promptly at five-thirty, the group of four arrived at the wharf and went aboard the "Albemarle Lady" with Mr. Jameson at the helm. The ride to the blind lasted about twenty minutes. Mr. Jameson piloted the boat to a carefully camouflaged platform at the mouth of the Roanoke River and left them well before sunrise. William and Thomas took the little dory and set the decoys while Sam and Ray prepared everything in the blind.

Sam yelled at William, "Come on, the sun will rise in fifteen minutes. Hurry up with those decoys."

"Hold your horses, Sam. We'll be finished in just a minute.", William retorts.

The boys finished setting out the decoys and returned to the platform. William and Thomas covered the dory with reeds to camouflage it after tying it up at the back of the blind. Taking their places in the blind, Sam handed them their guns and sat down beside Ray to wait for sunrise.

Ray asked, "What time should we start seeing birds since it won't be light for at least another thirty minutes?"

"Well, Ray, the birds will land within the decoy pattern between now and daylight. You will be able to hear them splash as they land.", Sam replied.

Just then, a group of about ten birds splashed amongst the decoys. With day slowly dawning, Ray looked out of the duck blind and saw about twenty or thirty ducks swimming in and around the fifty or so decoys.

Will asked in a whisper to no one in particular, "Who gives the word when to stand up and scare the birds to flight?"

Sam quietly responded, "I will give the word when it is time to stand and scare the birds to flight. I want to take time to figure out what species of ducks we are looking at before shooting. We can only legally take forty ducks between the four of us."

Thomas rebutted, "We know about the bag limits, Sam. Why are you telling us stuff we already know...?"

"Because Ray has never duck hunted and he doesn't know the regulations. After I know what we are looking at, I will give the word to stand and shoot. Now, BE QUIET!", Sam said softly.

The sun had just peeked over the eastern horizon when Ray looked out to see a large raft of ducks swimming in the decoys. The old 12-gauge side-by-side shotgun felt comfortable in his hands, and he awaited the signal to stand and shoot. Sam judged there were about thirty ducks, mostly canvasbacks and mallards, in the spread.

He then quietly said to Ray, "Remember, just like shooting doves or quail, pick out one bird at a time and kill it before moving to the next one."

"Thanks for the tip. I tend to forget that.", Ray whispered.

Sam said, "By the paper, sunrise today is at seven-fifteen which is five minutes from now. At that time, all of us will stand and flush the birds off the water. After the volley, William and Thomas will retrieve the birds with the dory."

The group nodded anxiously at Sam. They picked out which birds they were going to shoot as they lifted off of the water. Everyone stood and flushed the ducks to flight at seven-fifteen. Ray picked out the duck closest to his side of the blind, drew a bead, followed through, and watched the mallard splash in the water after two shots. Sam with his Winchester pump shotgun, killed two out of three ducks in quick succession as they took flight. William and Thomas each knocked down a canvasback duck with their shots. Five ducks were taken in the first flight of the morning. With the birds out of shooting range for the time being, William and Thomas picked up the downed birds while Sam poured Ray a cup of coffee from the thermos.

Ray said, "Sara tells me that the Army is going to pay for you to finish medical school at Duke before requiring your services as a doctor. When do you think you'll finish the program? And, what are the Army's requirements after you complete it?"

"I thought about enlisting immediately which is what Sara tells me you are going to do. I think finishing school is the best thing to do since I'm a full year into the three-year medical program. The Army and Navy need doctors to care for the wounded. The local draft board got in touch with the War Department on my behalf who said that I could join now and I would be assigned as a medical orderly or a frontline medic. Or, the Army would pay for an accelerated year-round medical program at Duke as an officer in the Army. I will finish the accelerated medical program designed by the Army, Navy, and medical schools sometime in the fall of 1943.[1] After completing the program, I will be assigned as a medical officer either near the front lines or in a military hospital. This is best option for me and if the Army needs me elsewhere, they can always assign me to fill that need. I will be required to serve in the Army for six years.", Sam replied.

---

1 • Accelerated Medical Education Program - http://repository.countway. harvard.edu/xmlui/handle/10473/1784

"That sounds like a great program for you. Combat surgeons have one of the toughest jobs in the military. I certainly wish you luck.", Ray replied.

Sam asked, "Sara told me that you will be joining the Marines like your father did in 1917 right after Christmas. I have to ask, why not wait until your spring semester is finished?"

"I thought about waiting, but I see the need our country has to mobilize its forces for the defense of the country. My father joined the Marines very soon after President Wilson declared war in 1917. He felt that he had to serve when the country called. Part of my decision is with this in mind and the other part of my decision lends itself to hoping the sooner I get in; the sooner I get out. I don't know what the chances are of the latter happening though it is my fervent hope that I get home to Sara as soon as I can."

Sam replied, "I do hope your service can be completed quickly and you can get home to Sara safely. She is scared for you because she loves you very much. She'll worry until you're home. Good luck, Ray."

William and Thomas joined the two men back on the platform with the ducks they had taken earlier.

"These ducks are some of the prettiest I've seen this year. Look at how full the plumage is on the redhead and canvasback. Ray, would you like to have your redhead mounted by our taxidermist? It shouldn't cost that much.", Thomas asked while he poured himself a cup of coffee.

Ray replied, "I think that is a great idea since I don't know when I will get to hunt again. The mount would make a great memory of today."

William poured himself a cup of coffee then said to Ray, "I overheard what you told Sam about volunteering immediately; especially the part about getting back home as quickly as possible. I was initially angry about the surprise attack and wanted to volunteer immediately. Then, after discussing the attack with my professors and parents, I came to the conclusion that this war is going to be a long, drawn out, bloody affair. That discussion helped me decide to wait until I have finished this year at school. During summer I can decide if I want to volunteer, continue college, or go to work in one of the deferred positions. I don't turn twenty-one until July 10, 1943. I am willing to do my part, but I've not figured out exactly what part I must play."

"William, unless you know for sure what you want to do, that's the best plan. The decision I made suits me and your decision will suit you. I told a friend of mine last Sunday that people may serve differently but all are pulling in the direction of victory.", Ray replied

Sam said, "Get ready, it looks like some more ducks are settling in our decoys."

Looking up just in time to see a flight of buffleheads and canvasbacks set their wings for the decoys, everyone managed to scrape down at least one duck. William ably killed a second one as it flew directly over the blind.

Three more flights came in that morning and the boys downed a few more. Ray's shooting improved as the morning progressed. With the last flight, Ray knocked down two ducks with two shells. The final tally was ten canvasbacks, seven mallards, five redheads, and four buffleheads.

William said to no one in particular, "These ducks will make great Christmas eating for us. I bet Mom and Eloise will even cook a couple for dinner tonight."

The brothers agreed that this was a great way to get to know their prospective brother-in-law. The ride back to the wharf flew as the boys relived every shot of the morning.

Thomas popped off at Ray, "Hey, Ray, where did you learn to shoot, a Cracker Jack box? It certainly looked at times like you couldn't hit the broad side of a barn. How many ducks did you get?"

In a good natured retort, Ray responded, "Well I did manage to bring down five ducks with my Cracker Jack shooting. Towards the end, I was getting the knack of leading the ducks. I finally managed a double on the last flight. All in all, I had a great time."

A good chuckle was had at Ray's expense which he took good-naturedly.

· ·

As Mr. Jameson tied the boat at the dock, Sara arrived to meet them. It made her happy to see all of them laughing. She was unsure how Ray would take to her brothers, but she saw that she had nothing to worry about.

Sara said, "Ray, I think we should have lunch while we are in town."

Sam, grabbing Ray, said, "You know, Ray, you have to help clean ducks before we can go home."

"Sara, the guys took me hunting and it is only fair that I help them clean the birds. Sam, you'll have to show me how to do it, but I will definitely help. Maybe we can have one or two tonight for dinner. Which species makes the best meal? And, which one should I have mounted?", Ray replied.

"Ray, I think you should have the redhead mounted. The best ducks for eating are the canvasbacks and mallards. We'll clean all the birds except your redhead.", Sam explains.

Ray replied, "Sounds good with me. I'm sorry, Sara, but I need to help the guys."

Sara, a little hurt but understanding, said, "I understand, Ray. You do need to help them. I'll see you when you get home."

The boys showed Ray the best way to clean the birds and within forty-five minutes, they had the birds table ready.

On the drive home, the group stopped by the taxidermist's shop to drop off the redhead.

Mr. Sampson, the local taxidermist, told Ray, "That's as beautiful a redhead duck as I've seen this year. I can mount it as a flying mount and it will cost $75.00. I just need a $25.00 deposit to get started. It'll take about three to six months to complete the mount. Who do I call when I'm finished?"

"Mr. Sampson, here's the deposit and let any of the Peabodys know when it can be picked up. They'll know how to get it to me since I'll be serving in the Marine Corps.", Ray responded.

"Thanks. Wish you all the best in the Marines. That's the best fighting outfit we have at present to handle the Japanese. I'll let the boys know when I'm done.", Mr. Sampson commented.

They wished Mr. Sampson well, drove back to the house, put the ducks in the cooler, washed their hands, and sat down to lunch. Mrs. Peabody served ham sandwiches, fried potatoes, and deviled eggs.

PEABODY GUEST HOUSE ~ EDENTON, NORTH CAROLINA
SATURDAY, DECEMBER 20, 1941 - 1:00PM
• • • • • • • • • • • • • • • • • • • •

Finishing lunch, Ray excused himself to clean up after the morning hunt, but before he left he said, "Sara, what are our plans after I clean up?"

"I would like to go visit some friends and neighbors in town."

"That's fine with me, Sara. I am a little tired so I hope I can take a little nap when we get back."

"We won't be gone long, Ray. I want to visit folks who aren't able to come tomorrow."

"I'll get cleaned up and be ready to leave soon."

Ray left Sara and her mother talking in the kitchen. He knew he had to hurry if they were to visit everyone on Sara's list. As he sat down in the luxurious hot water of the antique Clawfoot tub, he was overcome by weariness and was asleep within minutes. He was sleeping soundly in the tub when Sara and her mother entered the guest house to check on him about an hour later.

Sara yelled through the door, "RAY! RAY! ANYTHING WRONG?"

"RAY! ARE YOU ALL RIGHT? ANSWER US!"

Groggily, Ray began to awaken from the sleepy fog that shrouded his mind in the rapidly cooling water of the tub.

"RAY! WHAT'S WRONG?"

"Mom, go get Daddy, PLEASE. We need to check on Ray. He might have drowned in the tub!"

"Be right back. I'll get your Dad to check on him."

Her mother rushed into the main house to find her husband or one of her sons. Meanwhile, Sara kept banging on the door until Ray responded.

"Yes. Yes. Who is it?"

"Ray, ARE YOU ALL RIGHT?"

"Yes, I am fine. Why?"

"I've been waiting on you for over an hour! We're LATE NOW," she angrily retorted!

Escalating the tension, he responded, "SARA! I fell asleep, I told you I was TIRED! Give me fifteen minutes and I'll be ready to go."

Sara huffily left the guest house without a response.

Ray was in the main house fifteen minutes later with Sara's anger and frustration evident on her face. She gave him a look of cold fury that would kill any normal man.

Ray saw the look, defused it with a quick smile, and said, "I'm sorry I fell asleep in the tub. I couldn't help it. When my tired body hit that hot water, I was out like a light. I promise I'll make it up to you. Can you forgive me?"

Sara's anger melted with each apologetic word Ray uttered and she responded, "I thought you'd drowned or something when it took ten minutes of yelling and banging to wake you. I was angry thinking that you didn't want to go visiting this afternoon. I'm sorry too."

Ray took her in his arms and said, "I'm looking forward to meeting everyone, and I don't want anything to spoil it. I'm ready to go."

"We can leave now. We'll have to cut our visits short but, we'll be able to visit my grandparents and maybe the Crafts.", Sara said.

SARA'S GRANDPARENTS' HOME ~ EDENTON, NORTH CAROLINA
SATURDAY, DECEMBER 20, 1941 - 2:30PM
• • • • • • • • • • • • • • • • • • • •

Sara said, "Let's go to my Dad's parents' house first since they don't get out too often due to Grandpa's health. We won't stay more than thirty minutes because grandma tires very easily, too."

"All right. Was it Grandfather Peabody who fought with the Army in Cuba during the Spanish-American War and tells great stories of his time in the Army? I thoroughly enjoyed talking with him at the picnic during my last visit. He seemed so spry and healthy. What happened?"

Sara commented, "Yes, Grandpa Peabody did serve in the Army during the Spanish-American War and he thoroughly enjoys telling his old war stories. He got sick late in the summer and has been very weak ever since. Grandma tries to take care of him, but she's worn herself out trying to care for both of them. Dad pleads with her to hire some help but she'll hear nothing of it. Telling Dad, 'I married your Father for better or worse and I will take care of him myself.' They've always had servants doing the cooking, cleaning, and grounds keeping around the old home place, but Grandma says that she'll be the only one to take care of Grandpa."

The couple drove up the long circular driveway bordered by tall pine trees. Each time Ray saw the stately pines lining the driveway, it gave him the impression that he had traveled back in time to that wonderful antebellum period of the Old South. A house servant waited to greet them at the door and showed them into the massive Victorian home with its vaulted ceilings and massive stairway in the foyer.

The negro doorman said, "Good aftern'oon Miss Sara, come in. Let me take your coats and I will show you to the sitting room while I fetch Missus Leona. Mister John is reading in the study."

Sara replied, "Thank you Robert. You can show us both to the study. Please send Grandma there."

Robert announced Sara and Ray at the door of the study, and her grandfather looked up and saw his favorite granddaughter enter the room with the young man he met last summer.

Greeting them, he said, "Good afternoon, Sara, how is my favorite granddaughter today? That looks like the nice young man I met last summer at the picnic. Is it?"

"Very happy, Grandpa. Yes, you met Ray last summer at the picnic," Sara replied.

Ray said, "Mr. Peabody, it is good to see you again. At the picnic, I enjoyed your stories about the Spanish-American War and the history of this area and the Albemarle Sound. How have you been, Sir?"

"Ray, I have been feeling poorly since a bout with pneumonia and heart troubles hit me just before dove season opened. I had to take it easy and missed opening day of dove season for the first time in forty-five years. Doctor's orders keep me stuck in a chair somewhere in the house or on the veranda all day. I need to get out every once in a while, but Leona will not hear of it. She thinks it will tire me out. How can riding in a car tire me out?", Mr. Peabody responded.

"John, you know what the doctors said. The only way to regain your strength is for you to rest. Gallivanting around in the car will only exhaust you," Leona told John.

Turning to Sara and Ray, she said, "How's my granddaughter? You look well."

"I'm doing well, Grandma. I am glad to be home for Christmas. How are you?", Sara replied.

Her grandma says, "Been tired lately and cannot seem to get enough rest. I have got to watch your grandfather every minute or he would sneak away for an afternoon with your dad or brothers. I cannot let him tire himself out."

"Grandma, Ray and I would like to take Grandpa with us to visit the Crafts for afternoon tea. Would you care to join us? It would be good for both of you to go visiting," Sara asked.

Her grandpa replied, "It has been a while since we have visited your brother and sister-in-law. We should go visit and I promise I will not tire myself."

"All right, John, we will go for afternoon tea but we cannot stay too long," Leona responded.

Ray, Sara, and Robert helped her grandparents into the car for the short trip.

The small contingent arrived at the Crafts promptly at three-thirty for afternoon tea. The Craft's friendship with the Peabodys dated back to before John Peabody married Leona Craft in 1893 and joined the families.

The Crafts' butler answered the door and said, "Welcome Mistah John and Missus Leona, so glad to see you today. Who do you have with you?"

"You know Sara, my granddaughter, and this is her beau, Ray Johnson. Andrew, where's my brother-in-law this fine day?"

"They are in the sittin' room preparing for afternoon tea. Lets me take your coats and show you in."

Andrew took their coats and walked them into the sitting room in a manner keeping with the Antebellum traditions of the area.

Arthur greeted John with, "Glad to see you can get out and about after your illness, John. I am happy you could liven up our tea time this afternoon. You look great!"

"Thanks, Arthur. Leona has kept me on a short leash since my illness. How are you doing, Grace?"

Grace replied, "Doing well John. Glad you could make it today. It is good to see all of you today. You need to visit more often. We miss the conversations of the old times before all these crises plaguing us started. Who is the handsome gentleman joining us today?"

"I apologize for my rudeness; I should have introduced him as we came in. This young man is Sara's beau, Ray Johnson. Ray is from Montcross, North Carolina and is studying textile management at State College. I apologize."

Ray shook hands with Mr. and Mrs. Craft and responded, "No apologies necessary, Mr. Peabody. I am happy to meet you, both. I have heard so much about you, Mr. Craft, from textile leaders who tell me that Mr. Arthur Craft is one of the smartest textile businessmen in the state. I hope after I get discharged from the

Marines, I will be able to sit down with you and talk about modern textile manufacturing. Thank you for allowing me to join you today."

Everyone took their seat as Rosa served sweet iced tea and finger sandwiches. Light banter and deep conversation took up the majority of the next thirty minutes until Sara glanced at Ray to let him know it was time to leave.

Ray shook Mr. Craft's hand and commented, "Thank you for your hospitality and the information you shared about textile manufacturing in the state. I hope to see you again soon. Hope you have a wonderful Christmas."

Mr. Craft replied, "You are welcome, Ray. Come back to visit as soon as you get home from the war. I will be happy to set you up in one of the mills here after you finish the textile management program at State College. Tell Mr. Strathmore in Montcross, I said hello. Have a merry Christmas."

John said, "It was great to visit with you this afternoon. See you at church on Christmas Eve. Thanks again."

SARA'S GRANDPARENTS' HOME ~ EDENTON, NORTH CAROLINA
SATURDAY, DECEMBER 20, 1941 - 5:15PM
• • • • • • • • • • • • • • • • • • • •

Sitting in the library back at her grandparents' home, Sara checked her watch and exclaimed, "We'd better hurry, Ray. The family will be waiting supper if we don't leave now. You know how Mom is about having supper promptly at six. Grandma, Grandpa, we had a wonderful time and I will be by next week for a longer visit."

Leona whispered while hugging Sara, "You have a fine young man in Ray and I look forward to seeing more of him. I sure hope he takes care of himself while in the Marines. I love you, Sara, and will see you next week. Maybe we can go shopping."

Sara replied, "I love you too, Grandma. Yes, Ray is a fine man and I hope he gets back safely. Let's do go shopping. It will do us both good."

Shaking John's hand, Ray said, "Thank you for a wonderful visit Mr. Peabody. I look forward to seeing you as soon as I can return from the war."

"Ray, the pleasure was all mine. Like Arthur said, you are an upstanding young man who is going to go far in this world. Try to be as careful as you can while in the Marines and remember you have a place to come when the war is over. I wish you the best of luck and hope to see you real soon," Mr. Peabody replied.

PEABODY FAMILY HOME ~ EDENTON, NORTH CAROLINA
SATURDAY, DECEMBER 20, 1941 - 6:00PM
• •

Ray and Sara made it home in time for supper only to find that it would not be ready for another twenty minutes. The men moved to the den to talk while Eloise, Alma, and Sara finished preparing tonight's supper of fresh duck, rice, green beans, and yeast biscuits. Mr. Peabody sent Sam, William, and Thomas to get more firewood so he could have a private conversation with Ray.

Mr. Peabody asked Ray, "What did you think of my Uncle Arthur? He is a shrewd businessman who will be willing to help you in your textile career if you want to live in Edenton after the war."

"Mr. Craft is highly thought of across the state. When I told Mr. Strathmore of the Cronkite Mill in Montcross that I was visiting Edenton with Sara, he told me about the excellent record Mr. Craft had running mills in this part of the state. After meeting him today, I can see why he is so highly regarded by the textile business leaders of the state. I learned a lot in the short hour we visited. I cannot wait to meet with him again," Ray responded.

"What do you think you will do after the war, Ray? Would you like to come back here to Edenton and live?"

"I will have to make a lot of decisions, if I make it home safely after the war. I would be blessed to live here with Sara, if that's what God has planned for me, but, right now, all I can think about is doing my part."

"This war will be a long struggle and the country needs to prepare for things to get a lot worse before they start getting better. Somehow I believe you are going to survive and do just fine. We will be here praying for your safety. I want to know, do you intend to ask me for Sara's hand in marriage?"

Ray, shocked at the direct question and glad Sara was not in the room, stuttered, "Mr. Peabody, I would like nothing more than to ask your permission to marry your daughter. But, I do not think it is fair to Sara or your family to ask your permission with my future so unclear. I don't want to make Sara a war widow even before we've had a chance to make a life together. I want to wait until I make it home first."

Mr. Peabody, eyes glistening, responded, "Ray, there is nothing more I would like than to see you to marry my daughter. I know how hard it must be to not know what your future holds. Your character speaks volumes to me because a lot of men would have told me yes. Then they would have said that they wanted a quick wedding before they go off to war. I have seen a lot of young men in this area doing just this before they leave for the Army, Navy, or Marines. You told me that you love and want to marry my daughter, but you are putting her well-being ahead of your own. I am proud of you. When you are home safely from the war, you will have my permission to marry Sara; and I will be proud to call you my son-in-law. Please call me Samuel from now on."

"Yes, Sir. Thank you Mr. ..., Samuel. Life is not going to be easy but knowing that I have two families now, I couldn't be happier. I will do my best to make it home."

Sam, William, and Thomas returned with wood for the fire in time to see both men embracing.

Sam asked, "What's going on? Do I have another brother now?"

"You do not have another brother yet, but hopefully that's the case in the future. Ray told me that he would like to marry your sister only after he returns home. If something happened to him it would be bad enough on Sara, but he does not want to make it worse by marrying her now and possibly leaving her as a widow. I am proud of Ray. Now, tell me about the duck hunt."

As William started to talk about the duck hunt, Mrs. Peabody walked in and announced that supper was ready.

In the dining room, Sara noticed an air of mystery and an easiness between her dad and Ray.

This calmness and ease made Sara a little nervous and she asked, "Dad, what is going on? You and Ray seem like you've come to some understanding about something."

Her dad smiled when he looked at his daughter and said, "Sara, I know how much both of you care for one another. We had a conversation and came to an understanding. Ray said he wants to marry you only after he returns from this conflict because he does not want you to carry the risks and burdens of this conflict hanging over your marriage. He wants to have a clear future before you start your lives as husband and wife. Frankly, I am proud of Ray for thinking of you before thinking of himself."

Sara blushed and started crying, "Oh DAD! That's wonderful! I'm glad that you approve of Ray! I want to spend the rest of my life with him."

Her mom broke in and said, "I'm happy, too. Welcome to the family, Ray."

"Thank you, Mrs. Peabody. Today has been overwhelming for me. The boys treated me like I was part of the family this morning during the duck hunt. Mr. and Mrs. Peabody at tea this afternoon welcomed me like I was their long lost grandson. And now tonight, I will always strive to maintain the love and trust of this family. Thank you all for this wonderful Christmas gift," Ray gushed.

Thomas announced, "Now that all the mushy stuff is over, would someone pass the duck. I'm starved."

Everyone laughed as the talk gave way to eating. After supper, Ray and Sara excused themselves to take a walk down to the beautiful Edenton waterfront.

Edenton Waterfront ~ Edenton, North Carolina
Saturday, December 20, 1941 - 8:00pm

• •

Ray and Sara walked hand in hand to the waterfront and sat down on one of the lovely benches that overlooked the beautifully moonlit Albemarle Sound with its quiet serenity. Ray thought, *It is hard to believe that lurking just off the North Carolina coast are German U-Boats that have been sinking cargo and oil freighters by the score.* The scene was one of tranquility which was a direct contradiction of the death and destruction occurring all over the world. It had been a wonderful day for the couple and they needed some time to talk about all the momentous occurrences.

"Sara, I know you would marry me tomorrow, but we both know that is not the proper thing to do. I am very nervous about serving but I know that I cannot do otherwise. Will you wait on me? You know I love you and I will do everything in my power to return to you."

"Yes, Ray, I will wait on you. Nothing is going to happen to you; I love you too much."

"Let's have fun the rest of the weekend and try not to think too much about the future. Can we do that?"

"I'll try, but it will be difficult for me."

"Good, we need to get back home so that I can defend my shooting skills from this morning. Your brothers are probably telling your dad how badly I shot. Thomas loved ribbing me about missing several 'easy' shots this morning"

"You know it was not too long ago that William was ribbing Thomas about his shooting as well. I am glad you had a good time with my brothers. I am sure they will try to drag you out one more time while you are here."

They left the comfort of the bench with its tranquil view and walked home; lost in the bliss of the love they shared.

The Peabodys of Edenton

As Sara and Ray walked back into the warm house, the laughing banter of Sara's parents and brothers could be heard throughout the large Victorian home.

They overheard Thomas say, "Ray could not hit the broadside of the barn from the inside this morning. He was lucky to get five ducks during the hunt."

Ray winked at Sara, sneaked through the door, and said, "Hey, Thomas, your shooting wasn't that good either. How many ducks did you kill this morning? I know Sam killed nine birds, William killed seven, and I killed five which ironically is the same number you killed this morning. I think your shooting was just as bad. I have to admit though; I had a great time hunting with all of you today. Now since you woke me up at four-thirty this morning to abuse me, I do believe I will retire to my nice warm bed."

Thomas piped back, "I thought we were going snipe hunting tonight. What do you mean turning in early? I thought you were here to have a good time."

"Well, Thomas, I about got in trouble with Sara this afternoon because I fell asleep on duty. I wouldn't want to get in trouble with your mother for sleeping through church. I'll just have to pass on the snipe hunting since it is a well-known fact that snipe do not come out at night."

Mrs. Peabody interjected, "There will be no snipe hunting tonight. I think you all need your rest since we have the luncheon here tomorrow. Good night, Ray, and we are mighty glad to have you here."

Ray bid the family good night and Sara walked him to the guest house where he kissed her goodnight at the door.

"Good night, Ray. I love you."

"I love you too. Good night, Sara."

Sara returned to the house to talk with her mother. She found her mother in the sitting room talking to her dad about the day.

"Mom, can I talk to you for a little while.", Sara asked.

Her dad, a bit perplexed, was given the idea that maybe he should leave so the women could talk.

"Goodnight, Sara. Please do not keep your mother up too late."

"Goodnight, Dad. We'll not be too long. Hope you have a good night's sleep. I love you."

"Samuel, I should not be too long. Goodnight and I love you.", her mom replied.

"Mom, I am trying not to think about how everything in my life is going to completely change next week. I will not have Ray in Raleigh when school starts back. I will have to get used to going to church and luncheons alone. I do not know how I will handle it. Will I remain faithful to Ray while he is gone and will he remain faithful to me?" Sara asked.

"You are not first woman to ask herself these questions. I believe you love Ray with all your heart and will be faithful to him just like he will be completely faithful to you. As far as having to do things alone; remember that you can always write, phone, or telegram when things are especially rough. You should enjoy those activities that will help take your mind off of the separation. I am sure Ray's family will keep in touch with you while he is gone, and I know Ray will write you religiously while he is gone as well. Just try not to worry. Everything will be fine. I'm tired, I think we both need to go to bed since we have the Red Cross luncheon tomorrow. Goodnight, Sara."

"Thanks, Mom. I know I can count on you and Dad if I need anything. I love you, Mom, goodnight."

PEABODY FAMILY HOME ~ EDENTON, NORTH CAROLINA
SUNDAY, DECEMBER 21, 1941 - 9:00AM

The sun rose over the eastern shore of the Albemarle Sound on the second Sunday after the attack on Pearl Harbor. Ray awoke this morning with the thought of how wonderful this weekend had been so far. He was welcomed and accepted by Sara's family and friends. The sun shone in the window of the guest house and reflected off of the Victorian fixtures and furniture which temporarily caused Ray to think he had time-traveled back to a more genteel period. For a brief moment, he forgot there was a world war raging and soaked up the tranquility of the scene. He arose from bed, got dressed, and left the guest house to enter the kitchen for breakfast.

The smell of frying eggs and country ham greeted him as he made his way to the kitchen door. He entered the kitchen to join the rest of the family for breakfast. The banter was light this morning. Everyone was talking about the luncheon that they were hosting after church.

After breakfast, the family left for church. The morning was chilly but not too cold for the family to make the brisk five-minute walk to the Edenton Baptist Church. Sara was radiant in her winter dress, shawl, and hat with Ray by her side. The family arrived at a quarter of eleven and were warmly greeted by Deacon Smith and Deacon Trantham. In the sanctuary, they were shown to their seats in the sixth row of the center section which had been occupied by the Peabody family since 1875. Ray looked around the church, built in 1918, and he was awed not only by the limestone construction and the intricately painted ceiling border, but also the warm welcome he received. He was touched with the same warm feeling he received every time he attended First Baptist in Montcross, the feeling that he belonged.

The service lasted a little over an hour. Reverend Wells preached about the coming of Jesus on Christmas day and how the three wise men brought their gifts to the Christ child. Reverend Wells led a prayer for the young men who had volunteered and those about to volunteer for service with the United States military. The announcement of the Christmas Eve Service was made and the service concluded. Sara and Ray greeted the pastor and walked home. They knew they needed to hurry home to help her parents prepare for the luncheon. Everyone arrived at about the same time and helped Eloise finish preparing the meal.

PEABODY FAMILY HOME LUNCHEON ~ EDENTON, NORTH CAROLINA
SUNDAY, DECEMBER 21, 1941 - 1:00PM

• • • • • • • • • • • • • • • • • • • •

The annual luncheon brought together longtime residents, family, and friends to raise funds for community civic organizations. This year would be an exception because all funds would be donated to the American Red Cross. Eloise, Mrs. Peabody, and women of the community prepared the meal and everyone enjoyed the food and fellowship. The younger children moved to the play room upstairs for games after lunch. The men retired to the den for cigars and conversation while the ladies moved to the sitting room for fellowship. Ray, at the behest of Sara, moved between rooms to meet and greet everyone. As the luncheon wound down, Ray, Sam, and William were asked by Mr. Peabody to help him collect the donations.

Mr. and Mrs. Peabody believed that the need for the Red Cross would be greater than ever with the war and they wanted to get this year's drive off to a rousing start. The Peabody family including Sara's grandparents, John and Leona, donated over $250.00. Mr. and Mrs. Arthur Craft wrote a check in the amount of $200.00 for the fundraiser. The sum total of funds for the Red Cross from the luncheon exceeded $2,500.00. The donation was received by the Red Cross representative with profuse gratitude, and the Peabody family thanked everyone for making the luncheon a wonderful success.

PEABODY FAMILY HOME ~ EDENTON, NORTH CAROLINA
SUNDAY, DECEMBER 21, 1941 - 4:30PM

• • • • • • • • • • • • • • • • • • • •

The feeling of success was fleeting now that everyone had to help clean up. The moans and groans could be heard as dishes were collected, floors were cleaned, and the playroom was picked up. Ray and Sara worked in the sitting room where they cleaned out the ash trays, wiped off the wood surfaces where coffee cups and tea glasses left condensation, and swept the carpets with the rolling carpet sweeper. Mr. Peabody and the boys returned the folding tables and chairs to the storage room, then cleaned out the fireplaces to prepare them for use later. Some of the women stayed to help Mrs. Peabody and Eloise. As soon as the house had some semblance of order, Mr. and Mrs. Peabody made their way to the den to relax.

Ray told Sara that he should call his folks since they had not heard from him since Friday. Sara left Ray in the study to call his parents and check on everything in Montcross. Ray picked up the earpiece and tapped the receiver twice to get the operator. The operator set up the collect call between Ray and his parents at Montcross 344.

Raymond answered, "Hello, Hello"

The operator said, "Collect call from Ray Johnson, will you accept the charges?"

"Yes, Operator, I will accept the charges. Thank you.", Raymond replied.

"You are now connected." The operator responded.

"Hello, Ray! How is everything in Edenton?" His dad asked.

"Hello, Dad! Everything is wonderful here in Edenton. We just finished the Christmas luncheon here and $2,500.00 was raised for the local Red Cross. How is everything in Montcross?"

"Everything has been good here. I am feeling a lot better and looking forward to going back to work tomorrow. Jimmy has everything lined up to start his flying lessons. Mom and Elizabeth have been helping the ladies roll bandages for the Red Cross. Myra and Lillie have been driving everyone crazy asking about you and Santa."

"Glad you are doing better and I bet you are excited to go back to work tomorrow. Sara's brothers woke me up at four-thirty yesterday morning to take me duck hunting. I had a great time with Sam, William, and Thomas, and I ably bagged five ducks. One was so pretty, they talked me into taking it to the taxidermist. I met Sara's grandparents, John and Leona Peabody, who introduced me to Mr. and Mrs. Arthur Craft at a tea in the Craft home. Mr. Craft offered me a job in management at one of his textile mills after I get home from the war and graduate from State College. Tell Mr. Strathmore that Mr. Arthur Craft said hello if you see him before I get home. Not much else to tell from here, but I'll be on the bus Tuesday at eight in the morning and should be in Charlotte by seven that evening. Tell everyone I can't wait to see them."

"It is good to talk to you, Son. I am glad to hear you are enjoying your visit. You will have to tell me all about it when you get home. I love you, Ray. Goodbye."

"I love you too, Dad. Give my love to the rest of the family. Goodbye."

———————

Ray walked into the den to find Sara and her brothers in an intense game of Parcheesi. During a short break in the game, Ray quickly told Sara that everything was fine in Montcross and his dad would be returning to work tomorrow.

She smiled and said, "That's great. I am glad to hear your dad has recovered."

He sat down in a very comfortable chair to watch the game unfold. Pretty soon his eyes closed and sleep followed quickly. Ray did not know he had been caught snoring until he woke to everyone laughing and staring at him.

"Hey! What is everyone laughing at?"

"You've been doing some major lumber work sawing those logs. Your snoring could wake the dead. Have a nice nap?" Sam chuckles and replied.

"Well now, Sam, I did not realize I was tired until I sunk into the chair to watch the game. How long have I been asleep anyway? By the way, I don't snore."

"You got in here about 4:15 and it is now almost 6:00, I would say about an hour and a half. I am sorry to break this to you, Ray, but you snore like a freight train." Sara said.

Thomas cut in to give his remarks on Ray's snoring, "I am glad I do not have to share a room with you. You'd keep me up all night."

Ray laughed along with everyone about his snoring faux pas and sheepishly asked if he missed supper. Everyone had him believing he had until Mrs. Peabody came to the den and rescued him by announcing supper would be leftovers. Everyone had a good laugh as they turned on the radio for the latest news from around the world.

Supper was a quiet affair and everyone was in bed by eight-thirty after the long and exhausting day.

Sam knocked on Ray's guest quarters at seven and yelled, "Ray, It's seven bells and all's well! Rise and shine. It's a great day to hunt quail."

"I'm awake! I will be in for breakfast as soon as I'm dressed. Thanks for the loan of the hunting clothes."

Ray walked into the kitchen and saw ample servings of pancakes, eggs, and sausage on the breakfast table, and Sara's dad sipping coffee. Samuel waited until everyone was seated before he ate his breakfast.

Samuel said, "Well boys, I will be joining you this morning on the hunt."

Sam replied, "That's great, Dad! It will make the hunt that much more enjoyable!"

Sam went over the details of the quail hunt since they would be using Jake and Molly, their champion pointing dogs.

Sam told Ray, "The biggest thing about hunting over dogs and a group this size is to be sure of your target. Make sure that the angle of your shot will not hit a dog or another hunter. If in doubt about whether to shoot or not, the safest bet is not to shoot and let someone else take a safer shot. The last thing we need is to have to visit a veterinarian or a doctor to clean a gunshot wound."

Ray replied, "I will make sure I'm safe. This is going to be a great day with your dad along."

PEABODY HUNTING LODGE AND FARM ~ EDENTON, NORTH CAROLINA
MONDAY - 9:00AM

The group arrived at the Peabody Hunting Lodge which was situated on 1,250 acres of prime farm land and pine forests. A plethora of wildlife including whitetail deer, black bears, eastern wild turkeys, quail, rabbits, squirrels, and possum called the farm home. Peanuts, soybeans, corn, and alfalfa crops were rotated annually to keep the soil in place and safe from erosion. The entire acreage this year was planted in peanuts with an expectation of

$63.00 per acre of picked peanuts. The peanut plant cuttings helped to protect the quail from predators and allow the quail to produce quality chicks year after year.

Sam said, "Remember that the bag limit this year is ten birds per person and make sure that you have a clear target and a safe shot before shooting."

Mr. Thompson, the gamekeeper and guide, welcomed everyone to the ornately furnished lodge and gave Ray a quick tour and history of the home. As Ray walked into the lodge, he was awed by the vaulted ceilings and big game trophies lining the walls of the main room. He was impressed with how well the house was furnished; especially the fine Victorian furniture and well-appointed bedrooms. The house was originally built in 1837 by the Butler family who owned the surrounding acreage and numerous slaves who worked the Butlers' thriving cotton plantation. In 1867, due to the financial strain of Civil War Reconstruction, the Butlers had to sell the home in order to pay off exorbitant taxes and family war debt. James Peabody, a Yankee carpetbagger who was named regional overseer by the federal government, bought the house and one hundred acres at federal auction for a little over ten-thousand dollars, and the house and land had remained in the Peabody Family since that first dubious purchase. Since 1867, several Peabodys had purchased surrounding land as it came available. The Peabody farm was one of the must see attractions for northern hunters because of the quality of the hunting.

After the tour, Mr. Thompson had everyone climb aboard the horse-drawn wagon to ride out to the first hunting area. Mr. Peabody released his two champion pointing dogs, Jake and Molly, to work the area for quail. The group on the wagon followed the dogs until they spotted Jake, with his tail held high, pointing a covey of quail hidden in a brush pile on the edge of a pine forest. The first group of shooters were Mr. Peabody, Sam, and Ray. They disembarked from the wagon and walked with Mr. Thompson. Mr. Thompson positioned everyone in a semi-circle around the dog at a distance of about ten yards to prevent the chances that an errant shot could hurt someone or a dog. Mr. Thompson walked in and flushed the covey of fifteen quail. Mr. Peabody with his gorgeous twenty-gauge over and under knocked down two birds on the rise with each of his shots. Sam with his pump-action twelve-gauge luckily harvested one bird with two shots. Ray knocked down one bird himself with the same side-by-side twelve-gauge double barrel that he had been loaned for the duck hunt. Four birds were in the bag, and the dogs were released again to find the next covey.

Mr. Thompson drove the four-horse hunting wagon down the winding farm road until the group spotted Molly pointing another covey in the high, thick grass at the side of the road. Mr. Peabody, William, and Thomas got off the wagon and set up to shoot at this covey rise. This group of quail numbered twenty-five or so birds and again Mr. Peabody brought two down. William, with his side-by-side twenty-gauge, beautifully knocked down two birds as they rose to shooting level. Thomas missed wildly with all three shots from the pump-action twelve-gauge he carried. After Jake and Molly retrieved the downed quail, the two dogs were loaded into their kennels on the wagon and allowed to rest. Mr. Thompson's Champion English Setters were then released to find the next coveys of quail.

The group found six coveys during their hunt and flushed well over one hundred birds. Mr. Peabody, shooting on each covey, had his limit of ten birds after five consecutive covey rises. Ray bagged four birds which included an extraordinary double on the last rise. Sam's shooting was magnificent this morning with five birds on three coveys as well. William was five for six on his three coveys and Thomas only bagged two birds with his three chances. On the wagon ride back to the lodge, Sam and William immediately heckled Thomas about his atrocious shooting. Ray would not rib Thomas because he knew he was lucky to bag four birds.

As the boys continued their harassment, Thomas snapped, "SO I HAD AN OFF DAY! Get off my back!"

Thomas' dad jumped immediately into the conversation and said, "Thomas, you need to apologize right now. I did not hear Ray get upset when you were giving him such a hard time about his shooting on Saturday. As a matter of fact, he took it like a man and laughed with you boys."

Thomas, immediately chastened, apologized, "You are right, Dad. Ray, Sam, William; I apologize for snapping like I did. After hurrahing Ray on Saturday, I know I had it coming with my shooting skills today. I couldn't hit the broadside of the barn if I were standing inside it."

The wagon arrived back at the lodge where Mr. Thompson gave the quail to the negro bird boys to clean and prepare for eating. The men walked into the lodge to wash up and prepare for a hunter's lunch of country ham sandwiches, fried potatoes, and deviled eggs. Conversation was light with everyone reliving their favorite moment of the morning's hunt. After lunch, Sam took the cleaned and prepared birds and placed them in the cooler. Mr. Peabody thanked Mr. Thompson for another wonderful quail hunt and told him to expect some northern executives out after Christmas for three days of hunting.

Ray said, "Thank you, Mr. Thompson. I will remember this hunt with great admiration and will look forward to coming back after the war is over. Have a Merry Christmas."

Mr. Thompson replied, "Ray, you're welcome. I hope you are able to come back soon and good luck in the Marines. Merry Christmas to you as well."

PEABODY FAMILY HOME ~ EDENTON, NORTH CAROLINA
MONDAY - 2:00PM

• • • • • • • • • • • • • • • • • • • •

Sara began pacing at the Peabody home around one-thirty. She waited on Ray to return from hunting with her Dad and brothers, and the more she paced, the angrier she got. Ray knew she wanted to go shopping in town before the party that would start at six-thirty. The great quail hunters arrived at two-thirty and Ray was met by Sara's wrath.

"RAY! You knew I wanted to go shopping this afternoon; yet, you wasted the entire day hunting! You've been so inconsiderate while you've been here! WHY?", Sara barked.

Ray, taken aback by the barrage from Sara, flushed with anger himself.

"Sara, I have been overwhelmed by the generosity of your Dad and brothers; they've tried to include me in everything that happened this weekend. I came here this weekend to get to know your family better and to spend time with you before I leave next week for God knows how long. It almost seems you are jealous of the time I spent with your Dad and brothers. Is that the reason you think I've been inconsiderate?"

"Ray, you spent half a day on Saturday hunting ducks with my brothers; and now today, you spend another half day hunting at the lodge. Yes, you've not spent enough time with me because you've been too busy having fun with my family. Call it jealousy! I call it inconsiderate. Just stay here while I go shopping with my Mother.

"Go shopping then. I will be ready to go to the Wright party when you get back. I need time to cool off."

Mr. and Mrs. Peabody entered the sitting room just before Sara's diatribe finished and they heard Ray's response.

Mr. Peabody announced their presence and said, "Sara, I heard just a little of why you are upset with Ray. He has worked hard to become a part of this family by doing what we've asked. Just because there has not been enough time to spend with you does not mean his love for you is any less. Everyone of us has pulled on him so that we could get to know him better. It is not Ray's fault that we got home late today. If anything it is mine because I spent a little extra time with Mr. Thompson to check on things at the lodge after the hunt. If you want to be mad at someone, you should be mad at me. Now, you go shopping with your Mother and calm down. Things like this happen all the time when you are married. Right, Mother?"

Mrs. Peabody responded, "That is right, Sara. You need to understand that while Ray is here, he feels obligated to do things with all of us in order to get to know us better. Are we going to stay here and be angry? Or, are we going shopping?"

"I think we should go shopping, Mother. I need to think a little anyway. Ray, we will be back in about two hours to get ready for the party."

"I will be ready when you get back so that we can spend a little time talking before we have to leave. I think it will do us both some good."

"Thanks, Ray. I agree."

Sara and her Mother left the house and Ray talked with Mr. Peabody for several minutes about whether he should apologize to Sara or not. Mr. Peabody let him know that an apology was not required for this argument, but there would be times when an apology would definitely be required to ease tension and open communication between them. Except for the last thirty or so minutes, Ray thought about how much he had enjoyed the time here in Edenton with Sara and her family. He knew the memory of this trip would stay with him while he served in the Marines.

"Samuel, I believe I will go clean up and get ready for the party tonight. Thanks again for a great hunt and coming to my rescue."

"Ray, the pleasure has been all mine and don't let Sara's tirade upset you because she's definitely scared about your future. Take your time cleaning up because I know that it will be a couple of hours before Sara and her mother return from downtown."

"Thank you, Sir."

PEABODY FAMILY HOME ~ EDENTON, NORTH CAROLINA
MONDAY - 3:30PM

. . . .

After Sara and her mother left to go shopping downtown, Ray started walking to the guest quarters to clean up. As he passed the den, he heard Sam, William, and Thomas in conversation about how well their father shot this morning. Ray walked into the den to give them his observation on why he thought their dad shot so well.

Ray said to Sam and William, "I have a theory on why your dad shot so well this morning. I watched him closely and saw that he took his time taking the first shot. After the first bird was down, he continued his follow through until he picked and shot the second bird while he continued his swing. We were more erratic on our shots. The next time we go hunting I will be practicing what your father showed me today."

William responded, "I watched him a couple of times and saw what you described; with Dad taking the first bird then following through to the second bird without stopping. I tried it on two coveys myself and was able to double up on each covey when I maintained my pull through both birds. It was amazing how much better I shot when I kept that in mind."

Sam then said, "Dad has taught all of us how to shoot quail by continuing the follow through from one bird to the next. I was finally able to slow down enough today to put it in practice. The technique made all the difference in the world."

Ray looked at the clock which said four-fifteen and he knew that he had to excuse himself to get ready for the party.

Ray told them, "I have enjoyed getting to know all of you this weekend and I will be looking forward to seeing all of you again when I get back. I want to thank you for making me feel like a member of the family. I better get ready for the party tonight if I want to stay on speaking terms with your sister. Thanks again for everything."

Sam spoke for all of them when he said, "We have really enjoyed getting to know you as well. Thanks are not necessary because we enjoy your company as well. I know I speak for William and Thomas when I say, we hope you come home safely to Sara."

Ray left the boys talking about the morning hunt and their plans to go Christmas shopping tomorrow.

It was four-thirty when Ray made his way into the guest house to get ready for the party. He opened the ornate closet to look through the three suits he brought on this trip. He decided on the dark blue suit with gray pinstripes, white shirt, black braces, matching bow tie, and black and white Oxford shoes for tonight. Quickly finishing the bath, he dressed and returned to the main house.

PEABODY FAMILY HOME ~ EDENTON, NORTH CAROLINA
MONDAY - 5:30PM

As Sara walked in from shopping, she was struck by how handsome Ray looked in his suit. She knew Ray was trying to make amends for their argument earlier.

Sara said, "You look absolutely handsome tonight, Ray. I'm sorry about what happened earlier."

"I love you, Sara, and I know we are facing a very scary future. Tonight, let's enjoy our time together at the party and try not to worry about the future."

Sara replied, "I will try, Ray."

Sara excused herself to get dressed for the party. Mr. Peabody took the time while the women were shopping to get ready, and now he had Ray join him in the den while they waited on Sara and his wife get ready.

Ray said, "Samuel, I would like to thank you and Mrs. Peabody for the wonderful time this weekend. I look forward to many future and happier visits after the war is over."

"Ray, the pleasure has been all ours and we hope you will come home safely once the battle is won. I know there will be many trying moments in the days and weeks to come, but remember that there is a family in Edenton who loves you and is praying for you."

"Thank you, Sir."

Mr. Peabody turned on the radio to check on the latest news. CBS Radio announced that Winston Churchill was in Washington to discuss war plans with President Roosevelt and that the heroic marine garrison on Wake Island was still holding out against an overwhelming Japanese invasion force. As the broadcaster finished a news segment, Mrs. Peabody and Sara came into the den and both ladies looked lovely in their new hats. Ray was awestruck by the beauty of Sara's dress and it took him a few extra seconds to catch his breath before rising. Ray offered Sara his arm to escort her to the car, and she was pleasantly surprised by a momentary shudder when she took his arm. At the car, Ray opened Sara's door and seated her beside her mother, and then joined Mr. Peabody in the front seat for the short drive to the Wright home.

THE WRIGHT FAMILY HOME ~ EDENTON, NORTH CAROLINA
MONDAY - 6:30PM

• • • • • • • • • • • • • • • • • • • •

Mr. Peabody turned left onto the Wright's long tree lined drive which ended in a circular drive in front of a large one-hundred-year old plantation home which had been in the Wright family since 1839. As the car came to a stop, Albert, the Wright's valet, was there to greet the family and escort them into the party. Inside the spacious home, the group was escorted to the large ballroom where Mr. and Mrs. Wright were greeting their guests. Ray was introduced and he thanked Mr. and Mrs. Wright for allowing him to attend their Christmas Gala. Sara was escorted into the spacious ballroom on Ray's arm, and she directed him to a group of young women on the edge of the dance floor which included Mary Wright, a beautiful eighteen-year-old freshman at East Carolina Teachers College, who was Sara's best friend.

Sara said, "Hello, Mary, I would like to introduce you to my beau, Ray Johnson, of Montcross."

Mary extended her hand to Ray and said, "Pleased to meet you, Ray. Sara has told me a lot about you. Welcome to our Christmas party, and I hope you enjoy yourself tonight."

"Nice to meet you as well and thank you for allowing me to join Sara at this magnificent event."

"You're welcome. If you'll excuse me, I see that Mother needs my help."

Ray and Sara made their way to the dance floor as the band played a waltz. Ray and Sara danced several of those beautiful waltzes, and then joined her parents at their table.

Mr. Wright announced, "Dinner will be served in about ten minutes. Please be seated and thank you all again for joining us for this most festive of holiday occasions."

Dinner was served by a well-dressed wait staff and consisted of she-crab soup for an appetizer and a main course of oysters Rockefeller, veal cutlets, boiled potatoes, and cauliflower au gratin.

Ray said, "This is a wonderful meal. Some of these delicacies are only served in the restaurants of Washington or New York. Even then, they are probably out of my price range."

Samuel replied, "I agree, Ray. A meal like this in one of those restaurants would probably cost upwards to fifteen or twenty dollars. The Wrights go all out this time of year to welcome everyone into their home for their Christmas Gala."

After dinner, the music resumed for more dancing and socializing until about ten when Mr. Wright called for silence to announce the names of those young men who had volunteered or were about to volunteer for military service. He asked them all to stand so that the group could say a prayer for victory and their safe return.

Mr. Wright said, "Thank you all for joining us to celebrate Christmas in our home. We hope everyone has a wonderful and merry Christmas. Good luck, young men. We will all be praying for your safe return home."

As they left, Samuel and Alma Peabody thanked Mr. Wright and his wife for the wonderful meal and wished them a Merry Christmas. Albert delivered their car to the front door, and Samuel and Ray escorted the ladies to the car. On the drive home, everyone commented about the wonderful party and hospitality.

PEABODY FAMILY HOME ~ EDENTON, NORTH CAROLINA
MONDAY - 11:00PM

Ray and the family arrived home exhausted, and he knew he needed to be ready to leave by eight the following morning. But, he wanted to spend some time talking with Sara before retiring for the evening. Mr. and Mrs. Peabody reminded the couple not to stay up too late, and wished them both a good night's sleep. Mrs. Peabody excused herself to go to bed while Mr. Peabody did a little office work.

In the sitting room, Ray said to Sara, "I know you are having a tough time with my decision to join the Marines. Please understand that I will do my best to come back home to you. I don't know what the future has in store, but I know I love you. As soon as I get home from the Marines, I want to start planning our wedding if you still want that when that time comes."

"I love you very much, Ray. Not knowing what is going to happen after you leave is really difficult for me to handle. Mom tries to comfort me, but she never had to deal with this type of separation since Dad was unable to serve in the Great War. I know I will be going back to school this spring, but it will not be the same without you. When the war is over and you come home safe, I will be happy to plan our wedding with you. In the meantime, how do I get through each day of separation since we will only be able to exchange letters or telegrams?"

"I am going to take it one day at a time and you should too. When you are feeling lonely or anxious, know that you will always be on my mind and in my heart. I am scared because I do not know whether I will measure up to what it means to be a Marine, but I will work hard to make you proud. I love you too, Sara. I promise I will write as often as I can, and I hope you will do the same because those letters will be my lifeline home."

"I will write you every day if I can. I will also write your Mom and sisters."

Ray hugged and kissed Sara then said, "I love you, Sara. I need to get to bed so that I can catch my bus on time in the morning. Goodnight."

After the long kiss ended, Sara said, "I hope you sleep well and I will see you in the morning. I love you, too."

Ray left Sara at the kitchen door and continued the short walk to the guest quarters.

Sara found her dad in the study and said, "Goodnight, Dad."

"How are you doing, Sweet Pea?"

With tears flowing like a faucet, Sara replied, "Dad, I am so scared of what may happen to Ray. What will I do if he does not make it home? How will I live my life without him? I am so scared!"

He held his daughter in an embrace and tried to comfort her fears, but he was also afraid of what might happen to this young man whom he looked upon as another son.

"Your mother and I will be right here for you. We know that the Johnson family thinks of you as another daughter, just like we think of Ray as another son. When everything seems it is falling apart, you will have the support you need. Please try not to worry, and we will be here to walk with you on this journey. Go to bed and try to get some sleep, I love you, Darling."

Sara sobbed, "Thanks, Dad. I will try to get some sleep and I feel better knowing that Mom and you will be here to help me through this. Goodnight, Dad. I love you, too."

Sara haltingly shuffled off to her bedroom as her dad did the same.

PEABODY FAMILY HOME ~ EDENTON, NORTH CAROLINA
TUESDAY, DECEMBER 23, 1941 - 6:30AM

The alarm clock buzzed in a vain attempt to arouse Ray from his exhaustion-fueled slumber. The incessant noise finally broke through Ray's foggy curtain of sleep. When he looked at the clock, it showed six fifty-five. He was going to miss his bus if he did not hurry. Bypassing his normal routine, he picked out a nice pair of pants and a white collarless shirt with blue stripes to wear on his trip home. The morning was crisp with a temperature around thirty degrees and a cold ten-knot wind. As he stepped out of the guest quarters at seven-thirty with his luggage, the morning chill surprised Ray. He was greeted by Eloise as he entered through the kitchen door. She was cooking eggs, grits, and sausage for breakfast. Mr. Peabody, already seated at the table, greeted Ray warmly as Eloise poured Ray a cup of coffee.

"Good morning to you as well, Samuel. I want to thank you and Mrs. Peabody for your wonderful hospitality this weekend. I hope the next time I visit that the war will no longer hang over our heads.", Ray says.

"Ray, it has been great for us as well. It seems you are running a little behind schedule this morning. What time do you have to be at the bus station?"

"Yes, I am running really late. My bus leaves at eight-fifteen so I need to be there no later than eight o'clock. What do you think?"

"Eight o'clock would be good, but I think if we are there by eight-ten, you will be just fine. I have not heard Sara stirring this morning; do you want me to go wake her?"

"No, I don't think that will be necessary. I will write her a note if she is not downstairs when we get ready to leave. We can leave as soon as I finish breakfast. Thank you again, Samuel."

The conversation died as Eloise served breakfast to the two men. Ray ate his breakfast quickly and was ready to leave when Sara hurried into the kitchen.

Sara breathlessly said, "I'm so glad you haven't left yet. I will write you every day while you are gone. I love you and I will miss you."

Ray hugs Sara and said, "I love you, too. I will write as much as I can, and I cannot wait until I can return. If I am going to make my bus, we need to leave now. Are you going to see me off here or at the station?"

"I will await your return and say my goodbyes here. Have a safe trip home. Goodbye and good luck, Ray."

They hugged each other once more and Ray gave Sara a peck on the cheek on his way out the front door.

Ray pulled on his woolen overcoat and grabbed his luggage for the short walk to the car. Sara was still at the front door when Ray blew her a kiss. Samuel and Ray arrived at the bus station at eight-ten as the bus was just warming up to leave. Ray bid Samuel a hasty goodbye, loaded his luggage into the baggage compartment and climbed aboard the bus as it was getting ready to leave the station.

BUS TRIP FROM EDENTON TO RALEIGH
TUESDAY - 8:15AM TO 1:15PM

. . . .

The bus trip was uneventful and Ray passed the time talking to an older gentleman who was keenly aware of the politics of the state and a veteran of the Great War. Ray asked the gentleman what he did for a living and the gentleman responded that he sold textile machinery. The textile machinery salesman introduced himself as Ed Martin from Philadelphia, Pennsylvania. He told Ray that he had been living in Raleigh for fifteen years. Ray introduced himself as well, and they talked about the war. Ray told Mr. Martin that he would be leaving after Christmas to volunteer for the Marines. Mr. Martin recounted his service in the All-American Division during the Great War and how the war left its mark on his life because he had been caught in a gas attack. The conversation lasted for the better part of two hours until Mr. Martin faded off to sleep.

As Mr. Martin started snoring softly, Ray was able to think about the weekend with Sara and the happenings that had such a great effect on him.

I can't believe how well the weekend went and I am so glad that I made a good impression on Sara's dad. I thoroughly enjoyed the hunting trips with them and I hope the brothers never second-guess their decisions about the war just like I hope to never second-guess my decision. Lord, please let me come home safe.

RALEIGH TRAIN STATION ~ RALEIGH, NORTH CAROLINA
TUESDAY ~ 2:15PM

• •

The bus pulled into the station in Raleigh at 1:30, and the Charlotte train, on-time, was about to leave the station as Ray picked up his ticket at the counter. He barely made it aboard with his luggage, and by the time he was seated, the conductor was checking tickets and found that Ray was supposed to be in a first-class Pullman Car berth located towards the front of the train.

Ray asked the conductor, "I purchased a regular ticket and know that I am not entitled to a Pullman Car. Are you sure this is correct?"

The conductor said, "Yes, your ticket is correct. It was upgraded and I will take you to your seat now."

The conductor seated Ray next to the gentleman who was going to Gastonia to sell his textile spinning machinery.

Ray reached out his hand and said, "Thank you, Mr. Martin, but I have not done anything to deserve this."

Mr. Martin replied, "You may not have been in battle yet or even started serving, but your willingness to sacrifice yourself in the defense of the country is deserving of my thanks. You need to remember that you are fighting for your buddies in your squad and platoon, and you should strive not to let them down."

"I will remember that, Mr. Martin, and I will also remember your generosity today. Thank you again."

CHARLOTTE TRAIN STATION ~ CHARLOTTE, NORTH CAROLINA
TUESDAY - 6:45PM

• •

When the train pulled into the Charlotte Train Station at six forty-five that evening, Ray's dad and his brother Jimmy were waiting for him, and Ray was welcomed immediately by them. They started telling him all about the happenings in Montcross while he had been gone. Ray stopped them long enough to introduce them to Mr. Martin whom he had met on the train from Raleigh. Ray thanked Mr. Martin again for upgrading his ticket and wished him a Merry Christmas.

In the car, Ray could not wait to hear what had happened since he left last Friday, and Jimmy was bursting with news about his flying lessons.

Jimmy said, "I'm very happy that I will be instructed by Mr. Mayerhofer. During the Great War, he was a German fighter ace in the Deutsche Luftstreitkräfte until he was shot down and captured in the summer of 1918. As a prisoner of the Americans during the war, Mr. Mayerhofer saw that Americans treated prisoners with dignity and respect. This dignified treatment as a prisoner planted a seed in Mr. Mayerhofer that one day he might want to move his family to America. In 1925, Mr. Mayerhofer and his family emigrated from Germany to the United States; and they gained their United States citizenship five years later."

Ray responded, "I have seen Mr. Mayerhofer around town, but I didn't know any of this. Does he still have family in Germany?"

"Mr. Mayerhofer's family is Jewish and they are from the small town of Rheydt which happens to be the German Propaganda Minister's, Joseph Goebbels, hometown. Mr. Mayerhofer's parents and brother still live there and he has been worried about them since the Nazi's started persecuting the Jews during the Kristallnacht riots in 1938."

"That's an amazing story about Mr. Mayerhofer and I can see why you are happy to take flying lessons from him. You're lucky to have such a great pilot as your instructor. Dad, how have you been feeling?"

"I have been doing very well, Ray. I went back to work yesterday and the boys in the yard had taken care of everything so I did not have too much to worry about when I got there. Your sisters have been driving me crazy with wanting to get the Christmas tree put up early, but I reminded them that we always put the tree up on Christmas Eve. I am not working tomorrow so we can get a tree at the Strathmore farm like we always do."

"Sounds good, Dad. Let's make the tree a big one and place it in the foyer so everyone who passes by our house can see it. Glad everything is going well at the rail yard, too."

All too quickly, they were pulling into their driveway in Montcross.

• • • • • • • • • • • • • • • • • • • •

The car was barely parked before Bessie, Elizabeth, Myra, and Lillie were outside wanting to find out all about Ray's trip to Edenton. Bessie was the first to greet Ray and she gave him a big hug. Elizabeth, Myra, and Lillie all took their turns hugging Ray and welcoming him home. Jimmy grabbed Ray's luggage from the trunk as the family made its way into the house.

Bessie asked Ray, "Have you eaten supper yet? I think Elva left some fried chicken and potato salad in the ice box. Would you like me to make you a plate?"

"Mom, that sounds wonderful since I've not eaten anything since lunch which was a couple of sandwiches packed by Mrs. Peabody."

Elizabeth, Myra, and Lillie wanted to know all about the trip, but Ray only wanted to eat a bite, unpack from the trip, and retire for the evening. He promised the girls that he would tell them all about his trip tomorrow.

Little Lillie blurted, "Did you bring us anything, Ray?"

"Yes, Lillie, I brought all of you something; your Christmas presents. You will have to wait until Christmas to open them."

Lillie retorted, "THAT'S NOT FAIR! I DON'T WANT TO WAIT!"

Bessie intervened, "Lillie, you will have to wait. Your brother bought your presents in Edenton, and he did not bring you any other surprises. It is time for you to get your bath and get ready for bed. While I get Ray his supper, Elizabeth, will you run Myra and Lillie's bath, please?"

"Yes, Mom, I will take care of helping them with their baths." Elizabeth replied.

The girls left for their baths while Bessie prepared a plate of leftovers for Ray.

Bessie and Raymond sat down with Ray while he ate his dinner to talk about Ray's enlistment.

Raymond said, "Have you reconsidered your decision to join the Marine Corps? What came of your discussions with Sara about marriage?"

"Dad," Ray replied, "I still firmly believe that I have to do my duty and help this country overcome the Japanese treachery committed at Pearl Harbor. The only way we overcome our enemies is if young men like me take the initiative and volunteer. I will be enlisting on Friday in Charlotte at the Naval Recruiting Station. As far as Sara and marriage is concerned, I had a long conversation with Mr. Peabody about marriage. The fact is I did not want to leave Sara as a war widow before we even had the chance to build a life as husband and wife. Sara and I talked about it as well this weekend and while she was for a quick wedding before I left, she agreed that waiting was the most prudent thing to do. My belief is that I want to get married only after my military service is completed. That way we start our life together without the war hanging over our head. I love her very much and would have married her as soon I finished school had the Japanese not flung us into war."

"How did Mr. Peabody take it when you told him you wanted to wait until your service was completed?", his father asks.

"Mr. Peabody told me how proud he would be to have me as his son-in-law as soon as this dreadful war is over. He seemed genuinely happy that I did not want to rush marriage like so many others in Edenton and the surrounding communities were doing. Mr. Peabody asked me to write the family often to let them know how I was doing and if I needed anything. Sara is a bit perturbed because she does not know how she will cope with the separation. I let Sara know that Mom would be able to help her since she has been through this before. Is that all right, Mom?" Ray replied.

"That is just fine, Ray. I will make sure to write Sara and I will also call her mother to give her guidance on how to handle the various situations that might arise while you are away. Did you send them a wire letting them know you had arrived home safely?" Bessie asked.

Ray told his mother that he sent one as they were leaving the train station. Ray finished the last of the fried chicken and potato salad on his plate and thanked his mother for the finest meal he had eaten all day. He washed his own dishes and put them away so Elva would not have to do them in the morning. Ray, exhausted from the late night and the travel, excused himself to get ready for bed. While telling him goodnight, his mom and dad told him how much they loved him and how happy they were to have him home.

Jimmy was kind enough to carry Ray's luggage to their room so Ray could spend time with their parents at the dinner table. As Ray entered their shared bedroom, he saw that Jimmy was busy reading the Civilian Pilot Training Program Manual. Jimmy was trying to get a jump on his flight training. As Ray started unpacking, he thanked Jimmy for bringing his luggage from the car.

Jimmy looked up briefly from his book and asked, "Ray, are you ready to go to bed?"

"Yes, Jimmy. It's been a long day on top of a short night's sleep last night. I need to get some sleep so that I'm ready for everything we have to do tomorrow."

"I understand. We will have a long day tomorrow since we have to get the Christmas tree and go to the church for the Christmas Eve service. Goodnight, Ray."

As soon as Ray's head hit the pillow, he was blissfully sleeping. His only thought. *It feels so good to be in my own bed tonight.*

Christmas in Montcross

JOHNSON FAMILY HOME ~ MONTCROSS, NORTH CAROLINA
WEDNESDAY, DECEMBER 24, 1941 – 7:00AM

- - - - - - - - - - - - - - - - - - - -

After a restful night's sleep, Ray awakened refreshed and looked forward to the day which would include picking out their Christmas tree at Mr. Strathmore's farm. Jimmy awoke to the sound of Ray brushing his teeth in their adjacent bathroom. Both of them had chores to do and Ray was the first one out the door to milk the cow and gather the eggs. He walked downstairs quietly so that he would not disturb the rest of the still-sleeping family. As he walked into the kitchen for a cup of coffee, Elva and his mother greeted him. They were already preparing the Christmas Eve dinner of baked ham, mashed potatoes, green peas, and deviled eggs.

Ray's mother asked, "How did you sleep last night?"

"I slept well and I'm ready for today's festivities. Jimmy should be right down. Is Dad awake yet?"

"No, Ray. Your Dad is not awake yet, but I know he will be shortly because he wants to go get the Christmas tree this morning. You need to bring in the eggs before milking Gertrude so that we can have French toast for breakfast."

"I will gather the eggs now and be right back. Elva knows French toast is my favorite and I'll not miss it."

Ray walked to the chicken coop and found that the chickens had been busy overnight. Ray gathered seventeen eggs this morning, and he placed them gently into the basket. His dad was drinking his coffee and talking to Jimmy when he walked back in the with the eggs. Ray handed the basket of eggs to Elva, and she started preparing breakfast. His dad greeted him heartily and told him that they would be going to the Strathmore farm after the chores and breakfast were finished. Ray finished his cup of coffee before going to milk Gertrude.

Raymond and his two sons left to harvest the Christmas tree after breakfast. Raymond told the boys that they should try to find a tree that would be a little over seven feet. After the group arrived at the Strathmore farm, they were shown this year's crop of trees. Taking their time, Ray and Jimmy found one that would fit the bill for this year's tree. The tree was about four feet wide and about seven and a half feet tall which would cut down to the perfect size for the foyer. Ray grabbed the tree saw from the car trunk and after his dad approved the choice, started cutting it down. With the tree on the ground, Ray and Jimmy worked to get the tree safely secured in the car trunk for the ride home where the girls would decorate it for tonight's festivities.

JOHNSON FAMILY HOME ~ MONTCROSS, NORTH CAROLINA
WEDNESDAY - 10:30AM

Raymond parked the car close to the walkway leading to the front porch. The boys unloaded the tree onto the porch, and he told the boys that he would be right back. By the time he returned from parking the car, the boys had the tree standing upright on the porch and were waiting to place the tree in the stand. Raymond placed the stand upright on the porch and removed the screws that would hold the tree level. Ray and Jimmy picked up the tree and placed it in the base until it hit the bottom of the stand. Raymond replaced and tightened the screws until the tree was held firm. The men stepped back to admire their handiwork and to make sure that the tree was standing perfectly level. Once satisfied, they moved the tree to its place of prominence in the foyer. Raymond always put the electric lights on the tree and tested them before allowing Bessie and the girls to add the garlands, icicles, tinsel, and ornaments to the tree. With the lights fully tested and water in the basin of the tree stand, Bessie and the girls started decorating the tree with Lillie haphazardly throwing tinsel onto the lower half of the tree.

Ray needed to borrow the car to pick up a couple of last minute gifts from the mercantile for Jimmy and his father. Sara had helped him shop for his mother and sisters while he was in Edenton. After he dropped his dad off at the rail yard for their annual Christmas luncheon, he drove downtown to pick up the last few items on his list before the stores closed at noon.

DOWNTOWN MONTCROSS ~ MONTCROSS, NORTH CAROLINA
WEDNESDAY - 11:15AM

Ray saw Mr. Strathmore at the counter talking to one of the clerks of the Strathmore Mercantile while he was looking for the items he needed to fill out his Christmas purchases.

Ray walked to the counter and said, "Good morning, Mr. Strathmore. Merry Christmas to you and your family."

Mr. Strathmore replied, "Thanks, Ray. I hear you and your family picked out a nice tree from the farm this morning."

Ray replied, "The tree was perfect for our foyer and Dad will be calling you later to thank you, but I want to thank you as well."

"Your family is very welcome. By the way, I spoke to Arthur Craft on Monday and he told me about meeting a nice young man from Montcross. I understand that he offered you a job after your military service was complete. It is a high honor to earn the respect of a man like Arthur and you should be proud that he offered you a position with his firm, Ray. There is always a position at the Cronkite as well."

"Thank you, Sir. I was honored to meet Mr. Craft and get to know him while I was in Edenton visiting my girlfriend, Sara Peabody, and her family. He definitely understands the trends of textile manufacturing and told me that his mills are gearing up for a lot of war work. Did I read in the Montcross Weekly Gazette that the Cronkite and Majesty are getting big contracts as well?"

"Yes, war mobilization contracts have our mills running at full capacity turning out cotton yarn in the various sizes and grades for everything from uniforms to bandages. I know you have decided to join the Marines as your father did in 1917, but I want to offer you a job managing a shift in the Cronkite if you were to change your mind. It will mean a full deferral since you will be a position deemed in the national interest."

"Mr. Strathmore," Ray replied, "thank you for your offer and while it is very tempting, I feel that I need to do my duty. I hope that you would hold that job for me until I return. Thank you, again, Mr. Strathmore."

"Ray, you are welcome and I know you will make a fine Marine. You will always have a job waiting at the Cronkite, Majesty, or any of the other mills under my ownership. Good luck, Ray, and Merry Christmas."

"Merry Christmas to you too, Sir."

JOHNSON FAMILY HOME ~ MONTCROSS, NORTH CAROLINA
WEDNESDAY - 12:30PM

•••••••••••••••••••••

As he passed the front of the house, Ray saw that the tree was nicely lighted and decorated. Ray pulled carefully into the driveway to prevent Lillie from having an accident while she rode her bike around the carport. When Lillie saw the car, she stopped riding and rushed to see if Ray had any surprises for her.

"RAY!" The six-year-old exclaimed, "Do you have any surprises for me?"

"Not this time, Lillie. I had to pick up Christmas presents for Dad and Jimmy and pick up cards for Sara's family."

"Oh! I like Sara. Is she coming to visit us soon?"

"She probably will come visit while I am on my trip. I like her too."

"Where are you going, Ray? You just got back from a trip." Lillie naively asked as Ray tried not to tell his littlest sister about the war and military service.

"I will be going on a long trip after Christmas."

"Oh, that's nice," she said, "I wish I could go on trips like you, Jimmy, Elizabeth, and Myra do."

Bessie came to the door and told them to hurry in and wash up; lunch was about ready. Ray helped Lillie put her bike up and grabbed his presents. A lunch of Elva's meatloaf, macaroni and cheese, lima beans and sliced bread waited in the kitchen for everyone to eat.

At lunch, Ray told his mom and sisters how good the tree looked from the road and that he thought Dad would be impressed. Jimmy told Ray that he had been accepted into the pilot ground school at Montcross College that was part of the Civilian Pilot Training Program. The Civilian Pilot Training Program was a federal program that trained pilots for both the Army and the Navy. He would still be able to take the flight portion of his training from Mr. Mayerhofer. Ray could hear the excitement and pride in his brother's voice because of acceptance into this prestigious program. Ray congratulated him on the acceptance and asked when the ground school started.

He said, "I have to finish up the Army enlistment paperwork, but I will not have to start my term of service until I complete the program. The ground school at Montcross College starts on December 29th in one of the classrooms. My flying lessons will be every Saturday starting on December 27th. I can't wait; and when I complete the program, I will be required to join the Army's flight training program."

As everyone finished lunch, the phone rang. It was Raymond calling to ask Ray to pick him up. Ray asked his mother if there was anything she needed while he was out.

She said, "No, I have everything I need for this evening."

He picked up his dad from the rail yard and was only gone for twenty minutes. Ray spent the rest of the day wrapping gifts and taking the cards to the post office. The family had to leave the house at five o'clock for the First Baptist Christmas Service so he needed to hurry back home after he dropped the cards in the mail.

• •

The family arrived for the Christmas service and were seated in their normal pew by an usher. Raymond's parents, Mr. And Mrs. Robert Johnson, were already seated in the pew and they looked forward to spending Christmas Eve with their grandchildren. The service opened with Lillie in the children's choir singing, *O' Little Town of Bethlehem*. After the song, the members of the children's choir returned to their parents. From that old tattered King James Bible that Reverend Kelton had carried since Baptist seminary, he delivered the scripture readings from the Old and New Testaments.

The Old Testament reading came from the book of Isaiah, chapter nine, verse six which said, "For unto us a child is born, unto us a son is given: and the government shall be upon his shoulder: and his name shall be called Wonderful, Counsellor, The mighty God, The everlasting Father, The Prince of Peace."

The New Testament reading came from the book of John, chapter three, verses sixteen and seventeen which read, "For God so loved the world, that he gave his only begotten Son, that whosoever believeth in him should not perish, but have everlasting life. For God sent not his Son into the world to condemn the world; but that the world through him might be saved."

Reverend Kelton's Christmas message on this Christmas Eve was a reminder that Jesus had come to bring light to the world and in this time of trial and struggle, the need for Jesus' light was great. He ended his message with a reminder that there were many Americans facing hardships and many American soldiers facing determined enemies on foreign shores who needed their prayers. The service ended with the passing of the peace and the lighting of candles as the congregation sang *Silent Night*. The congregation recessed from the church with candles lit signifying God's sending of Jesus to bring light to the world.

Christmas in Montcross

The family gathered around the big dining room for the meal prepared earlier by Elva and Bessie. Ray's grandfather, Robert, said the blessing and prayed for the safety of all the servicemen who were not able to be with their families tonight. Dinner was a boisterous affair especially from the younger members of the Johnson Family. Myra and Lillie were very excited about the thought that Santa Claus was coming tonight.

Myra excitedly asked, "What time is Santa coming? Are we opening any gifts tonight?"

"Myra," Bessie replied, "Santa will be here sometime tonight. We are all opening one gift tonight and the rest will be saved until tomorrow. That goes for you too, Lillie."

"Mommy, why can we only open one gift tonight? I want to open all my presents tonight!" Lillie exclaimed.

"Now, Lillie, what will you do in the morning while everyone else is opening their gifts if you open all yours tonight?", Bessie asked.

"I will open Grandma and Grandpa Stuart's presents and I will have my Santa presents.", Lillie said, getting the better of her mother with her logic.

"Well, Miss Lillie, you will only open one present tonight and you will open the rest in the morning. Grandma and Grandpa Stuart are not coming here tomorrow. We will be visiting them tomorrow afternoon."

The children's banter continued throughout supper until Ray reminded everyone that the President was going to give his Christmas Eve proclamation to the nation with Prime Minister Churchill of Great Britain at nine o'clock. After dessert, everyone filed into the living room to open a single present from their grandparents and listen to the President's proclamation on the radio.

Raymond announced this year they were changing the order of opening the gifts. This year Ray would open his gift first, then opening would proceed down the line to Lillie, who was none too happy about this unpleasant turn of events.

"WHY DO I HAVE TO GO LAST THIS YEAR? I HAVE ALWAYS OPENED FIRST!"

Raymond said, "Young Lady, unless you apologize right now for your outburst, you can go on to bed. We are changing the order this year because Ray is the oldest and he should go first."

With crocodile tears running down her little face, she said, "I'm sorry, Daddy. I promise I will be good if you let me stay and open my present when it is my turn."

With the outburst under control, Raymond gave Lillie a big hug and told her, "I love you, Sweetie. You can ask Ray if he needs your help opening his present."

Ray gave his father a knowing wink as Lillie asked nicely if he would like some help opening his present.

Ray said, "That would be nice. I need some help with this present from Grandma and Grandpa Johnson."

Lillie sidled over to Ray's chair and helped him pull off the bow. Ray finished opening the gift which was an aluminum waterproof compass that was engraved, "To Ray ~ With Love and Hope, Grandma and Grandpa", along with an aluminum waterproof lighter; practical gifts that would come in handy in the Marine Corps. Ray thanked his grandparents and gave each a hug. The other children opened their gifts and when the time came for Lillie to open her gift, she asked Ray for some help. Lillie's gift from her grandparents was a new doll with eyes that opened and closed with a wardrobe to match.

She rushed over to Grandma and told her, "Thank you, Grandma, I will take good care of my new dolly. Her name will be Margie."

Lillie gave her grandma a big hug and a kiss. With the presents opened and the time for the President's address approaching, Myra and Lillie were sent off to bed. There were no protests from either child because they knew the faster they got to sleep; the sooner they would wake up to the joys of Santa Claus and Christmas morning.

The family gathered around the radio in the den to listen to the President's Christmas Proclamation. The Christmas proclamation was in the classic Roosevelt style as he implored the American people to continue to be a light for the rest of the world. After the address, Grandma and Grandpa Johnson walked to their home next door. Christmas morning would bring Ray one day closer to his destiny of becoming a Marine, and the apprehension, he felt, kept him awake long into the night.

As Christmas morning dawned, the youngest girls awoke first and wanted to rush down the stairs. They were eager to see what Santa brought them but knew they must wait until their parents called them down the stairs. Lillie, in her excitement, rushed into her brothers' room in an effort to speed up the morning process by waking them. Ray awakened with a start from a restless night's sleep when Lillie shook him.

Through bleary eyes and a sleepy fog Ray sees Lillie and exclaimed, "Lillie, why are you waking me? What time is it? It is still dark outside!"

Lillie looks at the clock by Ray's bed even though she cannot tell time and says, "The little hand on the clock is on the six and the big hand is on the one. You need to get up so we can go downstairs! I'm sure Santa has come!"

Jimmy was somewhat awake by now with all the excitement in the room and looked at Lillie with a grin on his face.

He said to Ray, "Don't you remember what it was like to be her age and the excitement that comes with Christmas morning? I remember that until I was about twelve years old, I woke you every Christmas morning before the rooster crowed so we could get downstairs and see what Santa brought."

"I remember, Jimmy.", Ray replied, "I didn't sleep well last night because I was thinking about the future, Sara, and what life would be like soon."

Ray looked at Lillie and smiled.

"Let me go check to see if Mom and Dad are awake and if they are I will see how long until you and Myra are allowed downstairs."

"THANKS, RAY!", Lillie exclaimed.

Ray went downstairs to his parent's room and found them still asleep. He knew better than to wake them before seven this morning. He walked back to his room and told Lillie, Myra, and Jimmy that their parents were still asleep.

Lillie asked, "Why can't you wake them, Ray?"

"Mom and Dad told us last night that we were not to wake them before seven this morning if they weren't already up. It is six-fifteen right now and we have to wait until seven o'clock. I am going to do my chores and when I come back in, it should be time. So, go back to your room and wait until I come get you."

As Ray stepped out of the kitchen door, he was hit by how cold and dreary it was this morning. The weather seemed to match his mood on what should be an exciting and joyous day. He could not stop thinking about all he had to do before he left for the Marines. He grabbed the milk can and the egg basket from the kitchen porch and carried them with him to the hen house and cow shed. The hens had laid overtime, it seemed, as he gathered about twenty eggs this morning. Gertrude gave him about half of an eight-gallon milk-can of milk for which Ray thanked her. He fed Gertrude and the chickens then took the eggs and milk back to the house. He placed the egg basket and milk can in the kitchen. When he looked at the clock and saw it was seven-fifteen, it meant that it was safe to wake his parents for the Christmas morning celebration. Ray walked towards his parents' bedroom and passed their room as his mother was getting out of bed.

Ray said, "Good morning, Mom. How did you sleep?"

"Good morning, Ray. I slept just fine. I am surprised Lillie and Myra have not been down already to wake us up."

"Well, Mom, Lillie blasted me out of bed at about six this morning and I came down to see if you and Dad were awake. When you were not, I reminded Lillie and Myra that Dad told us not to wake you until after seven this morning. I told them to stay upstairs until I finished my chores and made sure you and Dad were awake. Should I go up and get them?"

"Go up and tell Jimmy and the girls to get dressed before coming down. That should give us enough time to set everything up for them. Thank you, Ray."

Ray quietly walked upstairs to his waiting brother and sisters to let them know that the Johnson family Christmas celebration would commence as soon as everyone was dressed.

Lillie said, "Look at me, I am already dressed for the day!"

Ray took one look at her in that hopelessly mismatched outfit and said, "You need to get Elizabeth to help you get dressed. After breakfast we will be going to Granny and Granddaddy Stuart's and you need put on your nice outfit."

Elizabeth had been awakened by Lillie a little over thirty minutes ago, and she walked into the youngest girls' room to find Lillie's outfit so hopeless that all she could do was laugh.

Elizabeth said, "Lillie, we need to get you changed into a different outfit because that one is too small for you. I think this outfit with the Christmas red sweater will really look good today."

Properly attired, the entourage walked downstairs to find wondrous gifts from Santa. Lillie, temporarily sidetracked by the need to change outfits, was still the first one downstairs. Bessie and Raymond were sitting in their favorite chairs waiting on the children to gather before handing out presents. Lillie's eyes lit up as she spied a brand new bicycle with training wheels that had her name attached to the handlebars.

She said in awe, "Santa must have gotten my letter! This bike is just what I asked for! Thanks, SANTA!"

Myra had asked Santa for a smaller sized piano and there in the living room was a children's piano with a great sound that could be used to learn how to play piano. Her excitement, like Lillie's, was barely contained when she saw the magnificent gift. The older three siblings, Ray, Jimmy, and Elizabeth, allowed the two youngest the time to savor the wonder of the morning before they opened their gifts. Elizabeth opened her first present which was a light blue wool dress and a green and red plaid woolen scarf which would look nice to wear when school reopened after January first. Jimmy opened his gift from Ray to find a pocket knife and a leather cover for his flight logbook.

Jimmy said, "Ray, this is a perfect gift, thank you."

"You're welcome, Jimmy. Thank you for the nice pen and pencil set with personalized stationery that I will definitely use while I am away."

Ray's gifts from his parents were practical in nature as well, including a pocket knife, billfold, pocket notebooks, and a pocket Bible. These gifts would be perfect for his time in the service because he wanted to keep a journal of his experiences. With the gifts opened, Bessie told everyone that breakfast would be served in about ten minutes. Christmas breakfast was bacon, sausage, pancakes, eggs, and orange juice. The banter around the table was about what Granny and Granddaddy Stuart would have for Christmas lunch and whether or not their aunts, uncles, and cousins would be there to share in the celebration.

Reflecting on the peaceful atmosphere and thinking of the future, Ray absently said, "I don't think I shut Gertrude's gate. I need to go check on that."

Raymond replied, "Would you like some company, son?"

"Sure, Dad. That would be nice."

Ray and his Dad left the house to check on the cow shed.

"Son, I can see that you are not having as much fun this Christmas. Why?"

"Dad," Ray replied, "I'm thinking about a lot of things this Christmas; knowing that my life is about to change when I enlist in the Marines. I am questioning whether I am doing the right thing. Did you know that Mr. Strathmore offered me a job in one of his mills in order to keep me out of harm's way? Were you the one who suggested this?"

"Ray, I wouldn't do anything to try to change your mind about serving, but I think the offer came from Mr. Craft on behalf of Sara's family so that you would be safe during this conflict. I believe that you are doing the right thing because you made the decision on your own once you heard of the attack on Pearl Harbor. Your Mom and I have talked about your decision and want you to know how proud we are about it. Are you still sure you want to serve?"

"Yes, Dad, my decision hasn't changed. I'm serving because to do otherwise would make me feel like I let the country down."

"Then, Ray, you answered your own question about if you were doing the right thing. In your eyes, you are doing the only thing you can do; so go make the most of your service. Know that your Mom and I will stand with you and pray for your safety as you serve. We love you, Ray."

"I love you and Mom very much too. Thanks, Dad!"

The time with his Dad did wonders for Ray's sagging morale as the day to leave crept ever closer. After finding that Ray had indeed shut and locked the gate, the two walked back to the kitchen to gather the family to leave for Staunton.

GRANNY AND GRANDDADDY STUART'S HOME ~ STAUNTON, NORTH CAROLINA
CHRISTMAS DAY - 1:00PM

Raymond, Bessie, and the family arrived at one o'clock for Christmas lunch in Staunton, and Ray's aunts, uncles, and cousins welcomed them with open arms. Ray was excited to see Aunt Linda and Uncle Bill, who were his favorites. They had always given him unconditional support through their love and kindness.

Ray greeted them, "Hello, Aunt Linda and Uncle Bill, hope your Christmas has been good!"

Uncle Bill replied, "It has been wonderful so far and you look well. How has school been treating you?"

"School has been good, and after spending the first week of my break in Montcross, I was able to visit my girlfriend, Sara and her family in Edenton this past weekend. I am glad to see you both and want to thank you for the moral support you gave me last semester when I had trouble with economics history and how to remember the different economic principles. I scored an A in that class thanks to your help."

Uncle Bill responded, "Glad to hear I could help you make the grade. I hear that you are joining the Marines, is that true?"

"Yes, it is. I feel like it is my duty to serve just like you and Dad did during the Great War. I am not looking forward to it because of what Dad went through. But, I know I must serve in order to help the country."

"Your aunt and I will be praying for your safe return. We know it will be tough to defeat the Axis, but I believe our country will be able to do it. Good luck, Ray. If we don't hurry inside, we will miss the turkey, dressing, and other succulent dishes that Granny prepared."

"Thanks, Uncle Bill.", Ray replied.

Lunch was wonderful and the camaraderie around the table made Ray forget for a moment that he would be leaving soon. Granddaddy Stuart asked Ray to say the blessing and Ray blessed the food and all young men who were serving in harm's way. This Christmas dinner was more subdued for the adults because they sensed that this would be the last one that had everyone around the table. Ray and several of his cousins would be volunteering soon. Oblivious, the younger children's excitement of opening presents after dinner was scarcely contained as they hastily finished their meal and waited impatiently until the entire family gathered for the opening of gifts and the passing of the traditional Christmas blessing by Granddaddy Stuart.

Granddaddy said, "Dear Lord, thank you for bringing our family home again this year. Thank you for all the blessings you have given this family and especially for allowing Raymond to remain with us. We ask that you protect and bless those family members who will be leaving us for trips which might put them in harm's way. We thank you for the birth of Jesus that we celebrate today and we look forward to many more celebrations. In Jesus name, I pray. Amen."

After they exchanged gifts, the various families left the comfort of the Stuart home with the love of family traveling with them in their hearts. Ray was thankful for the time he had spent with his grandparents as he knew this would be the last time he would visit them until the war was over.

JOHNSON FAMILY HOME ~ MONTCROSS, NORTH CAROLINE
CHRISTMAS DAY - 6:30PM
• •

When the family arrived home from Staunton, Elva had supper waiting for them like she always did on Christmas Day. She had celebrated earlier with her family and then came to the Johnson home at five to prepare the evening meal.

After supper, Ray and Jimmy moved to the den to listen to the radio and talk for a while.

Jimmy said, "Ray, when are you going to Charlotte to enlist?"

"Well, Jimmy, I'm taking my paperwork to the recruiting station tomorrow and I hope that they will set my departure date for Monday."

"Are you scared?"

"I don't know that I'm scared, but I know that I'm a little apprehensive about what's to come. I should be able to physically handle the Marine Corps training, but I am concerned about mentally withstanding training and combat." Ray replied then continued, "I need to call Sara and wish her a Merry Christmas. I also need to thank her for the gift of the Cross medal with the inscription, 'To Ray, this Cross signifies the love of Jesus and my love for you. Yours always, Sara'."

Ray left the den and went to the study to call Sara.

He picked up the receiver and tapped the handle twice until the operator answered.

"Number, please.", the operator asked.

Ray said, "Mrs. Bass, I would like to make a long distance call to Edenton, NC E-676, please."

Mrs. Bass replied, "Ray, how is Mr. Johnson doing after his spell?"

"Doing just fine, Mrs. Bass. Hope you've been doing well." Ray replied.

"Just fine, Ray. Merry Christmas to you and your family."

"Merry Christmas to you and your family also, and thank you for asking about Dad."

"Hold one moment while I connect your call." Mrs. Bass replied as she started working with the operators up the line to connect the call to the Peabody home.

Mrs. Bass was finally connected to the operator in Edenton and asked, "Please connect me to E-676, the Samuel Peabody residence."

The Edenton operator responded, "Hold one moment, ringing the Peabody's now."

Sam, Sara's brother, answered the phone, "Hello."

The local operator responded, "Long distance call from Montcross, connecting you now."

"Thanks, Mrs. Laney. Hello." Sam responded.

In Montcross, Mrs. Bass told Ray, "Your call is connected, let me know when you disconnect. Thanks."

"Thanks, Mrs. Bass. Hello.", Ray replied.

"Hello, Ray, this is Sam. Have a good Christmas?"

"Sure did, Sam. It has been a wonderful day here. What about Christmas for you and your family?"

"We had a great day here as well. I'll get Sara so that you don't run up a big phone bill."

"Thanks, Sam. Merry Christmas to you."

Sam finds Sara in the sitting room with her mother who asked, "Who was on the phone?"

"They are still on the phone. Do you want to talk to Ray, Sara?" Sam slyly asked.

"Yes! Ray is on the phone?", Sara exclaims.

"Yes, Ray is on the phone. I would not keep him waiting considering the cost of long distance calls." Sam replied to Sara's back as she dashed to the phone.

Sara picked up the receiver and practically yelled, "Hello, Ray!"

"Hello, Sara. I just opened my gift from you and that medal is wonderful. Thank you so much! How was your Christmas?"

"You are welcome. Mom helped me pick it out. I wanted something special that you could carry with you. Thank you for the nice comb and brush set with my initial engraved on them. Christmas has been very nice except you're not here to share it with me. I miss you."

"I miss you too and you're welcome. I've been thinking of you a lot while I've been home; especially today, when I wanted to show you all the practical gifts I received. I'm enlisting tomorrow and will try to call you one more time before I leave. I love you."

"I love you too, Ray. You should be getting a letter or two in the next couple of days. I hope you have the opportunity to call before you leave for training; otherwise, send me a wire with your new address."

"Merry Christmas, Sara. Goodbye.", Ray says.

Sara responds, "Merry Christmas to you too, Ray. Goodbye."

They hung up and Ray let Mrs. Bass know that the call was complete by clicking the handle twice. With the bittersweet feeling of not having Sara close to him, he returned to the den to resume his conversation with Jimmy.

When he walked into the den, he saw that his father had finished putting Lillie's doll house together and was talking with Jimmy.

Raymond asked Ray, "How is Sara? Did her family enjoy their Christmas today?"

"Sara is doing well and her family had a wonderful Christmas. Sara asked me to tell everyone Merry Christmas and let you know she is thinking of all of you today." Ray replied and continued, "Dad, I am going to deliver my enlistment paperwork tomorrow and ask that I be inducted on Monday."

"I'm glad everything is good with Sara and her family. I would hope that you can get your induction set as Monday because I think you need the next several days to tie up loose ends.", his dad responds.

"Thanks, Dad. That was my thinking as well. I hope the Marine recruiter will allow me that choice; because once I'm in the Corps, personal choice goes out the window."

At eight-thirty, Bessie poked her head into the den and announced that she was ready to retire and had already sent the young ones to bed. Ray decided that it would be a good time for him to go to bed as well since he did not get a lot of sleep last night. Bessie and Ray told Raymond and Jimmy good night.

Ray mused, *I hope I can get a good night's sleep tonight so I can be on the ball tomorrow.*

JOHNSON FAMILY HOME ~ MONTCROSS, NORTH CAROLINA
FRIDAY, DECEMBER 26, 1941 - 8:00AM

Jimmy was up first so he could get to the airport to pick up all the air mail that was coming in this morning and deliver it to the post office. Ray awoke as Jimmy was walking out of the bedroom and asked him the time. Jimmy told him that it was about 8:00 and that he needed to get moving.

Ray asked Jimmy, "Did my chores get done? It felt so good to sleep after Lillie woke me up so early yesterday."

Jimmy's response was almost self-serving when he said, "I took care of them for you this morning. Mom thought you needed your beauty rest."

"Thanks, Jimmy." Ray responded, "I needed my sleep, and after the next few days I won't be sleeping on my schedule any more for a while."

Jimmy asked, "Seems like you're having second thoughts about joining the Marines; are you?"

"Not second thoughts, but I'm very nervous for some reason. I don't know what is going on with me these days. It seems the closer I get to the possibility of leaving; the scarier the decision looks. Maybe if I had enlisted immediately, I wouldn't have had this bout of nerves."

"If you had joined immediately, you may not have had this case of nerves, but there would be some other issue to lose sleep over. I have to leave if I am going to get the airmail to the post office on time. When are you leaving for the Marine Recruiting Station?"

"I'll be leaving after breakfast and try to get there by eleven this morning for induction today. I will let you know how it goes."

As he left the house, Jimmy took his flight training manual so he could study with Mr. Mayerhofer after he delivered the mail to the post office.

━━━━━━━━━

"Good morning, Elva. Is there any breakfast left?" Ray asked.

"I saved you some eggs and sausage links. Looks like you slept good. "

"Yes ma'am, I slept very well. Thank you for saving me some breakfast. Do we have any coffee?"

"You are welcome. There is coffee left and I will make more if you need it."

"This should be enough, thank you."

Ray's dad had been gone a couple of hours to catch up on freight car repairs and train traffic that had been steadily increasing at the rail yard. Jimmy took the Model-A to use in delivering the mail and to take Bessie and the girls to roll bandages for the Red Cross. Ray would have to borrow the family car from his dad to take his paperwork to Charlotte.

Ray picked up the receiver and taps the handle twice and heard Mrs. Bass pick up and say, "Operator, number please."

"Hello, Mrs. Bass. Can you get me the rail yard, Montcross-406?"

"Hold one moment. Ray, that line is busy. Do you want to wait or leave a message?"

"I will wait to see if the call ends soon."

After about two minutes, Mrs. Bass came back and said that his call had been connected.

The secretary and rail yard switchboard operator, Miss Maier, answered the phone, "Montcross Rail Yard, how may I help you?"

"Miss Maier, this is Ray. Is Dad available to take a call?"

"Hello, Ray. How are you doing? I'm sending someone out to get your dad.", Miss Maier replied.

"I am doing well and if I can borrow the car from Dad, I'm going to go to Charlotte to enlist in the Marines."

"Good luck, I will be praying for you. I will connect you to your dad now."

"Hello, Ray. Overslept this morning didn't you, son?"

"Yes, I guess I needed it after Lillie woke me up before dawn yesterday. Can I borrow the car to complete my enlistment? I will be gone a couple of hours."

"When do you want to leave? Are you going to walk down here to get the car?"

"I want to leave within the hour so that I can get there by 11:00 or 11:30. I'll walk to the yard to get the car."

"That's fine. Just come by my office to get the keys. The keys will be in the center drawer of my desk if I am not in my office. If I do not see you before you leave, good luck."

"Thanks, Dad. Goodbye."

They hung up and both men let the operators know that the phone line was free.

"Elva, I'll be walking to the rail yard to get the car to go to Charlotte to enlist, but should be home by supper."

———————————

It was a brisk fifteen-minute walk to the rail yard and his dad was waiting in his office when he arrived.

"Hey, Dad, thanks for loaning me the car. Any last minute advice?"

"Just answer the recruiters questions truthfully and make sure that you have all the paperwork filled out correctly."

"Would you look the paperwork over one time before I leave? I think I have everything the Marines require to complete my enlistment."

His dad looked over the paperwork; found everything in order and handed him the car keys. Trying to stay upbeat, Ray told his dad goodbye and left the office to get in the car for the drive to the recruiting station.

MARINE RECRUITING STATION ~ CHARLOTTE, NORTH CAROLINA
FRIDAY - 11:30PM

Ray arrived at the Marine Recruiting Station at eleven-thirty and waited less than fifteen minutes before being seen by the recruiting sergeant. This was the same recruiting sergeant that Ray had spoken to on December 15 and the sergeant seemed to be in the same mood. The sergeant's last name was Yardley according to the nameplate.

At the head of the line and in front of the recruiting sergeant's desk, Ray said, "Sergeant Yardley, I am here to enlist in the Marines Corps. Here is my paperwork, Sir."

Sergeant Yardley took the paperwork, looked up and noticed Ray.

He said, "You are the baby who took his paperwork home for mama to fill out, right? She say it's all right for you to join my Corps?"

"Sir, I am here of my own volition and did not need my parents' permission to join. I'm here to serve just like my father did in the Great War. He served in the First Marine Division and was decorated with the Silver Star during the Battle of Belleau Wood. I am proud of his service and want to do my duty. That is all."

The sergeant's expression changed the instant Ray mentioned Silver Star and Belleau Wood. That was the old Corps doing what the old Corps did best, fighting and winning.

Sergeant Yardley spoke to Ray a little more reverently, "Mr. Johnson, I fought at Belleau Wood and there was a group of men that saved my platoon from sure destruction when they took out a couple of machine gun nests. I seem to recall that there was wounded soldier named Johnson. Was that your father?"

"Yes, Sir. He was wounded in the stomach during the action that cleared the nests and was sent back to England to recuperate. After twenty years of asking him to tell us about his time in the war, he finally told us what he went through so long ago in France. I'm here because of what he sacrificed during the Great War and I want to do my part.".

Yardley went over his paperwork with a fine tooth comb to make sure everything was in order, and when he came to the date that Ray wanted to leave for training which was Monday, December 29, 1941, he said, "We DON'T do things in the CORPS on your schedule! You will be here Sunday morning at nine o'clock to leave for training. Now step forward and be inducted!"

"Yes, Sir." Ray responded.

This date was not what Ray wanted, but he knew he could not put conditions on his enlistment. He accepted what the sergeant told him and followed the other recruits down the hall for his physical.

He walked into the examination area where a group of about twenty recruits waited, and at twelve-thirty, several Marine doctors and a Marine Corporal walked into the room. The Corporal had the recruits follow him into the examination area and strip for their physicals. At this point, Ray knew he was about to become a member of the Corps. This demeaning process was part of the molding of a Marine. Twenty naked men in line went from medical station to medical station getting poked, prodded, and surveyed in order to determine if they met Marine requirements. Out of the twenty men who started, only twelve, including Ray, were deemed acceptable for induction. The eight deemed physically unfit were sent on their way after the sergeant destroyed their paperwork. Ray and the other eleven dressed in the same communal area and returned to the waiting area where the oath was administered by Sergeant Yardley.

Ray raised his right hand and repeated, *"I, Raymond Johnson, Jr., do solemnly swear that I will support the constitution of the United States. I, Raymond Johnson, Jr., do solemnly swear to bear true allegiance to the United States of America, and to serve them honestly and faithfully, against all their enemies or opposers whatsoever, and to observe and obey the orders of the President of the United States of America, and the orders of the officers appointed over me."*[1]

With that oath, Ray was in the Corps and Sergeant Yardley reminded everyone, "The bus to Parris Island leaves promptly at nine Sunday morning, you 'boots' better be here in plenty of time to get on it!"

After the ordeal of the physical and the enlistment process, Ray got in the family car to return to Montcross all the while thinking, *What have I gotten myself into? I hope I am tough enough to make it through six weeks of this type of degrading experience in order to come out a member of the elite First Marine Division.*

The drive back to the rail yard in Montcross seemed quick and as he was parking the family car, his father stepped out of the shop, walked over, and asked how everything went with the recruiter.

"Well, are you in the Marines?"

"Yes, I passed the physical exam and have taken my oath of enlistment. The bus leaves from Charlotte on Sunday morning at nine for Parris Island. Sergeant Yardley made a point to tell us 'boots' that we should be at the Recruiting Station early to make sure we don't miss it."

---

1 • http://www.history.army.mil/html/faq/oaths.html

"Well that sounds like the Corps, I knew, and you probably stood in a room with twenty or so men and were told to strip to take your physical. You endured the short arm inspection, were poked, prodded, and probably even talked to a psychiatrist in order to make sure you were fit for duty. Right?"

"You are absolutely right, Dad. Why didn't you warn me?"

"If I had warned you, it would have given you one more thing to worry about during Christmas. The only thing you have left to do is break the news to your Mother that you are leaving Sunday. I am proud of you, Ray.", his dad says.

"Thanks, Dad. I'm going to go to the Hotel Montcross dining room for lunch. I'll see you tonight."

"Sounds fine, Son. Enjoy your meal and I'll see you at home."

DOWNTOWN MONTCROSS ~ MONTCROSS, NORTH CAROLINA
FRIDAY - 2:30PM

· · · · · · · · · · · · · · · · · · · ·

Ray walked to the diner at Hotel Montcross and ordered the lunch special from Mrs. Gullickson who was waiting the tables this afternoon.

"Hello, Ray. How's your dad doing since his scare the other week?"

"He is doing just fine and is back to work already. Thank you for asking."

"That's wonderful news. I hear you're joining the Marines. When do you leave?"

"I completed my enlistment this morning and leave Sunday morning for Parris Island."

Mrs. Gullickson wished him well and shuffled off to get his food. The lunch special was just what Ray needed after the ordeal at the recruiting station. Finishing lunch, he thanked Mrs. Gullickson for another delicious meal, paid his fifty-cent bill, and walked home.

Ray thought during the walk, *I'm nervous about my conversation with Mom, but I'm sure she will understand. At least, I hope she does.*

• •

Ray found that his mother and sisters had been home since two o'clock. They were cleaning up and putting away the Christmas decorations so they would be ready for next year. Lillie spied Ray as he was walking up the driveway and screamed in delight when she saw him.

Lillie yelled, "Ray, where have you been?"

"I have been down to see Dad at the rail yard and had lunch at the hotel. What have you been doing?"

"We rolled bandages this morning with Mommy and other ladies. We came home, had lunch, and Mommy made us clean up the decorations. I wish I could have had lunch at the hotel."

"I will take you for lunch after I get back from my trip."

"Thanks, Ray!"

Ray caught his mother's eye and nodded that he would like to talk to her. She understood and told the girls that she needed to check on something upstairs with Ray.

"Girls, I will be back down shortly. Continue cleaning up the decorations, please."

"Yes, Mom. We will get everything cleaned up." Elizabeth replied.

As Ray and his mother walked upstairs, he broke the news that he was leaving for Marine training on Sunday morning.

She told Ray, "After the attack on Pearl Harbor, I knew this day would come. I want you to know how proud I am of you. I have always been able to count on you when I needed help with the children or when something at the church needed doing. I know you are traveling into the unknown, but I want you to know that I will be praying for your safety. I heard you tell Lillie that you are going on a trip. Are you sure that is the right thing to tell her?"

"Thanks for everything you taught me growing up. I know this separation will be just as hard on you as when Dad left to serve in the Great War. As far as Lillie goes, I know how much she looks up to me, and I don't want to say anything that might scare her or make her think I may not come home. I am calling it a trip instead of telling the truth that I am going to war because of the chance I may not return. What do you think I should do?"

"Ray, I will tell you now that we should have a family meeting like we do when we try to decide where we want to go on vacation and at that time, you should tell everyone the truth. I know Jimmy and Elizabeth understand the risk that you are taking and I will be putting a Blue Star Flag in the window once you leave on Sunday. I firmly believe you should tell Myra and Lillie the truth in words that they can understand."

"I think that is the best way to handle it. I'll try not to scare Myra and Lillie. Please ask Dad to call the family meeting tonight so we have a day before I leave to help the girls understand. I love you, Mom."

"I love you too, Ray! Now we cannot show any fear at all and we must have happy faces tonight during the meeting."

They hugged. His mom went downstairs to finish supervising the clean up. Ray stayed in his room to contemplate the future.

At about five thirty, Jimmy and Raymond arrived home and cleaned up for supper. Bessie pulled Raymond aside to ask him to call a family meeting after supper to discuss Ray's enlistment so the young ones would know exactly what was happening. Bessie relayed to him the crux of the discussion she had with Ray that afternoon. Raymond agreed that it was a good idea to call the meeting to help the family understand.

As the family gathered around the dinner table, Raymond announced, "After supper, we are going to have a family meeting to talk about the war and what part our family will play in it."

Jimmy asked, "Dad, what is this all about? I know what part I plan to play in the war. Ray has made his decision as well."

"Jimmy, the girls have to know what part they are going to play. This meeting will help them understand the choices you and Ray have made."

With the questioning from Jimmy quelled, the family went back to enjoying supper. After finishing her meal, Bessie left Elva to clean up the dishes so she could join the family in the den.

Much like the smaller family meeting that occurred two Sundays ago, this meeting would help the family understand what the next few months and possibly years might mean for the family.

Raymond said, "Myra and Lillie, your mother and I want you to know what Ray means when he says he is going on a long trip. I think you went with your mother to roll bandages for the Red Cross this morning. Do you know that the United States is currently fighting a war against Germany and Japan?"

Myra piped up and said, "My teacher told our class that a country bombed our ships somewhere. I cannot remember where she told us, Daddy. She also told us our country has to fight them. Who will fight them, Daddy?"

"Myra, your teacher told you correctly that a country bombed our ships. That country is Japan and the place they bombed was Pearl Harbor in Hawaii. In our country, we have a military made up of the Army, Navy, and Marines. The men who are in the military have to go and fight the people who bombed our ships. Those may not get to come home to their families for a long time. Ray joined the Marines today and will be leaving Sunday morning to go help protect our country."

Little six-year-old Lillie piped up and bawled, "Daddy, why does Ray have to do that? I want him to stay here with me!"

At this point, Ray said, "Lillie, I made the decision to join the Marines so I can keep you and Myra safe. I need to do my part to protect you and the family."

Lillie replied, "I don't want you to go! When will you come back home?"

"I will get home as soon as I am able. You need to remember to pray for me every night. I promise to write and tell you what is happening. Will that be all right?"

Lillie responds, "I guess."

Raymond said, "Girls, if you don't have any more questions, you can go outside and play."

Elizabeth had been awfully quiet throughout the conversation with the young children. Now, nothing held her back, "Ray, why didn't you tell me when you got home earlier that you were leaving on Sunday?"

Ray replied, "Elizabeth, you noticed that I asked Mom to go upstairs to talk with her privately. I didn't want to say anything in front of the little ones. She recommended that Dad call this meeting to tell everyone all at one time. I'm sorry that I did not tell you then, but I did not keep you in the dark on purpose."

Elizabeth said, "Promise me that you will be careful and try to stay safe. I don't want to tell Sara something bad has happened to you."

"I will, Elizabeth. I don't want Sara to worry either. I'll have to call her to tell her that I'll be leaving on Sunday."

Ray was not the only one with news, Jimmy told everyone that his first flight lesson would be tomorrow. He was definitely excited knowing that he was part of the Civilian Pilot Training Program. The program would automatically grant him officer status in the Army Air Corps when he finished.

Jimmy said, "Since I am a part of the CPTP, I do not have to pay for anything except fuel. Fuel will cost seven dollars a lesson instead of the original fifteen. I can get more training hours now because I'd saved enough to pay for the entire program at fifteen dollars an hour."

Ray congratulated his brother and wished him well in training. He asked him to write often so he could follow his progress. Bessie and Raymond took a long look at their sons; and with a sense of pride, told them both how proud they were. Elizabeth even said she was proud to have such fine brothers. The family meeting was adjourned and Ray went to the study to call Sara.

Ray had the operator place a long distance call to the Peabody residence in Edenton, North Carolina

Ray said, "Hello."

Mrs. Peabody responds, "Hello, Ray. How are you doing?"

"Doing fine, Mrs. Peabody, just calling Sara to let her know I leave on Sunday for training at Parris Island. Is she available?"

"Yes. After you and Sara are finished, do you think I could speak to your mother?"

"Hold on and I'll get her now. After you are finished, I can talk to Sara. That might be better. Will that be all right?"

"Yes, Ray. That would be better. I'll wait."

Ray went to the den and asked his mother to speak to Mrs. Peabody.

Bessie answered, "Hello, Alma. How are you?"

"Hello, Bessie. I am doing fine. I want to take just a minute to ask you what might seem like prying questions. I need to know how I can help Sara while Ray is away in service."

"Yes, Alma. I will be happy to help you." Bessie replied and continued, "The hardest part will not be while Ray is at Parris Island. The hardest part will be when he is deployed to a war zone and the letters slow down or stop completely due to censorship in the battle zone."

"That makes sense; so what should I tell Sara when that happens?"

"You tell her to continue writing Ray. As soon as the mail catches up with him in the war zone, he will get all those letters which will raise his morale. Tell her to never put any guilt or sorrow in those letters as that will only make his life more difficult; in other words, keep everything upbeat even though she misses him terribly. Depression for a soldier can cause them to make mistakes and not remain diligent. I learned that from Raymond after he got home."

"Thanks, Bessie. This will help me help Sara. May Sara and I call or visit while Ray is gone?"

"Absolutely, Alma. Any time you or Sara want to talk about what is happening, you may feel free to call or visit. If we get information about Ray that is important, I will make sure you are informed. Understand that Raymond and I believe this war is going to be a long, drawn-out affair and it will take all of us maintaining our positive morale here at home."

"Thank you so much for taking the time to help me understand how to help Sara. Have a good evening. I will go get Sara so Ray can give her his news."

"Keep me posted if you need anything. Goodnight, Alma."

Ray's wait was brief and then he heard Sara say, "Hello, Ray. You have news about your enlistment, right?

"Yes, Sara. I completed my physical and my paperwork today. I will leave Sunday morning at nine for Parris Island."

Sara asked, "What does that mean?"

"I get on the bus at the recruiting station on Sunday morning. I travel to Parris Island for six weeks of basic training. I will get advanced training before deploying either to a war zone or a naval vessel." Ray replied.

"I understand that but I am scared that something will happen to you or you will find someone else while we are separated.", Sara cried as she told Ray one of her deepest fears.

Ray tried to comfort her by saying, "Sara, I love you more than anything in the world. I promise I will do everything in my power to come home safe and sound. Do not worry about me being unfaithful because I want to spend the rest of my life with you as your husband. I have my own concerns as well about you possibly finding someone else while I'm gone. I know you love me and am believing that you will remain faithful, too."

Sara choked up and said, "I love you and I promise that you are the only man for me. Good luck, Ray. I will be praying for your quick return to your family and me."

"Thank you. Our Moms talked before we began our conversation and I know both of them will help make this separation bearable for you. Please write me often; the letters will help me maintain my morale. Good night, Sara."

"Good night, Ray. I will write every day and tell you all the happenings at Meredith and Raleigh. Goodbye. I love you.".

"I love you, too. Goodbye." Ray said, as he hung up the phone.

JOHNSON FAMILY HOME ~ MONTCROSS, NORTH CAROLINA
SATURDAY, DECEMBER 27, 1941 - 7:00AM
• • • • • • • • • • • • • • • • • • • •

Ray arose at his normal time to get his chores done and gather what he would take with him to Parris Island. Jimmy was up and getting ready to take his first flying lesson at the Montcross Airport. They looked at one another and knew that this morning marked one of those changing tide moments of their young lives. One would be fighting on the ground in the Marine Corps and the other would learn to fly so he could fight in the air.

Ray said, "What time is your lesson today? Are you nervous?"

Jimmy replied, "Mr. Mayerhofer scheduled my lesson for eleven this morning. I have been on a couple of flights to the Charlotte Airport to pick up packages for the textile mills with Mr. Mayerhofer. I am not that nervous even though I know the training is going to be tough. I have to be diligent if I want to succeed and gain acceptance in the Army Air Corps as a pilot."

"Good luck. I hope your first lesson goes well and I hope you will tell me all about it when you get home. I need to ask Dad what I should pack for boot camp. I imagine he has a pretty good idea what is appropriate."

While Jimmy was still dressing, Ray pulled on his heavy mackinaw and left the house to do the chores.

―――――――

After Ray left, Jimmy had a moment to think about what his older brother would be facing in the not so distant future and he hoped he could be as steadfast in his commitment as his brother had been when he enlisted in the Marines. Today would be the first test to determine whether or not he had the ability to become a pilot. In actuality, Jimmy was extremely nervous about his first lesson even though he had told Ray otherwise. Jimmy finished dressing and went to the kitchen for breakfast which smelled of bacon, fried eggs, pancakes, and coffee. Raymond was at the table sipping his coffee when Ray walked back in the kitchen door with the eggs and milk. Bessie was helping Elva finish cooking breakfast while Elizabeth and the girls filled the glasses with milk and juice.

Ray said, "Dad, do you need a refill on your coffee before I sit down? It's certainly chilly outside this morning."

"That would be good, Ray. Thanks. I know, the paper says it might snow in the next day or so."

The family sat down at the table and the dishes of food were placed on the lazy susan for the older members to serve themselves.

Bessie said, "Myra, what would you like for breakfast?"

Myra replied, "I want two pancakes and a bowl of fruit, Mama."

"All right, Myra. Here is your plate and bowl." Bessie said as she placed Myra's breakfast in front of the ten-year-old.

Lillie said, "Mama, I want one pancake, eggs, two pieces of bacon, and a glass of milk."

Bessie prepared Lillie's plate and placed it in front of the six-year-old, saying, "Here you go, Lillie."

Once the youngest had their plates, Raymond said the blessing. Breakfast was a lively affair with everyone talking about their plans for the day. Myra and Lillie wanted to go to the movies this morning to watch the weekly cartoon serials which started at ten o'clock. Bessie told them since they had been extra good this week, she would take them. Elizabeth had volunteered to help the draft board with registration of eligible candidates and she had to report to the office by nine this morning for her three-hour shift.

Raymond asks Ray, "What are your plans for the day?"

"Dad, I need to know what I should take to Parris Island with me. I hear horror stories about guys having their bags and clothes confiscated for not being appropriate. Can you help me?"

"I will be happy to help you figure out what you should pack. I would guess if the Marines are still like they were in 1917, you won't need to take much. Everything you need will be issued."

"Thanks, Dad."

"Jimmy, are you ready for your first lesson, Son?

"Dad, I am a little nervous about my lesson but this is just a basic introduction to the airplane and basic flight maneuvers. Mr. Mayerhofer will probably describe the instruments in the airplane before we leave the ground; then he will demonstrate a maneuver and have me attempt it. The lesson should take about an hour."

"Good luck and be careful, Son. Flying is dangerous, but I know that Fred will keep you as safe as possible."

As the family finished breakfast, Ray asked his dad for the family car so he could drive Elizabeth to the draft board office for her shift.

During the short drive, Elizabeth asked Ray if he would come pick her up at noon so that she could be home in time for lunch.

"Dad or I will be there to pick you up."

After dropping Elizabeth off at the draft board office, Ray went directly to the post office to buy a three-dollar sheet of one hundred stamps. From the post office, Ray walked to Belk's to pick up a couple of things. While there, he was stopped by Mr. Linkenburg, the owner of the Montcross Rail Yard.

Mr. Linkenburg said, "Hello, Ray. I hear that you will be leaving us tomorrow for the Marine Corps. I want to wish you luck and safe travels. We are certainly proud of you."

"Thank you, Mr. Linkenburg. I am nervous about my decision and hope I don't let anyone down.", Ray replied.

"I do not think you need to worry about that. I have known you since you were a little boy and have watched you grow into a fine young man with a good head on his shoulders. You will do just fine, and I hope you will occasionally send us a letter at the rail yard to let us know how you are doing."

"I will certainly do that, Mr. Linkenburg. Thank you again for your kind words. They mean a lot."

While Ray was gone, Jimmy took Bessie and youngest two to the movie theater and then went on to the airport for his lesson. Ray arrived home at ten-fifteen ready to have a serious conversation with his father about what he would face in basic training. Ray found his dad in the den listening to the Saturday morning news report on the radio. With the newscast over, Ray clicked off the radio and started a conversation with his father.

"Things are sure looking bad for the country and our troops in the Philippines. Do you think any relief will get to them before they have to surrender? Will MacArthur be able to escape? What do you think the Marines Corps role will be in this war? I know we have not had much time to talk since you told me about your service in the Great War, but I want to know what you think I should expect in basic training. "

His father thought for a little while before he responded, "Ray, I don't think the Navy will be able to get to the Philippines to relieve the garrison, but I hope the President orders MacArthur to leave the Philippines and escape because his loss would completely drain our morale. As far as boot camp goes, I think it will be the hardest six-weeks of your life. You should only pack enough clothes for one night. I would not take the compass and knife you received for Christmas. Everything you will need will be issued by the Corps. Once you are assigned, you can write us and tell us what you need before you are shipped out. You have signed up for one of the toughest assignments in the military, and it will take all the mental strength you have. The drill instructors will make you believe you can't do anything right and you are worthless. Remember, that is the method they use to mold you into a Marine. You have everything within you to come through as long as you keep the Lord close and understand that you can do anything."

"Dad, I hope I am mentally tough enough to make it through not only training, but combat. My biggest fear is I will freeze when I face combat for the first time and let everyone down. How did you make it through your baptism of fire?"

"My baptism of fire came so quickly that I didn't have time to think, which probably helped me. After the soldier on my left went down from a bullet, I knew I had to move forward and fight my way through the fusillade if I wanted to stay alive. In the action where I took out the machine gun nest, my sergeant knew what needed to be done and ordered us forward in great haste. There was no time to think; I had to do what I was ordered. That will be the same for you. Just keep your head, do what you are told, and you will be fine."

In the Marines, Ray knew from this conversation that he would have to follow orders because to do otherwise could have dire consequences.

"Thanks, Dad. I love you."

"Your Mom and I love you, too. We will be praying for your safe return to us and for victory in the war. Now get packed for tomorrow."

MONTCROSS AIRPORT ~ MONTCROSS, NORTH CAROLINA
SATURDAY - 11:00AM

Jimmy arrived at the Montcross Airport at ten-thirty for his lesson at eleven. Mr. Mayerhofer was in the air with another student, and Jimmy decided to continue reading the *Civilian Pilot*

Training Program Manual while he waited. At ten-fifty, Jimmy looked up to see that Mr. Mayerhofer had returned from the previous lesson and was seated behind the counter in the airport office.

Jimmy walked to the counter and said, "Mr. Mayerhofer, I think I'm prepared for my lesson. I re-read the part about the pre-flight inspection in the *Civilian Pilot Training Program Manual*. I also studied the chapter about the flight training requirements. Is there anything else I should study before we start today?"

Mr. Mayerhofer with his thick German accent said, "No, I do not think so. I saw you studying when I came in from my lesson and did not want to interrupt you. Did you read and study the chapter about parachutes yet?"

"No, Sir. I glanced at the chapter on parachutes, but I did not study it like I've done the other chapters. Should I do that before we start?"

"No, Jimmy. But, you will need to demonstrate putting it on properly and explain how to use it before your next lesson. For today, we have a basic demonstration flight," Mr. Mayerhofer replied.

They discussed the fine points of the lesson then walked out to the J-3 Piper Cub tandem-seat airplane.

Mr. Mayerhofer walked with Jimmy around the bright yellow Piper Cub and showed him all of the control surfaces. They discussed how to manually check for movement in the control surfaces that was neither bound or extremely loose in the ailerons and rudder because either issue could cause serious consequences in the air.

Mr. Mayerhofer asked, "Jimmy, do you have any questions about the movement of the ailerons or rudder since both of those control surfaces help you maintain stable flight?"

Jimmy responds, "Yes, Mr. Mayerhofer. When you say that I should not fly an airplane that has either bound movement or very loose movement in the ailerons or rudder, what constitutes too loose? Does it mean that the control mechanism has possibly worked loose, releasing the tension on the control cable? Could that cause loss of control if the connection is completely severed?"

While Mr. Mayerhofer had taken Jimmy on various flights to pick up packages in other airplanes without much instruction, he saw that Jimmy was even more diligent about flying than he originally thought. He liked what he saw and the questions that he asked.

"Yes, a control surface that is too loose could signify that a cable has worked loose or is working loose which could be catastrophic if the connection fails. With the Piper Cub, you need to pay attention to everything about this airplane from the fabric on the fuselage to gasoline in its tank because a problem with any of them can result in a crash. Why don't we get you seated in the airplane and go over the various instruments that we will use in your basic flight training."

Jimmy, hardly able to contain his enthusiasm, replied, "I understand what you mean and that tells me that I have to ALWAYS make sure everything looks and feels right."

Mr. Mayerhofer opened the cockpit door, seated Jimmy in the front seat, and helped him properly fasten and tighten the safety belts; then he began his instrument introduction by saying, "The instrument in the center of the panel with a ball in it is called a bank indicator and you should always pay close attention to it. It shows whether you are in a coordinated turn or an uncoordinated turn. Do you have any questions about this instrument?"

Jimmy replied, "Just to clarify that I understand it, if I bank the airplane to the left with too much aileron and not enough rudder, then the ball in the bank indicator will move to the left. If I make a right turn with too much rudder and not enough aileron, then the bank indicator will also move to the left. Is that correct?"

"Yah! That is correct and you will be able to see it once we are flying. We need to look at the other instruments in the panel. The next instrument which is mounted directly beneath the bank indicator is the magnetic compass. The compass will keep you on course when flying cross-country. To the left of the compass is the airspeed indicator which will tell you how fast the wind is entering the pitot tube of the airplane. This speed is known as indicated airspeed. Next to the airspeed indicator is a tachometer which tells you how many RPMs the engine is running and will be used to test the spark to the engine from the magnetos. To the right of the compass is the altimeter which measures your altitude against sea level. You will need to know the altitude of the airport. You will set that altitude in the altimeter prior to take off. The two gauges on the right hand side of the dash are the oil temperature gauge and the oil pressure gauge. Why do you think these two instruments are important?"

"If the oil temperature is too high then you run the risk of having the engine seize and shut off just like you do in a car. The same with the oil pressure. If it happens in a car, you can pull off to the side of the road but if it happens in an airplane, you have an emergency and must try to safely land the aircraft as a glider. Will I be taught how to do that?"

"That is correct. You will learn to handle this type of engine out emergency. In an emergency, you need to remain calm and do no harm. The airplane can glide for some distance if you take care not to panic. Are you ready for your first flight?"

"Yes, Sir! I am ready to fly!"

"We need to get your parachute from the hangar and fit it properly. The Civilian Pilot Training Program requires all instructors and students to wear a parachute every flight and know how to use it in the event of an emergency."

After Jimmy was briefed by Mr. Mayerhofer on the use of the parachute, they walked back to the airplane wearing their parachutes. After demonstrating the pre-flight inspection, Mr. Mayerhofer climbed into the back seat of the tandem-seat Cub and fastened his safety belts. Jimmy positioned himself in the front seat and followed the procedure to fasten his safety belts. They closed the door and Mr. Mayerhofer started the airplane with help from the airport attendant. Without electric start, the Cub required someone to pull the prop through in order to start the engine.

With the airplane running, Mr. Mayerhofer yelled, "The first thing you do is make sure the airplane is running smoothly, then you test the magnetos to make sure they are firing properly."

After allowing sufficient time for the engine to warm up, Mr. Mayerhofer checked the magnetos and said, "Jimmy, we will taxi to the end of the runway. Notice you cannot see over the nose so you have to look out the side window to make sure you are taxiing straight."

They taxied to the end of the runway and positioned the aircraft into the wind for takeoff. Mr. Mayerhofer demonstrated a proper takeoff even though Jimmy probably would not remember all the steps. Once the airplane reached a safe altitude, Mr. Mayerhofer began Jimmy's flight maneuver training.

Mr. Mayerhofer spoke loud enough for Jimmy to hear him and said, "I am going to show you a coordinated right turn, then you can try the turn."

Mr. Mayerhofer slowly banked the airplane to the right and fed in enough right rudder to keep the ball centered in the bank indicator. He turned the airplane 180 degrees on the compass.

"Jimmy, take the stick and make a coordinated right turn another 180 degrees."

Jimmy took the stick and banked the airplane to the right while forgetting to add right rudder causing the ball in the bank indicator to move to the right. In Jimmy's mind everything was moving too fast and he had forgotten to add rudder until Mr. Mayerhofer's gentle reminder. As Jimmy slowly added right rudder, he saw the ball start moving to the left, but Jimmy did not stop his rudder input when the ball was centered and added too much rudder. While trying to complete his turn, Jimmy inadvertently started a climb which caused the airplane to slow.

Mr. Mayerhofer yelled, "My airplane! Let go of the stick!"

Mr. Mayerhofer reestablished control, and Jimmy started slowly making progress in his maneuvers. Mr. Mayerhofer flew the airplane back to the traffic pattern, walked Jimmy through the landing checklist, and landed. Once the plane was on the ground and stopped, Mr. Mayerhofer and Jimmy walked back to the terminal.

Jimmy sheepishly asked, "Are all student pilots as bad as I was on my first flight? I felt completely out of control and everything seemed to happen so fast."

"Yes, Jimmy, most students think everything is moving too fast and they forget everything while trying to maintain balanced flight. But, I can tell you have been studying your training manual because you were able to answer my questions. By the questions you asked, you know that flying is not simple and mistakes can kill you. When you were learning to drive, did you just get in the car and drive? Or, did it take time to learn?"

"When I was learning to drive, it took time. Things happened just as fast in the car in the beginning as they did in the airplane today. I had to learn how to get the car moving properly with the correct inputs to clutch and gas. It took me several months to master and once I was proficient at starting, stopping, and driving short distances, everything started to fall in place and slowed down. Will the same thing happen in the airplane?"

"Over time with practice, you will learn to fly the airplane and things will slow down. Do not expect it to happen in the first few weeks. It will only happen with diligent work and practice on your part. Do you have any more questions about your first flight?"

"No."

Mr. Mayerhofer continued, "Today's demonstration of the coordinated turn is very important. It requires diligent practice. You add bank to the airplane with the stick and you follow it with rudder to keep the ball centered. In this type of maneuver, you set the wing's angle of bank while adding rudder, check the bank indicator, and apply any corrections needed to keep the ball centered. Periodically in the turn, you will need to check the compass and the altimeter to make sure you do not overshoot the turn and you are not climbing or descending. Any questions?"

"No, Sir. I understand that all turns need to be coordinated. I know I have to look outside and scan the instruments throughout the flight to make sure everything is in balance."

"Yes, that is correct. Just be patient, Jimmy, everything will start working together. I will be with you every step of the way and I will train you like I trained my comrades. I will see you Monday for ground school and your next flying lesson is Saturday at eleven."

"Thank you, Mr. Mayerhofer. I hope to be better prepared next time."

Jimmy was completely wrung out and hoped next week would be better. He knew it would take work and effort on his part if he wanted to become a pilot, but his confidence that he could complete the course had been bruised.

Christmas in Montcross

Raymond picked up Elizabeth at noon from the draft board office and returned home for lunch. Ray had gathered everything he was going to take to Parris Island, and with each passing hour, Ray's apprehension of boot camp and the unknown increased. Raymond, Elizabeth, and Ray gathered in the kitchen, and as Elva was placing the food on the table, Jimmy walked in looking a like a whipped puppy.

Raymond took one look at Jimmy and asked, "What's wrong, Son? You look like you've been through the wringer."

"Well, Dad, it certainly feels that way after my first lesson. Mr. Mayerhofer demonstrated a coordinated turn then turned the controls over to me and my turn was so uncoordinated that he had to retake control of the airplane in order to stabilize it. I felt like a failure even though Mr. Mayerhofer tried to lift my spirits by continuing to allow me to try until I finally completed the maneuver. When I completed that last turn almost correctly, Mr. Mayerhofer determined it was time to land. I feel I failed my first lesson although Mr. Mayerhofer said I had done fine. He told me I performed just like his other students during their first lesson."

"Jimmy, if Mr. Mayerhofer said you did fine for your first lesson then you did. I know you want to succeed, but flying is an art that will take practice. Remember the best way to accomplish your goal is to remain calm and patient and you must take every bit of training and advice Mr. Mayerhofer imparts to you. That is the only way you can succeed in learning to fly."

"Thank you, Dad. I read everything about the bank indicator and knew what I had to do based on the book, but when I got in the airplane, everything I had studied vanished and I couldn't remember a thing and that scared me."

His dad replied, "Fear is a good thing because you know a mistake can hurt or even kill you. You can't let the fear control you though. When you know you are scared, take a deep breath, remember your training from Mr. Mayerhofer and the manual, and you will do just fine. When is your next lesson?"

"My next flying lesson is Saturday at eleven, and my first ground school class is Monday night at seven. I think once I talk to other students, I'll be fine. I know it takes time to learn a new skill and flying is no different. Mr. Mayerhofer is an excellent instructor and pilots who have completed their training under him have told me that he made them better pilots."

Bessie, Myra, and Lillie came in and sat down with the others to eat. Even with all the upheaval, the banter was light and calm. This family knew that their future was unknown, but with the love they shared for one another, the family knew they could survive anything life threw at them.

MONTCROSS DRUG ~ MONTCROSS, NORTH CAROLINA
SATURDAY - 4:30PM

• • • • • • • • • • • • • • • • • • • •

After lunch, Ray, Jimmy, and Elizabeth went to the Gem Theatre for a movie and later to Montcross Drug for a soda and to talk. Jimmy ordered himself a vanilla milkshake even though it was pretty cold outside. Ray ordered his favorite and a Montcross Drug special, the orangeade.

Elizabeth ordered a bottled coke and said, "Are you sure you're ready to go in the morning?"

Ray replied, "No, Elizabeth, I am not sure, but I am now at the point of no return because I've already signed my enlistment papers and passed my physical. I'll be honest; I'm scared. This is not like going to school because I knew that whenever I wanted or needed to come home, I could. With military service, I only get to come home when they say I can. What are you going to do for the war effort?"

Elizabeth said, "I am going with Mom to roll bandages every chance I get and I will be working every Saturday at the draft board to help with the paperwork. Every spare penny I save from my odd jobs will be used to buy war stamps to support the war effort. I will make sure Mom and Dad have all the help they need. Ray, you know Mom will have a very difficult time if anything happens to you."

Ray replied, "I know they will, but I cannot think about that if I am to do my job. I will write as often as I can and I am going to keep a journal that will tell my story after I get home. In Mom's conversation with Mrs. Peabody, she said, 'those who remain behind on the home front should always write cheery, upbeat letters to help keep the morale of soldiers at their highest level. When a soldier receives a letter that is downcast or disheartening, that soldier is more likely to let his guard down and do something that could get him hurt or killed.' I am beginning to see the truth in this because when you're safe, you can deal with both positive and negative things more easily since your life is not a constant struggle against an enemy or an environment. I am asking you to help keep Mom and Dad as upbeat as best you can."

The group sipped their drinks and enjoyed the short time they had together.

Ray tried to lift Jimmy's spirits by saying, "Hey, Jimmy, you remember how hard it was to ride your bicycle as a kid? Flying an airplane is more like riding a bike than it is about driving a car."

Jimmy replied, "How do you figure that?"

Ray then responds, "What is the hardest part about riding a bike?"

"Well, I think the hardest part about riding a bike is probably keeping it balanced," Jimmy replied.

"That's it; you have to keep the bike balanced in order to ride it with proficiency. What is the hardest part about flying an airplane?"

Jimmy thought interminably about what Ray just asked and when the conversation seemed to be sinking irretrievably into sullen silence, said, "Balance! I have to keep the airplane balanced which is the same as riding the bike. I haven't ridden a bicycle for so long that I had forgotten you have to keep your hands and feet coordinated so you don't fall. When we get home, I'm going to pull out my old bike and take it for a spin. That should help with my coordination. Thanks, Ray!"

The siblings were happy they had the opportunity to share this time together and made the most of it. Ray had always been the one to keep everyone in line and upbeat, and he was still doing that today. Jimmy, always the tempestuous one, needed someone to calm him and show him there were consequences to his sometimes rash actions. Elizabeth had gone from being the youngest in the family to being the oldest of the three girls, and from this day on would be assuming more of a leadership role within the family. Her diligence and studiousness would be needed in the days to come.

With their drinks finished and a new found understanding, they started home safe in the knowledge that although the changing currents and changing tides of life may separate them, they would still have each other to cling to for support.

JOHNSON FAMILY HOME ~ MONTCROSS, NORTH CAROLINA
SATURDAY - 6:00PM

• • • • • • • • • • • • • • • • • • • •

Bessie and the girls had done chores all afternoon; one of which was baking chocolate chip cookies. The youngest girls loved being able to help their mom and Elva with the baking. They always got to lick the spoon of leftover batter after the cookies went into the oven. Bessie told the girls that these chocolate chip cookies were special because she was sending them with Ray on the bus to Parris Island to share with his new friends.

Bessie said, "We need a big batch today so Ray has enough cookies to share. These cookies will show him how much we love him."

Myra replied, "Yes they will, Mommy! Maybe they will help make the other soldiers happy, too."

With tears welling up, Lillie said, "I don't want Ray to go! I want him to stay here with me!"

Bessie tried to calm the six-year-old by saying, "We talked about this, Lillie. You know he must go and protect us. You need to remember that Ray loves you very much, and you don't want him to see you crying. He will have trouble doing his job if he thinks you are sad that he is leaving. So put on a smile, and lick this spoon; it is full of cookie dough."

"Ok, Mommy. Ooh! That is a full spoon, THANKS!"

While the cookies were being baked in the kitchen, Raymond sat in the den all afternoon thinking about what Ray's departure would do to the family. He was extremely nervous about what could happen to his son in battle since he had witnessed it first hand during the Battle of Belleau Wood.

He said a silent prayer, *"Dear Lord, I come to you a sinner who is saved by your grace and mercy asking that you protect all my children during this time, especially Ray, as he leaves tomorrow to serve our country. I ask that you guide his heart and protect his body, in Jesus name I pray. Amen."*

Raymond made his way to the kitchen to see what Elva and the girls fixed for supper. As he took his seat at the kitchen table, he saw Ray, Jimmy, and Elizabeth walking up the driveway. The three siblings joined everyone around the table, and their dad asked if they had a good time at the movies and the drug store.

Elizabeth said, "We had a wonderful time and it was just great to spend time together."

Ray smelled the chocolate chip cookies and asked, "Are those chocolate chip cookies for me? Mom, you know I love your cookies."

Lillie gleefully said, "Myra and I made them for you. You must share them with everyone on your bus. We made a lot!"

"Thank you, Lillie and Myra. I will share them with the people on my bus. Mom, I know you had a hand in this. Thank you!"

Bessie replied, "You're welcome. I hope you enjoy them. It does my heart good knowing you will have a touch of home, if only for a little while. Supper's ready. Raymond, will you say grace?"

Raymond said, "Yes, Mother. Dear Lord, we come before you on this the last evening before our family becomes one less with thanksgiving in our hearts for the bountiful blessings you have bestowed upon us. Bless this food to the nourishment of our bodies and us to your service. In Jesus name, we pray. Amen."

After dinner, Ray went into the study to call Sara to have one last conversation before he left for basic training. Ray picked up the phone and tapped the receiver twice getting Mrs. Ann Lionel, the town's other operator and biggest gossip.

"Number, please," Mrs. Lionel asked.

"Good evening, Mrs. Lionel. Long distance call to Edenton-676, please," Ray replied.

Mrs. Lionel insolently asked, "Ray, do you have your parent's permission to make a long distance call? You know they are expensive."

Ray, a little peeved, replied, "Yes, ma'am, they are aware that I am making a long distance call to Edenton. Would you please connect me, now?"

Mrs. Lionel, showing unusual obstinacy, replied, "I cannot connect you until you put one of your parents on the phone to authorize this call. You know the rules, Ray. I can only allow authorized bill holders to place long distance calls."

"Hold on, Mrs. Lionel, I will get my Dad," Ray said.

Ray left the phone dangling and walked into the den.

Ray said, "Dad, Mrs. Lionel is not allowing me to make a long distance to Edenton without having your approval. Mrs. Bass has never asked me if I had permission to make a long distance call."

"I'll take care of it, Ray."

Both men walked back to the study and Raymond picked up the phone, saying, "Good evening, Mrs. Lionel. Ray says you need my help."

Mrs. Lionel replied, "Did you know that Ray wanted to make a long distance call to Edenton? Who does he know in Edenton that makes a call at this late hour necessary?"

"Mrs. Lionel, I knew Ray was making a long distance call to Edenton and I would appreciate it if you would put the call through. If any of my children request that you put a long distance call through, please do so without harassing them like you did tonight. By the way, it is none of your business who my son is calling in Edenton and it's rude for you to ask. I will speak to Mrs. Bass when she comes on duty tomorrow to see what we can do to prevent this from happening in the future. Now, will you please connect the call to Edenton-676?"

Mrs. Lionel stuttered and stammered as if all the air had been knocked out of her. Never had she heard someone get so upset with her for following the rules even though it was out of sheer nosiness and not necessity that she did it.

She replied, "Mr. Johnson, I want to apologize and let you know that I will put through any call from your phone without question in the future. Please do not talk to Mrs. Bass tomorrow about my behavior and I will never let this type of thing happen again."

"Mrs. Lionel, I will be talking to Ouida tomorrow about this. We have wasted enough time on this already; please put the call through immediately."

"Yes, Sir. Again I apologize. Putting the call through, now."

"Thank you, Mrs. Lionel," Raymond replied and handed the phone to Ray, saying, "You should not have any more problems with Mrs. Lionel tonight. Tell Sara the family says hello."

"Thanks, Dad, I will," Ray replied and removed his hand from the mouthpiece as he put the phone to his ear. Ray heard Mrs. Lionel working with the operators up the line to put the call through to Edenton-676.

Ray finally heard Mrs. Lionel say, "I have you connected to Edenton-676. Thank you for your patience."

Ray said, "Thanks, Mrs. Lionel. Have a good evening. I will let you know when I have hung up by tapping our receiver twice."

Mrs. Lionel, whose nosiness kept her from unplugging from some calls, replied, "Disconnecting now. Have a good evening."

Ray said, "Hello."

Mrs. Peabody replied, "Hello, Ray. How are you this evening?"

"Doing fine, Mrs. Peabody. I am calling Sara tonight to talk one last time until boot camp is over. How is she doing?"

"She is doing fine and I know she appreciated the letters and card she received. We are nervous about what the future holds, and we will keep you in our prayers. How is your family?"

"Thanks, Mrs. Peabody. Everyone in the family is a little nervous as well, but doing well otherwise. Mother says she is going to invite you and Sara for a visit soon. Is Sara home?"

"No, Ray. She is not home now. Sam, William, and Thomas cajoled her into going to the Wright home for a church youth get-together. They thought it would do her some good to see old friends. She should be home by nine thirty. Would that be too late for her to call you back? I know she wants to talk to you."

Ray thought for a moment about whether the time would be too late for Sara to call back and decided that since the girls would have been in bed for at least an hour that a call then would not be appropriate.

"Mrs. Peabody, that will be a little late to call me back because the girls will be in bed and the phone might disturb them. Let her know that I love her very much and I will do my best to be careful. I will write her often to tell her how everything is going and call her the first chance I get."

Mrs. Peabody, knowing that Sara would want to talk to Ray, said, "I know Sara wants to talk to you so I will call over to the Wright home and let her know you called. She will call you back shortly."

"Thank you, Mrs. Peabody. That will be nice because I really don't want to leave without talking to her. Our number here is Montcross-344. Thank you again for your hospitality last weekend. Give everyone my love."

"You're welcome, Ray. We love you too and I will have Sara call as quickly as she can. Goodbye."

"Goodbye."

They hung up and Ray let Mrs. Lionel know that the line was free.

PEABODY FAMILY HOME ~ EDENTON, NORTH CAROLINA
SATURDAY - 7:30PM

• •

As soon as Alma hung up, she picked the phone back up and tapped the receiver to call the Wright home.

The operator, Mrs. Margaret Owens, picked up and said, "Number, please."

"Margaret, this is Alma, can you get me the Wright Home, 469? Please," Alma replied.

"Yes, Alma, I can. Hold one moment.", Margaret replied.

Margaret looked at the line to the Wright home and noticed that it was busy and replied, "Alma, the Wright's phone is busy, do you want to wait?"

"No, I don't need to wait, just let me know when the line comes free. Can you do that?"

"Yes, I will ring your phone when the line comes free."

"Thank you, goodbye."

"You are welcome, goodbye."

While she waited on the return call, she found Samuel in the sitting room reading the latest edition of the newspaper.

"Samuel," Alma said, "I might need you to go pick Sara up and bring her home so she can call Ray. Tonight is his last as a civilian, and he wants to talk to Sara before he leaves tomorrow for the Marines."

Samuel replied, "Yes, I can pick Sara up if I need to and take her back after she talks to Ray. I think she should talk to Ray before he leaves. Heaven knows when she will get to talk to him on the phone or in person again."

Alma replied, "Thanks, Samuel."

About ten minutes later, the phone rang and it was Margaret saying she had the Wright home connected.

Mrs. Nora Wright answered the phone, "Hello."

"Nora, are Sara and the boys still there? I need to speak to Sara to let her know that Ray called this evening."

"Yes they are all here. Ray is the nice young beau of Sara's, right? Isn't he leaving for service, soon?"

"Yes, Nora, Ray leaves tomorrow morning and he wanted to talk to Sara before he left. Can you get me Sara so I can see what she wants to do about calling Ray? If she calls from your home, I will have Margaret set up the call to bill to our number."

"I will have Sara call Ray from here. Do you still need to talk to her?"

"No, I do not need to talk to her if you will let her know to call Ray at Montcross-344"

The two women said goodbye and Alma set up to have the called billed properly with Margaret.

Mrs. Wright found Sara with Mary and a group of young ladies in fierce discussion about the various branches of service and which soldiers looked the most handsome in their uniforms.

Mrs. Wright got Sara's attention and said, "Your mother just called and she told me that Ray called 30 minutes ago and would like for you to call him back."

"Mrs. Wright, is it ok if I use your phone to call him back since it is a long distance call?"

"Yes, it will be just fine. The billing has been taken care of by your mother. I will take you to the study where you should not be disturbed."

Mrs. Wright escorted Sara into the study and Mrs. Wright closed the door as she left.

Sara picked up the phone to get the operator.

"Number, please," the operator responded.

"Mrs. Owens, this is Sara Peabody and my mother told Mrs. Wright that the long distance call I am about to make to Montcross 344 will be billed to our phone and not the Wright phone. Is that correct?"

"Yes, Sara, that is correct. Your mother and I worked that out. I will now connect your call. Hold please."

Mrs. Owens worked about three minutes to get the call connected to the Johnson family home and routed the call through the Peabody home in order to get the billing correct.

When she had the Johnson home, Mrs. Owens said, "You are connected to Montcross 344. Please let me know when the call is complete."

"Thanks, Mrs. Owens. I will let you know. Hello."

"Hello, Mrs. Johnson. This is Sara. I am calling Ray back. Is he available?"

"Yes, Sara. How is the get-together at the Wrights?"

"It is wonderful and has done me good to see old friends and classmates. How are you doing?"

"Everything is wonderful here and we are enjoying our Christmas time together. How are you doing?"

"I'm nervous about Ray leaving for training, but Mom told me what you said to her. I will try not to give Ray the impression that I am upset in any way. I know for the sake of his morale and the safety of our troops, I need to have an upbeat attitude in the letters I write and during the few times we might have the opportunity to talk."

"That is exactly how you need to handle things no matter how upset you are by the separation. I am here for you and your mother if you need someone to talk to about the pain of separation. It was wonderful to talk to you; I'll get Ray."

"Thanks, Mrs. Johnson. I'm sure I'll be calling you because I do not know how well I will handle everything."

"You will do just fine and Ray will be right here."

Mrs. Johnson laid down the phone and went to the den to get Ray. Ray thanked his mother and rushed to the study to pick up the phone.

"Hello, Sara, hope you are enjoying your evening at the Wrights."

"It has been a great evening and I've caught up with many of my friends from church. Are you nervous about tomorrow?"

"Sara, honestly, I am petrified about tomorrow and my upcoming training. I hope I can mentally and physically handle the pressure that I am sure the instructors are going to inflict. I want you to know that whatever happens; I will always be thinking of you."

"Ray, you will do fine. You are an athlete and you are prepared to do whatever it takes to succeed. I have watched you think through various problems and make the best decision. The things you are going to face may require quicker decisions but you will make it because I want you to come back home to me."

They conversed about how things would be after tomorrow and how each one would work hard to keep the other informed through letters and telegrams.

"I'll not be able to write you much, if at all, the first week because of getting used to the daily training regimen. I know that it is a six-week training program followed by assignment to a unit, but I don't know if I'll get a furlough before I am shipped to my duty station for advanced training."

"Everything will be just fine, Ray. I know that you will write or call when you can. Also, I have your Mom to talk to if the separation becomes unbearable. Just do this for me, work hard; and do the best you can not to worry."

"Thanks, Sara. That means a lot because I am going to worry about how you are handling everything. I can tell you myself that I am not going to do well with it, but I know I'm doing the right thing. I just didn't know that it would be this scary."

Sara thought for a moment about this sign of weakness from Ray and said, "Don't worry because you will have us praying for your safe return, and you know that with Jesus all things are possible. I will be here for you and I know we will begin our lives together forever once you return."

They talked a little longer about how their families were doing and professed their love for one another. They felt better after talking and hung up knowing what they needed to do to make everything bearable.

JOHNSON FAMILY HOME ~ MONTCROSS, NORTH CAROLINA
SATURDAY - 9:00PM

• •

Ray found his mother in the sitting room with her needlepoint and took a chair to spend some time talking with her.

"Mom," Ray said, "do you have a minute to talk?"

"Yes, I have plenty of time for you. What do you need?"

"I'm pretty scared about leaving tomorrow for boot camp. I don't know what it is going to be like even though Dad explained what he went through. Is this normal?"

"I would've been concerned if you had not come to me with some fear because you are about to embark on something that could kill you or leave you crippled. I think it is very normal to be afraid, but you need to channel that fear so that it does not overwhelm you. I believe you will do just fine; because you have excelled in everything you have chosen to do, and this will be no different."

"Thanks, Mom. I accomplished my Eagle Scout and excelled in all of the outdoor activities required by the Boy Scouts, but this is different because I will not be able to come home if things get too tough. I hope I am tough enough to handle it."

"You are, Ray. Do you remember when you played the second half of the 1938 State Championship game with that broken arm? You did not want to come out of the game until it was over because you felt like you could still make plays. You had three tackles and you tackled the quarterback before he could throw during that half. You will need to use that same mental toughness to make it through training and whatever happens afterwards."

Ray had always felt that he had played better after the injury even though he could not receive a pain injection. Opioid painkillers were prohibited without parental permission for high school athletes. He always felt he had been mentally sharper due to having to block out the pain. He began to see what his mother was saying about mental toughness which would help him throughout his training.

"Thanks, Mom. Your memory of my championship game performance has given me a little better feel for being mentally tough enough to make it."

"I know you can do it and just remember when the going gets tough, the tough get going. You are tough. You might want to go on to bed so that you are refreshed and ready to leave by seven-thirty."

"Good night, Mom. Thank you and I love you."

"I love you too, Ray. I'm proud of you. Good night."

WRIGHT FAMILY HOME ~ EDENTON, NORTH CAROLINA
SATURDAY - 9:00PM

After finishing the phone call with Ray, Sara decided to call her mom before returning to the party.

Her father answered and Sara said, "Hello, Dad, is Mom there?"

"Yes, Sara, your Mom is standing right here. Do you want to speak to her?"

"Yes, Dad. I would like to talk to her for a minute before I return to the party."

Samuel handed the phone to Alma and she said, "Hello, Sara. Did you get in touch with Ray?"

"Yes, Mom. I was able to talk to him. He seemed really nervous, but I tried to lift his spirits by telling him he would do just fine. I followed the instructions that you relayed to me from Mrs. Johnson. I did tell him I would miss him and I made sure to let him know that I would always be here for him. I asked him to remember that his service comes first before thinking about any problems here at home."

Her mother replied, "That was exactly what you needed to do because the training will be tough enough without having him worry about anything here. I know you miss him and you want to be close to him, but this separation will only make both of you appreciate the love you share even more. Now go and enjoy the time with all your friends. I am glad you were able to spend a little time on the phone with Ray."

Sara thanked her mom and returned to the party.

As she walked into the large ballroom, her brother Sam saw her and walked over.

He said, "I noticed that Mrs. Wright came in and escorted you out; where have you been? Is everything all right?"

"Yes, everything is just fine. Ray called our house earlier and wanted to talk to me before he leaves in the morning. Mom set it up for me to call Ray from here and Mrs. Wright made sure I was able to use the study to make the call."

"How is Ray doing? I need to write him soon myself. I want to let him know that I am thinking of him and hope his training goes well."

Sara thought about her response because she did not want to betray Ray's confidence of being scared of what tomorrow and the future would bring.

So she said to Sam, "He is nervous about the unknown starting tomorrow, but he thinks that he should do fine as long as he keeps his wits about him."

"That's good, Sara. I know he will do fine because he showed us his toughness when he was here a week ago. We tried to tire him out and make things difficult on him but he met every trial with a grace that usually only comes from men twice his age."

"Thanks. I figured you, William, and Thomas were testing him while he was here."

Mary saw Sara had returned and asked her to join them in the last game before the party ended. Sara had a wonderful time and won the last game. The prize was a one dollar War Stamp which she would add to her War Stamp Book. As the party ended, Sara agreed with her brothers that she felt much better for having attended.

JOHNSON FAMILY HOME ~ MONTCROSS, NORTH CAROLINA
SUNDAY, DECEMBER 28, 1941 - 6:30AM

· · · · · · · · · · · · · · · · · · · ·

Ray slept soundly after his conversation with his mother, and he awakened refreshed on a day which dawned cold with the temperature hovering around thirty degrees. Ray arose from his bed and readied himself to face the day and his destiny. Jimmy was still sleeping soundly when Ray suddenly threw a pillow at him to wake him.

"Hey, Jimmy, you going to sleep through the day? It is already six thirty and we need to get our chores done if we want to have time for breakfast."

Jimmy, bleary eyed, looked at his brother and laughed, saying, "I didn't realize you were so excited about leaving that you would be up before the sun to get your chores done. I'll humor you this morning especially since Elva is preparing your favorite breakfast of French Toast, bacon, and fruit cocktail."

Jimmy popped out of bed and dressed quickly while Ray finished packing his suitcase. Ray told Jimmy he was going out to do his chores and should be back in for breakfast about seven-fifteen.

Ray placed his suitcase on the back porch to make it easy to grab and put in the car when it was time to leave. He walked to the cow shed to milk Gertrude and he hummed a little ditty as he talked to the cow. He tried to warm his hands sufficiently to not give her a start. She dutifully stood in her stall while Ray gathered his milking stool and the milk bucket. She had worked hard overnight and gave him five and a half gallons of creamy milk. Ray thanked her and poured the milk from the bucket into milk can for delivery to Elva and his mother. About that time, Jimmy joined him in the shed and cleaned Gertrude's stall and refilled her feed and water buckets. Ray gathered the eggs from the hen house as Jimmy followed behind him cleaning out the nesting areas of dirty straw and replacing it. With the eggs gathered and the small barnyard clean, Ray and Jimmy walked back to the house with the milk and the eggs.

When he walked in with the milk and the eggs, Ray saw everyone was downstairs and dressed like they had some place to go besides church this morning.

Ray looked at his dad and said, "Good morning, I did not expect everyone to be down and ready to go this morning. What is going on? Did I miss the memo that there is early Sunday school today?"

Lillie in her zeal blurted, "No, Ray! We are going to Charlotte to see you off! You didn't think you were going to go by yourself, did you?"

Ray, a little flabbergasted, looked at his siblings with admiration because this was their small way of showing how much they loved him and how much they would miss him while he was gone.

Ray says, "Thank you, all. This will be a wonderful memory for me while I am away. Now, let's eat if I am to get to the bus on time!"

Everyone laughed at the last line about eating. Elva delivered one of her signature breakfasts of succulent French Toast with plenty of syrup and honey. Ray was so hungry that he ate six slices of the delectable toast and four slices of his favorite thick bacon while washing it all down with two cups of coffee and a glass of orange juice.

Everyone piled into the family car at seven forty-five to take Ray to the recruiting station. Bessie remembered to grab the two tins of cookies the girls baked yesterday for Ray and his fellow enlistees. Elva packed him two ham sandwiches, deviled eggs, potato chips, and a couple of dill pickles in a brown sack for lunch.

As Ray stepped into the car, Elva said, "Ray, my prayer and hope is that I will see you again very soon. Good luck and may God bless your endeavor."

"Thank you, Elva, I will remember you always and will look forward to the day that I can sit down to one of your dinners again."

Elva, with a tear in her eye, gave Ray a hug just like she did while he was growing up after he skinned his knee or was upset.

Ray embraced her just as strongly saying, "You take care, Elva, and I will see you as soon as I can."

After everyone was in the car, Mr. Johnson backed down the driveway. It was a silent trip to Charlotte as everyone contemplated what might happen to Ray once he was a front-line soldier in the Marines.

CHARLOTTE MARINE RECRUITING STATION ~ CHARLOTTE, NORTH CAROLINA
SUNDAY - 8:30AM

• • • • • • • • • • • • • • • • • • • •

Ray was one of the first recruits to arrive at the recruiting station, and Sergeant Yardley was there to greet the contingent of boots who were leaving this morning for the hell which was Parris Island recruit training.

Ray walked up to the sergeant and said, "Good Morning, Sergeant Yardley, recruit Raymond Johnson, Jr., reporting for duty, Sir."

His dad had warned him not to use any rank this morning when he reported for duty because as a "Boot", he was lower than the lowest pond scum on the Marine totem pole of rank.

"Welcome aboard BOOT! Gather your gear and report to the corporal over there for boarding instructions. If you've got any goodbyes to say and crying to do, do it now before you report to the corporal. After this there will be no crying in the ranks. You look like a MAMA'S BOY and all a MAMA'S BOY is good for is crying and washing out of my CORPS," Sergeant Yardley spat.

Ray was not taken aback in the least because he knew he loved his mother and that he probably was a mama's boy. From here on though, he would be one hundred percent Marine and would do everything the instructors told him to do.

Ray walked over to his family and said, "You heard the Sergeant. I am going to tell you goodbye now so that you can make it back in time for Sunday school."

Ray lifted Lillie up to give her a big hug saying, "Now, Lillie, you be a good girl while I am gone. Please remember to write me often to tell me what you are doing."

Lillie started crying and said, "I love you, Ray. Be careful and come home soon. I will miss you."

Ray, holding back tears, said, "I love you too, Lillie. Will you write me to tell me how you are doing?"

"Oh, YES," Lillie replied!

Ray put Lillie down and leaned down to hug Myra. He said, "Myra, I am going to miss you while I am gone. Remember to write me like I asked your sister to do and tell me all about school. Good luck this quarter. Remember to save your stamps for a war bond to help the country win the war."

Myra cried, "BE CAREFUL, RAY! I LOVE YOU!"

She tore away from him and ran to their mother.

Ray, on the verge of losing control of his own emotions, quickly hugged the rest of the family.

He said to his parents, "Keep me in your prayers and keep me posted on everything in Montcross. I love you all and will miss every one of you while I am gone. Thanks for all the goodies for the bus ride. I will mail you a letter as soon as I have my new address."

Jimmy and Elizabeth wished Ray well and told him that they would write often.

His mom said, "Ray, remember what we talked about last night and you will do fine. I will help Sara in any manner necessary. You do not need to worry about her while you are gone. Good luck, Son. I love you."

His dad said, "Your mother just about covered everything I was going to say, but I will add just this, your best bet is to listen and follow every instruction that your drill instructor gives you. He knows what he is talking about. You will do just fine by just following orders. I love you very much and the family will keep you posted about everything happening in Montcross. Good luck and God speed."

Ray choked back his tears and said, "I love you all and I will remember everything you and Mom taught me. Mom, I promise to go to church services every Sunday they are offered, and I will read the New Testament that Reverend Kelton gave me every night."

Jimmy stepped up and gave Ray a couple of books by Hemingway and Melville to toss in his bag saying, "I know you've not read Hemingway's, <u>For Whom the Bell Tolls</u>, so I picked that up last week to give to you for reading on the bus. I know you have not read <u>Moby Dick</u> lately either, and I hope you enjoy them both. Good luck, Ray."

Ray replied to Jimmy, "Thanks, Jimmy. These books will come in handy on the long bus ride and will stay with me throughout my service. Good luck with your flying and definitely let me know how you are doing."

Ray picked up his luggage and walked to where the corporal was stationed to fall in with the rest of the recruits. Ray waved goodbye to his family as he boarded the bus.

―――――――――

On board the bus, Ray picked out a window seat in the front third of the bus so he could hear any instructions that might be given by the corporal in charge.

Once everyone was on board and seated, the corporal said, "Next stop Parris Island, you 'boots' aren't worthy to be Marines. You all look like a bunch of pantywaists and mama's boys. Hope you survive the first week, you big babies."

The bus pulled out on schedule as a couple of recruits were seen arriving just a minute too late. The bus did not stop for them and they were left at the recruiting station to deal with Sergeant Yardley.

Ray said to the person sharing his seat, "Looks like those boys are going to be in trouble if they don't make it to Parris Island by the time our bus does. By the way, my name is Ray Johnson."

His seat mate replied, "My name is George Mason. Yes, it certainly looks like it. Wonder what the punishment will be if they don't make it to camp."

Ray thought for a moment then said, "I don't know, but it will not be good for them. Maybe they will be given the opportunity to get to Parris Island by other means and avoid punishment. I don't dare ask the corporal because it really is none of our business."

The corporal over-hearing several conversations on the late recruits piped up, "Those recruits will be given two choices, first choice will be to figure out some way to beat the bus to its first stop and get on board there or to beat the bus all the way to Parris Island and fall out with the rest of you idiots. Otherwise, they'll be spending some time in the brig until they can be attached to a new training battalion. And the boot who told his neighbor that it is none of our business was absolutely right. You 'boots' need to know not to go nosing into things that don't affect you!"

The corporal resumed watching the road signs pass knowing that the bus would pick up other recruits on the trip and he would have to rearrange the bus based on each location.

George, Ray's seat mate, looked a little nervous Ray thought and judging by his looks, Ray thought he might be about 16 or 17.

Ray asked, "George. Where is home?"

George, in need of some talk, said, "I'm from Kannapolis; what about you?"

Ray replied, "I am from Montcross. I have been attending State College in Raleigh. What about you?"

George said, "I was a junior in high school at J. W. Cannon until Pearl Harbor. I decided I wanted to join the Marines even though I'm only 17. My parents are dead, so it didn't take much to get my

Aunt and Uncle to sign the papers allowing me to enlist. It will give them one less mouth to feed. Now, though, I am a little nervous about the whole thing."

"Well, I can say even at 20, I'm nervous as well. I think as long as we follow the instructions that are given us by the drill instructors, we should be just fine," Ray replied.

The conversation continued with each asking the other about what they thought boot camp would entail. Both men thought the six-week timetable seemed awfully short to mold a Marine. Both men were slowly building a friendship during this long ride to Parris Island. Traveling about an hour, the bus stopped in McBee, South Carolina to pick up five more recruits. Those on the bus were allowed a brief break to use the bathroom before the bus departed.

Two recruits on the bus from Charlotte disappeared in McBee, and the corporal took note during roll call that George Mason from Kannapolis and James Frasier from Monroe did not return to the bus. Ray told the corporal that he thought George might have gotten scared or lost track of the time while using the bathroom. The corporal told the driver to stop before the bus pulled completely out of the parking lot and assigned Ray and several others the job of locating the miscreants.

As the bus stopped and the door started to open, the corporal saw George running from the bathroom back to the bus screaming, "Don't leave me, I took too long in the bathroom. Sorry, Corporal, Sir. I'm not running away."

The corporal looks at George, saying, "Good grief, BOOT! You have delayed my bus because of taking too long to shit. Get on my bus right now and your privileges to leave the bus for any reason including defecation are hereby revoked until further notice. You'll have to use the head that is located at the back of the bus. It smells like last year's hog leavings. Now let's go find the idiot who might actually be running and hiding from the Marines."

George dutifully climbed back on the bus and took his seat beside Ray again. After ten minutes, the corporal and the other group of recruits returned with James Frasier who was doing all he could to undo his enlistment in the Corps.

The corporal told everyone, "Until further notice, all you idiots on my bus will not have any privileges to get off until we get to Parris Island. You can thank James Frasier and George Mason. Get in your seats and thank these two idiots for making this bus late."

The guys who are sitting around Frasier are giving him so much grief that he starts crying and tries to move to a safer location.

Everywhere Frasier moved on the bus, the heckling continued unabated until he finally blurted, "Goldarnit! Shut up guys, you don't have to keep rubbing my nose in the fact I am a coward. Next person who says something is going to get his block knocked off."

The corporal yelled at Frasier, "Frasier get your ass up here. You get to sit next to me for the rest of the trip. After we are unloaded, you can just spend a little time in the brig until the training commander figures out what to do with you. Congratulations, Sissy!"

For another hour the trip passed without conversation. Ray decided he might liven up the trip by sharing his first tin of chocolate chip cookies.

Ray took two cookies out of the tin and passed it to George, saying, "Here, George, have a couple of fresh homemade cookies, and pass the tin to the next guy; tell him he can have some, too."

George replied, "Sure thing, THANKS! Nothing like homemade chocolate chip cookies."

Before long, each recruit on the bus had a couple of Bessie's homemade cookies.

One recruit said, "Hey, where did these cookies come from?"

Ray piped, "They came from me! My Mom and two younger sisters made them for us. What do you think?"

The recruit replied, "I sure hope you have more, Buddy, because these things are delicious! Thanks!"

Even cowardly Frasier and the corporal had a couple of cookies each and the cookies thawed the ice between them.

Frasier spoke to the corporal, "I know I'm scared, but if you will give me another chance, I won't disappoint you, Sir."

The corporal replied, "So, you are telling me that you want to be allowed to start training as if nothing ever happened and that if I do that, you won't try to jump the wall the first chance you get."

"No, Sir. I will be the model recruit and I will work hard to earn the trust and respect of my training group," Frasier replied.

"Ok, Frasier, against my better judgement I will allow you to be assigned to a standard training battalion. I hope to God you don't disgrace me by failing to live up to your part in this bargain. If you don't live up to it, I will show you a wrath the likes you have never seen before," the corporal responded adding a few more epithets for emphasis.

After six hours and forty-five minutes of travel, the bus pulled through the main gate of Parris Island past several squads of recruits and some who were lounging after the day's training.

They were all saying basically the same thing, "You'll be SORR-REE. Fresh meat for the grinders, good luck you lousy 'boots'."

The bus stopped at the edge of the parade ground and the new recruits disembarked and milled around the baggage compartment to get their luggage and other personal effects.

The corporal formed the group into ranks with each guy holding his belongings like his life depended on it.

A burly drill sergeant walked up and yelled, "BOYS! I's wants to tell ya'll something. Give your hearts to Jesus, cause your ass belongs to me."

With that greeting from the sergeant, Ray knew he was in the Marines and that his training had begun.

Ray Enlists in the Marine Corps

PARRIS ISLAND MARINE DEPOT ~ PARRIS ISLAND, SOUTH CAROLINA
SUNDAY, DECEMBER 28, 1941 - 6:00PM

● ● ● ● ● ● ● ● ● ● ● ● ● ● ● ● ● ● ● ●

After the long ride and unceremonious introduction to their drill instructor, Sergeant C. J. Garrett, the group of sixty recruits was hustled to the dining hall for supper. As Ray sat down, he noticed that the potential runaways, James Frasier and George Mason were not in his training platoon. Ray thought this was due to the issues on the trip today and probably earmarked them for a more restrictive training platoon. Supper consisted of bologna, lima beans, and coffee or tea. As Ray tasted his food, he realized he would miss the delicacies and delectable food Elva prepared daily for the family.

Ray, daydreaming about home, had his repast rudely interrupted by Sergeant Garrett when he yelled, "Training Platoon 276, time to go ladies! Form up outside, immediately!"

Ray and everyone else in his training platoon number 276 rushed into the biting cold with their suitcases and formed disorderly ranks.

Sergeant Garrett bellowed, "You mama's boys don't know how to form ranks to save your asses. Right face! Forward HAARCH!"

With some recruits turning left and others turning the prescribed right, Sergeant Garrett soon sorted everyone out and with their suitcases in tow, marched them to the quartermaster building.

The sixty raw recruits arrived in the quartermaster building and were told to strip and pack the clothes they wore on arrival into their suitcases, fill out a mailing tag, and attach it to their suitcases. Ray's wallet was inspected and he was allowed to keep that; everything else was shipped back to Montcross. Ray stood naked among sixty other naked recruits and received his sea bag. In the sea bag was assorted Marine Corps clothing including white shorts, t-shirts, uniform shirt and pants, socks, sweatshirt, and overcoat. Ray was given the opportunity to try on the various articles to make sure they fit appropriately and he exchanged those that were either too small or too large while the DI bellowed how to fold and pack each article in the sea bag. Ray finally got everything together and fitting properly when the group was sent through the barber line where everyone's head was shorn of hair. Ray was already concerned about how he would make it through the next six weeks with everything thrown at him at break-neck speed with no concern for the individual. Ray filled out his payroll paperwork and learned he would receive twenty one dollars per month in pay, but much to his surprise, his steel bucket and toiletries including a scrub brush, soap, shaving articles, sewing kit, etc. cost him twenty five dollars. He realized that it would be at least a month before he saw a paycheck. Before he left this morning, his dad had given him thirty dollars to tide him over until he started getting paid. Ray wondered if there would be any need for that money anyway since it already looked like he was going to be stuck inside the confines of the Marine Training Base for the duration of his training.

After the platoon was outfitted, they were marched about a two and half miles to their brand new steel Quonset hut barracks.

During the interminable march to their new quarters, the recruits heard, "You'll Be SORR-REE", from every lounging Marine they passed.

The drill instructor watched them closely as they staggered under the weight of the new sea bags. When one or two started to weaken, he chastised the whole group by calling them mama's babies, weaklings, and any other number of epithets he could think of to berate them. As the exhausted recruits arrived at their barracks, the DI told the boys to find a bunk and stow their gear.

Looking upon his new quarters, Ray thought, *Not the Ritz Carlton, but definitely better than a tent during a South Carolina coast winter with its wind and cold rains.*

Ray slowly got to know some of the members of his training platoon and figured out that three-quarters of the guys were from New York and Massachusetts. They all had a laugh at the funny accent of the Bostonians. Ray was assigned a bunk next to one of the New Yorkers, Harry Weichel, who seemed to be a good guy. Ray got his gear put away and his bunk squared away just as the DI bellowed that was time for lights out. He let the little girls, as he called them, know that reveille was at five in the morning and everyone was to be up and dressed within thirty minutes.

Parris Island Marine Depot ~ Parris Island, South Carolina
Monday, December 29, 1941 – 5:00am

• •

It felt to Ray that he had just fallen asleep when reveille was blown and the DI moved through the barracks kicking everyone out of their racks. Ray was bleary eyed and tired from tossing and turning on the miserable thing the Marines called a mattress. He knew he must move with haste if he wanted to get a shower and shave before breakfast. His bunkmate, Harry, was trying to catch a few more minutes of shut-eye and that got rudely interrupted by the DI. Sergeant C. J. Garrett nonchalantly turned it over and dumped the unsuspecting recruit into the floor. Harry came up sputtering and ready to fight until he saw the DI glowering at him. With a menacing look only a dyed in the wool Marine DI can give, Ray knew Harry better start moving if he wanted to survive until breakfast and it was almost comical to Ray that Harry looked like he could not remember how the DI showed them to make their bed.

Ray continued to watch this little tête-à-tête with minor amusement and a smile on his face until he caught the eye of Sergeant Garrett who bellowed, "What the hell are you smiling at boy?! This ain't nothin' to be smiling about; your buddy is about to get an ass chewing for not recognizing my reveilley and not hopping TO!"

"Nothing, Sir.", Ray stammered as he rushed quickly out of the line of fire to the showers hoping to escape the wrath of his instructor.

Lord, I hope I make it through without getting on this guy's bad side. I would hate to have him mad at me, Ray contemplated as the welcoming water from the shower washed over him. With an unpracticed haste, Ray was in and out of the shower and ready to go in what for him was a record. Ray joined the ranks in front of the barracks in less than the prescribed thirty minutes.

After this most inauspicious start, the DI had everyone do a calisthenics and a physical training routine before marching the platoon two-and-a-half-miles to the main camp for breakfast. While Ray marched, he thought about home and wondered what Elva had cooked for breakfast. Elva's meals were one of the many things he would miss, but he knew that he had become part of something bigger than himself. The motley group of recruits finished marching to the mess hall for breakfast which consisted of powdered eggs, sausage, and grits with coffee, orange juice, or water to drink. Ray definitely did not care for the powdered eggs because they tasted nothing like the real thing that he gathered every day at home.

Seated with Ray at the table was Harry who said in a severe New England accent, "I am from Gloucester, Massachusetts which is on the coast and home to one of the largest fishing fleets in the country. I'm a fourth generation Gloucester fisherman and third generation soldier. My family has fished for everything from tuna to whales over the last hundred-plus years. I joined because my father was in the Army during the Great War but never made it overseas. My grandfather served in the Spanish-American War in the Navy. I joined the Marines because they are the first ones into battle when things are going bad. What about you, Ray, where are you from and why did you join?"

Ray replied, "I am from Montcross, North Carolina which is a small town that boasts some of the largest textile manufacturing facilities on the East Coast. Until the attack on Pearl Harbor, I attended State College in Raleigh, North Carolina studying textile management and playing football. My father was a Marine in the First Division during the Great War and served in France where he earned the Silver Star and the Purple Heart. I joined the Marines primarily because this was his branch and I wanted to be trained by the best and fight with the best. Say, how old are you?"

"I am 19 years old and have been working on my family's boat full-time since I graduated from high school in 1940...", Harry was saying until they were rudely interrupted by their DI who was gathering his platoon for more drill.

Outside, the DI had everyone fall in to ranks and start marching towards the parade ground where it seemed they were being continuously belittled and berated for not keeping in step to the "Threeee...Fourrr...Yah left!", cadence of the drill instructor.

After an hour and a half of marching with his newly issued 1903 Springfield Rifle with the serial number 458761, Ray began to wonder if the drilling and serial number recitation would ever end. It was drilled in the new recruits that above all else they best remember and be able to recite the serial number of their rifle at a moment's notice.

Sergeant Garrett bellowed, "You's all nuthin' but a bunch of lousy BOOTS and if you don't get in line and stop acting like whiney ass Mama's boys, you sure as hell won't make in my CORPS!"

For Ray, the morning seemed to fly from one training exercise to another until the recruits were in step and marching as one back to the mess hall for lunch. Again Harry and Ray sat together discussing the morning's exercises and everything they learned. Learning these lessons would make tomorrow easier as they became attuned to the vagaries of Marine boot training. Lunch was eloquently called "shit-on-a-shingle" or SOS which is creamed chip beef on toast by those veteran recruits of two or three weeks. Ray thought it was pretty good although he was not sure how his stomach would react once they returned to the parade ground for more physical training and drill. Ray had begun to figure out that no matter when one got through the chow line, everyone ended up having fifteen minutes to eat before the DI was pushing them back outside for further instruction.

The afternoon and evening passed so quickly that Ray barely had time to think about anything. Slowly his vestige of self was broken down with each mistake and every epithet hurled at him about being a pansy, a baby or even a mama's boy. If the goal of the drill instructor was to strip the individual of his identity and self-worth, Sergeant Garrett was doing a bang up job on Ray.

As Ray climbed into his rack for his second night on Parris Island he thought, *What am I doing here? Am I that worthless a human being that I do not deserve to be a Marine? Mom was right, I need to believe in myself even when those around me doubt my ability. I will make it just like I made it through the state championship game with the broken arm. One day at a time and one drill at a time.*

After Ray said his prayers, he fell asleep hoping that he would make it through whatever the next six weeks threw at him.

MONTCROSS COLLEGE ~ MONTCROSS, NORTH CAROLINA
MONDAY, DECEMBER 29, 1941 - 6:45PM

Jimmy noticed that Mr. Mayerhofer was going to assist with instruction as he walked into his first Civilian Pilot Training Program ground school class. Jimmy was a lot more comfortable with this development even though the instructor would be Mr. Joe Rosen of Gastonia. Jimmy knew that Mr. Rosen was a stickler not only for safety in flight but also that the student knew and understood the various flight instruments and characteristics of the airplane.

Jimmy observed most of the students were of college age and seem to be as interested in flying as he.

Jimmy asked one of his fellow students, "Why are you taking this course?"

The student replied, "I want to fly fighters for the Navy and take off of carriers; but if I wash out, I will be happy flying bombers for the Army Air Corps. I just want to fly and contribute to the war effort that way. What about you?"

"I fell in love with flying from my first flight. Since then, all I want to do is earn my pilot's license. My goal is to be an Army Air Forces fighter pilot and like you, I just want to fly. My first flying lesson was Saturday and it was thrilling and scary. Keeping the airplane coordinated and balanced will take some practice. Have you had a flying lesson yet?" Jimmy replied.

The student said, "No, I have not had a flying lesson and to tell the truth, I've never been in an airplane. So I don't know how I will do once my flying lessons start in about three weeks."

They talked a little longer about flying until Mr. Rosen, promptly at seven, announced it was time for class to begin. The students took their seats and Mr. Rosen announced they should open the Civilian Pilot Training manual to chapter one – Theory of Flight. Mr. Mayerhofer and Mr. Rosen handed out CPTP manuals and Bulletin 22 – Digest of Civil Air Regulations for Pilots to those students who had not received the two required texts.

The first half of the class tonight was a lecture on the principles of flight and the characteristics of the airplane. Mr. Rosen discussed aerodynamics which explained how the airplane was able to maintain flight even though it was heavier than the air around it.

Mr. Rosen pointed out that the definition of aerodynamics from the CPTP manual was, *"Aerodynamics may be defined as the science or study of the forces produced by relative motion between the air and an object."*

Mr. Rosen continued and showed in the manual that the forces involved and the effects produced are identical whether the air moves by the body or the body moves through the air. An airplane in motion, according to Mr. Rosen and the manual, moved through a body of air but engineers could also test the aerodynamics of a planned design by using a wind tunnel. A student raised his hand at this point to ask a question.

The student was recognized by Mr. Rosen and asked, "How can a wind tunnel be used to test a design if there is no room for the airplane to move through the body of air like it does in flight?"

Mr. Rosen replied, "As we have read, the effects of aerodynamics are identical whether the air moves by the body or the body moves through the air. In the case of a wind tunnel, the air moves by the body thereby simulating the same effect of the body moving through the air. If the air is moving over the wing at 90 miles per hour, the wing will show the exact same characteristics of an airplane wing that is being moved through the air at 90 miles per hour. Either way, the characteristics of the wing are identical and can be studied in the safety of a wind tunnel. Do you understand now?"

The student replied in the affirmative and Mr. Rosen continued the lecture.

Mr. Rosen posed a rhetorical question at this point, "Why are aerodynamics so important to flight?"

He paused briefly then answered the question this way, "The amount of air going across the wing will determine how much lift the airplane is able to generate for a given speed. At various altitudes, the density of the air changes due to the barometric pressure which will determine how much speed is required for safe flight. A stall occurs when not enough air flows across the wing to maintain flight. This occurs when the airplane has slowed down too much or a stall can occur at higher speeds due to a misconfiguration of the airplane which prevents only one portion of the airfoil from maintaining flight. At low altitudes, these mistakes can be deadly. Remember the airplane must have enough speed moving through a body of air to maintain flight. These speeds will be located in every manual of every airplane produced and should be studied to the point that the speeds are committed to memory."

About halfway through the class period, the students were allowed a ten-minute break and Jimmy sought out Mr. Mayerhofer to ask him a question about aerodynamics.

"Good Evening, Mr. Mayerhofer, I have a question." Jimmy said.

Mr. Mayerhofer replied, "Hello, Jimmy. What's your question?"

"I have been thinking about what you demonstrated on Saturday in the airplane as it pertains to maintaining the proper airflow across the wing as described by Mr. Rosen tonight. When the airplane is in uncoordinated flight during turns as I demonstrated by accident Saturday, the plane could stall at higher speeds because there is not enough air moving across a wing due to lack of coordination. I noticed that at one point you took the airplane over rather quickly during one of my maneuvers; was that because I had the plane in a configuration where it could stall more easily?"

"Yes, Jimmy, you had the airplane climbing and turning which degraded your airspeed along with not having the plane coordinated. Another thirty seconds could have seen the airplane in a stall-spin which takes practice to recover. You will learn to make that type of recovery only after you can demonstrate controlled flight and recovery from straight ahead stalls." Mr. Mayerhofer replied.

Jimmy thanked Mr. Mayerhofer for answering his question and realized that he needed to be more diligent in maintaining balanced flight in all his maneuvers.

The lecture continued with more discussion about the airfoil and how an airplane flew within certain set criteria. Mr. Rosen talked about the angle of attack of the wing which allowed for more efficient climbing and less drag when trying to gain altitude. The biggest takeaway he wanted to give his students during this lecture was that it was necessary to make sure that the indicated airspeed was indicating correctly for a standard 500 feet per minute climb. The biggest safety advice Mr. Rosen gave tonight was in order to maintain safe flight, the pilot needs to maintain a balanced aircraft with the proper throttle setting for that phase of flight. Takeoff and climb out require more power than level cruising flight. Turns and altitude changes should start with an increase in power and then coordinated inputs of rudder and aileron to maintain a smooth turn. The lecture ended with a pop quiz on aerodynamics and the students could not leave until they received their grades and if their grade was below 80 then those students would be required to attend the first session again on Wednesday while the other students would not return until Thursday for the next class. Jimmy made an 85 on his pop quiz, missing only three questions. This upset him and he vowed he would study more to finish at the top of his class which guarantees first choice of assignments in the Army Air Corps.

Johnson Family Home ~ Montcross, North Carolina
Monday - 9:15pm

• • • • • • • • • • • • • • • • • • • •

After the short drive down Main Street from Montcross College, Jimmy pulled the brothers' Model-A into the driveway. He had a lot on his mind and wondered how Ray was doing after his first full day of boot camp. Jimmy knew he had a long way to go if he was going to fly fighters in the Army Air Corps. With the score he made on the first pop quiz, he knew he had to study harder and take flying seriously. Jimmy would have to improve the mediocre B average he currently held at Montcross High School to a more acceptable A average because his grades in the CPTP Ground School along with high school transcript would be taken into consideration when he made the transition to Army Air Corps pilot training.

He parked the car in the garage and walked into the house not expecting anyone to be waiting up for him. He was surprised to find his father still awake and looking over paperwork on his desk with a scowl on his face.

Jimmy stepped into the study and asked, "Dad, why the look of disgust on your face? Did one of us do something wrong?"

His dad looked up and said, "No, Son. None of you did anything wrong. I am working on rail yard paperwork this evening. I cannot schedule enough men to maintain the trains that are running because another four left today for military service. The draft-eligible men that are left in town are the bottom of the barrel and unwilling to do the type of work that is demanded in the rail yard. Randy Hamstead has been a good worker and I have decided to put him on full time. I hope he sticks with me for the rest of this year and maybe I can find some men willing to work as hard as he does. I need to add men quickly in order to maintain our current schedules, let alone handle any additional trains as the need arises. The older guys who served during the last war that I have working are still with me, but I need ten more good men. I plan to talk to Mr. Linkenburg tomorrow to see if he can get some good men from the mills to work in the yard on a shift that does not conflict with their current textile work. Our textile mills are really producing the yarn as a sub-contractor for all those plants manufacturing uniforms, bandages, and other textile products for the military, and we have not had an empty train leave Montcross in the last two weeks. Well enough about my troubles, how was your first CPTP class?"

With a grimace due to his embarrassment over his first test grade, Jimmy sat down and told his father, "Well, Dad, Mr. Joe Rosen is my ground school instructor and Mr. Mayerhofer is his assistant. There was a lot of material covered on the science of aerodynamics and how it pertains to powered flight. I learned a lot about wing loading and what the airplane requires to remain safely aloft. I figured out why Mr. Mayerhofer quickly retook control of the airplane in one of my maneuvers last Saturday and that really scared me. I had the airplane in such an unbalanced condition that it was about to stall and spin. A stall-spin can cause an accident leading to injury or death. I hope I do better in my second lesson. I passed the pop quiz at the end of the class with an 85. I found out the best student in the ground school along with their high school or college grades will get their choice of assignment in the Army Air Corps. I am going to have to do better all the way around if I want to have my assignment of choice. Dad, I am really doubting myself right now. I don't think I have ever really applied myself to my studies or my hobbies. I've coasted along doing just enough to get by. I don't know if I know how to dig deep and really work even though this is something I want more than anything in the world."

His dad gave his son a look of great understanding and pride, then said, "Jimmy, I have often wondered if you would ever realize how much potential you wasted growing up by doing just enough to get by but not enough to be great. Now that you have seen something that you want beyond anything else; you realize that doing just enough to get by will probably put you in the bottom of the class and unable to fulfill your dream. I am not going to say it is going to be easy to accomplish, and only you will know if you are giving all you can to make it happen. I do know, just like Ray, you have a hidden reserve that will allow you to overcome any obstacle placed before you. Ray has tapped his reserve before and knows what it takes to bring that extra effort to bear. You have never been tested where you needed that extra push to get you over the hump. You will figure out how to tap it and what it takes to make your dream a reality. I know you can do it; now you must determine you ARE going to do it."

Jimmy had not realized his dad knew that he had always coasted along. Jimmy blushed with extreme embarrassment at having this character flaw laid bare by his father; but he understood that only he could change it. The change would be a must if he was going to succeed.

He replied to his dad, "I am embarrassed, Dad. I always thought until now that I was doing all that I could do, but after sitting through class half listening and then getting an 85 on the test; I saw I was falling into the trap of doing just enough to get by. Coming home, I promised myself that I would put my mind and body to work in order to succeed in getting my choice of assignment and the top grade in all of my classes. Thanks for listening and telling me not what I wanted to hear which is that I am doing enough, but telling me that I could have always done better. There will be pain I'm sure, but I will give one hundred percent of my energy to this pursuit. If I fail, it will not be for a lack of giving it my entire focus."

With new vigor Jimmy asked his dad what he could do to help him find men to work at the rail yard. His dad thought he could get by with some of the recent high school graduates who were not required to register for the draft and might not be ready to enlist in the service. Jimmy let his father know that he would check with some of his friends to see if they would like a job at the rail yard.

"Jimmy,", his dad said, "the job at the rail yard will pay 35 cents an hour and will be hard work. Mr. Linkenburg and the other owners know that we need quality labor to maintain our schedule and have promised that, throughout the year, they will give bonuses to the ablest employees. We have two shifts available. The morning shift is from six to three and the evening shift is three to eleven. Everyone gets a half-hour for lunch and two fifteen-minute breaks during their shift. New men hired will have to work a two-week probationary period before being put on full time and receiving their military deferrals. Thanks, Jimmy."

Jimmy replied, "I will check with some friends tomorrow and see if I can find some who are interested in helping the war effort by working in the yard."

His dad replied, "Thanks, Jimmy. Let me know what you figure out. I think it is time I retire. I am relieved you might be able to help me. Goodnight. Jimmy, do not stay up too late studying."

PARRIS ISLAND MARINE DEPOT ~ PARRIS ISLAND, SOUTH CAROLINA
TUESDAY, DECEMBER 30, 1941 - 4:30AM

• • • • • • • • • • • • • • • • • • • •

As Ray awoke to reveille, he was quickly reminded that he was in the Marine Corps because the DI ran through the Quonset hut rousting everyone out and into their physical training gear for their morning run. The run this morning was two and a half miles up to the main base and back again before breakfast and must be completed in an hour. Anyone who did not complete it was subjected to extended physical training every day they failed to meet the criteria. Ray had not run this much since the fall football season at State College, but he felt pretty comfortable that he could average the twelve-minute mile required for this morning.

When reveille sounded, Ray got up quickly and yelled at Harry to wake up and prepare for inspection. Harry ignored him and went on sleeping which led to another dumping of his rack and epithets from Garrett.

Garrett, naturally easily riled and expecting respect, was dumbfounded when Harry adjusts his blanket and goes back to sleeping on the floor until Sergeant Garrett gave him a swift kick in the ribs, yelling, "WHAT'S YOUR PROBLEM WEICHEL? SLEEPING THROUGH MY REVEILLE AGAIN! I TOLD YOU BOY, YOU SLEEP THROUGH MY REVEILLE AGAIN AND I WAS GOING TO HAVE YOUR ASS! TODAY AFTER TRAINING, YOU WILL GET TO SHOW ME HOW WELL YOU WORK! YOU GET TO DIG SOME DITCHES AND CLEAN OUT LATRINES SINCE YOU THINK YOU'S AN ALL FIRED IMPORTANT MAN WHO DOESN'T HAVE TO FOLLOW ORDERS! IS THAT CLEAR!"

Harry who was now fully awake to the predicament he had gotten himself into started crying and breaking down in the face of wrath being dealt by Sergeant Garrett.

Harry sobbing, muttered, "Yes, Sir! It won't happen again, Sir."

Sergeant Garrett who hated crybabies says, "On second thought, Weichel, I think you just need to quit because I don't want or need any babies in my outfit who might get their buddies killed with their cowardice. While your platoon is doing what they came here to do, pack your gear and get the hell out of my outfit. You are a loser and don't deserve to be in my Corps! Report to the front gate for instructions on how to quit and get a crybaby discharge."

Ray, watching the entire exchange, knew now that he must never let Sergeant Garrett see any weakness. He knew the sergeant would pounce on it as quickly as he did on Harry. Ray felt bad for Harry; but after yesterday he knew that Harry did not have the fortitude to endure this rigorous training even though he came from a family of hearty Gloucester fishermen.

Ray had little time to think about it before Sergeant Garrett inspected his rack and stowage with satisfaction saying, "Good job, Johnson! I know you will sleep better after that piece of shit is gone. I'll get you a new buddy to train with later."

With another inauspicious start to the day, Ray and his training platoon started the arduous five-mile run to the main camp and back, leaving Harry to collect his gear. After making it up to the main camp, the platoon started the run back to the barracks. On the return trip, they passed Harry with his sea bag and rifle. None of the 'boots' dared look at the disgraced failure because they knew all too well that the same fate could await them between now and graduation. For their first run, they made it in record time. The last 'boot' crossed the line at forty-five minutes which beat the record of forty-eight minutes by the previous group of second day 'boots'. The sergeant, proud of his boys, told them that they might be all right; now that they had gotten rid of the dead wood. They had thirty minutes to shower and shave before marching to breakfast. While showering, Ray thought about how he could force himself to better handle the problems that had occured.

The only thing he could think of was that he needed to fall back to what a coach once told him, *As long as you do the best you can and follow my instructions, you will never have anything to worry about.*

Ray knew that every one of the recruits was being broken down every day to insure they had the mental and physical fortitude to do what this war would require. He knew at some point, the sergeant would start putting them back together as Marines. This current fire was required to weed out the weak-minded and cowardly individuals among them and that is exactly what happened this morning. Ray was sure he would see more fall by the wayside as the training continued.

With each passing day, Ray became more adept to what the drill sergeant and other instructors expected from the 'boots'. The first week passed without his drawing unwanted attention from the drill sergeant, but he had not had time to write to Sara or the family, either. With permission from the sergeant, he sent the short telegram that gave the family his address. By Friday, three more recruits had been discharged for failing to live up to the expectations of the Corps and their sergeant. Ray had been at the top of his group in physical and mental aptitude and he made sure he followed every instruction from anyone in charge to the letter without question and was becoming more self-assured every day. With each passing grade and excellent report, the sergeant tried harder to break Ray down mentally and physically because the sergeant was trying to find Ray's breaking point. After only three days, Ray was contemplating whether he had enough reserves to withstand the latest onslaught from the DI. While it was only the first week, Ray was beginning to think that he might not make it through three more weeks of this type of mental and physical torture. The 'boots' knew that the last two weeks would be spent on the rifle range perfecting the shooting positions required by Marine riflemen. Lying down in his rack on Friday night, Ray slept well knowing that he was on his way to becoming a Marine if he could continue to persevere.

JOHNSON FAMILY HOME ~ MONTCROSS, NORTH CAROLINA
SATURDAY, JANUARY 3, 1942 - 9:00AM

Jimmy was about to leave the house to take his second flying lesson and he knew that this lesson could jumpstart the process to realize his dream. Since Monday, Jimmy had been diligent in his studies and scored a ninety-five on the quiz at the end of Thursday's CPTP class which put him in a tie for third in the race to the top score. His new attitude had also shown at home where he had picked up Ray's chores as well as his own so that his dad could have more time to manage the increasingly busy rail yard. During the week, Jimmy found fifteen young men who were willing to work at the rail yard and sent them to his father for an interview. His dad was greatly impressed with all these young men and gave all fifteen an opportunity to earn one of the ten positions available in the yard and shop. So far the number had been whittled down to thirteen because two of the young men decided, after all, to join the military. It was a good week for Jimmy now that he had applied himself to achieving his goals.

As Jimmy left to go to the airport, his dad handed him a ten-dollar bill, puzzling Jimmy.

He asked, "Dad, what is this for? I have money I earned for my flying lessons and that is what I have planned to use."

His dad replied, "Jimmy, I thought I might help you out a little with your flying lessons after you helped me solve my problem this week at the rail yard and shop."

Jimmy looked at his dad with a grin and replied, "Thanks, Dad. I appreciate your help."

Telling his dad goodbye, Jimmy stuffed the ten-dollar bill in his pocket and picked up his flight manuals and log book. He had been thinking seriously about today's lesson, especially after the class on Thursday which dealt with various maneuvers and the airplane's flight instruments. This week he had made himself a cardboard cutout of the J-3's dashboard and worked on scanning the instruments while "chair flying" in his room. Jimmy was sure this extra "flying" would help him today during his lesson with Mr. Mayerhofer.

MONTCROSS AIRPORT ~ MONTCROSS, NORTH CAROLINA
SATURDAY - 10:00AM

· ·

Jimmy arrived an hour early for his lesson so that he could get permission to sit in the spare training Cub and familiarize himself further with the configuration of the cockpit. Jimmy believed that more seat time, even if the airplane was not moving or flying, would help him improve his skills quickly. Jimmy did not believe in shortcutting any part of the flight instruction because any mistake could be fatal.

Mr. Mayerhofer saw Jimmy walk in and said, "Is my schedule wrong? I thought your lesson was at eleven this morning. Why are you here so early?"

Jimmy replied, "My lesson is at eleven this morning but I wanted to get here early so I could sit in the airplane and get more familiar with the instrument panel. I have been practicing my scan at home with a cardboard J-3 dash in order to get my hands and feet to move in sync. While you are teaching the ten o'clock student, I was hoping to get some seat time in the other J-3. Will that be alright?"

Mr. Mayerhofer replied, "I think that would be great and I think it will help you understand the coordination required to keep the airplane balanced. Whenever you are ready, just go out to the flight line and get in NC275 for your practice. I will see you in about an hour for your lesson."

After Mr. Mayerhofer took his student out for his lesson in the primary J-3 Cub, Jimmy walked out and climbed into NC275 for his "ground" flying. Jimmy went through the procedures to properly fasten the seat belts and position the seat where he could comfortably reach the rudder pedals and the stick. Completing the preliminaries, he looked at the instruments in the cockpit and started making imaginary turns to both the left and the right being careful to add what he thought was the correct amount of rudder, all the while, scanning from outside the cockpit to the instrument panel inside and back again. For the next thirty minutes, he continued this practice of making sure that he did not add any back pressure or forward pressure on the stick which would cause the airplane to climb or descend in a turn. This practice, Jimmy decided, would be repeated before each lesson because he believed this extra "flying" would help him in his lesson.

Jimmy thought at this point, *Tme will tell if this practice will help, but I do feel better after spending time this morning in the airplane alone.*

Jimmy climbed out of the cockpit of the Cub about ten minutes before his lesson was set to begin and walked back to the office to await Mr. Mayerhofer's arrival.

Mr. Mayerhofer and his student walked into the office at ten-fifty to debrief the previous lesson, and the look on the face of the student showed that the lesson must not have gone well. Jimmy overheard part of the debrief, and it seems the student made some dangerous mistakes in his landing maneuvers in preparation to solo. From what Jimmy heard, it sounds like the student was questioning the veracity of Mr. Mayerhofer's issues with his flying. Jimmy decided it might be best if he moved out of ear shot of the debrief in order to prepare for his lesson.

Mr. Mayerhofer exited his office and hands the previous student his log book, saying, "I think you might want to finish up your flight training with Mr. Joe Rosen, because I am unable to make you understand that what you are doing could get you killed and I do not want that responsibility."

The student replied, "I have already taken lessons from Mr. Rosen and he sent me to you. What should I do now that two out of the three best instructors in the county have washed me out?"

"You could change your approach to your lessons and start listening to your instructors. We will not do anything in your training that could compromise your safety or our safety. Are you willing to start listening to my instruction?", Mr. Mayerhofer replied.

The student thought for a moment and replied, "I will try Mr. Mayerhofer. Can I have one more lesson next Saturday to prove that I can listen and follow your instruction?"

"I will see you on Saturday at ten o'clock in the morning and if you follow my instruction and fly properly like I know you can, then we will continue your training. See you then.", Mr. Mayerhofer acquiesced.

———————

Mr. Mayerhofer looked at Jimmy and said, "Are you ready for your lesson, Jimmy?"

Jimmy replied, "Yes, Sir. I'm ready. I took thirty minutes to practice my scan and maneuvers making sure that I kept my hands and feet in sync when making turns so I can keep the plane coordinated and neither climbing or descending in the turn."

"That sounds good, let's get our parachutes on and see how well you do once we are up in the air.", Mr. Mayerhofer replied.

They both put on their parachutes, pre-flighted the airplane, and seated themselves securely before Mr. Mayerhofer received help starting the engine. He allowed the Cub's engine to warm sufficiently before checking the magnetos in preparation for takeoff. After takeoff and climbing out to 5500 feet, Mr. Mayerhofer demonstrated left and right level turns again for Jimmy to copy.

Mr. Mayerhofer yelled over the engine noise, "Jimmy, your airplane! Turn the airplane 180 degrees to the left and level the wings at a compass heading of 90 then wait thirty seconds before turning back right to a heading of 270."

Jimmy took control of the airplane and leveled the wings on a 270 heading before starting his left turn. He started his left turn with a quality scan of the instruments and input the proper amount of rudder to maintain a coordinated turn. As he scanned the instruments, he noticed that he was climbing slightly and released a little pressure on the stick in order to stop the ascent while returning the airplane to the 5500 feet altitude. As he approached the reverse heading of 90, Jimmy started rolling out of the turn a little late and overshot the 90 degree heading requested by Mr. Mayerhofer, but he quickly recovered and lined the airplane up on the 90 degree heading. For thirty seconds, Jimmy flew the 90 degree heading before he started his coordinated right turn back to a heading of 270 degrees. The right turn was a lot smoother and Jimmy rolled out exactly on 270 degrees and the airplane had not changed altitude.

Jimmy yelled, "Your airplane," then raised his hands letting Mr. Mayerhofer know that the airplane was now his to control. Mr. Mayerhofer demonstrated several other maneuvers including a straight ahead stall and recovery. Mr. Mayerhofer then walked Jimmy through the stall and recovery with control in Jimmy's hands. As he was practicing the stall and recovery, Jimmy inadvertently unbalanced the airplane which caused it to drop the right wing and spin. Mr. Mayerhofer told him to let go of the controls which he did immediately. Mr. Mayerhofer immediately pulled the power, dropped the nose, and applied full left rudder to recover from the spin with only a loss of a thousand feet of altitude. This incident undid Jimmy and he asked Mr. Mayerhofer to go back to the airport and land. Mr. Mayerhofer told him no and let him know that they were going to climb back to 5500 feet for another try at the straight ahead stall and recovery. In Jimmy's second attempt at a straight ahead stall, he got everything coordinated and correctly completed a smooth stall and recovery, and Mr. Mayerhofer had him fly the airplane back to the airport and descend to 2500 feet. Jimmy was still a little undone by creating the spin, but did very well in the descent and the minor course turns required to get back to the airport. Mr. Mayerhofer landed and taxied the airplane to the ramp.

———

As they were walking back to the office after parking the airplane, Jimmy said, "I know what I did that caused the plane to spin. I had right rudder added and a little right aileron as the plane reached stall speed. Therefore, the airplane fell off to the right because that wing stopped flying first. I noticed that you pulled all power then let the controls reset and finally used full opposite rudder to make the recovery. Only after the recovery from the spin did you add power back. Was that your procedure?"

"Yes, Jimmy, your unbalanced control caused the right wing to stall before the other wing and created the spin. Your review of the procedure was exactly how I recovered from the stall. You made progress today in your flying but you still have a lot to learn. Starting next week, we will be working on more airplane control with you adding and decreasing power. We should have the "Gosport" tube and helmet next week for instructor to student communication. With this device, I won't have to yell instructions to you anymore making cockpit communication easier which in turn should make instruction and flying easier. Great work on learning to scan and being able to describe what happened in the stall-spin."

Jimmy thought for a minute then replied, "Thanks, Mr. Mayerhofer. I believe that the time I took sitting in the airplane helped me understand the scan and what the airplane was doing based on my control inputs. I felt that the airplane was unbalanced just before the right hand stall-spin. I panicked before you had me let go of the controls. You calmly recovered the airplane from what I thought was going to be a fatal crash. Will I ever get to that point where a spin does not seem like a deadly mistake?"

"Panicking will get you killed in an airplane quicker than anything else; that is why I made you go through a few more maneuvers before returning to the airport. You needed to regain your confidence and to understand you are making progress in learning to fly. You did great work today and you will continue to improve over the next few lessons. See you next Saturday at eleven.", Mr. Mayerhofer replied.

Jimmy paid and thanked Mr. Mayerhofer for the lesson and replied that he would see him next Saturday.

Jimmy was extremely happy with the lesson today even though he had panicked when he caused the airplane to spin. He was glad that Mr. Mayerhofer did not let the lesson end before he successfully demonstrated a straight ahead stall recovery. Pulling into the driveway at home, Jimmy was thinking about Ray and wondering how he was doing. He decided he would write Ray a letter to let him know everything that was happening in Montcross and ask him how his first week in boot camp had gone.

JOHNSON FAMILY HOME ~ MONTCROSS, NORTH CAROLINA
SATURDAY - 1:00PM
• •

Jimmy walked into the kitchen and found the family gathered around the table for a lunch of Elva's fried chicken, black-eyed peas, and mashed potatoes.

Raymond looked up as Jimmy entered and said, "Well, Jimmy, how was your lesson today?"

Jimmy replied, "It was better than last week and Mr. Mayerhofer had to demonstrate how to recover from an inadvertent spin after I made a mistake. That mistake added to my healthy respect of the airplane where any mistake might be fatal. He let me know in my debrief that even though I panicked when the spin happened, I was able to mentally recover enough to finish the lesson and make good progress on the basic maneuvers. I am a lot happier after this lesson than I was last Saturday. I believe I have made some progress towards my goal of becoming a pilot."

"That sounds good, Jimmy. I think we are all writing Ray a letter this afternoon. Would you like to take part? We will mail them all in one envelope so we will be sure that Ray receives them all.", his dad replied.

Jimmy said, "I was thinking about writing Ray myself this afternoon, so this fits into my plans. I will add my letter to the collection today. What time are we taking them to the post office?"

"I will take them to the post office on Monday." His dad replied.

Lillie piped up and said, "I am going to draw him a picture of Myra and me that shows him how much we love and miss him."

Bessie replied to Lillie, "That will be wonderful, Lillie. I am concerned that we have only received the telegram and his suitcase since Ray left. I would have thought that he would have written us a letter by now."

"Bessie, if boot camp today is anything like it was for me, Ray will not have time to write us until possibly this weekend. I would not worry that he has not written. The first chance he gets, I am sure he will write Sara and us." Raymond replied.

Bessie said, "That makes sense, because I recall it was two weeks before I heard from you while in boot camp. I hope he is doing well and will make it through the tough training that he is receiving."

Bessie helped Elva with the dishes while Jimmy, Elizabeth, Myra, and Lillie rushed off to write letters to Ray. Raymond moved into the study to write his own letter and he asked questions about the training to figure out if toughness and ruthlessness were still part of the DI handbook for training 'boots'.

Ray Enlists in the Marine Corps

Parris Island Marine Depot ~ Parris Island, South Carolina
Saturday, January 3, 1942 - 10:00am

Ray's training platoon was up before dawn for the five mile run that had become the standard pre-breakfast drill for training platoon 276 and daily, they improved on their times. Each day Sergeant Garrett tried to break Ray down and wash him out of the Corps, but Ray actually reveled in the challenge and got tougher mentally and physically. After breakfast this morning, the platoon was required to complete the obstacle course in three minutes, and failure would result in the immediate wrath of their drill sergeant. Ray slipped going over a wall and injured his ankle which cost him valuable time. He did not complete the course in the allotted time and faced the wrath of the DI for screwing up the platoon's perfect record.

The DI yelled at Ray, "What's your problem, Crybaby Johnson? You could not complete my course in time because of a little thing like a sprained ankle. You have two choices, you can go back and run it again or you can take yourself to the base dispensary. If your ankle is only sprained then I expect you to come back and complete the course; otherwise, if it's broken, you will be excused from our platoon and you will wait until the next group comes through."

Ray replied, "Let me wrap it and I will complete YOUR obstacle course in less than three minutes; then we will see if it is broken, Sir."

The DI with a little hint of admiration told him, "Johnson, get the ankle wrapped up and if you beat three minutes then I will give you the afternoon off to get it checked out at the base dispensary."

Ray had help wrapping the ankle and then repeated the course. The pain in Ray's ankle was excruciating, but he completed the obstacle course in two minutes and forty-five seconds and then reported to the DI.

The masochistic DI brought the entire platoon to attention, saying, "Crybabies, look at Johnson here! This is what a Marine does when he thinks he can't. He makes it through an obstacle course on a bum ankle without complaint in the fastest time for the entire platoon. If you babies can't make it any faster uninjured, I think you should just quit now. Anyone willing to try? Or, are all you whiney butts going to QUIT MY CORPS?"

The entire platoon responded, "SIR, NO, SIR!"

The entire platoon returned to the start line of the obstacle course and ran it again. The last one completes it in two minutes and forty-five seconds. This made the DI proud.

———

Sergeant Garrett marched the platoon back to the barracks and said, "Boys, while you might not make Marines, you have shown me that you've got heart. Everyone except Johnson has ten minutes to prepare the barracks for inspection! Johnson get in that vehicle for a ride to the base dispensary. Platoon dismissed!"

The rest of platoon grumbled about going through another meaningless inspection while Ray was taken to the base dispensary.

Ray reported to the doctor at the base dispensary for a diagnosis of his injury. The doctor was pretty old and minor injuries just aggravated him. He thought all complainants were trying to get out of training. Once the doctor removed the wrap, the doctor knew this was a pretty severe injury. The doctor ordered a radiograph to see if the ankle or leg had been fractured. Ray waited hours for a diagnosis, and when the doctor finally returned to the room, he told Ray that his ankle was severely sprained and it would take at least a week to heal.

Ray asked the doctor, "How am I to maintain the pace of training if I have to be off of the ankle for a week? I want to finish training with my platoon."

The doctor replied, "If you can handle the pain then you need to keep training; otherwise you will have to be reassigned to the next training platoon which is a week behind yours. Your choice is for me to sign a reassignment paper to the next platoon or continue with your platoon with the injury."

Ray decided that regardless of the pain that he wanted to train and complete the course with his platoon. The doctor noted the injury in Ray's military personnel file; then wrapped the ankle.

The doctor said, "Every day after training, you will report here so that I can check the progress of the injury and replace the wrap. Sign this paperwork and you can return to your unit."

"Thank you, Doctor." Ray signed his paperwork and with the doctor's diagnosis, reported back to his training platoon.

Sergeant Garrett said, "Johnson, looks like I owe you an apology. You really is injured and you's not a shirker like most of these pantywaists! To think you want to return to my outfit instead of taking the easy way out makes me proud! You will still need to complete all the work and I sure as hell won't go easy on you, injury or not. Now get your bunk ready for inspection and report back here in ten minutes!"

Ray replied, "Sir, Yes, Sir! Thank you, Sir!"

Ray prepared his area for inspection making sure that everything was in its proper place and his rifle was cleaned spotless for inspection. Ray, with his rifle, reported to the sergeant for inspection. Sergeant Garrett marched him back to his bunk and held an individual inspection. Ray passed without a single mark down and the sergeant dismissed Ray for the afternoon.

PARRIS ISLAND MARINE DEPOT ~ PARRIS ISLAND, SOUTH CAROLINA
SATURDAY - 3:00PM

The morning mail call brought Ray a letter from Sara who had been keeping their writing promise better than he had been able to do. With the rest of the afternoon free, Ray took the time to read Sara's letter and respond. He wanted to tell Sara and his family everything that had happened during his first week. In his letters home, Ray was careful not to give the wrong impression, nor give the idea, he was anything but happy with his decision. Sara's letter was rather long at three pages and he savored every word. Propping his foot on a pillow, he made himself comfortable enough to read it.

December 31, 1941

Dearest Ray,

It has been a long week since last we spoke on Saturday night and it is only Wednesday. Sam, William, and Thomas helped me pack everything last night and drove me back to Meredith today. The spring semester starts on Friday. There is orientation tomorrow even though it is New Year's Day. I want to get acquainted with my instructors since some have changed due to military service. Tomorrow will give me that opportunity.

I want you to know how proud I am to be your girlfriend. I know that this separation is going to be tough. We will overcome it together. I cannot wait for the day you come home and we can start our lives together. At church, Sunday, the pastor led a prayer for all servicemen who are currently serving at home or abroad. Mom and I added your name to the list of local servicemen who need prayer. At Easter, Thanksgiving, and Christmas, the Ladies Auxiliary will put together care packages so our men, who are serving, will have a little taste of home during those holidays.

I know this first week for you has been busy trying to get acclimated to the Marine way of doing things and I want to hear all about it. What was it like when you arrived at Parris Island? Has anything interesting happened during your introduction to the Marine way of doing things? What is training like, tough? Please tell me all about it.

Well, Ray, I will close now as it is getting late and I have to be up early tomorrow to get breakfast and walk through orientation. I hope you are doing well. I love you very much and I miss you.

With love and support,

Sara

Ray, thrilled with the letter from Sara, started moving towards the writing desk to reply when the entire platoon rushed in from their latest training exercise. As one, they came to immediate attention at their bunks.

Ray looked at one of the guys as if to say, "What is going on?"

Instead of getting a response from all the wild-eyed guys, Ray instinctively knew he would find out quickly. He too should be standing at attention at the foot of his bunk. He put away his writing materials and smoothed out his bunk. He barely made it to his position of attention when the extremely angry DI walked in with an equally angry officer.

"Platoon, ATTEN-HUT!" Sergeant Garrett bellowed.

Every member of the platoon came to attention at the foot of their bunks as the officer began speaking, "Boys! What just happened is a bad thing! Boot Hollman is dead because he did not follow orders to keep his head down during the barbed-wire crawl! Sergeant Garrett gave you a direct order to keep your head down as you crawled the course. Hollman had to go and raise his head because he couldn't stand crawling through blood and guts in the trench. His lack of fortitude and inability to follow orders, killed him. The Marines are a volunteer organization which means you won't find any draftees here. The Corps knows draftees don't make good Marines. If you are unwilling to follow orders, you are more than free to quit now. Take one step forward if you think you have what it takes to become Marines. After today, I don't want any more dumbass mistakes and crybabies messing up my training platoon. Is that clear?"

"Sir, Yes, Sir", came the response from Ray and the platoon as all but three men failed to step forward at the Lieutenant's order.

The three were summarily dismissed by the sergeant and told to pack their gear. They had been three of the worst members of the platoon and were derided all the way to the front gate. In less than a week, the training platoon that started at 60 men had dwindled through attrition to 45 men. The men had either quit or were forced out as unfit for Marine Corps duty.

Ray was thinking about this when Sergeant Garrett bellowed, 'Fall out for a repeat of this afternoon's drill in the barbed-wire obstacle course. Johnson, YOU TOO!"

Ray replied, "YES, SIR!", and he put on his dungarees to prepare for the 'blood and guts' course as the men call it.

Ray and his platoon had run through it several times without live ammunition. Today was the first time live ammunition was being fired about eighteen inches over their heads. From the other 'boots', he figured out that Hollman did not like how the entrails felt and was scared to place his face and body flat into them. That is why he lifted his head when he felt he could go no further in the gunk.

One fellow said to Ray, "Sergeant Garrett let us all know that they was firing live ammunition and to keep our heads down and keep moving. He also told us that anyone who pokes his head up was apt to be killed. Lo and behold, ole Hollman rises up and dies with a bullet in his brain. Idiot!"

The training platoon double timed to the barbed-wire trench course and stood at attention. Sergeant Garrett once again went over the rules for this exercise.

Sergeant Garrett yelled, "It only took one crybaby to screw up a perfectly good training exercise this afternoon, now you babies listen and LISTEN GOOD! You have one minute to crawl the course. THERE WILL BE LIVE AMMUNITION FIRED OVER YOUR HEADS, SO KEEP YOUR DAMN HEADS DOWN! Johnson, with squad one, GET YOUR GUYS MOVING!"

Ray and his squad prepared to crawl the course as instructed. Ray's ankle was hurting him, but he spread out his squad and prepared them to push through course. On the sergeant's command, they ran into the course at full speed. Ray had never been comfortable crawling through the pig entrails and blood, but he knew if he were to make it through the entire Marine training program then he had to push his entire squad through the course in less than a minute.

Ray yelled to his guys, "Come on, let's go. Push boys, we can beat the record if we try!"

His squad mates surged forward as if spurred by some unforeseen force and completed the course without mishap in less than forty-five seconds which was the fastest time of the entire platoon. They stood at attention at the end of the course awaiting completion of the course by the remaining squads.

Sergeant Garrett bellowed, "Johnson's squad did it again, fastest time of all you pantywaists. Johnson's squad is dismissed while the ladies of the other squads run the course until you can finish it quicker than fifty seconds. Good luck, girls. Johnson, take your squad and get them cleaned up."

Ray replied, "SIR, YES, SIR!"

Ray marched his squad back to the barracks for a shower and some down time. He removed the wrapping from his ankle and stepped into the shower to clean up. After his shower, Ray put a fresh wrap on his ankle, washed his dungarees, and cleaned the old wrap. He was ready for supper when the sergeant marched the rest of the platoon back to the barracks. The 'boots' were dragging when they returned and had barely enough time to clean up before they had to report to march to supper. Outside, Ray and his squad were the first in formation when Sergeant Garrett bellowed for everyone else to get outside, too. The platoon marched double time to the mess hall for their 'nightly hash' as some of the boys called it.

After supper, the platoon was allowed a little recreational time that each man could use writing letters, playing ping pong, or generally goofing off until lights out. This was the first break the men of platoon 276 enjoyed since their first rude awakening on Monday. Ray chose to take this time to write several letters to Sara and his family. He was sure after reading Sara's letter earlier today that they were beginning to wonder how he was getting along in training. He decided that his first letter would be to his Mom and Dad because he knew they were as anxious as Sara for news.

Saturday, January 3, 1942

Dear Mom and Dad,

This first week has been an eye-opener to say the least when it comes to the Marine way of doing things. Got here Sunday night and they marched us straight to the mess hall for supper which was bologna, lima beans, hash browns and toast. Supper was a far cry from Elva's wonderful meals. After supper, we were assigned our training platoon which started on Sunday with sixty men and is now down to forty-five. Some of the guys could not handle the way the Marines do business. Training has been as difficult as I expected; especially now that I have been appointed to lead a training squad. Sergeant Garrett is pushing me to see how much I can take mentally and physically.

During the obstacle course run earlier today I sprained my ankle pretty badly. Since I did not make the qualification time, the sergeant demanded that I run it again on my bad ankle. I completed the entire obstacle course in two minutes and forty-five seconds which was the fastest time of my entire platoon. After that run, the sergeant sent me to the post dispensary to get checked by the doctor. The doctor put me through the wringer to make sure that the ankle was actually injured. There have been a large group of malingerers and whiners going to the post dispensary for the smallest ache or ailment. After about an hour and a half, the doctor declared my ankle sprained, wrapped it, and gave me the choice of taking a week off and joining the next training platoon coming or continuing with my current platoon. I chose to continue and Sergeant Garrett told me he would not cut me any slack in the training. I guess that means I am going to have to tough it out, no matter what.

This has been one of the hardest weeks of my life. I have to say it taught me a lot about myself and how much I can endure both mentally and physically. Hope everyone is well back home, and enclosed, find letters to Jimmy, Elizabeth, Myra, and Lillie.

Your loving son,

Ray

Ray wrote letters to Sara, Jimmy, Elizabeth, Myra, and Lillie to tell them in his own special way how he was getting along. In all the letters, he did not mention the kid killed in the barbed wire obstacle course run nor did he mention anything about how some nights he had gone to bed wondering if he would make it through the six-week course. His letters to anyone, but his parents, would be cheery and full of optimism. He did not want Sara or his siblings to worry about him even though the possibility existed for him to be hurt or even killed.

He was finishing up his letter to Lillie when the sergeant came into the Quonset hut and bellowed, "Lights Out!"

With that command, Ray's brief respite ended and he knew that tomorrow would bring another hard day of training. There would be a break at eleven in the morning for those men who wanted to attend church. If you did not attend church, you would be assigned a work detail. Ray knew he would attend the protestant service conducted by a Baptist chaplain from Swansboro, North Carolina and an Old Breed Marine. Ray had begun making friends with some of the guys in his training platoon especially those members of his squad, and he learned that while they all have different reasons for joining, they joined for the love of the country and the feeling they must somehow do their part. As Ray fell asleep, he was in a reflective mood and understood that in joining the Corps, he was doing exactly what he must and was happy with his decision.

PARRIS ISLAND MARINE DEPOT ~ PARRIS ISLAND, SOUTH CAROLINA
SATURDAY, JANUARY 10, 1942

• • • • • • • • • • • • • • • • • • • •

The second week passed very quickly and the training was taking on an urgency not known in the first week. His ankle was healing very slowly, but several times during the week, he thought that he would not be able to make it though the rougher stretches of training. Somehow, Ray overcame the pain and pushed through to continue leading the platoon in physical acuity and mental toughness.His times decreased with each repetition except the five-mile run. Due to the length of the run, his ankle was almost not able to hold up. Although he had never fallen below the required threshold, there had been some close calls during the week. The cohesion of his squad continued with the men pulling together to get everyone through the tougher exercises.

This week, Ray received mail from his family in one big envelope. The letter from Jimmy was at first encouraging because of what he said about applying himself more, but then became somewhat troubling when he mentioned the difficulty he had with his lessons. His dad wrote a separate letter from his mom, and sealed it in its own envelope, inside the larger envelope with all of the other letters. That seemed strange until he read it.

Saturday, January 3, 1942

Dear Ray,

Hope this letter finds you well. I hope you have taken to the Marine Corps life as well as I did back in 1917. I am pretty sure by now you know all about how the Marines treat new recruits, and that is lower than some folks treat negroes. I will bet the first evening you got there that they marched you to supper and then after supper you were marched to a building and told to strip. Then you were issued all sorts of Marine Corps gear including your uniform and accessories. As you stood there naked and freezing, you probably thought about how humiliating this whole process seems to be; but understand it is just the Marine Corps way of breaking a man down in order to build him up again in the Marine Corps image.

Training during the first week is hell on earth with the DI waking you up every morning somewhere between three and five to push you on a five or ten-mile run either in full gear or in physical training uniform. I am sure by now you have experienced what I just described. Later on in your training you will have to crawl through a barbed wire enclosed obstacle course where the wire is stretched about eighteen inches above your head. The first few times you crawl through, they will be shooting blanks over your head, and then they will start shooting live ammunition which can kill you quickly if you are not careful. Remember to always stay low during this training, no matter what. I was unfortunate enough to see a young man have his brains splattered everywhere in '17 because he did not follow orders and keep his head down. I hope you do not have to endure this. It will leave a lasting image of the cost of training and war.

I am writing you this in a separate envelope because you and I will now be inexorably linked because of our service in the Corps. Maybe I can tell you some things about training that I could not tell you while you were here because of the many happenings during Christmas.

I hope you are doing well and I want you to know how proud your Mother and I are of you. Keep up the good work and if you need to send me a letter for my eyes only, send it to the rail yard so that your Mother will not be tempted to read it.

With Love,

Dad

After reading his father's letter, Ray reflected on his short time in boot camp and realized that his father had written exactly how his training had progressed. He decided he would write to his dad always at the rail yard except for some missive to his dad included in his weekly letters home. The letter did give him a sense of pride that he had not known before, and he realized his dad was now viewing him as a man and not just his son. At that moment, Ray determined to do everything in his power to continue to earn his dad's respect.

Jimmy had worked hard this week to improve his flying skills through his practice and spending time at the airport observing some of the other student pilots in training. He arrived at the airport this morning prepared for his next lesson. He greeted Mr. Mayerhofer as he came out of the office with his troublesome student in tow for another practice flight of takeoffs and landings.

Jimmy yelled across the tarmac at Mr. Mayerhofer asking, "Can I prepare for my lesson as I did last week by seat flying the spare J-3?"

Mr. Mayerhofer responded, "That is just fine, Jimmy. I will see you right at 11:00 for your lesson."

Jimmy thanked Mr. Mayerhofer and walked into the office. He waited there until Mr. Mayerhofer and the student took off for their training flight. Once that flight was off the ground, Jimmy made his way to the spare Cub to practice his seat flying.

While Jimmy practiced, Mr. Mayerhofer and the student, who would not listen to his instructor, were practicing touch and goes. Out of the corner of his eye, Jimmy saw the Cub turning final, suddenly stall, drop the left wing, and spin into the ground right at the end of the runway. Jimmy quickly jumped out of the airplane and ran to the wreckage as other people joined him to do what they could to help. The man in the office called the local fire department and ambulance service for help. As Jimmy reached the wreckage, he could see that Mr. Mayerhofer was trapped in the back seat with his neck at a crooked angle. The student in the front was bleeding profusely from a cut on his head but seemed to still be alive. The sight of the blood and Mr. Mayerhofer's mangled body was almost more than Jimmy could stand.

Jimmy turned and yelled, "Where is the ambulance? Do we have a doctor here yet?"

The group murmured that they had not arrived yet, but that it did not seem like there was anything anyone could do for the injured men. Jimmy stifled the urge to vomit and noticed that there was a very real chance of fire with the amount of fuel flowing off the wings.

Jimmy looked at the crowd and said, "There's a chance of a fire from the fuel! Let's get them out of the airplane! Be careful, we don't want to injure them any more than they are already."

A couple of men helped Jimmy carefully extract the injured instructor and student from the airplane and they placed them gently on blankets safely away from the airplane.

The ambulance arrived at about the same time the doctor did. The doctor checked the student first and declared that he was in critical condition with a broken arm, broken legs, and might have internal injuries. The doctor helped the ambulance attendants load the student and sent them off to the hospital in Charlotte. The doctor examined Mr. Mayerhofer and found somehow that he was still alive with what appeared to be a broken neck. The doctor knew time was of the essence in Mr. Mayerhofer's case and did everything in his capacity to stabilize him. The doctor gently loaded Mr. Mayerhofer into the ambulance and rode with him to the hospital in order to monitor him during the trip. After the ambulances left, Jimmy was overcome by the tragedy and he walked back to the office to call his father. He knew he was in no condition to drive. Jimmy asked the man in the office if he could use the phone and the man replied that it would be all right considering the circumstances. Jimmy picked up the phone and had the operator put through the call.

Jimmy's dad answered, "Hello."

Jimmy replied, "Hello, Dad, can you come pick me up at the airport? There has been a terrible accident involving Mr. Mayerhofer and another student."

His dad replied, "I am on my way and are you all right?"

Jimmy replied, "Physically I am fine but I was the first one to the crash. It was horrible. Mr. Mayerhofer may not survive his injuries and the student was touch and go as well. Do you think we could go pick up Mrs. Mayerhofer and take her to the hospital? I do not think they have anyone who will help them if something happens to him."

"Sure, Son, I think that will be fine. I will be there in about ten minutes," his Dad replied.

Jimmy's Struggle

About fifteen minutes later, Jimmy's dad arrived to pick him up. His dad took one look at him, saw the blood on his clothes, and knew his son witnessed something horrific.

"Are you all right, Son? Whose blood is on your shirt?"

"I am physically fine but mentally, it will take me a long time to get over what I witnessed today. It is the student pilot's and Mr. Mayerhofer's blood. I was the first person there and tried to help them the best I could. There was so much blood and Mr. Mayerhofer's neck was bent at a weird angle and after a couple of minutes his face became a terrible shade of gray. I hope he is still alive when we get Mrs. Mayerhofer to the hospital."

His dad drove them to the Mayerhofer home and knocked on the door while Jimmy waited in the car. Margaretha Mayerhofer answered the door and her face was pale. She had just received the phone call from the hospital notifying her of her husband's grievous injuries.

Raymond said, "Mrs. Mayerhofer, my son, Jimmy, saw the accident and tried to help the student and Fred out of the airplane. He thought you might need a ride to the hospital since you do not drive. Would you like us to take you to the hospital?"

Margaretha replied, "That would be good. The doctor just called and told me Fred might not survive the next few hours. Let me tell Eliana and Michael where I am going."

Raymond asked, "Before you tell them you are leaving, would you like them to come with us as well? Or do you think it might be too much for them?"

Margaretha replied, "That probably would be good since we do not know the extent of his injuries and there is a possibility he might not survive. Thank you, Mr. Johnson."

Margaretha gathered her two children, Eliana and Michael, and told them their father had been hurt in a plane crash. She also told them that the prognosis was not good and that the Johnsons were taking them to the hospital to be with their father.

Mercy Hospital ~ Charlotte, North Carolina
Saturday - 1:00pm
• •

Raymond pulled the car into the emergency entrance at Mercy Hospital and let Margaretha and her children out to go inside and find out about her husband. He and Jimmy parked the car before joining the Mayerhofer family in the waiting area. Raymond found Margaretha and asked her if she had any news about Fred yet. Margaretha told Raymond that the doctor had let her know that Fred was in surgery right now to stop the internal bleeding and to attempt to stabilize his fractured spine. Mr. and Mrs. Thomas Cameron arrived just a little later to check on their son, Tom, the student pilot involved with Mr. Mayerhofer in the accident. Mr. Cameron spoke to the doctor about the prognosis of his son and found that his son was also in surgery to repair his broken legs and attempt to stop the internal hemorrhaging. The doctor spoke with Margaretha and told her Fred was still holding his own in surgery and that he would let her know when she could see her husband. At this point, Mr. Cameron came over to speak to Jimmy and Raymond because he noticed Jimmy had blood on his shirt and that the two men were keeping Margaretha company.

Mr. Cameron said, "I would like to introduce myself, Mrs. Mayerhofer. I am Thomas Cameron, and this is my wife, Lucille. Your husband, along with Joe Rosen, has been giving my son flying lessons. Do you know what happened today to cause the accident?"

Mrs. Mayerhofer responded, "Mr. Cameron, I do not know what happened to cause the accident, but I know that Jimmy Johnson was there, saw what happened, and pulled both my husband and your son to safety when it seemed the airplane might catch fire. He is sitting over there beside my children and his father. You may want to talk to him. He might be able to give you some details about what happened."

Jimmy and his dad were quietly talking about what happened earlier in the day when Mr. Cameron walked up and introduced himself.

Mr. Cameron spoke to Jimmy, "Mrs. Mayerhofer pointed you out to me. I am Thomas Cameron and this is my wife, Lucille. She said you might know what happened, Mr. Johnson."

Raymond answered, "Mr. Cameron, my name is Raymond Johnson and this is my son, Jimmy. He saw most of what happened and has told me a little about what happened. He has been in shock since it happened so if he does not want to talk about it, I will not allow you to press him."

Mr. Cameron replied, "Mr. Johnson, I would hope he could tell me what happened or at least what he saw because my son was very close to soloing."

Raymond looked at his son and said, "Jimmy, do you think you can talk about what happened from your vantage point?"

Jimmy replied, "Dad, I will tell Mr. Cameron everything I saw to the best of my recollection since it seems to be all a blur."

His dad replied, "Do your best, Son. I know that it was a very shocking experience."

Jimmy cleared his throat and started, "Mr. Cameron, from my vantage point in a J-3 Cub sitting on the ramp, I saw your son and Mr. Mayerhofer practicing touch and goes in order to, I assume, prepare for his solo flight. They made several passes as I was practice flying in the spare Cub on the ramp. On that last pass, I noticed the airplane out of the corner of my eye turning from the base leg to the final approach, and as the airplane was making the left turn to land, it suddenly rose, dropped the left wing, and made about a half revolution spin before crashing at the end of the runway. I may have heard the engine rev, then die, during the stall when they tried to recover. I got out of the plane and rushed quickly to the crumpled wreck where I was the first to arrive. Your son had a nasty gash on his forehead and seemed to have broken his arm and both legs. He was unconscious and unresponsive when I got there and Mr. Mayerhofer, in the back seat, looked worse because his head and neck were at an unnatural angle. People soon arrived and helped me extricate both men from the airplane. After the doctor and the ambulance got there, everything from then on is a blur. I am sorry I do not remember any more."

Mr. Cameron replied, "Thanks, Jimmy. I appreciate this information. Could you tell me more about whether you knew if his flying was going well before the crash?"

Jimmy remembered that he overheard Mr. Mayerhofer telling Tom that the way he flew approaches could get him killed because he was coming in too slow but Jimmy did not think it was appropriate to tell Mr. Cameron about it.

Jimmy replied, "Other than the few touch and goes I saw this morning, I do not know how his lessons were going. I am sorry."

"I appreciate you taking the time to talk to me. Thank you." Mr. Cameron replied.

Mr. Cameron joined his wife to continue the wait as Mrs. Mayerhofer came back over to sit with them.

Jimmy looked over at his father after about an hour of waiting and said, "Dad, can you and I take a walk? I need some air."

"Sure, Jimmy, we can walk and stretch our legs."

They excused themselves from Mrs. Mayerhofer and her children and exited through the emergency entrance to walk around the grounds.

After a short distance, Jimmy said, "Dad, I need to tell you something. I withheld information from Mr. Cameron earlier when he asked me if I knew how Tom's flying lessons were going. I did not think it was appropriate to tell him I overheard a conversation between Mr. Mayerhofer and Tom. Mr. Mayerhofer, after his lesson last Saturday with Tom, told him that the way he was flying his approaches could cause him to have an accident. Tom was turning to final too slow. He wanted to argue the point that he knew what he was doing and that he would be fine. It was like Tom was unwilling to listen to the instruction of Mr. Mayerhofer. Mr. Mayerhofer told Tom last Saturday, as his instructor he could no longer work with him since he was unwilling to follow his instruction. Tom replied to Mr. Mayerhofer that Mr. Rosen had ended his training with him and now Mr. Mayerhofer was doing the same. He stated that if the two best instructors in the county would not train him, he was pretty sure he would be unable to find another willing instructor and asked Mr. Mayerhofer to give him another chance. That chance came today and look what happened. Should I have told Mr. Cameron?"

His dad took a long time to think about his response then said, "No, Jimmy. You did the right thing since what you overheard may not have been the entire conversation. Let us hope both men pull through. How are you doing?"

Jimmy replied, "I am in shock, Dad. I do not know if I will be able to get into an airplane for a while because of what I witnessed. Would you be overly upset if I took some time to figure out what I want to do as far as flying is concerned?"

"I think that is sound reasoning, Jimmy. Take all the time you need. Your experience today will stay with you for a long time even if both men survive their injuries. I think it is time we got back to Mrs. Mayerhofer and her children."

Mercy Hospital ~ Charlotte, North Carolina
Saturday - 4:30pm

• • • • • • • • • • • • • • • • • • • •

While the small group was waiting for news on the two crash victims, Raymond took the time to call Bessie and tell her what had happened with Mr. Mayerhofer and his student. He let her know that Jimmy was the first to the scene and was in shock now from the trauma. Bessie asked Raymond if she could do anything for the Mayerhofer or Cameron families. Raymond told her everything was all right now but this would be a long ordeal. As Raymond returned from his conversation with Bessie, he saw a grim-faced doctor walking towards where Mrs. Mayerhofer and the Camerons were sitting. Raymond arrived just in time to hear the doctor tell Mr.

and Mrs. Cameron that their son had suffered numerous fractures and he had a collapsed lung and bruised heart from the trauma of the crash. The doctor told them that Tom was now in recovery and the next twenty-four to forty-eight hours would be critical to his survival. The doctor told them if he survived the next couple of days there was a good chance he might recover. Tom's doctor left the Camerons with the hope that they could see their son within the next few hours once he was out of recovery.

The vigil continued for Mrs. Mayerhofer, her children, Raymond, and Jimmy until another doctor came to update them on Fred's condition.

The doctor, clearing his throat, said, "Mrs. Mayerhofer, it is my sad duty to inform you that your husband has succumbed to his injuries. We did everything in our power during surgery to prevent this outcome, but the injuries he sustained in the crash were too great for his body to overcome. I am truly sorry."

Mrs. Mayerhofer, with typical German stoicism, replied, "Thank you, Doctor. We appreciate everything you did to try and save my husband's life. Can my children and I see him to tell him goodbye?"

The doctor replied, "Follow me and I will take you to him. Let me warn you that he does not look good."

The doctor led Mrs. Mayerhofer and her children away to view the body of her husband and their father. After they left, Jimmy broke down and wept while his dad tried fruitlessly to comfort him.

Jimmy railed, "Dad, it is just a senseless loss. That idiot student would not listen to the instructions from Mr. Mayerhofer and now Mr. Mayerhofer is dead! It's not fair for the student to survive and one of the best men I have ever known to be lying dead in that cold sterile hallway!"

His dad, fearing that Mr. and Mrs. Cameron would overhear and want to know what Jimmy was talking about, tried to quiet his son but that was impossible. Mr. Cameron did overhear the tirade and walked over to ask Jimmy what he was talking about.

Jimmy looked up squaring his shoulders and said, "Mr. Cameron, I did not tell you earlier but I overheard a conversation between Mr. Mayerhofer and your son last Saturday. Mr. Mayerhofer told your son he would not instruct him anymore because he was a dangerous pilot. According to the part of the conversation I overheard, your son has a dangerous habit of coming in too slow from base to final which could lead to an accident like we had today. I distinctly heard Mr. Mayerhofer tell your son that he needed to listen to and follow his instruction if he wanted to continue as one of his students. As a matter of fact, Mr. Mayerhofer had ended his lessons with your son last Saturday only to have your son talk him into one more chance by promising to follow Mr. Mayerhofer's instructions to the letter. I believe the accident is your son's fault and it cost the world a fine man. Now, please leave me alone and let me grieve in peace."

Mr. Cameron, at a loss for words and put out by Jimmy's impudence replied, "You are wrong; I am a pilot myself and I have spent time practicing with my son. He has always followed every procedure to the letter when I am in the airplane. You do not know what you are talking about."

Jimmy snapped, "Sir, if you want to know the truth, call Mr. Joe Rosen because he also stopped giving your son lessons for the same reason. Your son's flying is dangerous. I am truly sorry I blurted this out in my grief, but now that it is out, there is no reason for me to sit here and listen to your defense of your son. Dad, please get me out of here."

Jimmy's dad looked at Mr. Cameron, "At this point, the conversation is over and I do not appreciate your implication that my son is a liar. Please go back and sit with your wife and allow my son to grieve in peace."

Mr. Cameron replied, "Mr. Johnson, I did not mean to imply that your son is a liar but I will not have my son's name sullied either. I will talk to Mr. Rosen as your son has suggested. I am truly sorry that Mr. Mayerhofer died and I hope someone will be able to determine the cause of the accident."

With that, Mr. Cameron rejoined his wife with the knowledge that their son was still alive while Mrs. Mayerhofer had lost her husband and only source of income.

When Mrs. Mayerhofer and her children returned, she asked Raymond, "Mr. Johnson, if it is not much of an imposition, can you help me make funeral arrangements for Fred? I have never done anything like this and I do not know what to do."

Raymond replied, "Let me take you and your children back to our home and we can call Mr. Frith at the Strathmore Funeral Home to make arrangements."

Mrs. Mayerhofer replied, "Are you sure that this will not inconvenience you? How much do you think a funeral with a burial plot will cost?"

Raymond thought for a minute, "It will not inconvenience us at all; especially knowing how much Jimmy respected your husband. As far as the cost goes, I do not know how much a funeral costs, although I know a plot in Greenwood Cemetery is ten dollars. I think Mr. Frith can arrange this for you, Mrs. Mayerhofer."

"Thank you, Mr. Johnson, I hope I can afford to pay for my husband's funeral and still have money to live on," Mrs. Mayerhofer replied.

Raymond said, "There are many fine people in Montcross who will help. Your husband is highly respected in the community for the way he helped others in their times of need. Let's get everyone and start home."

After Eliana and Michael had seen their father, they lapsed into a shocked quiet that Jimmy tried to break. He knew well what these two children were feeling, since he was feeling the grief and loss as well. The trip to the Johnson family home was made in silence. The events of the day and the death of Mr. Mayerhofer had completely overwhelmed everyone.

JOHNSON FAMILY HOME ~ MONTCROSS, NORTH CAROLINA
SATURDAY - 6:00PM

• •

As the car pulled into the driveway at the corner of Main Street and Todd Street, the passengers were enveloped with a surreal quiet that almost suffocated them. Raymond, Jimmy, Mrs. Mayerhofer, Eliana, and Michael got out of the car and walked into the house. Bessie, there to greet them at the door, saw her husband's face and knew immediately that something was terribly wrong.

Bessie said to Margaretha, "I am so sorry, Margaretha. Can I do anything to help you?"

Margaretha replied, "I cannot think of anything right now Bessie except that I will ask if you can feed my children dinner. They have not had anything to eat since lunch."

"Sure, Margaretha. Elva has a dinner of boiled ham, potatoes and lima beans ready for everyone. I will have her set three more places. You and your children are welcome to stay here tonight if you would like." Bessie replied.

"I think that would be good. Raymond said he would call Mr. Frith at the Strathmore Funeral Home to help with Fred's arrangements. Thanks."

The family and their guests made their way into the dining room for supper. The girls tried to engage Eliana in conversation while Jimmy tried to engage Michael, but the trauma of the day was too much to overcome. Supper passed in silence and Margaretha and Bessie cleaned up the table while the children went to play in the den.

In the study after supper, Raymond called Mr. Frith at the funeral home to make the arrangements for Mr. Mayerhofer's funeral. Raymond picked up the phone and had Mrs. Bass connect him to Wayne Frith's home.

Wayne Frith answered the phone, "Hello."

"Hello, Wayne, this is Raymond Johnson. I am calling to set up funeral arrangements for Mr. Fred Mayerhofer. He died today in a plane crash." Raymond replied.

"Raymond, it's good to hear from you. I am sorry to hear about Fred Mayerhofer. What type of arrangements are you going to need? Do they need a plot?"

"I don't think Mrs. Mayerhofer has a lot of money. Fred did not make much managing the airport and giving flying lessons. She will need a burial plot, and I will personally guarantee payment. The funeral should be Jewish and I will have Mrs. Mayerhofer get in touch with the Rabbi in Charlotte to officiate. What do you think that will cost?"

"Raymond, the burial plot in Greenwood Cemetery will be ten dollars and the cost of the funeral will be about $300.00. Where is the body now?"

"Fred was taken to Mercy Hospital in Charlotte where he succumbed to his injuries while in surgery. Can you pick him up there and prepare him for burial? I will let Mrs. Mayerhofer know the cost."

"I will have someone pick up Mr. Mayerhofer's body later this evening. I will call you back and let you know when Mrs. Mayerhofer can set up the funeral and view her husband."

"Thanks, Wayne. I appreciate your help. I will await your call. Goodbye."

―――――――――――――

Raymond joined Bessie and Margaretha in the sitting room.

Raymond sat down and said, "Margaretha, I have spoken to Mr. Frith at the funeral home. He will go pick up Fred's remains and prepare him for burial in the proper Jewish custom. He will call me back after they have picked him up and prepared him for burial. The cost for the burial plot and funeral will be $310.00 and you will need to get in touch with your Rabbi to plan the funeral service. Is this acceptable?"

Margaretha replied, "That is more money than I have right now and I do not know when or how I will make more. Will I be allowed to make payments?"

"Margaretha, you do not have to worry about paying for the funeral, yet. We will help you through this very difficult time."

Margaretha stifled a sob, saying, "Thank you, Raymond and thank you, Bessie. The arrangements sound fine and I will call the Rabbi. Do you think Jimmy would be a pall bearer at Fred's funeral?"

"He would be honored to serve as a pall bearer." Raymond replied.

With this settled, they talked about the children, Eliana and Michael. They would have to bear the loss of the father they both adored, and that would be tough for a while. Bessie volunteered to let Michael and Eliana stay with them until after the funeral so that they would be around other children who could empathize and commiserate with them. Margaretha thought that was a nice gesture and she believed it would do her children good to be around others their own age. With the funeral arrangements tentatively planned, the small group said goodnight. Bessie showed Mrs. Mayerhofer to the guest room, Michael to Jimmy's room to sleep in Ray's vacant bed, and Eliana to Elizabeth's room to sleep in the spare bed there. Bessie and Margaretha wished the young children sweet dreams, as they tucked them into bed.

JOHNSON FAMILY HOME ~ MONTCROSS, NORTH CAROLINA
SUNDAY, JANUARY 11, 1942 - 7:00AM

Sunday morning dawned cold and dreary with a dusting of snow on the ground. The dreariness of the day matched Jimmy's mood as he milked the cow and gathered the eggs. The crash and its aftermath still weighed heavily on his mind along with the way that he had talked to Mr. Cameron at the hospital. The more Jimmy thought about the conversation with Mr. Cameron, the more he wanted to apologize for his rude behavior. He rushed through the rest of his chores hoping he could talk to his father before church. Jimmy returned to the house as everyone gathered for breakfast.

His dad asked, "How much milk did we get today?"

Jimmy replied, "Gertrude was in a very giving mood, she gave me three-quarters of a milk can, and the chickens were just as generous with their eighteen eggs. They must know that we need to feed an army."

Raymond chuckled, "Well, that might be the case. How did you sleep last night? I think I heard you pacing a couple of times during the night."

Jimmy gave his dad a grim look and said, "I did not sleep very well and I was pacing. Can we talk after breakfast?"

Knowing that his son does not normally ask to talk unless something is really bothering him, his dad responded, "That's fine, Son. Looks like breakfast is about to be served."

Mrs. Mayerhofer and her children came down to breakfast looking very weary. None of them were able to get much sleep because it had finally hit them that the head of their family was never coming home.

As Margaretha sat down at the table, she said, "Raymond and Bessie, thank you for your help yesterday and last night. I think that after breakfast we need to get home and start putting our lives together without Fred. I called the Rabbi of our synagogue in Charlotte this morning and he said he will send someone to pick us up for worship today. That will help us more than anything because our faith is strong. Will you take us home after breakfast?"

"Margaretha, I will be happy to take you home. Jimmy, will you ride with me? We can pick your car up at the airport after we take the Mayerhofers home."

"That sounds good to me."

Breakfast was a quiet affair with everyone lost in their own thoughts about the tragedy and what they must do the be able move forward. Jimmy and his dad helped Mrs. Mayerhofer, Eliana, and Michael into the car so they would get home in time for the ride to the synagogue. After the short ride, Raymond and Jimmy dropped the Mayerhofers off at their home and they thanked Raymond and Jimmy for their kindness.

Raymond said, "Margaretha, if you need anything over the next few days, please do not hesitate to send us a message or call. We will be happy to help you with whatever you need."

Margaretha replied, "Thanks, Raymond. I appreciate the support that you and Bessie have given us."

"You are welcome. You have my family's sympathy."

"Eliana, I will pick up your school work and bring it by to you so you will not have to worry about falling behind."

Eliana looks at Jimmy with gratitude, saying, "Thank you, Jimmy."

"You are welcome. Mrs. Mayerhofer, I will come by tomorrow and split wood for your fire."

Mrs. Mayerhofer thanked Jimmy and he got into the car with his dad.

On the drive to the airport his dad started the conversation by saying, "Jimmy, I knew you needed to talk by the look on your face ,and the request you made at breakfast. What is troubling you?"

Jimmy cleared his throat and replied, "Dad, every time I fell asleep last night, I kept seeing the crash and Mr. Mayerhofer's face in the back seat of that airplane, when I first got to it. I cannot put the accident out of mind. Is that normal?"

"Yes, Jimmy, that is very normal. You remember the story I told you about my service in France? After twenty plus years, I still remember the boy I killed in the trench. That is why it is very hard for me to talk about my service. I put it so far back in my mind that it is out of reach and one day you will be able to do the same thing."

MONTCROSS AIRPORT ~ MONTCROSS, NORTH CAROLINA
SUNDAY - 9:30AM

When Jimmy and his father arrived at the Montcross Airport to pick up his car, there seemed to be something inexplicably drawing Jimmy to the crash scene one more time.

Jimmy got out of the family car saying to his father, "Dad, I think I will walk over and take a look at the crash site again. Will you join me? I need to see if anything is there that belongs to Mr. Mayerhofer or Tom Cameron."

His dad replied, "Are you sure you want to walk to the crash site this morning? I know this tragedy has affected you in ways you are not even aware of yet. Are you going to church this morning? You know your mother will be upset if you miss church, especially today."

"Dad, I need to look over the site one more time. If I am going to finish my pilot training, I will have to put this accident behind me. I am dressed for church already. I will make sure that I am in our pew for the worship service. I need to hear Reverend Kelton's message this morning. He is so in tune to the message God wants him to deliver to the congregation."

His dad, understanding his son's grief, said, "I need to take your Mother and the girls to Sunday school, so I am going to go on home and pick them up since it has started snowing. I do not think they should be walking to the church in this weather today."

"I will see you at church, Dad. Thank you for listening and helping me."

Jimmy walked to the office to see if anyone was working today before going to the end of the runway to look at the crash site. Jimmy found the Sunday attendant in the office working on some paperwork which included a form for the Civil Aeronautics Authority about the accident yesterday.

"Hello, Jimmy", the attendant said in greeting.

"Hello, Truett. I want to go look at the crash site again, will that be all right?" Jimmy asked.

"Jimmy, it is all right with me, but I want you to know that the Civil Aeronautics Authority will be convening an inquiry in the next few weeks to figure out what happened. I had to list you on this CAA form as being the first person to the crash yesterday and an eyewitness to the accident. You should expect to be called as a witness in the inquiry." Truett replied.

Jimmy thought a moment before responding, "Do you know where they will hold the inquiry? Have you ever been part of one of these inquiries?"

"Jimmy, I think they will probably hold it at the Montcross Court House since they will need a court reporter and all witnesses must be sworn for their testimony to be heard. I wanted you to be prepared to receive some sort of request to appear."

"Thanks, Truett. I will wait and see what happens. I am going to walk to the end of the runway and see the crash site. I did not see the airplane when we pulled into the parking lot, where is it?"

"The airplane is being stored in the CPTP hangar and all lessons have been suspended until the cause of the accident is determined."

Jimmy thanked Truett and left the office to walk to the end of the runway.

At the crash site, Jimmy noticed a tree limb about halfway up a pine was broken off and he began to wonder if that tree helped Tom survive the crash by slowing down the descent or changing the angle of impact of the crashing airplane. Jimmy looked from the crash site to the J-3 Cub that he had been sitting in and practicing to determine how far away he was from the crash. He looked around to see if there were any personal effects left on the ground after the fire department cleaned up the crash site yesterday.

Jimmy thought, *I wonder why Tom would not listen to his instructors when they told him the way he flew landing approaches was dangerous. Why did Mr. Mayerhofer continue to give him lessons if he thought there was a possibility that his landing procedure could lead to an accident? I will never know the answer to either question but I hope I can put this behind me. I do not know if I will ever get into an airplane again.*

As Jimmy was about to leave the crash site, he noticed a glimmer in the grass and walked over to see what caught his eye. He bent over and found a ring on the ground with a fine chain passing through the center. Examining the ring closely, Jimmy found it was a Great War Deutsche Luftstreitkräfte flyer's badge made into a ring which commemorated Mr. Mayerhofer's service in the air arm of the German Empire. Jimmy had seen this ring many times around Mr. Mayerhofer's neck and at one point was able to ask him about it. Mr. Mayerhofer told him this ring was manufactured in the early 1930's by people wanting to remember their service as flyers in the Great War, and his parents had sent him this one to commemorate his service. Jimmy hoped, even though the United States was at war with Germany, that people would remember, even though Mr. Mayerhofer served in the Deutsche Luftstreitkräfte during the Great War, that he was a United States citizen and had been doing everything in his power to help train the pilots that would be needed to defeat Hitler.

Jimmy vowed, *I will do everything in my power to keep the good name of Mr. Mayerhofer unsullied by any accusations that may come out of the inquiry into the accident. Mr. Mayerhofer was one of the finest men I have ever known and I want everyone to see what this man did to help me and others like me.*

Jimmy placed the chain with the ring on it around his neck and planned to deliver it to Mrs. Mayerhofer this afternoon. Jimmy walked back to his car and saw that the time was ten twenty-five, and he needed to hurry in order to make it to the First Baptist Church worship service on time, this morning.

Jimmy's Struggle

• •

After the worship service, Jimmy and the family arrived home for a lunch of country style steak, mashed potatoes, green beans, and oven rolls prepared by Elva before she left to go to her church. All Bessie had to do was heat the food and serve it to the family. Elizabeth helped her mother with heating the food and putting it on the table. Lillie and Myra helped the best they could by setting the table.

Jimmy changed his clothes and said to his dad, "After lunch, I need to return this ring and chain I found today at the crash site to Mrs. Mayerhofer. I also promised her I would split some wood for them as well. Will it be all right if I went over there this afternoon?"

"You should call them first to make sure it is convenient for you to go visit. If Mrs. Mayerhofer says that it is all right to visit, then it will be fine with me."

The family gathered around the table for lunch and the banter started with Lillie saying, "Mommy, I wonder what Ray is doing today at boot camp. Do you have any idea?"

Bessie replied, "I bet he has been in church just like you and is now having lunch in the mess hall before exercising this afternoon. What are you going to do this afternoon?"

"I am going to play with my dolls and then play some games with Myra." Lillie replied.

Raymond looked at Elizabeth, "What are your plans for this afternoon, Elizabeth?"

Elizabeth replied, "I need to finish reading The Scarlet Letter by Nathaniel Hawthorne and write a book report by Tuesday. I am about halfway through the book and really need to buckle down and finish it today."

The family talked about other happenings around Montcross and shied away from talking about the accident. With lunch complete, Raymond retired to the den to listen to the radio and read the newspaper while Jimmy called Mrs. Mayerhofer.

Mrs. Mayerhofer answered, "Hello."

Jimmy said, "Hello, Mrs. Mayerhofer, this morning I found Mr. Mayerhofer's pilot's ring that he wore around his neck. May I return it to you today and get a head start on some of that wood I promised to split?"

"That is nice of you to offer, Jimmy, but the Rabbi is here helping us make plans for Fred's funeral. Can you bring it tomorrow when you bring Eliana's homework?"

"Yes, Ma'am. That will be just fine."

"I want to thank you and your family for all of their support. Eliana, Michael, and I certainly appreciate it."

"You are welcome, Mrs. Mayerhofer. If you need anything, please do not hesitate to ask. Have a good afternoon."

"Thanks, Jimmy. Goodbye.".

They hung up and Jimmy walked into the den to tell his father that the Rabbi is at the Mayerhofer home helping make plans for the funeral and Mrs. Mayerhofer wanted him to wait until tomorrow to bring the ring and split the wood.

"I think that is probably best. You need your space to grieve just like the Mayerhofers do. Anything happen at the airport? I saw you go into the office, as I was leaving."

"Yes, Dad. Truett told me that there is going to be a formal inquiry into the accident by the Civil Aeronautics Authority sometime in the next few weeks. I might be summoned as a witness in the proceedings. I asked Truett if he had ever been a part of an inquiry like this and he told me that he had not. Where do you think an inquiry like this will be held?"

"Jimmy, I think an inquiry is going to be the best thing for everyone especially after what you said, in your grief, yesterday to Mr. Cameron. It will probably be held at the Montcross Courthouse and the testimony will be sworn and recorded for public record and I hope the public good."

"Dad, I regret what I said to Mr. Cameron last night; especially with his son lying grievously injured in the hospital. Should I speak to Mr. Cameron and apologize? I think I need to after my outburst and the disrespect I showed him in the hospital waiting room."

Raymond contemplated his answer for a full minute before saying, "Jimmy, your outburst was out of grief over the loss of your mentor and friend, Mr. Mayerhofer. As long as you told the truth last night which I firmly believe you did, I think you should wait until the inquiry before saying anything more to anyone unless the investigator requests an interview before the proceedings."

"Thanks, Dad. I always want to do what is right and I am embarrassed I let my emotions get the better of me last night at the hospital. I know I told the truth. You always taught Ray and me never to compromise the truth with a lie. I wonder how long we have to wait until they start the proceedings."

"I think it will take a few weeks. They probably want to wait until Tom Cameron is firmly on the road to recovery. I think they will conduct interviews of everyone who witnessed the accident and the other students of Mr. Mayerhofer. I will not speculate more than to say it will take some time before we know the findings of the accident investigation."

"Thanks, Dad. I am going to go upstairs to read my letter from Ray and probably write one as well."

"Jimmy, Ray has a lot of things to handle himself during boot camp. You might not want to tell him about the accident but I will leave that up to you."

Jimmy left the den thinking about what they had talked about this afternoon and went upstairs.

———————————

Once in the room he normally shared with his brother, Jimmy took out his CPTP Manual to study for his class tomorrow night. He wanted to continue the class until he could decide whether to finish up his flying lessons or not. He was leading the class with the highest average and wanted to maintain that with perfect attendance as both were taken into consideration when determining who got the coveted slot in the Army Air Corps. After an hour studying the upcoming material, he read Ray's letter.

Sunday, January 4, 1942

Dear Jimmy,

Hope this letter finds you well. My life has changed since I joined the Marines and not for the better. These last two weeks have been very difficult with the toughness of the training and the demeaning way the drill sergeant treats us. I sprained my ankle yesterday during the obstacle course but Sergeant Garrett made me run it again anyway just to prove I was not faking an injury. I completed the obstacle course in two minutes and forty-five seconds on an ankle that felt like it was going to fall off. The pain was intense during the run but I think I made the Sergeant proud by running the fastest time of the entire platoon. After I finished, he made everyone in the platoon run the course again and attempt to beat my record which most of the guys did with ease.

At the base dispensary, the doctor also tried to determine if I was just another slacker trying to get out of training but when he took a look at all the swelling and the radiographs, he knew I had injured it. He gave me the choice of waiting a week and joining the next training platoon or continuing with light duty for two days with my current platoon. I chose two days light duty to stay with my platoon. I know that the ankle will not be completely healed by then. I think I will be able to tough it out to complete the last two weeks of training before our time on the rifle range.

How are you doing with your flight training? I see from your last letter you are working hard to be at the top of your class. What else is going on in Montcross? Dad says that the mills are running full speed and he is down about five employees because they joined the Army or the Navy. Does Dad have any prospects for replacing them?

Hope all is well with you and I certainly miss you and the family.

Your brother with love,

Ray

After reading the letter and thinking about what his father told him about keeping Ray's spirits up, Jimmy knew that he should not tell Ray about the accident although it would do his heart good to write about it. Jimmy sat down at his writing desk and wrote his letter to Ray.

Sunday, January 11, 1942

Dear Ray,

Hope your ankle is healing up from your training mishap and you are doing well in your training. Things here have been good and I am at the head of my class in the CPTP Ground School. I have started working on getting my grades up in school as well. The CPTP Program requires not only my ground school grades but also my attendance and high school grades to be taken into consideration. I know I have coasted through life doing just enough to get by and now I have to do more than just coast, I hope I have it in me to prove to myself that I can work hard enough.

You asked about Dad and the railyard in your letter and if he was going to be able to replace any of the men who resigned to enlist in the military. This week I was able to find him fifteen young men who recently graduated from Montcross High. He put all fifteen to work, and while three left to enlist, the rest of the group seems to be doing a good job for Dad. They are about finished with the probation period Dad hired them under, and after they complete it, Dad will give them the deferral paperwork to file with the draft board allowing them an exemption from service.

I know we are not supposed to write bad news but I need to tell that there was an accident yesterday at the airport and Mr. Mayerhofer lost his life. A dangerous student who Mr. Mayerhofer had just about stopped teaching was practicing his landings and takeoffs in preparation to solo. Mr. Mayerhofer was in the airplane with the student when the student stalled the airplane and spun it into the ground. I was at the airport preparing for my lesson and I saw the crash happen. I was the first person to the scene and seeing Mr. Mayerhofer and the student bleeding profusely, I have to admit that I do not know how I was able to function to get them out of the plane. Luckily the airplane did not burst into flames and they both survived the trip to hospital only to have Mr. Mayerhofer succumb in surgery.

Mrs. Mayerhofer and her two children stayed here last night because she needed Dad's assistance making the funeral arrangements for Mr. Mayerhofer. Dad was such a help and I think it really calmed them to stay here. I left my car at the airport yesterday because I did not think I could drive home. Dad and I took them home before church this morning and I picked up my car at the airport.

I do not know if I will be able to get back in an airplane and finish my flying lessons, but I am going to continue the ground school program. Flying lessons have been suspended until after the inquiry into the accident. Good luck with the rest of your training and I hope you heal quickly.

Your loving brother,

Jimmy

After finishing his letter, he placed it in the envelope and he went back to the den and gave it to his father to mail.

"Dad, I wrote a letter to Ray and I did tell him about the accident because I think he needs to know why I might not be flying anymore."

"I think that is fine, Jimmy. Are you going to the ground school class tomorrow night?"

"Yes, Dad. I studied my manual before writing Ray because I want to be prepared for tomorrow night's class. I want to finish in the top of the class and when the CAA reinstates lessons at Montcross Airport, I can decide if I want to continue."

"I think that is a smart approach, and I know you will make the top of the class and earn the spot. I am glad to hear you will continue with the ground school classes."

Jimmy's Struggle

• • • • • • • • • • • • • • • • • • • •

After school, Jimmy hurried to the Mayerhofer home to split wood like he promised. Arriving at the front door, he knocked and Mrs. Mayerhofer answered the door.

"Hello, Mrs. Mayerhofer. I am here to deliver Mr. Mayerhofer's ring I found in the grass at the crash site yesterday and to split the wood for the fire place like I promised."

Mrs. Mayerhofer replied, "Thanks. Did you also pick up Eliana's school work for her?"

"Yes, Ma'am, I went to all her teachers. They asked me to tell you how sorry they are for your loss. They also said if your family needs anything, they would be happy to help."

"Tell them that we appreciate their support. I think Eliana and Michael will need a lot of support from everyone. Michael is having a tough time with this because he worshipped his father and Fred loved him dearly."

Jimmy handed Mrs. Mayerhofer the ring and the chain, saying, "I appreciated the story Mr. Mayerhofer told me about the ring and how proud he was of his service to his country during the Great War. I know both of you are United States citizens now, but he told me how much it pained him to see Germany fall into the trap of Hitler. I want you to know that Mr. Mayerhofer was not only my mentor when it came to flying, but he had also become my friend. I looked upon him as a hero. I know this is of little consolation now, but I want you to know that whatever you and your family need, I will be happy to try to provide."

Mrs. Mayerhofer, at a loss for words, just said, "Thank you, Jimmy."

"I will go get started on the wood pile and will try to split you enough wood for the next several days. I will leave Eliana's schoolwork on the table. There are a couple of lessons in math and history that I will need to explain to her."

He laid the schoolwork on the table and walked out the backdoor to the wood pile where he split wood for a solid hour. Jimmy piled up enough fireplace sized sticks to fill all the woodboxes in the house. Just to be make sure the Mayerhofers were taken care of, he left another full woodbox load stacked by the back door ready for use. Jimmy believed that this should be enough wood to last them for three or four days depending on how cold it got. Jimmy figured out quickly that they did not have a furnace in their house and would need a lot of wood for the fireplaces if they were to keep the house comfortably warm. According to the forecast in the "*Gastonia Daily Gazette*", he also knew the low temperatures were going to hover in the twenties and thirties with the highs only reaching fifty degrees. They would have to burn a lot of wood to keep the small home heated. After stacking the wood in the various woodboxes and at the back door, Jimmy walked back into the house and found Eliana sitting at the table about to start her school work.

Jimmy said, "Hello, Eliana, how are you doing?"

She looked up and replied, "I am trying to be all right, but it is hard knowing that my Father is never coming home again. Thank you for bringing my schoolwork to me."

Jimmy replied, "I am sorry about your father and if there is anything you need from me, please ask. Do you need me to explain any of your work to you?"

"I have read over my assignments and I think they are all pretty clear. I will probably not be going back to school until next week. Can you bring my schoolwork every day and take my assignments back to my teachers?"

"Yes, I will be happy to pick up and take your assignments as long as you are out of school."

"Thanks, Jimmy. I know my Mother wants to tell you about the funeral arrangements for my father before you leave."

Mrs. Mayerhofer told him that the funeral would be Wednesday afternoon at 2:00 at the Jewish Synagogue in Charlotte with Rabbi Kurtz performing the service. She advised him also that the Jewish custom of Shiva would be observed from Wednesday at 2:00 until Friday at sundown for her family and mourners.

"What is Shiva, Mrs. Mayerhofer?"

"Jimmy, Shiva is a Jewish mourning custom that is observed in the home and the family and close friends of Fred will come by and sit for a while. Unless Eliana, Michael, or I start a conversation with the mourner, they are to remain silent. Until the Shiva is over, we will not leave the house for anything and the children will not be in school. Rabbi Kurtz made sure that Mr. Frith would prepare Fred for burial in the traditional Jewish manner with a Tachrichim, which is a traditional Jewish shroud, and his Tallit, which is his prayer shawl along with a simple wooden coffin. Your father helped me with the burial plot. Tell him thank you for me, please."

"Thank you for your explanation. I will tell Dad you send your thanks for his help. Our family will arrive for the service by one-thirty on Wednesday. All of your woodboxes are full and there is almost another woodbox load beside the back door. Let me know when you need me to split some more."

"Thanks, Jimmy. That should be enough to last us until Saturday."

Jimmy looked at his watch and saw that it was almost five thirty. Knowing that he had his CPTP class tonight, he took his leave from the Mayerhofer home and drove home to eat dinner before his class.

Montcross College ~ Montcross, North Carolina
Monday - 6:15pm

• •

Jimmy arrived early for his Civilian Pilot Training Program ground school class tonight, and he hoped to see Mr. Rosen before the class started because he needed to ask some questions about what he witnessed on Saturday. Mr. Rosen had not arrived when Jimmy walked into the classroom and took his seat. Jimmy opened his manual to the material for tonight's session and began studying.

Mr. Rosen walked in at six twenty, saw Jimmy studying, and said, "Hello, Jimmy. What are you doing here so early?"

"Mr. Rosen, I was hoping I could talk to you for a few minutes about the accident involving Mr. Mayerhofer. Do you have time to discuss it with me before any students arrive?"

Mr. Rosen involuntarily grimaced when Jimmy mentioned the accident, then responded, "Jimmy, I have time to discuss what you witnessed on Saturday, but due to a request from the Civil Aeronautics Authority, I am not allowed to give you or anyone else my opinion on what led to the accident. If you are going to ask me what I think then we should not discuss it. I have my own ideas on the cause."

Jimmy thought for a moment then said, "So, it is ok for me to tell you what I witnessed. We can discuss the cause based on what I saw, but you cannot give me your opinion on why the accident chain was not broken before it happened. Is that correct?"

"Yes, you can tell me what you saw and what you think happened based on your eyewitness view, but I cannot tell you why I think the accident chain was not broken."

"That is fine. I can abide by those guidelines. I was practicing coordinating my scan with control manipulation so that I could become more balanced with the instrument scan and airplane control. The spare J-3 was about three-quarters of the way down the line facing the runway on Saturday's approach end. I would practice for a few minutes and then watch the touch and goes being performed by Mr. Mayerhofer and Tom Cameron. I had just completed another five-minute session of scanning and practicing when I saw the airplane on the downwind leg of pattern. The plane made what looked like a fine coordinated turn to the base leg. As the plane turned to final, I noticed the airplane had a higher than normal nose and seemed very slow. Suddenly the left wing dropped and the airplane made a half turn clipping one of the pine trees and falling to the ground. At that point, I leapt from the J-3 and ran to the end of the runway to see if I could help them. Both men were unconscious and bleeding profusely. I saw that Mr. Mayerhofer's neck was bent at a weird angle and he was bleeding from his mouth and nose. Tom had a bad gash on his forehead and was bleeding from his ears. By the time I noticed fuel leaking from the wing tanks, others were there to help me get them out. A couple of men and I lifted them both out and placed them on blankets. I grabbed a fire extinguisher and sprayed the wings even though the airplane was not on fire. I had read that doing so would help prevent the gas from igniting. My belief is that Tom Cameron slowed the airplane down too much and his base to final turn was uncoordinated which lead to a stall spin. Did I do the right things when I got to the crash site first? And, can I ask if my view of the possible issue with the base to final leg is a plausible scenario?"

Mr. Rosen, awed by this young man's eyewitness account and almost precise delivery, said, "Jimmy, you have broken down the accident better than anyone else who witnessed the crash on Saturday. No one mentioned that the airplane clipped the pine tree to me. Can I ask how you noticed that?"

"I did not see it clip the pine tree but I recalled the airplane's angle changed abruptly. When I walked the crash site yesterday, I saw that there were several limbs broken on one of the taller pine trees on the edge of the opening that begins the runway threshold. It clicked that the changing angle was caused by those tree limbs. I cannot tell you whether there was any attempt to recover because it happened in probably less that fifteen seconds."

"You have told me so much in your account that I now have a better understanding of what probably happened. You said that the left wing dropped suddenly as if the airplane was uncoordinated. How would you know that?"

"Mr. Rosen, in my second flying lesson we were at 5500 feet; Mr. Mayerhofer was teaching me stalls and recoveries. As I was slowing the airplane for the stall, I did not have the ball centered when the right wing stalled and we spun. I let go of the controls and Mr. Mayerhofer recovered the plane in less than a thousand feet of altitude. We did more maneuvers for me to regain my confidence. When he debriefed me, he asked me what I thought had happened. I told him that I must have inadvertently added rudder as I was pulling back on the stick and uncoordinated the airplane which caused the right wing to stall first causing the airplane to spin."

"Yes, Jimmy, you are absolutely correct and you do have an understanding of stall spins. As far as what you did when you got to the airplane, the first thing you did was not panic and the second thing you did right was that you looked for the immediate danger before trying to remove the injured flyers. Finally, you sprayed the leaked fuel and the wings with the fire extinguisher to prevent an inadvertent fire. By then, you had help to remove the injured flyers which increased their chances of survival. I am sorry Mr. Mayerhofer did not make it. I know how highly he thought of you and I can see why. Are you going to continue your lessons?"

Jimmy paused to let Mr. Rosen's last statement sink in before saying, "Until the accident investigation is completed, there are no lessons at Montcross Airport. I have decided to continue my ground school classes until the inquiry is complete and then I can make a decision on whether to continue to take the flight portion of the training. Is that acceptable in this program?"

"That is absolutely acceptable and will help you to know for sure whether you want to continue the flight portion. Good luck, Jimmy."

"Thank you, Mr. Rosen.", he remarked as he went to his seat because other students had started filing into the classroom.

The class was flying by for Jimmy tonight, but Mr. Rosen took the time to tell everyone in class about the accident that injured Tom Cameron and took the life of Mr. Fred Mayerhofer. Mr. Rosen told the students that there had been a temporary cessation of lessons at the Montcross Airport until the Civil Aeronautics Authority could determine the cause of the accident and hold an inquiry. He gave the students a short background on how an accident inquiry was handled. He says the inquiry would include the accident survivors, eyewitnesses, and other aeronautic experts. Mr. Rosen explained that all testimony was sworn and would be duly recorded by a court reporter.

"The upcoming inquiry likely will be held in the Montcross Courthouse. This is usually to find the cause of an accident and appropriate authorities can get involved if necessary for civil or criminal proceedings in the case of gross negligence. I don't think that will be the case here."

After his explanation, the planned lesson was presented with the standard pop quiz at the end of the class. Jimmy made a 95 on this quiz and now had a healthy eight point lead over the second place student. He left the classroom with a better understanding of what would happen as the inquiry proceeded.

Jimmy thought, *I do wonder how long this procedure will take and whether there will be any blame pointed at Mr. Mayerhofer for the accident. I do hope that Mr. Rosen is able to make the investigators understand that this may have been a dangerous student and not a negligent instructor.*

MONTCROSS AIRPORT ~ MONTCROSS, NORTH CAROLINA
TUESDAY, JANUARY 13, 1942 - 4:00PM
● ●

After dropping off Eliana's schoolwork on Tuesday afternoon, Jimmy rushed to the airport because he knew that Truett would need his help fueling airplanes and delivering the airmails to the post office. Truett and the only other office worker had been working overtime since the accident on Saturday. The Montcross Township owned the airport, and the town council decided to take their time finding the perfect manager for the job. Since Mr. Mayerhofer had been a beloved overseer, Mr. H. R. Brighton, the town's attorney, wanted the Civil Aeronautics Authority's investigation completed before opening the managerial position up for applications.

On Tuesday evening, Jimmy let Truett know that he would not be in Wednesday afternoon since he would be attending the funeral of Mr. Mayerhofer. Truett told him that he was closing the airport as instructed by the town council for the afternoon so that the entire staff could attend the funeral. Jimmy grabbed the fueling clipboard and walked out to the flight line to inspect the airplanes. Part of his job was to make sure that all of the airplanes based at the field were properly secured and had not been tampered with. While he walked the flight line, a man in a tweed suit came from the office and walked towards him. Jimmy noticed that he seemed to be trying to get his attention and walked towards the office in order to meet the gentleman halfway.

The man who looked like he was in his late thirties asked, "Are you Jimmy Johnson?"

"Yes, Sir. Can I help you?"

The man said, "Yes. I am Ernest Rawlings of the Civil Aeronautics Authority in Washington. I am here to investigate the fatal accident that occurred last Saturday. Do you have time to answer some preliminary questions now?"

Jimmy, not knowing what to say, replied, "I do not have time this afternoon. Tomorrow will be inconvenient as well, due to the funeral of Mr. Mayerhofer. Can we schedule a time on Thursday afternoon after four?"

Mr. Rawlings replied, "Can you meet me here on Thursday afternoon at five? Or, would you prefer another location?"

Jimmy, wanting his father present, requested, "Sir, Thursday afternoon is fine. Can the interview take place at my parents' home? I would like my father to be present for the interview. This is scary to me and I do not want to say anything that might be misinterpreted. Would that be acceptable?"

Mr. Rawlings replied, "Thursday afternoon at five is just fine. To answer your question about having your father present, that is acceptable. I cannot do meetings in private homes because I need my court stenographer. Can you meet me at the Hotel Montcross in their private banquet area? I will be holding other preliminary inquiries there before the formal inquest is convened at the Montcross Courthouse."

"Thank you, Mr. Rawlings. My Dad and I will see you at the Hotel Montcross on Thursday afternoon. May I ask you a question?"

Mr. Rawlings replied, "That's good. Yes, you may ask me a question and if I cannot answer it because of my position, I will just decline. Is that acceptable?"

"Yes, that is fine. What does your preliminary investigation provide to the inquest? Also, when do you believe the inquest will start?"

Having been asked these questions before in other accident cases, Mr. Rawlings is well versed in his response, "Jimmy, my preliminary investigation determines whether the inquest will be a presentation of my formal findings on the cause of the accident or will proceed with sworn testimony and a full investigation due to an unclear accident cause. I think my preliminary investigation will take about a week and I will need time to compile my data. The inquest will likely start in two weeks. May I recommend that you not talk to anyone other than me about the accident from now until after the inquest."

"Thanks, Mr. Rawlings. I will not discuss the accident with anyone outside of you and my father since I have told him what I witnessed on Saturday."

Jimmy went about his business of checking the rest of the airplanes. At five-fifteen, the airmail delivery arrived and he had just enough time to make the delivery to the post office before it closed. He told Truett that he would see him on Thursday afternoon at three-thirty and that he would have to leave early to go to his interview with CAA investigator. Truett said that he would work things out and that it should be just fine. Jimmy thanked him and took the airmail to the post office.

JOHNSON FAMILY HOME ~ MONTCROSS, NORTH CAROLINA

Jimmy's Struggle

Jimmy arrived home just in time for dinner with the family. Elva had already placed a delicious looking meal of London broil, mashed potatoes, lima beans, and dinner rolls on the kitchen table.

He walked into the kitchen, saw the feast, and asked, "What is so special about tonight? A dinner like this is reserved for a special occasion."

His dad looked up and replied, "After everything that has happened this week, your Mother thought it would be nice if she and Elva cooked one of your favorite meals. They both know how upset you have been and they thought a wonderful dinner would make you happy."

Jimmy, stunned, walked over to his mother, gave her a hug and a kiss on the cheek, and said, "Thanks, Mom. This is the best thing that has happened for me all week. This meal looks fit for a king. Thank you, Mom! I love you!"

Bessie tightened the hug and whispered, "Jimmy, this has been a tough few days for you and it will probably get tougher before everything is settled. We just wanted you to know that you are loved and supported by the entire family."

He blinked back a tear before saying, "Mom, I do not know what to say. I love all of you very much and hope everything works out."

He walked over to Elva and startled her with a big hug and kiss. She was so taken aback that she dropped the plate that she had prepared for Lillie.

Elva, in mocking impertinence, said, "Jimmy this meal twernt nothin'. I enjoys cookin' for you all. You shant startle an old woman like that, my heart caint take it. Lillie is going to have to wait for her meal now. You sees what you gone and done?"

He winked at her, saying, "Yes, Ma'am. Let me clean up the mess for you. I am sorry for startling you like that, but I wanted you to know how thankful I am for your thoughtful gesture."

Jimmy picked up the pieces of the broken plate and took care to clean the food off of the floor before sitting down with the family for dinner. During dinner, his dad tells the family that the rail yard was going to be adding more men to the repair shop because the railroad would be sending more engines and freight cars to Montcross to handle the increased shipments of textile goods. His mom told everyone of the new war bond drive that started. She chaired the women's committee that would man the war bond drive booths at the post office and other businesses around town. She let everyone know that the sales goal for the township was $100,000 in war bonds and war stamps.

Raymond said, "Jimmy and Elizabeth, do you think each of you could buy a twenty-five dollar bond? They only cost eighteen dollars."

In unison, Jimmy and Elizabeth responded that they could each buy two bonds which would help meet the quota and that pleased their parents.

Lillie piped up, "I have one dollar in my piggy bank. Can I use that for a bond?"

Bessie responded, "Lillie, you are not able to buy a whole bond, but you can buy a dollar war stamp and paste it in your war stamp booklet. Then you can add to it until you have filled your book which can then be turned in for a bond. How does that sound?"

Lillie, bursting with excitement, exclaimed, "GREAT! When can we get my stamp and my booklet, Mommy?"

Myra, not to be outdone, said, "Can I do the same thing as Lillie? I want to help too!"

Bessie replied to the two youngest, "We can all go tomorrow after school to pick up the booklets and your first stamps. We will all help Ray and the other soldiers win the war with our purchase of bonds."

Jimmy had hesitated during dinner to tell his father about his conversation with the accident investigator, Mr. Rawlings. Now that they were both alone in the den listening to the news on the radio, Jimmy decided that he needed to tell his father about the meeting and upcoming interview.

"Dad," he said, "an investigator, Mr. Ernest Rawlings, from the Civil Aeronautics Authority came to the airport today and wanted to talk to me. I did not want to talk to him without you so I asked if I could schedule a time to meet him for an interview. Can you go with me to the Hotel Montcross on Thursday afternoon at five o'clock to talk with him?"

Raymond, a bit perplexed, said, "I can go with you to the interview, but why do you need me there? You have a fine head on your shoulders, and you can handle yourself pretty well."

"Dad, the death of Mr. Mayerhofer has taken a lot out of me and I do not know if I will be able to handle the questions from Mr. Rawlings without breaking down. I really need you there for support. Will you go with me?"

"Yes, Son. I will go with you, but I will not help you answer the questions. I will only be there in case you are overcome with emotion. You really should not worry because I know you will do just fine."

"Thanks, Dad. I appreciate all of the help and support you have given me these last few days. I hope this investigation does not find that Mr. Mayerhofer did anything wrong."

With everything worked out for the meeting on Thursday, Jimmy went upstairs to complete his homework and work on his history report which would be due next week. His thoughts had been muddled the last few days and he continued to worry about the inquest and its ramifications for the Mr. Mayerhofer's family. Jimmy was hopeful that things would work out and that everyone involved could start healing after tomorrow's funeral.

JEWISH SYNAGOGUE ~ CHARLOTTE, NORTH CAROLINA
WEDNESDAY, JANUARY 14, 1942
· · · · · · · · · · · · · · · · · · · ·

Jimmy left Montcross High School promptly at twelve-fifteen to get home in time to change clothes and leave with his family for Mr. Mayerhofer's funeral in Charlotte. When he got home, he saw that his mom had laid out a black suit, white shirt, black braces, and his black oxford shoes and he dressed quickly so that they could leave at one o'clock. Elva and Elizabeth offered to watch the youngest children while they were gone. Raymond, Bessie, and Jimmy left Montcross for the twenty-five minute drive to the Jewish Synagogue in Charlotte. Arriving at one-thirty, the family was ushered to their seats just behind the family. Jimmy understood from the bulletin he was handed that this would be a typical Jewish funeral ceremony.

Rabbi Kurtz began the service with the reading of the 24th Psalm. After Rabbi Kurtz finished the Psalm reading, Ansel Meyer delivered a eulogy that touched on every aspect of Fred's life including the family he left behind in Germany. Jimmy was particularly pleased when Mr. Meyer eulogized Mr. Mayerhofer's life by saying, "Fred was one of those men who believed in helping others through teaching, donating his time, or helping them with his unique carpentry talent. In his death, we can see the way he lived his life as a testament to his faith."

Once Mr. Meyer finished his eulogy, Rabbi Kurtz returned to the pulpit and read the prayer of remembrance, El Maleh Rachamim. The funeral service ended with the congregation reciting the Mourner's Kaddish.

Rabbi Kurtz dismissed the mourners with the "Offering of Consolation" and then helped move Mrs. Mayerhofer and her children to the waiting car. Everyone left the synagogue and drove to Montcross for the burial. Jimmy rode with the other pall bearers to Greenwood Cemetery where a similar shortened service was performed before Mr. Mayerhofer's simple wooden casket was lowered into the grave. Mrs. Mayerhofer, Eliana, and Michael proceeded past the grave and threw a handful of dirt on to the casket before going home to begin the period of Shiva. The rabbi told the group gathered for the burial that a traditional mourner's meal would be held at six o'clock this evening at the Mayerhofer home. Once the service was over, Jimmy found his parents to see if they thought it appropriate for him to attend the mourner's meal.

His dad said, "Since we are not Jewish, I do not think it appropriate for us to attend. I would let this period of mourning pass and call the Mayerhofers on Saturday."

"Thanks, Dad, I was thinking the same thing. I will just go on home with you and work on my history report which is due next week."

The family arrived home at four-thirty and the girls were wondering if their mother was going to take them to the post office to pick up their war stamps and war stamp booklets. Bessie looked at the girls and told them that they could just make it to the post office before it closed to pick up their stamps and booklets. She asked them if they had their money.

Lillie said, "I have three dollars in my piggy bank once I counted it all. I think I will take one dollar and one fifty-cent piece to buy stamps."

Myra said, "I have five dollars in my piggy bank and I am going to take two dollars to buy stamps."

Bessie replied, "That is wonderful girls. Let me put my coat back on and we will walk to the post office."

Once his mom and the girls left, Jimmy walked up to his room to work on his report and to take some time to reflect on the service he witnessed today. He reflected that while he was a Baptist and Mr. Mayerhofer was Jewish, they both worshipped the same God and they were both loved by Him. The service today went a long way to help Jimmy continue the healing process. He picked up his history book, gathered his notes, and continued working on his report on the Battle of Waterloo.

HOTEL MONTCROSS ~ MONTCROSS, NORTH CAROLINA
THURSDAY, JANUARY 15, 1942 - 5:00PM

· ·

Jimmy and his father arrived at the Hotel Montcross promptly at five o'clock to meet Mr. Rawlings for the interview. Jimmy noticed Mr. Cameron leaving a private room with Mr. Rawlings and wondered what Mr. Cameron was doing here since he was not an eyewitness to the accident. He looked at his father in bewilderment because this seemed a little out of the ordinary if Mr. Rawlings wanted an unbiased report of the accident.

He whispered to his dad, "Should I ask him how Tom is progressing since the accident?"

His dad replied in a whisper, "Yes, I think you should. This seems a little out of the ordinary to me."

As Mr. Cameron approached the door to leave, Jimmy asked, "Mr. Cameron, how is Tom doing since the accident? I hope he is continuing to heal."

Mr. Cameron, looking a little shocked to see Jimmy here with his father, replied, "Why do you care? You slandered his name in front of everyone at the hospital Saturday by saying he was a dangerous pilot. I will have you know that I cannot get Mr. Rosen to speak to me; something about not answering any questions until after the inquiry."

Jimmy, with a look of utter bewilderment, calmly said, "Mr. Cameron, all I asked was how Tom was doing? Since you want to make this a personal attack, I will say again that I hope Tom does get well soon."

Mr. Cameron, shocked by the calm demeanor of this young man, replied, "Tom is getting better everyday and he will be able to give his own testimony very soon. As I told Mr. Rawlings, your testimony is biased and should be discounted as such. I would bet that you will not be totally truthful about about the accident in the hopes of protecting that kike Mayerhofer from being charged posthumously with gross negligence. Tom has told me Mr. Mayerhofer took control at the time of the base to final turn and it was his fault the plane stalled. I will make sure you never get your pilot's license and I will also make sure that my son's reputation is untarnished by your slanderous lies. I've told Mr. Rawlings that your testimony is biased and should not even be entered into the record."

As Mr. Cameron intimated that Jimmy might lie to protect his friend and flight instructor, Mr. Mayerhofer, Raymond jumped to his son's defense by saying, "Thomas, I will tell you now that you are out of line. My son will not testify to anything other than what he witnessed in the interview. We all know this is a trying time for everyone involved and we hope that this inquiry will answer all the questions about what happened last Saturday. I think you should leave and let Jimmy give his testimony to Mr. Rawlings even if, as you say, it will not be entered into the record because you think my son's testimony is biased."

Mrs. Gullickson and a couple of guests overheard the exchange and were already taking sides in this matter with most believing that Jimmy was the one being wronged in the exchange. Mr. Rawlings walked out of the private room just in time to hear Thomas Cameron's intimation to Jimmy about wanting to protect Mr. Mayerhofer, and that he had been told to disregard this young man's testimony. Mr. Rawlings knew now that whatever Jimmy witnessed must be very important if the father of the student was trying to get it dismissed on the grounds of bias towards protecting the instructor. In order to save the situation, Mr. Rawlings rushed up to Jimmy and his father to prevent the situation from escalating any further.

Mr. Rawlings said, "Jimmy and Mr. Johnson, it is so good to see you. Thank you for coming down for an interview."

Raymond replied, " Good evening, Mr. Rawlings, I am Raymond Johnson. Mr. Rawlings, if you have been told that my son's testimony is unacceptable due to bias then we can wait for the formal inquest since testimony given then is subject to the perjury laws of the state. My son has no reason to lie about what he saw on Saturday last."

Mr. Rawlings knew now that he had lost control of the situation before he even heard one word of this eyewitness' testimony and he said to Raymond, "Mr. Johnson, I apologize that you believe your son's testimony will be discounted for bias based on Mr. Cameron's statements. Will you join me in the private room that the Gullicksons provided for this investigation, I would appreciate hearing Jimmy's testimony. Rest assured, everything will be given serious consideration."

Raymond replied, "Thank you, Mr. Rawlings, for your understanding. I just want to make sure that this is a legitimate interview and Jimmy's testimony will be properly recorded."

Mr. Rawlings replied, "Yes, Mr. Johnson. I have a court stenographer who is recording in shorthand all testimony, and after the stenographer types it up, I will have the witness sign it. That usually takes a couple of days."

Raymond replied, "We will not hold you up any longer. Jimmy is prepared to give his testimony."

The three men entered the private conference room that was usually home to the weekly Montcross Rotary Club meetings. With the door closed, the court stenographer prepared to take the notes of the interview.

Mr. Rawlings began by saying, "Jimmy, I apologize to you for what happened in the lobby a few minutes ago, and I want you to know that I need your testimony since everyone I have talked to says that you were the first to the scene of the accident and saw it happen from start to finish. Will you accept my apology and understand that what you say will be used to determine the cause of the accident?"

Jimmy, out of the corner of his eye, saw his dad innocuously point at the stenographer then mime writing. Jimmy understood that his dad wanted this response on the record before replying.

Jimmy replied, "Before I say anything, can you instruct the stenographer to start recording with what I am about to say? It should be included in my signed affidavit."

Mr. Rawlings addressed the stenographer, "That is somewhat irregular but knowing the situation I understand. Miss Prater, will you start recording the interview now?"

Miss Prater responded, "Yes, Sir. I will record from this point forward."

Jimmy responded to the original opening questions, "Mr. Rawlings, I will accept your apology, and I understand that my testimony, contrary to what Mr. Cameron just said to my father and me in the lobby, will be used to determine the cause of the accident."

Mr. Rawlings, knew that the accusations of bias by Mr. Cameron would now be written in Jimmy's affidavit, still hoped to somehow rebuild the trust of this young man because he knew his testimony was crucial.

Thinking quickly, Mr. Rawlings said, "Do you want to record the reasons that you had for having that response added to your record before beginning the testimonial part of the interview?"

"Yes, Mr. Rawlings, I think that would be a good idea. My Father and I walked into the Hotel Montcross at five o'clock for my scheduled interview when we met Mr. Thomas Cameron leaving this office. I asked Mr. Cameron how his son Tom was doing after the accident and was verbally attacked for something I said in a moment of grief at the hospital after Mr. Fred Mayerhofer had succumbed to his injuries from the accident. For the record, I told Mr. Cameron of a conversation that I had overheard between Mr. Mayerhofer and Tom Cameron where Mr. Mayerhofer was ready to quit giving Tom flying lessons because he thought Tom was flying dangerously slow approaches and was not listening to Mr. Mayerhofer's admonition to keep his approach speeds up. I also heard Tom say that Mr. Rosen had stopped giving him lessons for the same reason. The reason was that Tom would not listen and follow the flight instruction of two respected flight instructors. I know that this is hearsay at this point, but that is what I overheard. Now, Mr. Cameron thinks that I am trying to slander his son. What happened was that I was grieving the loss of one of the finest men I ever knew and Mr. Cameron overheard what I said to my father and confronted me with it. I told him the same thing I just told you. Today during our brief encounter, Mr. Cameron told me that he had told you, Mr. Rawlings, that my testimony would be biased to protect Mr. Mayerhofer and that you need not record it because it was not going to be truthful and accurate. I can assure you that my testimony will be truthful and accurate based only on what I witnessed that day."

"Thank you, Jimmy. I understand more fully the situation I witnessed and I understand why you said what you did the night your instructor and friend succumbed to the accident. Now, can we get started with the deposition? State your full name and address for the record."

"Yes, Sir. My name is James Andrew Johnson of 4 Todd Street, Montcross, North Carolina."

"Thank you. On Saturday, January 10, 1942 at the Montcross Airport, there was an accident involving a J-3 Cub with a student pilot and instructor on board. Can you tell me what you witnessed regarding the accident to the best of your recollection?"

"Yes, Sir. I was sitting in an idle J-3 Cub practicing my instrument scan and coordinating the movements of both the stick and the rudder in preparation for my third flying lesson with Mr. Fred Mayerhofer. The airplane was facing the runway and I witnessed several successful touch and goes by Mr. Mayerhofer and his student. I had just completed a period of practice and was watching the Cub in flight on the downwind leg of its approach, saw the airplane turn base, and then start its turn to final. In the turn to final, the airplane seemed slower than the previous approaches and appeared to have more of a nose up attitude than the others. All of a sudden, the right wing dropped and the plane spun into the ground in less than a few seconds. I quickly unbuckled my safety belt from the idle Cub and rushed to the accident scene. I was the first to arrive on the scene of the accident since I was less than 200 yards away from it. I looked into the airplane first and noticed that Tom Cameron was bleeding from his head pretty badly in the front seat. I looked at Mr. Mayerhofer in the back seat and his head was twisted at an awkward angle. In less than three minutes others got there to help. We gently removed both Tom Cameron and Mr. Mayerhofer from the airplane. I noticed that fuel was leaking from the wings and grabbed a fire extinguisher and sprayed them down. Then the Dr. and the ambulances arrived. After the ambulances left, I called my father to come pick me up since I was unable to drive at that time."

Mr. Rawlings replied, "Thank you. Is there anything you would like to add to what you told me so far?"

Jimmy answered, "Yes, there is one more thing, but I did not notice it until I walked the crash site on Sunday morning. The top of one of the pine trees had a couple of freshly broken limbs and I recalled then that it looked like the angle changed abruptly during the crash. I am strictly speculating that the airplane clipped the trees in the spin which changed the angle of impact of the airplane. And, for the record, I could not tell from my vantage point who was in control of the airplane on any of the legs of that last approach nor could I tell on any of the other approaches either. That is all I can tell you about the accident."

Mr. Rawlings finished the interview by saying, "Thank you, Jimmy. Your testimony is the most detailed of anyone I have interviewed regarding this accident. I certainly appreciate you taking the time to give me your deposition. I will be in touch to let you know when you can come sign your affidavit. Where can I reach you?"

Jimmy replied, "You are welcome, Mr. Rawlings. You can reach me at my parent's home by phone, Montcross-344. I look forward to hearing from you."

Jimmy and his dad shook hands with Mr. Rawlings and left the hotel to return home for supper. Jimmy was thankful that his father had accompanied him to the interview; especially when he had the confrontation with Mr. Cameron in the hotel lobby. As they were walking home, both were thinking about the threat that Mr. Cameron made, but as of yet, did not think it was something they needed to worry about.

• • • • • • • • • • • • • • • • • • • •

At two o'clock on Friday morning, Ray and the entire platoon was awakened by Sergeant Garrett yelling, "Fall out platoon 276. Khaki pants, sweat shirt, and pith helmets. Don't dawdle you mothers' little babies, get your butts in formation!"

Ray dressed quickly and limped to the ranks with the rest of his weary platoon and stood at rigid attention.

Then Sergeant Garrett bellowed, "Sea Bag DRILL, you morons!"

Ray rushed back to his bunk, dumped his seabag on the deck, stripped his bed, and stuffed his mattress into his sea bag. He hustled back outside into ranks, but his fate, due to his ankle, was that he was the last one out and back into ranks. Garrett then jumped in his face and yelled, "You pussywillow, how is it you are the last one out tonight? You know better than that! Now get your ass back inside and do it again! Don't make these other pantywaists wait too long!"

Ray, with the assistant drill instructor, Corporal Andrews, went back into the barracks, unloaded the mattress from his sea bag, and repacked his sea bag as quickly as he could so that the other trainees did not have to stand outside freezing more than was necessary. Ray finished repacking and rushed back into the ranks.[1]

Once again Sergeant Garrett berated him, "You stupid baby! You know better than to be last out in my sea bag drill! What's wrong with you, Johnson? You had enough of boot camp? You want to quit, boy?"

Ray yelled in reply, "Sir, No, SIR! It won't happen again!"

Sergeant Garrett and Corporal Andrews had the entire platoon run around the parade ground counting cadence and waking up the other sleeping platoons who were lucky enough not to be involved

---

1 • Phillips, Sidney, You'll Be Sor-ree!, p. 21

in this ritual of torture meant to try men's souls. Ray's ankle had been healing slowly, and this morning with no time to wrap it before the run, his ankle felt like it was going to fall off. Ray thought to himself, "I can make it, I will not quit. Our training will only last two more weeks and once it is completed, I will have a little time to allow it to heal."

The entire platoon finished the run and the DI yelled, "FALL OUT! Inspection in ten minutes!"

The trainees rushed back into the hut and quickly made their bunks in the prescribed Marine Corps manner which when properly done, allowed a quarter to bounce when dropped on the bunk. Ray quickly made his bunk and was standing at rigid attention at the head of his bunk when the sergeant came to inspect. His bed failed inspection because the quarter only bounced a half inch.

Sergeant Garrett yelled, "Johnson, you are bound and determined to screw up tonight! My quarter only bounced a half inch and on every other bunk my quarter bounced an inch! You are a moron and mama's boy who hasn't done anything right lately! What's your problem, BOY?"

Ray was getting angry, not because he fouled up his bunk because he knows it was made correctly, but because the DI had been singling him out lately for minor infractions and it seemed he was trying to make him quit.

Ray, not being a quitter, yelled at the DI, "I HAVE NO PROBLEM, SIR! I WILL GET IT RIGHT!"

Ray removed the coverings from his bunk and remade it. This time the quarter bounced the prescribed inch.

Sergeant Garrett, glaring at Ray, said, "HOW THE HELL DO YOU EXPECT TO BECOME A MARINE IF YOU CAN'T MAKE A SIMPLE BUNK? GET YOUR MAMA'S BOY HEAD OUT OF YOUR MAMA'S BOY ASS OR YOU WON'T LIVE TO BECOME A MARINE! IS THAT CLEAR?"

Ray replied, "SIR! YES, SIR!"

The sergeant then said, "Hit the sack! You lazy good for nothing babies better be on the ball in the morning!"

After the lights went back out, Ray laid on his bunk thinking, *What is wrong with me? I can do everything the DI wants with my eyes shut. Does he really want me to quit? Or is he just testing me? I think I will write Dad and ask his advice. He will know what is going on. Tomorrow I'm also asking the sergeant if I can go to the dispensary to have my ankle looked at again. I am sure he thinks I am faking this injury and I wish I was, it would not be as painful.* Ray said a quick prayer before falling back to sleep.

Unbeknownst to Ray, the real reason Sergeant Garrett was pushing him was that he saw that Ray would be the kind of leader the Corps needed during this war. Sergeant Garrett wanted him as prepared as he could be to lead a squad in what could be some very tough fighting against the Germans or Japanese.

PARRIS ISLAND MARINE DEPOT ~ PARRIS ISLAND, SOUTH CAROLINA
SATURDAY, JANUARY 17, 1942

Saturday, January 17, 1942, at four-thirty in the morning, found Ray marching in a close order drill with the rest of his training platoon on the beach of Parris Island. The morning was a frigid thirty-five degrees and the sweatshirt and khaki pants were barely enough to keep them warm, but Ray knew this close order drill was just a prelude to what the rest of the day would bring. Sergeant Garrett is drilling them with his cadence and the platoon was working like a well oiled machine until he bellowed, "Left Face!" Someone deep in the ranks turned to the right and Sergeant Garret caught them. Immediately the culprit was summoned front and center.

Sergeant Garrett got into the face of the offender and yelled, "YOU ARE AN IDIOT! STAND HERE, SHOUT LEFT FACE, AND TURN IN A CIRCLE UNTIL I TELL YOU TO STOP! IS THAT CLEAR?"

The offender shouted, "SIR. YES, SIR!" The offender commenced to do left faces while the rest of the platoon was drilled around so that they could watch the poor guy shout, "LEFT FACE!" and turn in circles.

232

The punishment seemed to last forever and then some guy in the ranks was caught snickering at the offender. The DI blasts him into the circle of left faces with the order to shout, "I AM AN IDIOT!" on every turn. For fifteen minutes while the rest of the company looked on, the two offenders turned circles. Finally the DI called a halt to the punishment. By this time, the two have turned circles to the point they were up to their knees in a hole in the sand. Sergeant Garrett ordered the two offenders to fill in the holes and return to ranks. This punishment only needed to be repeated a few times before everyone made sure they were doing exactly what the sergeant ordered.[2]

Close order drill ended when the platoon reached the mess hall at six-thirty for breakfast. Once again, it was a breakfast of SOS with coffee. The more Ray had to eat this nasty concoction, the more he realized how much he missed Elva's wonderful meals and how easy her meals were on a man's intestines. Ray longed for his mother's and Elva's cooking but knew that was just a pipe dream as he was still imprisoned in boot camp with no sign of release. The platoon did more marching and close order drill until about noon when mail call occurred.

In today's call, Ray received five letters from his family and Sara. The rule was that any amount of mail over three pieces required the recipient to run through the dreaded belt line. Ray knew what was next when the sergeant yelled, "Johnson, five pieces of mail that smell just lovely."

Ray rushed quickly out of ranks to pick up the five pieces from the deck because the sergeant threw each piece up in the air after he called the recipient's name. With mail call completed, there were three trainees including Ray preparing to run through the painful punishment. The other recruits lined up in two lines with their belts and they were prepared to inflict punishment on the three offenders. Ray drew first position and led the parade by sprinting through the line as quickly as he could on his bad ankle to limit the damage from the belts. Every offender of the mail limit ran through the line and the platoon was dismissed for a little downtime.

---

2 • Phillips, Sidney; You'll Be Sor-Ree; p. 18;

Jimmy's Struggle

Ray's mail consisted of two letters from Sara and three from his family. He chose to read Sara's letters first and saved the letters from his family until later.

Monday, January 12, 1942

Dearest Ray,

How are you doing? I hope your ankle is healing and that you are doing all right. What is the training like? You have not told me what is happening with you other than your ankle injury since you have been in training. I want to share what you are going through. Can you please give some insight in what is happening with you.

My professors and house mother have asked about you and I have told them that you seem to be doing well. I have gone to church the past two Sundays at the First Baptist and I had lunch with the Redifers yesterday. They asked me to send their regards and let you know that you are on the soldier prayer list.

I miss you and school is a lot harder now that I do not have the opportunity to talk to you every day. It is really hard not knowing what is happening other than the letters which seem fewer and farther between from you. Is that because you do not love me any more or because the training is that tough? Why have you stopped writing?

I love you and I miss you.

Your sweetheart,

Sara

Ray knew after reading the second letter that he really needed to write Sara a letter that told her more about what he was going through so that she could understand the toughness of the training. He could see that Sara was feeling that he did not love her any more which was the furthest thing from the truth and he would work to quell that thought in his next letter to her. The letters from his family dealt with what was going on in Montcross and who had left to join the fight. Lillie's letter was a picture of him in his uniform with an American flag telling him how proud she was of him.

Before Ray could start writing his letters, Sergeant Garrett came in and ordered the platoon to fall out for more training.

MONTCROSS COURTHOUSE ~ MONTCROSS, NORTH CAROLINA
WEDNESDAY, JANUARY 21, 1942 - 9:00AM

• •

Jimmy and Raymond made their way downtown to the courthouse for the inquest into the accident. Raymond knew that today would be tough for Jimmy since he would have to repeat his eyewitness account for the members of Civilian Aeronautics Authority accident committee. The committee had been convened to review the facts of the accident.

Jimmy asked, "Dad, what is going to happen in this inquiry? Are they truly going to take all testimony into account without bias?"

Raymond replied, "I certainly hope that the committee will take everything into account before rendering its verdict on the cause of the accident."

They entered the courthouse and were greeted by Joe Rosen who was being called to testify to the facts of Tom Cameron's flying record. During the past few CPTP classes, Mr. Rosen had reiterated to the entire class to take the time to attend the accident hearings to see how the process worked. Waiting inside the courthouse lobby was Ernest Rawlings, the accident investigator, who would present the evidence and call the witnesses during the hearing. Mr. Rawlings knew that this was going to be a tough case because Thomas Cameron had already said that he would do his best to dissuade the members from believing the testimony of Jimmy and Joe Rosen. Since Jimmy had the blow up with Mr. Cameron at the hospital, Mr. Cameron had sworn to get even and disprove his testimony to the committee.

Promptly at nine o'clock, the committee convened the hearing with the statement from the chairman, "This hearing is convened to determine the cause of the January 10, 1942 accident that took the life of Mr. Frederick Mayerhofer and critically injured Thomas Cameron, Jr. This committee will hear all testimony in this case without bias. This committee will not condone any disturbances and are authorized by the laws of the United States to hold witnesses in contempt for perjury. This inquest will now come to order. Mr. Rawlings call your first witness."

Mr. Rawlings said, "James Andrew Johnson, please come forward."

Jimmy walked up to take the witness stand. Before he got to where the clerk was standing to administer the oath, Thomas Cameron, Sr. stood and yelled at the committee, "Jimmy Johnson is a liar and you should not even hear his testimony in this inquest. I will prove what I am saying beyond all doubt."

The committee chairman replied, "Order in the courtroom." Then asked "Who are you, sir? Why do you doubt the fealty of this young man's testimony even before it is heard? Step forward and approach the committee."

Mr. Cameron approached the committee, saying, "I am Thomas Cameron, Senior and this young man is a known liar. When Mr. Mayerhofer died at the hospital, Mr. James Johnson told me the most horrendous lie about my son and his flying ability. Mr. James Johnson told me that Mr. Joe Rosen could corroborate his story and I have asked Mr. Joe Rosen about what Mr. James Johnson said to me that night in the hospital. Mr. Joe Rosen refused, insisting that his testimony about my son's flying ability would be heard in front of this committee. Those two have conspired to protect that kike, Fred Mayerhofer, at the expense of my son and his possible flying career. I hope your committee will refuse their testimony because I am sure it is nothing but lies concocted to protect the dead Jew."

The chairman replied, "Mr. Cameron, in this hearing, you are out of order to use that language which is slanderous and will not be tolerated. Clerk, I ask that you add this note to the transcript, *Mr. Cameron states that Mr. James Johnson and Mr. Joe Rosen have conspired to commit perjury in this hearing. We will verify the fealty of this argument during cross-examination of these two witnesses.* Mr. Cameron, this committee will not tolerate another outburst from you and will eject you from these proceedings if you cannot give these hearings the deference they deserve. Am I understood?"

Mr. Cameron said, "You are understood, but I will not stand by and watch my son get railroaded by these two known liars and collaborators. Am I understood?"

The Chairman responded, "Then, at this point, you will be asked to leave. I will not have you disrupting these proceedings any further. Bailiff, escort Mr. Cameron from the court room please."

Mr. Cameron is escorted out by Officer Campbell of the Montcross Police Department, but not before Mr. Cameron says, "You have not heard the last of this, Mr. Chairman, I will be back with a court order that will require the redaction of their testimony from the record of these proceedings."

The chairman asked, "Judge Albright are you able to convene a hearing right now to determine the fealty of this gentleman's complaint so that this eyewitness testimony can be heard without the question of perjury hanging over these proceedings?"

Judge Albright stood and said, "At this point Mr. Chairman, I do not need to hold a hearing to vouch for the honesty and integrity of Mr. James Johnson. I will vouch that Mr. Johnson's testimony will be nothing but the truth. Will my personal guarantee of Mr. James Johnson's integrity suffice to continue the proceedings?"

The chairman responded, "Judge Albright, that is good enough for me. Mr. James Johnson, please take the stand. Clerk, please administer the oath."

The clerk said, "Mr. James Johnson, place your right hand on the Bible and lift your left hand. Repeat after me, I, James Andrew Johnson, do swear to tell the truth, the whole truth, and nothing but the truth, so help me God."

Jimmy repeated the oath then took the stand. Mr. Rawlings asked him for his account of the accident as he witnessed it on that Saturday morning. Jimmy repeated verbatim the witness testimony he provided Mr. Rawlings in the interview and continued his testimony about the issue with Mr. Thomas Cameron, Sr. as well. He gave his testimony without embellishment. He was then cross-examined by the committee to verify the veracity of his testimony and the entire committee was satisfied that Jimmy gave the facts without any speculation as to the actual cause of the accident. They commended him for his forthright testimony and he was released to return to his seat.

Once back to his seat, Raymond whispered to his son, "Jimmy, I am proud of you today. You did not let Mr. Cameron's outburst fluster you and you told the truth without any speculation. I am pretty sure we have not heard the last of Mr. Cameron."

"Thanks, Dad," Jimmy whispered.

The chairman had Mr. Rawlings call his next witness and that witness was one of the men who helped Jimmy get Mr. Mayerhofer and Tom Cameron out of the airplane. His testimony, while from a different perspective, was fairly close to Jimmy's eyewitness testimony and helped corroborate even further the veracity of Jimmy's testimony. Several more witnesses testified, based on their vantage points around the airport, that the airplane did indeed seem slow, pitched up suddenly, and spun into the ground exactly as Jimmy's testimony stated.

The next to last witness called for the hearing was Mr. Joe Rosen and his testimony was deemed critical to understanding the flight instructor's role in any accident as well as to testify to the critical phases of the landing procedure.

Mr. Rawlings asked, "Mr. Rosen, are you acquainted with the student pilot, Mr. Thomas Cameron, Jr., involved in the accident on January 10, 1942?"

Mr. Rosen replied, "Yes, Sir. Mr. Thomas Cameron, Jr. was a student of mine until I told him that since he would not listen to my instruction, then I could no longer give him flight instruction. In my opinion, Mr. Cameron is a dangerous pilot because he thinks he already knows everything there is about flying since he has been flying with his father for many years. Mr. Cameron, Sr. is a pilot and has supposedly instructed him that he is a natural pilot and does not need to listen to instructors who are charged with training pilots, because they do not teach anything other than what is in the manuals. Flight instructors are a burden to endure according to both father and son, and we cannot teach natural pilots anything."

Mr. Rawlings asked, "What do you think caused the accident in question after hearing all the eyewitness testimony?"

Mr. Rosen responded, "The cause of the accident is a classic approach stall-spin. Mr. James Johnson described the accident to me in minute detail during one CPTP ground school class; I was able to determine that the pilot in command allowed the airplane's speed to degrade too much and the pilot in command made an uncoordinated turn to final which caused the wing to stall before the rest of the airplane which resulted in a spin. A spin that close to the ground always results in a crash with the catastrophic results that were witnessed on that Saturday."

Mr. Rawlings asked, "The committee requests that you comment on the statement made my Mr. James Johnson that Mr. Fred Mayerhofer wanted to cancel Mr. Thomas Cameron's flight instruction as well. Is this true?"

Mr. Rosen responded, "I cannot comment on the conversation that was overheard by Mr. Johnson, but I can comment on a conversation that I had with Mr. Fred Mayerhofer on Thursday, January 8, 1942. I spoke to Mr. Mayerhofer prior to our CPTP Ground School class to see how his students were doing because we usually exchanged training tips based on the needs of our students. Mr. Mayerhofer asked me specifically about Mr. Thomas Cameron because he had allowed Mr. Cameron to talk him into continuing his lessons even though Mr. Mayerhofer felt the student was dangerous. The question he asked was, *how can I keep this student from killing himself? He insists on flying his approaches low and slow which leaves little margin for error and I do not want to be the cause of him hurting or killing himself or someone else.* I told him that if he was not comfortable flying with this student then it was his duty to wash him out of flight training or send him to another instructor. Mr. Mayerhofer told me that he was giving Mr. Thomas Cameron another chance the Saturday of the accident, and we are here today discussing the outcome of that lesson. I washed him out myself, and he found Mr. Mayerhofer would help him continue flying. That was a mistake made by a man willing to give someone second and third chances because he had been given a second chance when he immigrated to the United States and was welcomed with open arms into this community."

Mr. Rawlings said, "Thank you, Mr. Rosen. You may step down."

This was damning testimony from a flight instructor and it was clear that it was the truth. In Mr. Fred Mayerhofer's student logs for Thomas Cameron, Jr. there were many notations attesting to the lack of listening to instruction and unwillingness to change his bad habits which could get someone injured or killed if they were flying with this individual pilot. Those logs were also entered into the evidence of the committee's hearing.

Mr. Rawlings called the final witness, saying, "Mr. Thomas Cameron, Junior, please take the stand."

Tom Cameron, in a wheelchair still recovering from his injuries, was pushed to the witness stand by his mother since his father was no longer allowed in the courtroom. Tom took the oath and promptly tried to discount the testimony of Mr. Rosen with the claim that he was not there to witness the accident so how could he know what happened that day.

Mr. Rawlings asked, "Mr. Cameron, can you tell us who was in command of the airplane on the accident approach?"

Tom replied, "I was in command until the airplane started to stall and then Mr. Fred Mayerhofer yelled, *MY AIRPLANE*; then Mr. Mayerhofer took control of the airplane in an attempt to recover from the stall by applying power which caused the engine to quit. The next thing I remember is waking up in the ambulance on the way to the hospital."

Mr. Rawlings asked, "Why would an airplane engine quit when you apply power?"

Tom replied, "I don't know why an engine quits when power is applied because that does not happen normally."

Mr. Rawlings handed Tom a landing checklist for a Piper J-3 Cub and asked him to read it. Tom stalled on the very first item which stated, "Push Carburetor Heat ON prior throttling back for glide or for any other flight maneuver."

Mr. Rawlings asked, "Can you tell us if you pushed the carburetor heat on?"

Tom replied, "I do not remember."

Mr. Rawlings replied, "I can tell you based on the pictures from the panel after the accident that the carburetor heat was off which would cause the carburetor to build up ice and when power is applied to the engine again, the engine will quit almost every time due to this phenomenon."

Tom exclaimed, "Someone must have tampered with the controls! I would bet Jimmy Johnson pulled the carburetor heat off in order to protect Mr. Mayerhofer in this inquiry."

Mr. Rawlings stated coolly, "Mr. Cameron, these pictures were taken about five minutes after the accident by the newspapers and in all of those pictures the carburetor heat was in the off position. Mr. Johnson was too busy trying to save you and Mr. Mayerhofer to worry about tampering with the accident scene."

Tom protested some more that this was all a conspiracy to prevent him from ever getting the coveted pilot's license. Every argument he put forth was quickly dispelled by the preponderance of evidence and he was dismissed to return to his seat.

Mr. Rawlings rested his case at three-thirty in the afternoon and the committee recessed to deliberate. Jimmy and his dad walked to drug store for a coke and a pack of crackers while they awaited the verdict of the committee. At four-thirty, Mr. Rawlings sent messengers to find all the witnesses and have them return to the courthouse because the committee had come to a conclusion and was about to render its findings. Jimmy and his dad found their seats in the courtroom and awaited the reappearance of the committee.

The committee filed into the courtroom and took their seats at the table with the chairman stating, "This inquest is now called to order. We, the Civilian Aeronautics Authority Accident Committee, find that the student pilot, Mr. Thomas Cameron Junior, was grossly negligent in his approach to landing by not applying carburetor heat as required by the Piper J-3 Cub Manual. Mr. Thomas Cameron Junior was also grossly negligent in not maintaining a proper approach speed for his turn from base to final which contributed to the airplane's stall and crash. We, the committee, do hereby revoke the student flying privileges of Mr. Thomas Cameron, Junior. Mr. Fred Mayerhofer is not without blame in this accident because he should have noticed that the carburetor heat was not in the proper position, but it is the committee's finding that the student was preparing for solo and therefore given greater latitude as it pertained to control of the airplane. On Saturday, January 24, 1942, Montcross Airport can resume CPTP flying lessons. These proceedings are now closed."

Jimmy turned to his dad and said, "I am glad that the committee did not find that Mr. Mayerhofer was negligent except for the fact that he did not check the carb heat. Making sure the carburetor heat is on could easily be missed when an airplane is that low and slow with the possibility of an imminent stall. I do hate that Tom has lost his opportunity to continue his flight training although I think that is for the best."

His dad replied, "Be prepared, Jimmy. Your life just became very difficult because Tom's dad will not let this verdict rest and will do everything in his power to make your life miserable. I will tell you now that you should walk softly anytime you happen to come into contact with the Camerons. Understand?"

Jimmy replied, "Yes, Sir. I will not do anything escalate any confrontations with the Camerons."

Jimmy and Raymond left the courtroom and walked to their car to go back home. Jimmy could now put this ordeal behind him with a clean slate to decide whether he wanted to continue his flying lessons.

MONTCROSS AIRPORT ~ MONTCROSS, NORTH CAROLINA
SATURDAY, JANUARY 31, 1942
. . . .

A week and a half after the inquest concluded in favor of Mr. Mayerhofer, Jimmy decided that he wanted to continue his flying lessons and talked with Mr. Rosen after his Thursday CPTP class to schedule his first lesson for today at the Montcross Airport. Jimmy's lesson started at ten o'clock this morning and he was not going to be late. He pulled out of the driveway at nine-fifteen to leave for the airport in order to be there in time to prepare for his lesson.

At the airport, he found Mr. Rosen in the airport office preparing for his lesson. This situation had been just as hard on Mr. Rosen as it had been on Jimmy because both men knew Mr. Mayerhofer very well and thought highly of the quiet man from Germany.

Jimmy knocked on the office door and Mr. Rosen looked up from his log books, saying, "Hello, Jimmy. Are you ready for your lesson?"

Jimmy replied, "Yes, Sir, Mr. Rosen. I have to be honest though, I am a little apprehensive about this lesson since I have not been in an airplane since Mr. Mayerhofer died. Frankly, Mr. Rosen, I'm scared because I do not know if I will remain calm in the face of an emergency in the air."

Mr. Rosen replied, "Jimmy, I am glad to hear you say that because I would think you would be somewhat scared and apprehensive after seeing a good friend die in an airplane crash. From your studies and the questions you ask in class, I know that you have a good head on your shoulders which will make you a good and safe pilot. Unlike Tom Cameron, you are not brash and cocky which allows you to accept instruction and apply it."

"Thanks, Mr. Rosen. I am ready for my lesson now if you are."

"Let's go get our parachutes and get started. Do you have your logbook?"

"Yes, sir. Here it is."

He handed his logbook to Mr. Rosen and the two men walked out to the hangar where the parachutes were stored. The two men donned their parachutes in preparation for the lesson. They walked to the J-3 Cub and both did a pre-flight inspection of the airplane to make sure there were not any visible issues with the airplane. Once satisfied that the airplane had passed the pre-flight inspection, both men climbed into the cockpit with Jimmy taking the front seat and Mr. Rosen in the backseat. The new Gosport helmets and talking tubes made communication between the flight instructor and student a lot easier with the engine running. Truett pulled the propeller through to start the airplane engine and Mr. Rosen allowed the engine to warm up for about five minutes before checking the magnetos and gauges at 2100 rpm. With the engine check complete, Mr. Rosen had Jimmy taxi the airplane to the end of the runway using just enough throttle to get the airplane moving. Mr. Rosen kept his feet lightly on the rudder pedals just in case Jimmy had a problem and he needed to make a correction to prevent a ground loop or other taxiing accident. With the airplane positioned at the end of the runway, Mr. Rosen instructed Jimmy through the Gosport tube to loosen his grip on the stick and keep his feet loosely on the pedals and follow him through the takeoff procedure so that he could get a feel for what happens during takeoff. Mr. Rosen pushed the throttle forward until the engine's tachometer read 2300 rpm then he released the brakes to start the takeoff roll. At thirty miles per hour, Jimmy felt Mr. Rosen push slightly forward on the stick which brought the tailwheel off of the ground and Mr. Rosen started using the rudder to keep the airplane on the center line of the runway. At forty-five miles per hour, Mr. Rosen put a little back pressure on the stick and the airplane lifted off of the runway and started to climb.

Jimmy continued to follow Mr. Rosen's movements with his hands and feet and this really helped him get a feel for the airplane controls. At 4500 feet, Mr. Rosen reduced power and leveled off for cruising flight.

Mr. Rosen, through the Gosport, said, "Jimmy, I want you to give me a coordinated standard rate turn to the left until the compass has turned 180 degrees. Your airplane."

Jimmy replied, "Yes, Sir, my airplane."

He started the left turn by banking the airplane fifteen degrees to the left and used the rudder to center the ball in the turn and bank indicator. He constantly scanned the instruments to make sure that he was neither climbing or descending along with keeping the turn coordinated to the left. After a turn of 170 degrees, Jimmy started leveling the wings until the airplane was flying at exactly the 180-degree opposite course from where he started. For the first time, Jimmy felt like he was beginning to handle the airplane and maintain control without being nervous in the cockpit. Mr. Rosen instructed Jimmy to make a right turn for 180 degrees and come out on their original heading. Jimmy accomplished this as well and his confidence level soared.

Mr. Rosen said, "Now we are going to practice stalls and stall recovery. My airplane."

Jimmy replied, "Your airplane."

Mr. Rosen again instructed Jimmy to follow the movements of the stick and rudder in order to get a feel for a stall. Mr. Rosen pushed the carburetor heat to the on position and reduced engine power while gently pulling back on the stick until the wings started shaking which was an obvious sign of impending stall. The airplane abruptly nosed over and Mr. Rosen applied power until the airplane had regained enough speed to fly normally. He pulled the carburetor heat into the off position before instructing Jimmy to repeat the process of stalling and recovering the airplane.

Mr. Rosen said, "Your airplane."

Jimmy replied, "My airplane."

Careful to keep the airplane properly configured, Jimmy repeated the process that Mr. Rosen demonstrated and completed several stalls and recoveries while gaining confidence with each successful recovery. With the lesson coming to an end, Mr. Rosen had him use his basic pilotage skills to fly the airplane back to the airport and descend to the traffic pattern altitude where Mr. Rosen took over and landed the airplane. After parking and shutting the airplane down, they replaced their parachutes in the hangar and returned to the airport office to debrief.

Mr. Rosen said, "Your lesson today was one of the best of my group of students who have less than five hours of flight time. You made sure to scan all the instruments and keep everything in focus inside and outside of the cockpit. I want to commend you on a great job in your first lesson with me. You followed my instructions to the letter and you made sure to keep the airplane balanced which is one of the keys to safe flying. Any questions?"

"Thank you, Mr. Rosen. For some reason, I felt comfortable in the airplane today which made all the difference in the world. I have been studying my manual and my cardboard instrument panel since the time of the accident even though I did not know for sure whether I would continue with the lessons. I believe firmly that your instruction in the ground school and the work I have been doing on my own has really helped me take a big step forward in my flight training. I do not have any questions today, but I am sure by Monday's class I will have a few. Thank you again for taking me on as a student."

"You are welcome; keep up the good work. I will see you Monday and Thursday for ground school and Saturday at ten o'clock for your lesson."

Jimmy excused himself and walked to his car feeling confident that he had made a huge leap forward with his flying and vowed to continue to work towards attaining his pilot's license.

Ray's Assignment

* * * * * * * * * * * * * * * * * * * *

Ray had progressed through the various stages of boot camp while enduring the nagging injury to his ankle which he injured during the second week of training. He had been in rifle training for the last two weeks and had taken the training very seriously because he knew he would need the proficiency he was gaining in order to survive in combat. Today was the last of Marine rifle training in boot camp and tomorrow the entire training platoon would shoot for qualification. Ray was hopeful that he would shoot "Expert" in order to qualify for the additional five dollars in monthly pay which would make his pay, twenty-six dollars a month.

Throughout the entire six-week process, Sergeant Garrett had been pushing Ray harder than most of the other men in the training platoon and Ray could not figure out why. He knew that he had not done anything to get on the DI's bad side and he had worked hard to maintain the work load even with his injury so that he was not a burden on his fellow recruits. So when Sergeant Garrett jumped him after bayonet drill for a seemingly slight infraction, Ray took it with a grain of salt and did his penance of cleaning the barracks head with a toothbrush wondering the entire time, "Why is Sergeant Garrett still trying to break me?" Unbeknownst to him, Sergeant Garrett had seen the his leadership ability shine through in every exercise and had been pushing him harder than the rest of the men so that he would be prepared for the inevitability of combat.

Sergeant Garrett mustered the men out to the drill field to do more close order drill on Friday morning before marching everyone in the platoon to the rifle range for qualification. The day was a balmy 69 degrees, with clear skies and hardly any wind, when Ray and his training platoon went to the rifle range to qualify for their respective marksmanship badges. To be an expert marksman required shooting a score of 305 or more out of a possible 330 with the Marine issue 1903 Springfield rifle. Ray's squad was lined up on the firing line to shoot for score just after an altercation between a boot and the firing line officer. The boot was a new recruit firing a rifle for the first time in his life; he had inadvertently pointed the loaded rifle at another boot. The sergeant on the firing line immediately and forcefully rectified the situation by seizing the rifle and letting the boot know in no uncertain terms how stupid and careless he had been with his weapon.

With the firing line clear, Ray took his position to fire for qualification. Qualification consisted of firing sixty-six shots at target distances of 200, 300, and 500 yards. Fifty six shots would be rapid fire while ten would slow and steady. Ray fired steadily until he completed the qualification. The sergeant of the line read everyone's score and to Ray's astonishment, he shot a respectable 308 points which qualified him as a Marine Expert Marksman. About half of Ray's training squad was able to score expert rifleman which which would be a big boost to their wallets and their pride. Those who failed to qualify would not be allowed to graduate from boot camp tomorrow, Saturday, February 7, 1942, exactly two months after the bombing of Pearl Harbor, Hawaii.

While waiting for the rest of the training platoon to finish their qualifications, Ray took the time to clean and oil his rifle in order to prepare it for the inevitable inspection. The entire platoon marched back to the Quonset hut barracks in a route march and were ordered to fall out in five minutes in PT training gear for a three mile qualification run. Ray made the run with the rest of his squad within the allotted time. Again in route step, the platoon marched to the mess hall where they were once again served SOS and coffee. Ray was tired of the Marine fare and wished he could taste some of Elva's meatloaf or fried chicken. As he was eating his creamed chipped beef on toast, Ray tried to imagine that he was eating Elva's fried chicken. This thought of home cooking helped him stomach the vile concoction that every Marine felt certain had been dreamed up by some masochistic general to test the gastric capacities of the average soldier.

Saturday morning at two-thirty, there was one last sea bag drill which resulted in everyone being on time and Ray even making it out ahead of a quarter of the platoon. The last person out still had to repack his sea bag and return to the rest of the platoon already in ranks. Completed, everyone was allowed to sleep until reveille. Sergeant Garrett called an inspection just fifteen minutes after everyone was rousted out of bed. The entire platoon passed without a negative mark or negative reaction from the sergeant. The training platoon was told to pack their sea bags and all their gear because they would not be coming back to the barracks after graduation this morning. Ray packed his sea bag with all of his gear and shuffled outside to stand at attention for the march to the mess hall and then to the unknown. He had survived and thrived in boot camp and when the anchor and globe were pinned on his chest, he knew he was now a Marine and could not have been happier.

After the graduation ceremony, Sergeant Garrett pulled him aside and said, "Ray, I know you are probably wondering why I was harder on you than the rest of these lousy boots. Well, here's the dope, you have leadership potential that will make most generals green with envy. It ain't because you're brash or cocky, but it's that quiet manner in which you push everyone in your squad to succeed. Also, you help them succeed by putting the right people in the right position. Don't let what I said go to your head and good luck. I will be following your career with watchful eyes. Do nothing to let your buddies or the Corps down. Is that understood, Private?"

Ray replied, "Yes, Sir. Thank you, Sir. I will do my best to make you proud of the Marine you molded."

He received his assignment to the New River Marine Base, but it said nothing of the unit or division. One thing was sure though, he was one step closer to combat.

NEW RIVER MARINE BASE ~ JACKSONVILLE, NORTH CAROLINA
FEBRUARY 8, 1942

• • • • • • • • • • • • • • • • • • • •

After graduation from boot camp, Ray and the rest of his training platoon boarded a train at Yemassee Junction, South Carolina for the short ride to the New River Marine Base in Jacksonville, North Carolina. He was extremely happy that he had completed boot camp and might have time to let his ankle to heal. He knew that he was getting that much closer to going to war, and he was nervous, but pleased, that he was able to push through the tough training from Sergeant Garrett and succeed.

The train pulled in to Jacksonville after dark and the new Marines were loaded into trucks for the short ride to the base. Once on the base, each Marine was sent into a Quonset hut to speak to a corporal for assignment. Ray was assigned to the First Marine Division which made him proud. He had been assigned to the same Marine division of his father. He was assigned to G company, 2nd Battalion, 1st Marine Regiment and was directed to the company headquarters. At the company headquarters, he was assigned to the 2nd Platoon and reported to Sergeant Dick Hoggren for his bunk assignment. He found his hut and grabbed a bunk as other members of the 2nd platoon started filing into the building. He looked around to see if any members of his training platoon from Parris Island had been assigned to his active duty platoon, but he did not find a single person he knew from boot camp. With some permanence with his platoon, he would start building the new relationships that would shape not only his time in the Marine Corps but would affect the rest of his life. The first fellow he met was Private Lawson Jeffrey from Ringgold, Georgia.

As Private Jeffrey deposited his sea bag on the bunk next to his, Ray stuck out his hand and said, "Hello, I'm Private Raymond Johnson of Montcross, North Carolina."

Lawson shook Ray's hand, replying, "Hello, I'm Private Lawson Jeffrey of Ringgold, Georgia. Is it all right to take this bunk?"

Ray answered, "We are the first two here and I was told by Sergeant Hoggren to pick out my bunk. Did he not tell you the same thing when you were assigned?"

"Sergeant Hoggren told me to pick any bunk that has not been taken. It looks like this bunk is not taken so I will claim it." Private Jeffrey replied.

Ray replied, "Sounds good. Do you have any idea what type of platoon we are?"

Lawson replied, "Scuttlebutt has it that we are a rifle platoon."

"That makes sense because I earned my Expert Rifleman badge. What badge did you earn in qualification?" Ray replied.

Lawson said, "I earned the Expert Rifleman badge as well. I will bet if we take a poll of the others in our platoon that most will be either expert or sharpshooter because they want the best marksmen together in a platoon."

"I will agree with that assessment and I think we can look forward to being the first on the beaches we assault."

Lawson agreed with Ray and they both went about making their bunks in the prescribed Marine manner just in case there was a surprise inspection. More new assignees arrived in the hut until all thirty bunks were taken. The late arrivals were all assigned to the next hut until the platoon reached its full strength of sixty members. Once everyone had checked into their assigned bunk area, Sergeant Hoggren had the entire platoon march to the mess hall for supper. The supper tonight was bologna sandwiches and boiled potatoes with coffee to drink. Ray enjoyed the meal and was able to get to know more of the members of his platoon. He chatted with a few members of his platoon and found that about three-quarters of the platoon came from the southern states of Alabama, Mississippi, and Georgia. There are only three other North Carolinians and one was his bus mate from six weeks ago, Private George Mason.

Ray greeted George, saying, "Hello, George, I see you survived boot camp. Looks like we will be in the same platoon."

George replied while shaking Ray's hand, "It was touch and go a couple of times and I was not sure if I was going to make it through basic, but I remembered what you told me to do, 'Remain calm and believe that I could make it through.' I ended up shooting the best score in my training platoon at Parris Island during qualifications last week. Made Expert Rifleman and got the five-dollar a month raise in pay for it."

Ray looked at George, saying, "George, my advice may have helped but you still had to have the wherewithal to persevere. Thank you for the compliment. Congratulations on shooting expert, I got lucky and qualified expert too."

George replied, "I hope I am assigned to your squad when the platoon leader and platoon sergeant make those decisions."

Ray thought about that and said,"That would be good but I just hope that the squad to which we are assigned gels quickly and becomes a solid unit."

George agreed and they both finished eating. The platoon was given the rest of the evening to settle into the huts and prepare for the specialized training which would start tomorrow. Ray took the time to drop a postcard to his family and Sara to let them know his new address at New River. Lights were out at ten-thirty and Ray promptly fell into his rack. He was asleep in less than twenty minutes knowing that this place could be like Parris Island with their specialized training starting anytime between now and dawn.

NEW RIVER MARINE BASE ~ JACKSONVILLE, NORTH CAROLINA
FRIDAY, MARCH 27, 1942

• •

After a month and a half of intense training, Ray and his entire Second platoon were given seventy-two hour passes that would start at six o'clock this evening and would run through Tuesday at six o'clock in the morning. He knew that he would go to Montcross first to visit his parents, and then he would try to get to Raleigh to visit Sara, too. The first order of business on this Friday was to complete their training exercises which were beach landings from landing crafts at the south end of Onslow Beach at the mouth of the New River.

This morning they boarded the landing craft and trained diligently on beach assaults from those landing crafts. Ray's rifle squad seemed to be the first to come ashore and today was no different. The squad's objective, beyond not getting sick in the tossing landing craft, was to secure a piece of high ground on the south end of Onslow Beach that was held by a sister platoon. Ray's landing craft chugged out of the New River inlet into the ocean and circled for what seemed like forever to the men trapped on board. Many of the men on board had never been out in the ocean, let alone one that was this rough, and about half the group became seasick and green. One young Marine vomited on the windward side of the craft and sprayed half the platoon which led to a chorus of shouts, "Hey, buddy, use your damn helmet." That episode popped the cork on the others and pretty soon everyone except a few of the stronger stomached souls were following suit. Ray calmly placed his face in the wind and watched with Sergeant Hoggren as the landing craft made its way to the 'hostile' shore.

Sergeant Hoggren, looking around at his charges, bellowed, "Get your asses ready! No more clowning! One minute to the beach, hit it like you mean it!"

The landing craft ground ashore and Ray and the rest of the squad piled over the side of the landing craft as the noise from blank cartridges and the smell of cordite filled the air. Ray was over the side first with his 1903 Springfield and the sixty pound water-cooled machine gun tripod. In the best shape of his life, Ray sprinted to his assigned location with his thirty caliber machine gun squad; and in less than three minutes the squad had their position set up and in action. Shooting a belt of thirty caliber blank ammunition at a platoon of the "enemy" and attempting to take the strong point, the rest of the platoon out flanked the enemy and were preparing to close the noose when someone accidentally popped a live grenade in the middle of the assault force. Ray saw immediately what was happening and shouted, "LIVE GRENADE! SCATTER!", which was barely heard over the cacophony of the sea, mock battle sounds, and overall disorder. Marines scattered in every direction and luckily no one was injured as the grenade exploded harmlessly on a sand dune that ten seconds before held about eight marines. The platoon leader, Lieutenant Mercer, called a halt to the training exercise to make sure no one was injured and find out who threw the live grenade.

Lieutenant Mercer, steaming that someone would foul up his exercise, yelled, "PRIVATE JOHNSON, FRONT AND CENTER!"

Ray said, "Private Johnson reporting as ordered, Sir."

Lieutenant Mercer said, "Good job, Johnson! Glad you noticed that it was a live grenade. Did you see who threw it?"

Ray responded, "Yes, sir, it came from the squad that was protecting the enemy strong point. I did not get the fellow's name since as soon as he threw it, he took off running down the beach."

Lieutenant Mercer then said, "Private Johnson, you are dismissed. Rejoin your squad."

"Sir, yes, Sir."

Lieutenant Mercer asked, "Anyone injured, Sergeant Hoggren?"

Sergeant Hoggren replied, "No, Sir. Thanks to Johnson's quick thinking and shout."

"That's certainly good news. PLATOON, we were all briefed that only dummy grenades were being used for this exercise. Please check your grenades and if you find a live one, bring it here on the double."

The entire platoon checked their grenades and found that all of them were dummies. Lieutenant Mercer, seeing his platoon was properly outfitted with dummy grenades, dismissed everyone except Ray.

At the command post, Second Lieutenant Mercer reported to Captain Hargrave, "Captain Hargrave, I need to report an incident in our training area, Sir."

Captain Hargrave replied, "Lieutenant, I have heard of no incidents this morning! What incident are you reporting?"

Mercer responded, "One of third platoon's men threw a live grenade amongst our attacking force when everyone in our platoon had been issued dummies, Sir."

Captain Hargrave asked, "Did you witness the incident, Lieutenant?"

"No, Sir. Private Johnson witnessed it, sir."

Captain Hargrave noticed Ray standing at rigid attention just outside the door and said, "Private Johnson, front and center."

Ray walked in, snapped a salute to the captain, came to attention, and replied, "Private Johnson, reporting as ordered, Sir."

Captain Hargrave ordered, "At ease, Private. I would like to know how you saw a live grenade amongst all the dummy grenades being thrown this morning."

Ray replied, "In this exercise, my job was to protect my squad and platoon mates once our machine gun squad had the gun set up. I watched the action unfold and saw our platoon climbing the dune and saw from my position a defender throw a grenade at that dune. Sir, when we pull the pin, all our dummy grenades show green smoke for our platoon or red smoke for the opposing platoon. This grenade showed gray smoke, then immediately went out. I yelled to my squad and platoon, 'Live Grenade. Scatter.' Luckily everyone heard that warning and no one was injured."

"Private Johnson, are you always that observant? That was a helluva job this morning. Do you know who the perpetrator was?" Captain Hargrave replied.

"My job is to protect my buddies and that is all I was doing." Ray answered, "I do not know the perpetrator by name but I will recognize him on sight. He ran away down the beach once he threw the grenade."

Captain Hargrave replied, "Thank you, Private. We will come get you when we find the perpetrator of this almost disastrous act. You are dismissed."

"Thank you, Sir."

Ray came to attention, snapped another salute to the captain, and walked out the door to wait in the orderly area of the beach command post.

Captain Hargrave said, "Lieutenant, I think you need to make that young man a squad leader and promote him. Don't you agree?"

Mercer replied, "Yes, Sir. When he got here, I heard that he made it through boot camp on a bum ankle that he sprained the second week of training. According to Sergeant Garrett, the Private did not complain, did not shirk his duties, and he excelled at the training, while enduring all attempts to break him down and wash him out. He ended up leading his squad at boot camp and kept them going even during the toughest training. It is all in his personnel file. I gave him a break to allow his ankle to heal before pushing him myself to see what kind of Marine he would make. He has proven his DI's comments correct on every turn. He is a real leader, Sir."

"I will pull that young man's file when we get back to base to see for myself and then await your paperwork for his promotion to Private First Class."

Sergeant Hoggren and the rest of the platoon with third platoon's help went on a search for the man who threw the live grenade during the exercise. The platoons found the young man cowering in a sand dune trying to be as inconspicuous as possible. Sergeant Hoggren of second platoon and Sergeant Smathers of third platoon dragged the man out by his feet and began to beat the man up. Lieutenant Mercer and Ray were returning when they saw what was happening to the guy. Lieutenant Mercer jumped in and broke up the beating.

Mercer shouted, "Sergeants, stop that right now! Atten-Hut!"

Sergeant Hoggren, hearing his lieutenant and knowing beating up a soldier was strictly against regulation, stopped immediately and came to rigid attention. Sergeant Smathers of third platoon held on to the prisoner but stopped the beating as well.

In Sergeant Hoggren's face, Lieutenant Mercer yelled, "Sergeant, what the hell are you doing?"

"Beating the hell out of the idiot who tried to kill half our platoon, Sir."

"Johnson, front and center!" Lieutenant Mercer yelled.

"Private Johnson, reporting as ordered, Sir."

"Take a good look at that private," the lieutenant asked, "did he throw the live grenade?"

"Yes, Sir. He threw the live grenade this morning."

Dismissing Ray, the lieutenant yelled, "Sergeant Smathers, where the hell is your platoon leader?"

"Walking down the beach now, Sir." Sergeant Smathers replied, "I sent a runner to find him before we searched for my idiot grenade thrower."

Lieutenant Grantham strode up to the gathering and asked, "What the hell is going on, Sergeant Smathers?"

"Private numb nuts here threw a live grenade during the exercise, Sir."

Lt. Grantham said, "Lieutenant Mercer, is it true that this private threw a live grenade in the exercise?"

"Yes, Lieutenant Grantham, he threw a live grenade and without the fast thinking of Private Johnson, twelve to fifteen of my men would be casualties right now." Lieutenant Mercer responded while glaring at the private.

Lieutenant Grantham said, "Private Renton, front and center!"

Private Renton walked slowly to face the lieutenant, knowing that his punishment would be swift and severe, said, "Private Renton, reporting as ordered, Sir."

Lieutenant Grantham yelled, "What the hell were you doing with a live grenade? I know damn well none were issued for this exercise!"

Private Renton responded, "Sir, those guys are a bunch of babies if they don't know a joke when they see it. There was no charge in the grenade except what it took to light it off."

Lieutenant Grantham yelled, "WHY DID YOU THROW A LIVE GRENADE, PRIVATE?"

"It was a joke, Sir!" Private Renton lamely replied.

Lieutenant Grantham lost his temper and yelled, "PRIVATE, there is no such thing as a joke with weapons! So, why the hell did you do it?"

Private Renton replied, "Sir, I stand by my answer. It was a joke!"

Lieutenant Grantham lost his cool completely and seethed the words, "PRIVATE, LET'S GO LOOK AT YOUR JOKE!"

Both platoons were marched back up the beach to the point of the assault and the dune that took the entire force of the grenade going off. The blast zone of the grenade showed plainly in the area and there was a hole in the ground where the grenade exploded. Both lieutenants knew beyond a shadow of doubt that the grenade was not disarmed from the look of the ground and the shrapnel path where the dune grass had been blasted away. The platoons were brought to attention for review.

Lieutenant Grantham said, "Private Renton, your seventy-hour pass is revoked! From the looks of this ground, your grenade was 100% live and could have killed and wounded a lot of men. Private Johnson saved your ass! He saw what you did and yelled in time to save his platoon! Sergeant Smathers and Private Anderson, take Private Renton into custody! We will turn him over to the MP's for trial by court martial. Hopefully we will find out what his real motive was here."

Sergeant Smathers and Private Anderson took Private Renton into custody and marched him back to the landing craft. The group boarded it for the trip back to the base. The two platoons gathered their gear and loaded back into their respective landing craft. The boats churned off the beach and turned for the long ride back through the rough inlet and the relative safety of New River. Once back at the dock and unloaded, the platoons boarded their respective trucks for the trip back to the base.

———

Back on base, Lieutenant Mercer had Sergeant Hoggren summon Ray to company headquarters. He found Ray at chow and told him that he was needed immediately at company headquarters. They walked to the company headquarters building where the sergeant entered the lieutenant's office. The sergeant left Ray standing in the orderly room.

Sergeant Hoggren announced, "Private Johnson is here as ordered, Sir."

Lieutenant Mercer replied, "Send him in, Sergeant Hoggren."

The sergeant summoned Ray into the lieutenant's office.

The lieutenant said, "Private Johnson, your observation skills saved a lot of good Marines today. I want to commend you on a job well done."

Ray replied, "Thank you, Sir."

"Private, you will need to sign the witness affidavit being prepared by the company commander before you can leave the base. You will also need to be present for the court martial of Private Renton. Is that clear?"

"Sir, yes, Sir!"

"Private Johnson as of now you have been promoted one grade for your action today. You are now a private first class and you have been assigned as squad leader of your thirty caliber water-cooled machine gun squad."

Ray, a little perplexed at his good fortune because he was just doing his duty as he saw it, said, "Thank you, Sir."

Lieutenant Mercer asked, "Private Johnson, I have read your personnel file and saw that you had a tough time in boot camp because of your ankle, but you persevered and gained the admiration of your DI. Why did you join the Corps?"

Ray, wondering where this line of questioning was going, stated bluntly, "I joined the Corps because my Father fought in the First Division in the Great War. I wanted to fight this war with the best, Sir."

Lieutenant Mercer astonished, said, "Private, you are well on the way to making the Corps proud. Keep up the good work."

"Thank you, Sir. I will continue to do my best, Sir."

The lieutenant dismissed Ray with the admonition to get his new rank insignia sewn on his uniform before reporting back at four o'clock to sign the affidavit. Ray picked up his PFC insignia and walked back to his barracks to sew it on his uniform. At four o'clock that afternoon, Ray reported back to the company headquarters and signed the witness affidavit for the case against Private Renton. Completing that, Ray ate dinner and prepared to leave the base for his first seventy-two hour pass.

At six o'clock, Ray left the New River Marine Base in his khaki uniform to hitchhike to Wilmington where he planned to catch the late bus to Charlotte. Ray made it to Wilmington in time to catch the eight o'clock bus to Charlotte. He sent a wire to his parents to let them know he had a pass and would arrive in Charlotte at four o'clock in the morning.

JOHNSON FAMILY HOME ~ MONTCROSS, NORTH CAROLINA
FRIDAY, MARCH 27, 1942

The Western Union delivery boy walked up the front walk to the front door of the Johnson home and rang the doorbell. Raymond and Bessie answered the door and seeing the Western

Union delivery boy, both inadvertently gasped because they knew that this was how families were notified of a problem by the War Department. They both knew this young man and from his expression, they realized that this was not bad news.

Raymond said, "Hello, Ronnie, what do you have for us tonight?"

Ronnie replied, "I have a telegram from Ray in Wilmington."

Raymond took the telegram and gave him a dime to thank him for his delivery service. Raymond and Bessie were both wondering why Ray sent a telegram from Wilmington. Raymond opened the envelope and read the telegram that stated,

Mom and Dad,

Catching the bus in Wilmington. Have a seventy-two hour pass. Will be in Charlotte at four in the morning. Can stay until Sunday. Want to see Sara in Raleigh.

Love, Ray.

Raymond handed Bessie the telegram, saying, "Our son is coming home on a seventy-two hour pass, but will only stay until Sunday morning because he wants to see Sara in Raleigh, too."

Bessie read the telegram and said, "I think we need to invite Sara here instead. I want to pay for her bus ticket. What do you think?"

Raymond replied, "Give her a call and see if she will catch the bus in the morning or later tonight if there is one. Tell her we will pay for her ticket."

Bessie stepped into the study, picked up the phone, and made the call to Meredith College. After a short wait, Bessie is finally connected to Sara.

Sara said, "Hello, Mrs. Johnson."

"Hello, Sara, I have some good news for you. Ray is on his way to Montcross on a seventy-two hour pass and we would like to buy you a bus ticket to join us this weekend. Ray sent us a telegram that said he would leave Sunday to visit you. We would like you to visit us. Would you join us this weekend?"

Sara, flabbergasted and excited by the offer, said, "That would be wonderful! Can I leave tonight if there is a bus available?"

"Ray's bus arrives at four tomorrow morning in Charlotte and if there is a bus that leaves tonight, we will be happy to pick you up when you arrive."

"Thanks, Mrs. Johnson! I will call the bus station and ask what buses are available tonight or tomorrow. Can I call you back after I find out which bus I am taking?"

"You are welcome, Sara. Call us back with your bus information and we will take care of paying for it for you."

They both said goodbye and hung up. Sara immediately called her parents to let them know what she was going to do this weekend. Her parents were just as excited as she was that Ray's parents invited her to visit while Ray was home. She told her parents that she loved them and moved on to finding a bus to Charlotte. She called the bus station and found out that the last bus to Charlotte tonight would leave at nine o'clock with a five o'clock arrival tomorrow morning. She would have to hurry to make that bus.

After the operator connected the call, Sara said, "Mrs. Johnson, the last bus tonight leaves at nine o'clock and arrives in Charlotte at five o'clock. The ticket costs five dollars; is that all right?"

"That's wonderful, Sara! We will go to the bus station and pay for your ticket from here."

Bessie summoned Raymond into the study and sent him to the bus station to pay for Sara's ticket for tonight.

She said, "We will not tell Ray that you are coming in on the five o'clock bus so that it can be a surprise. How does that sound?"

Sara replied, "Sounds wonderful, Mrs. Johnson! I am going to pack so that I can make the nine o'clock to Charlotte. See you tomorrow! Thank YOU!"

"You are welcome and we cannot wait for you to get here! Goodbye, Sara."

"Goodbye, Mrs. Johnson."

Sara rushed up to her dorm room and packed quickly for the trip to Montcross. She made sure to include a dress for church on Sunday. Carrying her bag down to the reception area, she let her house mother know that she would not be back until Monday evening and would miss a couple of classes. Her house mother was happy that she had the chance to visit with Ray and would let Sara's professors know that she would be absent. The house mother called the taxi for Sara and she was delivered at the bus station at eight forty-five. She walked to the ticket counter; where the clerk asked if he could help her.

Sara says, "Yes, Sir, I have a ticket to Charlotte waiting on me. My name is Sara Peabody."

The clerk looked through his reservation cards and found Sara's reservation, saying, "Here is your ticket to Charlotte on the nine o'clock bus tonight. Five dollars, please."

Sara was surprised and said, "It should be prepaid by Raymond Johnson. Can you check on that?"

The clerk looked at the ticket closely and saw that it has been prepaid and apologized, saying, "I am sorry, Miss Peabody. The ticket has been paid for by Raymond Johnson. Have a good trip."

Sara replied, "Thank you, Sir."

Sara rushed to board the bus and once she was seated in the half-full bus, she allowed her emotions to flow. She would be seeing Ray for the first time since Christmas and she was overwhelmed that Ray's parents would buy her ticket to make sure she had the opportunity to visit with him. The bus pulled out of the Raleigh station, and after twenty minutes, Sara closed her eyes to try to sleep.

CHARLOTTE BUS STATION ~ CHARLOTTE, NORTH CAROLINA
SATURDAY, MARCH 28, 1942

The bus from Wilmington limped into the Charlotte Bus Terminal at four forty-five after enduring a series of breakdowns. Ray disembarked to see his dad waiting for him at another bus. He grabbed his sea bag and started walking towards him when he noticed his father talking to a beautiful young lady. Her face was obscured from view until he rounded the end of the bus and recognized Sara.

As he approached them, he yelled just loud enough for them to hear, "Hello, Dad! Hello, Sara!"

Both looked in the direction from which their names were called, they see a young man approaching in a khaki Marine uniform with private first class stripes. They instantly recognized him and Sara took two bounding steps into Ray's arms. Gently, he lifted her off the ground in a hug and kissed her with a passion she felt down in her soul. She involuntarily blushed. Ray had not been one for public displays of affection, but in an instant, Sara knew he was happy that she was here to meet him. He put her down and walked over to his father.

He shook his dad's hand, saying, "Hello, Dad! Wow! I am happy to be home!"

Raymond looked his son over approvingly, "Hello, Ray! Glad to have you home!"

"Dad, how did Sara get here before I did? I thought I would have to make the trip to Raleigh as I told you in my telegram." Ray asked, a little puzzled.

"You can thank your Mother. Once she read your telegram, she called Sara and invited her to spend the weekend here so that you could have a little more time together."

Overwhelmed by his mother's thoughtfulness, he said, "I will have to thank her when we get home. That was a wonderful gesture."

Still holding Sara's hand, he looked into her eyes and said, "Hello, Sara. I have missed you terribly and it is wonderful to see you!"

Sara returned his gaze and saw his love for her shining in his eyes, then said, "Hello, Ray. I love you and I have missed you terribly these past few months."

"Let's go home."

Ray picked up her suitcase and lithely slung his sea bag onto his shoulder as the three of them walked to the car. He put his sea bag and Sara's suitcase into the trunk and they drove back to Montcross.

Raymond pulled the car into the driveway at the corner of Main and Todd Street and Ray was briefly overcome by the joy of being home again. The only lights in the house were in the kitchen and on the back porch. Raymond parked the car in the garage and Ray retrieved the bags from the trunk. The three walked on to the back porch and into the house where Bessie was waiting to greet her oldest son. She appraised her son as he walked through the door and saw that he was twenty pounds lighter but had a hardness about him that told her that he had seen a lot in the last four months even though he had not yet been in combat.

She hugged him, saying, "Welcome home, Ray. Glad you are here."

He gave his mom a kiss on the cheek and said, "Mom, I am glad to be home. I have missed you and the family."

"You're looking a little thin. Does Marine food not agree with you?" His mother asked.

Winking at his dad, he replied, "Now that you mention it, I have not had anything to eat since supper. I have been waiting for one of yours or Elva's fine meals. Dad can tell you all about SOS and the other fine delicacies they feed you in the Corps. Anyone else awake yet this morning?"

A little perplexed over the term SOS but not willing to be embarrassed in front of Sara, Bessie replied, "I will let your father tell me about SOS and those fine delicacies. None of the children are up yet which will give us time for some conversation in the kitchen."

"Wonderful, Mom, and thanks for having Sara here waiting on me when I arrived this morning! That was a great surprise. I will get my chores done and be back inside shortly. Sara, would you like to help me?" Ray replied.

Before Sara could reply, Bessie, not to be put out, said, "Ray, you are welcome. Sara is like a daughter to us and it will give you more time to visit instead of riding on the bus. As for your chores, you will do no such thing! Jimmy can take care of them when he gets up."

Ray knew better than to argue with his mother but he was thinking that doing his chores would be an easy way to get Sara alone for a little while. He replied, "I do not mind doing the chores, Mom. It will do me some good to get back on the ball after being away. Besides I might eat more eggs than you have stored in the icebox for breakfast."

Bessie, seeing through Ray's ploy, replied, "Go ahead and do your chores but do not take too long. I will have the coffee ready when you and Sara get back."

———

Ray grabbed the milk can outside the kitchen door while Sara grabbed the egg basket and they walked hand in hand to the chicken house and cow shed to take care of the chores. Once out of sight of the kitchen and safely in the cow shed, Ray took Sara into his arms and kissed her deeply.

Sara returned the kiss breathlessly, saying, "I love you. I have longed for this moment since we parted in December."

Ray, breathless, replied, "I love you too. I've missed you more than you realize. When I saw you this morning at the bus station, I was happier than I have been in months."

They continued breathlessly kissing and the passion almost overwhelmed them.

Sara gently reminded Ray, "I think we need to milk Gertrude and gather the eggs before your mother sends out a search party."

He laughed uncontrollably and said, "You are right. I think we might need to do that before we get in trouble."

She gathered the eggs and he milked Gertrude, and they walked back to the kitchen for coffee. The couple walked in the kitchen door and saw that none of the children were awake yet. This gave Ray, Sara, and his parents time to talk.

———

Ray said, "It is good to be home even if it is only for a little while. Dad, what has been going on in town lately?"

"Ray, the big thing has been the inquest into the airplane crash of Mr. Mayerhofer and the student pilot. The inquest found the student pilot at fault based on the log notes of both the late Fred Mayerhofer and Joe Rosen. The inquest completed its inquiry about six weeks ago and Mr. Thomas Cameron, the boy's father, has tried to prevent Jimmy from getting his pilot's license. The crash was hard on Jimmy for a while."

Ray responded, "I know about the crash, Jimmy wrote me about it in one of his letters in January. I also know that he has started flying again and should be getting pretty close to soloing. Do you know how close he is?"

His dad replied, "I think he is very close and it might happen either today or next Saturday. Your Mom and I have supported him during this time and once the Civil Aeronautics Authority allowed lessons to resume at the Montcross Airport, it took a lot for him to get back in the airplane with another instructor."

"Well, if he solos today, I think I want to be there to see it. I am proud of all he has accomplished during what has to have been a tough situation to say the least."

His Dad, anxious about Ray's bootcamp and training experiences, asked, "Tell us about you. You come home twenty pounds lighter and looking like a block of granite. Seems like someone else has changed tremendously, too."

Ray, with ultimate understatement, replied, "It is just Marine Corps boot camp and training. I think you went through it in 1917. Nothing much to tell."

"I know what boot camp was like back in seventeen, but surely you are not using the same Springfield rifles and equipment we used. Have the DI's softened their approaches to breaking down recruits into a sniveling mass until they put them back together on the rifle range? Tell us about everything."

Ray said, "You know all about my introduction to boot camp and the issuance of my uniform. We still use the 1903 Springfield rifle and the Doughboy helmets of the Great War. Boot camp was tough Dad; especially after I sprained my ankle running the obstacle course. The post doctor gave me the choice of continuing with my training platoon or waiting for the next one to allow my ankle time to heal. I chose to stay with my platoon even though it took my ankle the rest of boot camp to heal. I will say it was tough and there were times I began to wonder why I chose to become a Marine. I have to say the food is not all that great but the friends I am making really help with my morale."

"When did you get promoted? I see you are now a Private First Class and not just a plain old buck private like I was during my service."

"I was promoted yesterday after an incident during a landing exercise. My machine gun squad was tasked with protecting our beach assault force and everyone was supposed to be using dummy ordnance. Our attacking platoon was charging up a dune when I saw one of the defenders throw a live grenade. All I did was yell for everyone to scatter and luckily no one ended up a casualty. The platoon leader called me into his office after we returned to New River and promoted me. I still do not think that I did anything that deserved the promotion or the assignment as squad leader of a water-cooled machine gun squad."

Sara and Bessie, listening to exchange, are in awe of what Ray just told them. Neither one of them could understand the nonchalance with which he just told the story of his promotion.

Bessie said, "Ray, you just told a hair raising story without even batting an eye, were you scared at all?"

"Mom, after everything boot camp teaches you, I was nervous, yes, but the DIs do not allow scared as scared will get someone killed."

His dad sat in awe of his son who just three short months ago was a civilian and now possessed the skills of a Marine and the attitude of a Marine. What made his dad especially proud was to see that his son had bought into the attitude and molding of Marine Corps Boot Camp. He decided that he would try to sit down with Ray alone while he was home to get the details.

JOHNSON FAMILY HOME ~ MONTCROSS, NORTH CAROLINA

• • • • • • • • • • • • • • • • • • • •

While Raymond, Bessie, Ray, and Sara were talking around the breakfast table, Jimmy walked into the kitchen and saw, much to his surprise, Ray and Sara. His parents had not told him or the other children that Ray was coming home because they wanted it to be a surprise for them.

Jimmy exclaimed, "Ray! When did you get here? How long can you stay?"

Ray replied, "Arrived by bus from Wilmington about an hour and a half ago and I am staying until Monday. I did not know that Mom and Dad had set it up for Sara to come down from Raleigh once they got my telegram last night until I saw her talking to Dad at the bus station."

"That is great! I want to talk to you this afternoon after I get finished with my flying lesson. I might even solo today. I have a lot to tell you about everything that has happened since Mr. Mayerhofer's death in the training accident."

"Can Sara and I go with you to the airport and watch your lesson? I would love to see what you have been working on for the last three months. I am proud that you are continuing to follow your dream. How are your grades? Did you score high enough on the CPTP exam to get first choice of assignment like you wanted?"

"If you want to watch my lesson, you can have Dad bring you to the airport because I do not want the added pressure of knowing you are there. Is that all right?"

Raymond interjected, "I agree with you, Jimmy. I think that would be the best thing. We will make that decision after you leave."

"Thanks, Dad. To answer your question, Ray," Jimmy continued, "I finished at the top of my CPTP class and the only thing that might hold me back are my grades and attendance at Montcross High School. Right now, one other CPTP student has me beaten in that category, but I do not know how much they weight that criteria. I think I have a pretty good chance of getting the top spot, and I know I am doing everything I can to make it happen."

"That's just great, Jimmy. I am proud of you for working so hard and overcoming the crash and its aftermath to make it happen. I do have one more question. Why are you sleeping so late and not getting your chores done on time? I have been waiting for someone to gather the eggs and get the milk so that we can have breakfast."

Jimmy started sputtering, "What do you mean? I normally get up at seven thirty in the morning on weekends to do my chores. Mom and Dad do not seem to have a problem with that schedule. Why should you? You are not here anymore to do them."

Sara and Bessie could not help themselves and burst out laughing with Bessie saying, "Jimmy, Ray is pulling your leg. He did the chores about an hour ago. Look at the egg basket and the milk can. He knew he could give you some grief about it because he has already done them for you."

Jimmy, in mock anger, said, "Ray! How dare you do that to me? After all those times during Christmas that I let you sleep because of everything that was happening, you have the gaul to give me grief over the chores. Thanks, big brother. I love you too!"

Ray replied, "Jimmy, you've done a great job keeping everything together with all you had going on. I did not mind doing the chores this morning. Where are Elizabeth, Myra, and Lillie? I would think they would be up by now."

"Elizabeth should be here any minute. She was getting dressed as I was coming downstairs. Lillie and Myra were doing the same thing. They will be surprised when they get down here."

Elva arrived at eight o'clock and was as shocked as Jimmy had been to see Ray and Sara sitting at the kitchen table drinking coffee with Raymond, Bessie, and Jimmy.

She took one look at Ray in his Marine khaki uniform and was overcome, saying, "Ray! It is so good to sees you. How's life in the Marines? Boy, you sure look thin. They's not feedin' you enough?"

He stood up and gave Elva a big hug, saying, "Every day, they feed us the same food, Elva. They have powdered eggs, a meat called SPAM, and a dinner called SOS. It is definitely not your cooking."

"How long's you here Ray? I'll have to try to feed you good while you's here. What do you want for breakfast this morning?"

"I am here until Monday about noon. If it is not any bother, I would love to have scrambled eggs, French toast, and sausage."

"Will you do with bacon because we ran out of sausage and I did not think we needed any this week?" Elva replied.

"That will be just fine. Thank you, Elva"

Elva set to work fixing breakfast and was surprised to see that the eggs and milk had already been delivered to the kitchen.

She said, "Jimmy, you sure was up early this mawnin' to have the milk and eggs gathered already. Thank you."

Jimmy sheepishly replied, "I just got here, Elva. You can thank Ray for the early delivery."

"You sha'nt have made him do the chores, Jimmy. He just got here from being gone oer' three months." Elva scolded.

"Jimmy, did not make him at all. He did them because he wanted to help this morning. I told him he did not have to do them." Bessie said.

Elva replied, "Thanks, Ray! The eggs will do fine for makin' your French toast and scrambled eggs. Anything else I can makes you for breakfast?"

"No, Ma'am. I will be happy with your wonderful French toast, eggs, and bacon. Thank you."

Elizabeth entered the kitchen and was shocked by the presence of Ray and Sara. She wanted to know how long Ray had been home and when he had to leave to return to his base. The conversation followed Jimmy's conversation almost to the word that Ray had to leave on Monday and that he was happy to see her as well.

Elizabeth asked Sara, "Can we spend some time this evening talking? I have really missed you since your last visit."

"We should be able to spend some time later today while Ray talks to Jimmy and your Dad. It will be great to catch up with you, too."

Myra and Lillie came downstairs with Elizabeth and they patiently waited their turn to speak. Lillie was overcome with glee that Ray had made it home for a visit.

She said, "Why didn't you tell me you were coming home? I missed you."

Ray replied, "I missed you too, Lillie. I told Mom and Dad last night that I was coming home and they wanted it to be a surprise. Did it surprise you to see me here this morning?"

"Yes, Ray! Why haven't you written me? You promised."

"Lillie, I am sorry that I have not written you as much as I promised. I have been busy trying to learn everything I can about my new job in the Marines. It has been tough, but I promise that I will do better. Will you forgive me and come give me a big hug?"

Before he could complete the sentence, Lillie was bounding into Ray's arms to give him a big bear hug. She hugged him with all her little might and he gave her a kiss on the cheek. She was overcome and started crying because she was so happy to have him home.

Lillie, through her tears, said, "I forgive you. Will you have time to watch me ride my bike without training wheels? I have gotten good at not falling."

Ray, a little overcome himself, replied, "I would love to see you ride your bike without training wheels. You are certainly growing up fast."

Ray put Lillie down and before he could sit back down, Myra, not about to be left out, was leaping into his arms for a hug as well.

"Ray, you have not written me lately either. Do you not love me anymore?" Myra asked, brushing tears out of her eyes.

He said in his most soothing voice, "I still love you, Myra, but I had to make it through a rough patch with my training. Letter writing has not been my strongest thing lately. Sara, Mom, and Dad have not gotten letters lately either. It is not that I do not love all of you like always but the Marines do not give you much time for writing with all the work we have to do. Do you understand?"

Stifling a sob, she replied, "I do not understand; you should write us every day like you promised."

Bessie tried to come to Ray's rescue when she said, "Myra, Ray loves you very much and with everything he has to learn in the Marines to protect our country from Germany and Japan, he is not able to write like he promised. I am sure he will try to do better. Be happy that he is home until Monday; I am sure he will spend some time with you. He might even take you to lunch later today. Would you and Lillie like that?"

Sara looked at Ray, stifling a giggle, when Myra replied, "That would be WONDERFUL! Where are we going to eat, Ray?"

Stuck between a rock and a hard place by his mother, he said, "Before I left, I promised Lillie that I would take her to lunch at the Hotel Montcross when I came home. I believe we will go about one o'clock for lunch. Will that suit you, Myra?"

She replied, "Great! I hope Sara is going, too."

Sara said, "I would not miss it, Myra. We will have a wonderful time at lunch."

Elva was cooking breakfast while Bessie made the third pot of coffee. The three girls took their seats, and breakfast was a lively affair; everyone was excited about having Sara and Ray in the house even if it was only for two days. Ray loved the French toast and after all of the Marine Corps powdered meals, he ate five pieces of it, a heaping portion of scrambled eggs, and six slices of bacon. With Ray's ravenous appetite, Elva was worried that she would run out of something, but she was immensely happy to see Ray eating so much and knew that she would put some weight back on him over the next couple of days. Finishing breakfast, Ray excused himself to take his sea bag and Sara's suitcase to their rooms upstairs.

After he came back downstairs, Elizabeth said, "Dad is taking me to the draft board to work. I look forward to seeing you and Sara tonight. I am glad to have you home, Ray."

He replied, "I am glad to be home and I will see you later this afternoon."

Ray pulled Sara aside and apologized that they had not had much time together since arrival. He promised that they would take a long walk tonight to spend some time talking about everything that has happened since he left for boot camp in December. Sara was understanding and said that she looked forward to spending whatever time they had together this weekend.

MONTCROSS AIRPORT ~ MONTCROSS, NORTH CAROLINA
SATURDAY - 10:30AM
•••••••••••••••••••••

Jimmy arrived at ten-thirty for his flying lesson at eleven o'clock with Mr. Rosen. Since the end of the inquest and the resumption of lessons, Jimmy had made steady progress towards soloing. Walking into the office, Jimmy noticed that Mr. Cameron was there with his son, Tom. Neither one had anything nice to say to Jimmy because his testimony along with Mr. Rosen's completely grounded Tom from flying. In return, Mr. Cameron was doing everything in his power to cost Joe Rosen his flight instructor privileges and Jimmy his position in the CPTP. Nothing that Mr. Cameron had done gained any traction in the local community, or at the Civilian Aeronautics Authority in Washington because the documentation in Fred Mayerhofer's and Joe Rosen's logs was indisputable evidence that Tom Cameron's piloting was dangerous. Every time the Camerons saw Jimmy, there had been some confrontation instigated by Tom or his father, and today would be no different. Jimmy, knowing what would inevitably happen, walked on into the office to prepare for his lesson. As soon as he walked through the door to the airport office, the abuse started with Mr. Cameron taking the lead.

Mr. Cameron spit every word of hate at Jimmy he could muster, saying, "I see the airport authority still lets liars and Jew lovers onto the premises! What are you here for today, you kike lover? Surely you don't think you will ever gain your flying privileges especially if I have anything to say about it!"

Jimmy, not rising to the bait, ignored Mr. Cameron and spoke to Truett, saying, "Truett, how is everything today? Has Mr. Rosen been in yet?"

Mr. Cameron, who not only wanted the confrontation but needed it because he had lost all credibility in the community with his public hatred of Jimmy and Joe Rosen, said, "Surely, you don't think you are going to take a lesson today, Jimmy. I have an injunction signed by my good friend and the town attorney, Mr. H. R. Brighton, that says you are no longer allowed to take lessons at the Montcross Airport. You will never get your pilot's license now that your lies and slander have ruined any chance my son has of making it into the Army or Navy flying program."

Jimmy, in order to avoid this confrontation, walked back outside to the pay telephone to call his father at home to ask his advice. Mr. Cameron followed Jimmy outside and confronted him again before he could make the phone call. Truett, seeing what was happening, called the Johnson residence to speak to Raymond.

Bessie answered the phone, "Hello."

Truett asked, "Can I speak to Mr. Johnson, please? This is Truett at the Montcross Airport."

"What's wrong, Truett? Jimmy did not have an accident, did he?" Bessie pleaded.

Truett replied, "No, Ma'am. Jimmy has not even started his flying lesson yet. Mr. Cameron is here trying to pick a fight with Jimmy and every move Jimmy makes to get away from the situation, Mr. Cameron follows and tries to push Jimmy into a confrontation. This morning Mr. Cameron said he has an injunction from the town attorney preventing Jimmy from taking lessons here at the airport. Can you send Mr. Johnson to the airport to diffuse the situation? I do not want to have to call the Montcross Police, if I can help it."

"Yes, Truett, I will send him to the airport right now. Please, see what you can do to calm the situation."

"I will do what I can, but I am not allowed to leave the office. Thanks, Mrs. Johnson."

After hanging up the phone, Bessie yelled for Raymond to come to the study and told him about the situation at the airport involving Mr. Cameron and Jimmy. Ray, hearing the fear in her mother's voice, volunteered to go with his dad to the airport. Raymond agreed that it might be a good thing because his temper was not what it used to be with this situation. As he had told Jimmy, this situation was bad because in a father's eyes a son can do no wrong, and to try to avoid confrontation at all costs. Raymond, Ray, and Sara left the house quickly for the short drive to the airport.

Meanwhile, Mr. Cameron was trying to get Jimmy to say anything to him, but had failed at every turn, because Jimmy just wanted to fly today. Joe Rosen pulled into the parking lot of the airport and quickly ascertained the situation, Jimmy was backed into a corner of the building with Thomas Cameron glaring, shaking and yelling at him. Joe decided now was the time to bring this issue to a head because Jimmy had done nothing wrong and had tried numerous times to keep the peace. Joe also knew that any further confrontation might hurt Jimmy's opportunity to solo today because of the stress Thomas Cameron was heaping on this fine young man.

As Joe Rosen stepped out of his car, he saw Raymond Johnson pulling into the parking lot. He was thankful that he would have help to diffuse the situation between Jimmy and the Camerons.

Raymond, Ray, and Sara quickly ascertained the situation. Jimmy was backed against a wall by Thomas Cameron, who was verbally abusing and holding Jimmy by the shirt collar to prevent any further attempts by Jimmy to walk away. Ray jumped out of the car before his dad could stop him and in less than twenty-seconds, Ray had grabbed Thomas Cameron and was backing him away from his brother. Raymond was taken aback by how quickly his son reacted, but saw that he was not doing Thomas Cameron any harm. He rushed to prevent a further escalation of the situation.

Raymond yelled, "Ray! What are you doing?"

"I am stopping this piece of shit from causing Jimmy any more trouble."

Looking Thomas Cameron squarely in the eye with two steel blue daggers, Ray said, "What the hell is your problem? My understanding is Jimmy tried to walk away from your attempts at confrontation numerous times today; yet you continued to confront him like you are spoiling for a fight. If you want one, I will be happy to oblige."

Thomas Cameron realized immediately that he had bitten off more than he could chew from the Marine and blustered, "Who are you to tell me what I can and cannot do? That boy, that you are protecting is a kike lover and a liar! He prevented my son from fulfilling his dream of flying in the military with his testimony. I will ask for you to take your hands off of me, or I will call the police and report an assault."

Ray replied tersely, "Go ahead and call the police because I think they would be interested to know that you instigated this confrontation. I would love nothing more than for you to make that call."

Raymond and Joe finally made it to the two men and noticed that Thomas Cameron's face was ashen from his confrontation with the Marine in the sharp khaki uniform.

Raymond, hearing Thomas's threat and Ray's reply said, "Jimmy, I think we do need to call the police. Will you walk in and ask Truett to make that phone call? Ask him to also summon Mr.

Brighton to the airport so that we can get this situation cleared up immediately. You will need to file charges against Thomas Cameron for assault. I saw that he had your shirt collar and was shaking you when we arrived. Did you see that too, Joe? Sara?"

Jimmy, shaken from the confrontation, replied, "Yes, Sir. I will have Truett make the phone calls."

Joe replied, "Yes, Raymond, I saw what was happening before the Marine stepped in to break it up. Who is that Marine?"

Raymond replied with a touch of pride, "That Marine is my oldest son, Ray. He finished boot camp a little over a month ago and has been assigned to the First Marine Division at New River."

Sara said, "Mr. Johnson, I saw the assault as well and will testify to it."

Raymond replied, "Thanks, Sara. I think we have enough witnesses to make the charge stick."

Now that Jimmy and Thomas Cameron had been bodily separated by Ray, Joe Rosen asked, "Thomas, why must you continue this Quixotic behavior? You know that you cannot prevent Jimmy from taking his flying lessons nor can you prevent my instruction. It was proven in the evidentiary hearing after the inquest when you submitted your formal charges of perjury and defamation of character against Jimmy and myself that neither one of us did anything other than present the truth."

Thomas Cameron regaining some of his bluster and giving no regard to the witnesses involved, replied, "Joe, I WILL NOT REST UNTIL I SEE YOUR LICENSE REVOKED! You and Jimmy have no right to the normal flying career that you have stolen from my son, Tom. I have an injunction that says Jimmy can no longer take flying lessons at this airport and it was signed by H. R. Brighton. Both of you helped slander my son's good name, damaged his reputation, and stole his right to fly. YOU BOTH WILL PAY FOR THAT!"

Joe calmly stated, "Thomas, we did not steal your son's right to fly. We told the truth. Why is that so hard for you to understand?"

Tom, who had been inside since the start of the confrontation between his father and Jimmy, slowly propelled himself to the group on crutches that were a constant reminder of the accident that took the life of Fred Mayerhofer and had left him broken physically and mentally. Tom saw the entire confrontation and knew, also, that the accident was his fault. He had even tried to tell his father a couple of times, but each time he tried, his anger at his own situation boiled over and he continued to blame Jimmy, Joe Rosen, and Fred Mayerhofer for his predicament.

Maybe today, Tom thought, *I should tell my father so that healing can begin for everyone. It was my fault that Mr. Mayerhofer died and I have been left with these scars. I do not know that I will physically be able to complete the rigorous military training, anyway.*

Jimmy made his way inside and said to Truett, "My Dad and Joe believe that you should call the police and have them come down. There will charges of assault brought against Mr. Cameron. Also, if you do not mind, can you have Mr. Brighton come to the airport as well to discuss the injunction."

"The police are already on their way. I called them after I saw the fellow in the Marine uniform jump Mr. Cameron. Who is he?"

Jimmy with pride, replied, "That's my brother, Ray, who is home on leave from the Marines. He sure moves fast to change a situation, don't you agree?"

"He sure does. I am surprised he didn't hurt Mr. Cameron. What stopped him from plowing him under?"

"I believe the only thing on Ray's mind was stopping the argument, which he did, without much trouble. Can you call Mr. Brighton?"

"I will call him now, do you happen to know where he might be today?"

"I would just ask the Montcross operator to locate Mr. Brighton if he is not at his home or office. Thanks, Truett."

Jimmy walked back outside to join the others in the group then said, "Truett says the police should be here any minute and he is working to find Mr. Brighton and have him come clear this situation up. Do you think I still need to press charges, Dad?"

His dad replied firmly, "Yes, I believe that charges are the only thing that Mr. Cameron will understand. Thomas, I hope that these charges will bring you to your senses because Jimmy has done everything he can to keep this from escalating; yet you continue to press for his disqualification with lies and slanders of your own.

At this point, I will be filing the charge of slander on behalf of Mrs. Mayerhofer and her children because of your anti-Semitic comments towards her late husband."

Thomas Cameron saw that he had backed himself into a corner with his behavior and it could cost him greatly if he did not back down, but his pride and love for his son would not let him contemplate such a move. He continued to bluster at Raymond, Jimmy, and Joe because he was certain he could bluff his way out of this situation with the same bravado that usually put him over the top in his business dealings. Little did he know though, that these three men would not be cowed by his bullying behavior and that in the end, he would only hurt himself and his family.

With this bluff and bravado in mind, Thomas replied, "I will be happy to go to court and prove that your kike loving son and Joe Rosen were the ones who committed slander against Tom and my family. Your son will never fly and now I will write a letter to your other son's commanding officer to tell him how he disgraced the Marine uniform by assaulting me. Neither one of them will ever make it here because I will do everything in my power to block their opportunities like Jimmy did for my son."

Officer Campbell of the Montcross Police department arrived with another officer to figure out what was happening and to make any arrest that was necessary. Officer Campbell saw that even though no one looked injured there was a tenseness about this situation that might take some work diffusing.

Officer Campbell asked the group, "What is happening here? Everything all right?"

Trying to put the situation in a favorable light for himself, Thomas Cameron stated, "I was having a conversation with Jimmy Johnson there and his brother jumped me from behind because he did not like how I was speaking to Jimmy. I would like to press charges against Ray Johnson, Officer; he assaulted me."

Officer Campbell knew what the dispatcher said on the call and started to question Thomas, saying, "Mr. Cameron, are you sure that is how the situation played out?"

Thomas replied in mock contempt, "What do you mean, am I sure that is how the situation played out? I told you that's what happened and I don't tell lies like others here."

Officer Campbell then interviewed Truett who contradicted everything Thomas Cameron had said. This put the light of guilt back on Thomas Cameron with his unprovoked attack of Jimmy, which ended when Ray bodily separated the two. The other officer received corroborated witness testimony from Raymond, Ray, Sara, and Joe Rosen which made it pretty clear what happened. Completing the witness statements, Officer Campbell had no choice but to arrest Thomas Cameron on an assault charge. Ray had been exonerated on the grounds that he was only protecting his brother from the bullying assault of Mr. Cameron.

Officer Campbell said to Thomas, "With all of the corroborating evidence, I have no choice, Mr. Cameron. You are under arrest for assault and you will have to come with me."

"I WILL NOT! YOU MEAN TO TELL ME YOU WILL TAKE THE TESTIMONY OF KNOWN LIARS OVER MY OWN! YOU ARE NOTHING MORE THAN AN IDIOT.", Thomas replied making the situation for himself even worse as H. R. Brighton walked up in time to hear the tirade against one of the town's finest police officers.

"What is going on here, Officer Campbell?" Mr. Brighton asked.

Officer Campbell quickly summarized the witness testimony of everyone outside and the corroborating testimony of Truett Ransome, and had concluded that the arrest of Thomas Cameron was called for in this situation. The officer knowing that Mr. Brighton overheard the tirade from Mr. Cameron asked him what he should do about that as well. Mr. Brighton told Officer Campbell that he should take him to the police station in downtown Montcross and book him immediately on the assault charge and add the charge of resisting arrest.

When Thomas heard that he was going to be booked on assault and resisting arrest, he blew up at the town attorney, saying, "You are an idiot too, Harmon! You gave me my injunction against Jimmy Johnson, and now you are having me booked on a trumped up assault charge and resisting arrest. I will see that you pay for your stupidity, as well. I have friends in high places who will make it hot for you if you don't change your mind. Furthermore, you better keep that injunction in place if you ever want to work in this state after your term expires in November."

Harmon knew that this was all bluff and bluster because he was the one who actually instigated the confrontations here today and said, "Thomas, are you sure you want to threaten me like that. I can always add communicating threats to the ever increasing list of charges. You might do yourself a favor and go downtown with Officer Campbell. As for the injunction, I planned to come down here today to let Jimmy and Joe know that I was lifting it after I read all of the evidence from the case last night. Thomas, you really need to drop this obsession because it is only hurting Tom and your wife."

Thomas replied, "Harmon, this is not done. You will never get me to give up my cause of seeing Jimmy and Joe ruined in the flying profession like they ruined Tom's opportunity. Officer Campbell will have to make me leave with him."

Tom finally had enough and broke down, saying, "DAD! I was the one who caused the accident that killed Mr. Mayerhofer. My flying was dangerous, and like you, I would not listen to anyone when they told me I was wrong. PLEASE STOP EMBARRASSING MOM AND ME WITH YOUR BEHAVIOR! I can't stand how it has made me feel. We are wrong and I have no one to blame but myself. Go with Officer Campbell now and stop making things worse."

Thomas Cameron's face lost all color after his son finished and the look of defeat came over him as Officer Campbell led him away to the squad car. Tom Cameron followed behind on his crutches and told his dad that he would drive home to let his mom know what happened today. Thomas Cameron was loaded in the back seat and the squad car left to go downtown to the jail.

Once Thomas Cameron and his son Tom had left the airport, the group gathered in the large main office of the airport terminal to discuss what happened earlier and how they wanted to proceed today. Joe Rosen asked Harmon Brighton to join the conversation now that the truth had come out about the accident from Tom Cameron.

Joe Rosen said, "Harmon, what do you think now that Tom has told the truth about the accident?"

Harmon Brighton replied, "I think at this point in order to make sure Thomas Cameron does not pull any more stunts with Jimmy, we let him think about what he has done over the last two months. I think he needs to be reminded that he is not above the law. I do not think we need to prosecute Tom Cameron for causing the accident because the young man is going to have to live with the accident for the rest of his life. What do you think, Joe?"

"I agree on all counts Harmon. I think like you said, just let Thomas sit in jail until bail can be set and as far as Tom goes, I think he will have to live with the accident and that will be punishment enough. Raymond, do you agree with our assessments?" Joe asked.

Raymond, thought for a minute, replied, "I agree as long as we can insure that Thomas Cameron does not harass Jimmy about anything from now on. I also think that Tom will be punished enough by his conscience and he does not need to be put through any more trauma as a result of the accident."

Harmon said, "I will put our plan into action. Joe, did you and Jimmy have a lesson scheduled for today?"

Joe replied, "We did have a lesson scheduled for eleven, but I think we will wait until two or three this afternoon, if that is all right with Jimmy. I think we both need time to recuperate from the episode with Thomas. Jimmy, will that suit you?"

Jimmy, who thought about the consequences and determined that waiting on the lesson was the right thing to do, replied, "Yes, I think that will be good. Can we have my lesson at three today?"

"Yes, we can have your lesson at three o'clock and it should give us more time to work on some of the things we talked about last week. I will see you then and maybe you can relax for the next couple of hours and prepare for your lesson."

"Thanks, Mr. Rosen. I will see you at three."

Raymond said to Ray,"We need to go home so that you and Sara can take the girls to lunch at Hotel Montcross. I will stay with Jimmy at home to help him prepare for his lesson."

"Sure, Dad, I think that will be good.", Ray replied.

Raymond, Ray and Sara told Jimmy goodbye and made their way to the car. Jimmy spent just a little more time at the airport and then went home himself.

• • • • • • • • • • • • • • • • • • • •

On the drive from the Montcross Airport to the home at Main and Todd, Ray brooded about what he did today without thinking. He assessed the situation and acted based on that assessment.

"Dad, I just realized that I reacted to Jimmy's situation based on the quick assessment of what I saw. I am a little shocked by my behavior, but I did not want Jimmy to have to continue to endure that harassment. My reaction in my opinion was the correct one for the situation. What do you think?"

"Ray, I know one thing, I was scared when I saw you rush up behind Mr. Cameron and grab him around the neck, I thought you might kill him. Instead, you elegantly backed him away from Jimmy and diffused the situation with a stare that would have made any DI proud. May I ask, how did you know what to do?"

"Well, Dad, I have been present when two Marines have been fighting and I watched as Marine Military Policemen broke up the fight using the same hold that I did today. I knew I was not going to hurt him, I just wanted him to stop assaulting Jimmy. I think I made my point."

"You made your point and I saw the old DI stare down that you employed as well. It worked the same way in boot camp when the wayward soldier was quickly put back in line with the ashen face to prove it. The biggest thing I have a problem with was your language. You have never used that language in the past, I do not like you using it now."

"Dad, Sara, I apologize for my language. I have learned a whole new vocabulary of swear words and epithets while I have been in Corps. I seldom use any of them except in a situation like we had today. I promise it will not happen again. Dad, please do not tell Mom. She would wash my mouth out with soap and I've always hated that taste."

Raymond and Sara had a good laugh at Ray's comment about not liking the taste of soap and they both poked fun at him by telling him that they were going to tell his mother so that they could watch the soap ritual. He squirmed a little in the front seat, but thoroughly enjoyed the good natured banter after the stress of the last hour and a half. Raymond pulled the car into the driveway and parked it in the garage. Bessie saw the car pull into the driveway and rushed to find out what happened at the airport.

———

She asked, "Is Jimmy all right? Did he get to take his flying lesson? What happened?"

Raymond said, "Slow down, Bessie. Everything is fine with Jimmy. No, he did not take his lesson. Joe Rosen rescheduled it for three o'clock this afternoon to allow Jimmy some time to recuperate from the incident. Thomas Cameron was arrested for assaulting Jimmy but would not go downtown. He resisted every attempt to diffuse the situation until young Tom Cameron came clean that he caused the accident that killed Fred Mayerhofer and that confession quickly diffused the situation. Thomas Cameron left the airport in the police car looking a man who had lost everything. Jimmy and I will need to talk about dropping the assault charge, which according to Mr. H. R. Brighton would be fully prosecuted, with a guilty verdict virtually assured. You would have been proud of Ray to see how quickly he reacted to stop Thomas from assaulting Jimmy. Thomas Cameron's face turned ashen gray as Ray gave him the classic drill instructor stare down. The stare, which comes straight of the Marine DI handbook, has struck fear in the heart of many a Marine boot, including me."

Sara interjected, "Only thing is Mrs. Johnson, Ray needs a little soap treatment for some of the salty language he used during the little tete a-tete. Do you think I could watch when you administer the punishment?"

Bessie looked from Raymond to Ray and then to Sara not knowing whether to cry or to laugh, but now that she knew Jimmy was all right, said, "I am glad everything turned out all right for Jimmy. Now, Ray! How dare you use salty language? I will give Sara the bar of soap and let her administer the punishment."

Ray, now on the defensive, but knowing Sara interjected to change the mood of his mom, said, "I thought we had an agreement, Sara. Dad, help?"

His dad just shrugged his shoulders like he could not help him, not even to save him from the humiliation of the soap treatment, said, "Sorry, Ray, you are on your own. I cannot come between your

Mom, Sara, and you when it comes to salty language punishment. Although, I would like to hear some of the epithets later to see if they match what I heard in seventeen." He chuckled, knowing that Bessie would not find the humor in his last comment.

Bessie laughed and in mock frustration, said, "Well, Raymond, I think I will give you the soap treatment as well, since your mind is dirty for wanting hear Ray's new vocabulary to compare it to seventeen."

Sara looked on in glee, saying, "I will not ruin your lunch with the girls, Ray, but as soon as we get home, I will love giving you the soap treatment with Myra and Lillie helping me."

In feigned frustration, he replied, "Wonderful. I cannot wait for the wonderful ivory soap taste."

The group moved into the house so that he and Sara could get the girls and walk downtown for lunch. Bessie and Raymond went to the den to discuss everything that happened in more detail.

Raymond thought about his two sons and mused, *Ray left a young man who was kind and polite who I thought he might be too soft for the Corps, but he proved to me today that he has learned his training well and will be all right when it comes time to fight on the field of battle. I am truly proud of the man he has become and proud of the way he handled the situation with Thomas Cameron. Jimmy has been so fragile since the accident and he did everything in his power today to try to prevent the escalation that occurred. I hope he is able to solo today because that would complete his recovery from the accident and its aftermath. I am proud of how he handled the situation today. I will let both of them know that they did everything right today and that I am proud of them.*

Hotel Montcross ~ Montcross, North Carolina
Saturday - 1:15pm

•••••••••••••••••••••

Lillie was so excited to eat lunch with her big brother, Ray, and his girlfriend, Sara, that she practically skipped the entire walk and chattered like a jaybird with her equally excited sister, Myra. Holding hands, Ray and Sara were a little more leisurely in their pace so that they could have time a little time to talk before lunch. He knew that he would probably be inundated with questions about not only the Marines, but also the disturbance this morning at the airport. In small towns like Montcross, rumors and gossip spread faster than the truth on most days. Even though this would be the case, he was happy to be home and happy to have lunch with Sara and his two youngest sisters.

He said with a note of sarcasm, "Sara, are you really going to wash my mouth with soap? I think I am a little too old for that treatment."

Sara replied, "You know better than that, silly. I just had to help change your mother's mood. She was upset with what happened and the fact that she could do nothing about it. I thought that might be the best way to help get her mind off Jimmy. I think it worked, too."

Knowing she was right, Ray replied, "Thank you, Sara. I have missed you very much and I know that I have not shown it in my feeble attempts of writing. I want you to know that I am happy that you made the trip last night from Raleigh to see me while I am here. We better hurry just a little if we want to keep up with Myra and Lillie."

They picked up the pace to catch up with the girls who had just about made it to the new post office at the corner of Catawba Street and Main Street.

Ray said, "Myra and Lillie! Stop so that we can catch up."

The girls looked back and saw that Ray and Sara were a half-block behind them and they patiently waited on them at the corner. Ray and Sara caught up and the entire group held hands to walk the rest of the way to the Hotel Montcross. The four of them walked into the dining room and were immediately greeted by Mrs. Gullickson who welcomed them.

"Hello, Ray, welcome home. Are you here for lunch with these three lovely ladies?"

He replied, "Yes, Ma'am. These three lovely ladies are my lunch dates this afternoon. Thank you, and I am happy to be home."

She seated the four at a table by the front picture window where the girls could watch what was happening on Main Street. It was a special treat for Lillie and Myra to have lunch at the hotel and they were going to make the most of it.

Lillie asked, "May I have a Coke to drink as my special treat?"

Ray said, "I think that will be just fine, Lillie. Mrs. Gullickson, can you bring us all Coke to drink?"

Mrs. Gullickson replied, "Yes. Here are your menus. Today's special is country fried steak or two pork chops with two vegetables. I will be right back with your Cokes."

"Thank you, Mrs. Gullickson." Ray replied.

Myra read the menu and figured out that she wanted a grilled cheese sandwich and fried potatoes. Lillie, who has been learning to read this year in first grade, decided that she would like a hot dog with fried potatoes. They asked Ray if that would be all right and he told them that those were some good choices for lunch, today. He reminded them that if they ate everything on their plate, they would be allowed to have ice cream for dessert. He decided that he would have the country fried steak with mashed potatoes and gravy and green beans. Sara decided on the pork chops with rice and gravy and collard greens for lunch. When Mrs. Gullickson returned with their drinks, Ray placed everyone's order. She told them that their lunches would be out shortly and she hoped they enjoyed them.

Sara asked, "How is school this year, Myra?"

"It is wonderful! I have learned more math and I can do my multiplication tables now. Would you like to hear?"

"That's great! Yes, tell me what four times two is?"

"That's easy, eight! Twelve times twelve is one hundred forty-four." Myra gleefully replied.

"I am learning math, too!" Lillie interrupted, "Want to hear what five plus five is?"

Sara replied, "Sure do, Lillie! Did you learn to read this year, too?"

Lillie, excited now that she was once again the center of attention, replied, "Five plus five is TEN! I am learning to read but it is hard. So is writing."

Sara replied, "Reading is wonderful, Lillie; especially those letters from Ray. I saw you read the menu by yourself. What are you reading, Myra?"

Myra replied before Lillie could get started, "Mom bought me The Secret of the Old Clock which is a Nancy Drew book. It is very interesting."

Lillie blurted, "I am reading my <u>McGuffey Reader</u>, but Mom has to help me with the big words when I get stuck."

Sara replied, "Wonderful girls! I loved the Nancy Drew books growing up, too. They are wonderful adventures. Looks like our lunch is coming now. Let's get ready to eat."

After the food arrived, Ray asked Lillie to say the blessing before they start.

Everyone bowed their head around the small table as Lillie prayed, "God is great. God is good. Let us thank Him for our food. Thank you God for everything. Amen."

The only sounds that emanated from the table were those of eating. Myra enjoyed her grilled cheese sandwich and Lillie devoured her hot dog. Finishing all of their lunch, the girls were allowed to order ice cream for dessert. Lillie chose chocolate ice cream and Myra ordered vanilla ice cream. Sara and Ray just drank some coffee while the girls enjoyed their special treats. Ray was extremely happy to get to spend this time with Sara and his sisters. He paid the bill and left a tip, and as they were leaving, he thanked Mrs. Gullickson for a delicious lunch and was even more thankful that no one had interrupted their lunch to talk about what happened at the airport.

Jimmy Solos

Jimmy pulled the old Model-A back into the parking lot of the Montcross Airport with some apprehension due to what had occurred this morning. Jimmy walked into the airport office and saw Truett behind the counter and Mr. Rosen in his office.

Mr. Rosen saw Jimmy arrive and said, "Are you ready for your lesson, Jimmy? I hope you have put this morning behind you because things similar to that will happen in military flying and you will have to overcome them quickly."

Jimmy replied, "Yes, Sir. I am ready for my lesson. I sat down with Dad after what happened and he said that I handled that situation with Mr. Cameron pretty well since no one could reason with him. I have put the incident behind me and am moving forward. Let's get started."

Mr. Rosen replied, "I believe you are ready so let's go."

The two men walked into the hangar to get their parachutes and the hangar still held the remains of the crashed J-3 Cub which was in the process of being rebuilt and repaired. There was very little conversation between the two men as they donned their parachutes and helmets. Mr. Rosen checked that Jimmy's parachute was properly fitted and the straps were tight. Jimmy then verified the same for Mr. Rosen. This was part of the safety protocol of the CPTP and must be adhered to for every training flight along with the pre-flight checklist. Jimmy walked out to the J-3 Cub that they would fly this afternoon and completed a pre-flight safety inspection of the airplane. The two men verified that the plane was ready to fly. To prepare for his solo flight, Jimmy got into the back seat of the airplane and Mr. Rosen sat in the front because the J-3 was meant to be flown from the back seat in solo flight. Jimmy attached the Gosport tube to his helmet and Mr. Rosen did the same so they could communicate with one another without having to shout.

Mr. Rosen asked, "Pre-flight check complete?"

Jimmy replied, "Pre-flight complete. All items satisfactory. Preparing to start."

Mr. Rosen said, "Start the airplane."

Jimmy started the airplane with Truett pulling the prop. Jimmy allowed the engine to warm up for about five minutes before checking the magnetos and other pre-taxi items on the checklist. The run up was completed and Jimmy taxied the airplane to the end of the runway to prepare for takeoff.

Jimmy finished the rest of the pre-takeoff checklist, saying, "Ready for takeoff."

Mr. Rosen replied, "Looks good. Ready for takeoff. Go ahead and takeoff."

Jimmy smoothly pushed the throttle until the tachometer reached 2300 rpm and the J-3 started accelerating down the runway and at thirty miles per hour, Jimmy pushed slightly on the stick to get the tail wheel off the ground. As the plane achieved a speed of forty-five mile per hour, Jimmy pulled slightly on the stick and the airplane gently left the ground and started climbing.

Mr. Rosen said into the Gosport tube, "Before we practice takeoffs and landings, climb to 4500 and show me stalls and recoveries."

Jimmy replied, "Yes, Sir," and continued climbing the airplane at fifty-five miles per hour to the designated altitude.

Jimmy completed a series of stalling maneuvers always making sure that the wings were level and ball was centered to prevent a spin. Jimmy did a series of coordinated turns in a race track pattern to simulate the landing pattern. Mr. Rosen instructed Jimmy to fly back to the airport and get into the landing pattern for no less than five touch and go landings. On descent to the traffic pattern, Jimmy pushed the carburetor heat on and started his glide to the traffic pattern carefully maintaining an indicated airspeed of fifty-five miles per hour. Jimmy crosses the airport and enters the downwind leg of the approach at 800 feet above the ground. Jimmy made a coordinated base turn and maintained fifty-five miles per hour. On final approach, he started milking off the power to land the airplane. As the plane crossed the end of the runway, he pulled all power from the airplane and gently landed the airplane on its two main gear. Promptly applying power and pulling off the carburetor heat, Jimmy did a smooth takeoff. Completing this procedure four more times, Mr. Rosen was satisfied that Jimmy was ready to solo and told him to taxi to the ramp.

On the ramp, Mr. Rosen said, "I know you are ready to solo; let me get out and you go show me three takeoffs and landings like you just completed. I will be watching from the ramp."

Jimmy, nervous and ecstatic, replied, "Yes, Sir."

Raymond and Ray were watching from the office when Mr. Rosen got out of the airplane and they saw that Jimmy was going to solo today. Both of them, happy and proud for Jimmy, said a silent prayer for Jimmy's safety and watched Jimmy complete his coming of age.

Jimmy thought as he taxied to the end of the runway, *All I need to do is maintain speed and control and I will have accomplished the first step in becoming a pilot. Just follow the procedure and everything will be fine.*

At the end of the runway, Jimmy verified that the airplane was configured correctly for a regular takeoff and started his takeoff roll. Once off the ground, Jimmy made sure the airplane's indicated airspeed was fifty-five miles per hour and he had an altitude of 800 feet above the ground before turning the crosswind leg to start the landing pattern. Maintaining his airspeed, Jimmy pulled the carburetor heat on and turned the downwind leg. On his base turn, he maintained the proper airspeed and verified that his turn was coordinated. Turning to the final approach, he made his descent into a smooth landing. Once on the ground, Jimmy reset the airplane and completed a smooth takeoff. After his third landing, Jimmy taxied to the ramp and it was then that he saw his dad and brother had watched the proceedings. Not forgetting that he must always fly and control the airplane, Jimmy kept his emotions in check until he reached the ramp and shutoff the engine. Once the engine was idle and quiet, his emotions overwhelmed him and he was proud that he had accomplished the first of many goals on the way to becoming a military pilot.

He unhooked the seat belt and shoulder harness to climb from the airplane. Little did he know what awaited him when he climbed out. Mr. Rosen was there to shake his hand and help him remove his parachute. With the parachute removed, the first solo ritual got under way.

Mr. Rosen said, "Congratulations, Jimmy. Welcome to the first-time solo club. Now turn around."

Raymond said, "Great job, Jimmy. You should be proud! I am proud of you!"

Ray said, "Jimmy, I am so glad I could be here to see you solo. You looked like a professional there."

Mr. Rosen turned Jimmy around, yanked out the tail of his favorite shirt, and produced a pair of shears to cut it off. Jimmy protested feebly that this was his favorite shirt and that he did not want to see it cut up. Raymond and Ray held the shirt tail tight while Mr. Rosen cut it off and with a grease pencil wrote, "Jimmy Johnson First Solo Flight, March 28, 1942 - Joe Rosen, Instructor". Mr. Rosen handed the piece to Jimmy who said he was going to remember this day forever. Raymond and Ray slapped him on the back and told him they were glad they could witness his first solo flight. After the back slapping and hurrahing, Jimmy and Mr. Rosen returned to the flight office to debrief his solo flight and plan his next lesson.

Johnson Family Home ~ Montcross, North Carolina
Saturday - 8:00pm
• •

Bessie, Sara, and the girls were in the sitting room visiting and playing games while the men took their places in the den to talk about the war, the occurrence at the airport, and congratulate

Jimmy on the safe completion of his first solo flight. Ray and Jimmy had been listening to the radio to hear the latest war news when Raymond walked in after he finished his rail yard paperwork. Before he sat down, he turned off the radio.

He opened the conversation with, "Jimmy, I am so proud of you for pushing past the crash and the harassment of Mr. Cameron and his son. Your perseverance should show you that you have the personal reserve to push through any obstacle that might threaten to derail your dream of military flying. What is the next step in the process to get your pilot's license?"

"Thanks, Dad. I made it through my solo today because of the help from you and Ray this morning. I appreciate that Ray grabbed and moved Mr. Cameron to allow me time to catch my breath. The actual flying this afternoon was easy compared to the harassment from Mr. Cameron. Dad, do you think we have heard the last of Mr. Cameron and his misguided idea that I caused his son to lose his flying opportunity?"

His dad replied, "Yes, Jimmy, I hope with Tom's confession to his father that the accident was his fault will bring closure to this difficult ordeal and allow everyone involved to heal. Mr. Brighton asked me if we wanted to drop the charges against Mr. Cameron after his son confessed. I told him that I would have to talk to you before letting him know whether to drop the charges or not. What do you want to do?"

"If you think I will not have to look over my shoulder every time I am at the airport to see if Mr. Cameron or Tom is there to harass me, then I think we should forgive them and move forward. This will be the best thing for everyone and like you said, it will allow everyone to finish the healing process without having the scab continuously ripped away only to have to restart the healing process."

Raymond told Jimmy and Ray that he would be right back because he wanted to call Harmon and let him know they would conditionally drop the charges provided that Mr. Thomas Cameron no longer harasses Jimmy anywhere. Raymond walked into the study and placed the call.

Harmon answered the phone, "Hello."

Raymond said, "Hello, Harmon. This is Raymond Johnson. Do you have a moment to talk about releasing Thomas Cameron?"

Harmon replied, "Yes, I do. What did Jimmy decide in this matter?"

Raymond said, "Jimmy says that he is willing to drop the charges with one caveat. That caveat is for Thomas to leave him alone and stop harassing him. Without this assurance from Thomas, we will continue with the charges. We are not asking for a public apology. We are asking that he stop harassing my son. Is that acceptable to you?"

"Raymond, I figured that might be the caveat that you would ask for to allow the charges to be dropped and I drew that up in the release order with Judge Albright's agreement. Thomas must agree and sign the release before he is free to leave the jail. Thomas asked for bail to be set earlier today, but I had Judge Albright hold him over until I knew for sure that Jimmy had completed his flying lesson today. Please give him my congratulations on his first solo flight. I will take the release document to the jail and release Thomas if he agrees to the terms. Otherwise, he will be staying in jail until his first hearing on Monday and will face all the charges brought against him for his behavior at the airport today. I will call you and let you know what happens."

"Thanks, Harmon. I will let Jimmy know and await your call. Have a good evening. Goodbye."

"Thanks, Raymond. Goodbye."

Raymond hung up the phone and walked back into the den to rejoin his sons.

Jimmy asked, "What did Mr. Brighton say? Is Mr. Cameron still in jail?"

"Jimmy, Harmon kept Thomas in jail to make sure you were able to take your lesson without any harassment and he sends his congratulations on your first solo flight. If Thomas signs the release Harmon drew up stating that Thomas will no longer harass you, he will be released tonight. Otherwise, all the charges against him will be prosecuted with his first appearance taking place Monday morning at the courthouse. I hope he accepts and signs the release so that everyone can put this behind them. Harmon will call us and let us know what he does.", his dad answered.

"I also hope he signs the release and then allows his son to heal now that Tom has accepted responsibility for the accident. Thanks for your help, Dad."

"Glad I could help, Son. Ray, I have a few questions for you especially after your demonstration this morning. What were you thinking when you grabbed Thomas Cameron? Were you going to hurt him or just stop him from attacking Jimmy?"

Ray thought for a moment, then replied, "Dad, at first my thought was just to stop the attack by Mr. Cameron without hurting him, but he seemed to be spoiling for a fight and I basically gave him the opportunity by saying, 'If you want one, I will be happy to oblige.' At that point, he cried that I was assaulting him when in actuality all I did was stop him from harassing Jimmy. I was not going to hurt him unless he chose to escalate the confrontation. At that point, I would not have taken any prisoners. Does that answer your question, Dad?"

"Yes it does, Ray. I saw your Marine training come out when you confronted Thomas. You put yourself in the most advantageous position and had leverage by grabbing him around the neck. I know you were shown in boot camp how to break an enemy's neck using that hold. I was very proud of the restraint you showed after you moved Thomas away from Jimmy. It showed me that you had learned the lessons of boot camp very well. The only problem is you reverted to the foul language of the corps during the confrontation and in front of Sara which is very rude and you know that. You need to watch that make sure you keep your tongue under control."

"I know, Dad. As soon as I said those words, I remembered that I was in Montcross and not in New River with my platoon mates. I apologized to Sara several times already and I apologized to Mom. Sara got her revenge when Myra and Lillie helped her wash my mouth out with soap. That really made the point to watch what I say."

Jimmy asked, "Ray, Dad told me that you have been promoted one rank which is usually unheard of for someone just out of boot camp. What did you do to get promoted?"

"I do not know that I did anything spectacular to get promoted, but in our training exercise on Friday I saved my platoon from being casualties when a defender threw a live grenade instead of a dummy grenade. After the two platoons found the perpetrator, I was asked to report to the company headquarters where Lieutenant Mercer promoted me one grade and made me the squad leader of a thirty caliber machine gun squad. Honestly, I did not think I did all that much to deserve a promotion and assignment as a squad leader, but I promised the platoon leader that I would do my best."

His dad interjected, "Ray, you may not have thought anything about what you did because all you were doing was protecting your platoon. Marine officers look for men who display quality leadership and your actions showed that you were engaged. To officers that is one sign of a good leader, but there is probably more that you do not know as to why you were promoted. Your actions in boot camp were recorded by your drill instructor and your time that you have spent at New River has also been observed. You would not have been promoted for just that incident but an accumulation of positive comments. That incident just provided the catalyst to promote you. Good job and congratulations. You have always been a natural born leader."

"Thanks, Dad. I feel like I struggled in boot camp once I hurt my ankle. My DI would not give me any quarter and at times it felt like he wanted me to quit, but somehow I made it through. On graduation day, Sergeant Garrett spoke to me before my bus left for Yemassee Junction and he said, 'I know you are probably wondering why I was harder on you than the rest of the lousy boots. Well here's the dope, you have leadership potential that will make most generals green with envy. It ain't because you're brash or cocky but it is that quiet manner in which you push everyone in your squad to succeed and you help them succeed by putting the right people in the right position.' His comments certainly surprised me but it helped me understand why he drove me as hard as he did even with my injury. I feel like his training has set me up well for wherever the corps sends me to do battle. What do you think, Dad; you have been in the corps too?"

His dad said, "Ray, you made a positive impression on your drill instructor and once you did, his goal was to make sure it was real and not some put on. You didn't quit or wait to heal but persevered through the pain and the hard training. You proved to yourself and your DI that you had what it took to be a Marine. I am proud of you for what you have accomplished and hope you have the same success on the field of battle."

Bessie heard the phone ring from the sitting room and walked into the study to answer it. It was Harmon Brighton calling Raymond back.

Raymond picked up the phone and said, "Hello, Harmon. How did it go?"

Harmon answered, "Thomas was very contrite when I presented the opportunity of being released without having any charges hanging over his head, as long as he ended his vendetta against Jimmy. Thomas let me know that since the incident this morning, and the fear of God your son, Ray, put in him, he knows that he was wrong to blame Jimmy for his son's shortcomings. He promised me that he would issue, Joe, the Mayerhofer Family, and Jimmy, a public apology in this week's Montcross Gazette. I told him that he did not need to do that. He said, 'I know but it is the least I can do after all the trouble I caused.' With that, I countersigned his release and he left with his wife and son. I truly hope this is the end of this sorry episode."

"Thanks, Harmon. I will let Jimmy know and I hope as well that this is the end."

Raymond walked into the den after his conversation and said, "Jimmy, Thomas signed the release agreement and Harmon told me that Thomas said he is going to issue a public apology in this week's newspaper. It looks like you no longer have to worry about Thomas Cameron or his son interrupting and harassing you during your flying lessons or around town. I hope that is the case."

"I do too, Dad. I am glad Mr. Cameron accepted the release agreement."

Raymond and the boys finished their conversation and said their goodnights. Sara and Elizabeth had already retired to their room for the night. At the top of the stairs, Ray knocked on Elizabeth's door to tell them goodnight and then walked into his room to sleep in his bed for the first time since December. Ray knew that being able to sleep in his own bed was going to be wonderful. He was asleep almost as soon as his head hit his pillow.

JOHNSON FAMILY HOME ~ MONTCROSS, NORTH CAROLINA SUNDAY, MARCH 29, 1942

Sara looked at him and said, "Ray, I love you very much, but what I have seen this weekend bothers me. You seem to have a new hardness about you and that bothers me. It is like the Marine Corps trained the loving spirit out of you. I do not understand how you can be so nonchalant about things that should be taken seriously."

"I love you too, Sara. Yes, there is a new hardness to me. I have seen four men die already in training because those young men did not follow orders. Boot Camp taught me that I need to push myself and block out pain in order to succeed. My ankle injury was worse than I let on to you and the family, but I could not quit nor could I allow myself to fall behind in training because I had to reach the goal of becoming a Marine. I developed that hardness in order to succeed. My drill instructor, Sergeant Garrett, told me as I was leaving boot camp after graduation that he pushed me harder than the other recruits because he saw something special in me and he knew with certainty that he could bring that leadership quality out if he pushed me to my breaking point. I promised him I would uphold the Esprit de Corps that he taught me in boot camp."

Sara said, "Four men dying, ankle injury, and a drill instructor pushing you to succeed; how did you make it through? And, how can you be so calm about what happened?"

"It wouldn't do any good to get upset about those things because nothing I could do would change the outcome unless I had decided to quit. Quitting was never an option, and it will not be an option while I have breath in my body. I promised you in December that I would one day come home to you and we would start a life together. The only way I can do that is to block out everything but the task at hand. Can you understand that?"

"Yes, Ray. I can understand that and now I have a better picture of why you are doing things this way. I will be waiting on you to come home for good, and I know now that you are doing the same thing your father did during the Great War in order to come home safely to your mother."

He took Sara in his arms and kissed her long and hard. She eagerly and forcefully returned the kiss, and their passion quickly overwhelmed them as they held one another in an embrace that neither one wanted to end. She did not want to stop the crescendo of feelings even though they were not married yet. She felt Ray stiffen through his khaki uniform trousers and the moisture of arousal began beneath her bloomers. She knew that they must stop before they both did something they would regret.

She pushed Ray away from her, saying, "Ray, this is not right. We need to stop before we go too far."

Through his fog of passion, Ray replied, "I know we do; I want our first time to be special and only after we are married. I love you, Sara!"

"I love you too, Ray! We need to get the chores done so that we have time to cool off before walking back to the house."

They took time to brush the straw off of their clothes and Sara gathered the eggs while Ray milked Gertrude. The young couple started the walk back to the house with the eggs and milk. They looked forward to having the full day to spend together. As the couple walked into the house, Bessie gave them the once over, knowing that it took them longer this morning to do the chores and hoping that they had not done anything they would regret. She decided that she would talk to Ray later today to make sure his moral compass was still intact.

First Baptist Church ~ Montcross, North Carolina
Sunday - 10:15am

• •

For the first time in three months, Ray was able to attend the Sunday worship service at First Baptist Church and he was going to make the most of it by visiting with friends after the service to see what was happening with them. Sara and Ray left earlier than usual to walk to church so that they could have more time to talk privately.

After the couple left, Bessie asked Raymond, "Do you think there is any chance that Ray and Sara committed a conjugal act this morning while doing the chores? They were gone an awfully long time to gather the eggs and milk."

Raymond, always the pragmatist, replied, "If they have done anything like that, we cannot change it. I trust Ray will not do anything that might affect his future with Sara and the Peabody family. I think they probably had a moment of passion, but I do not think either one of them would allow that moment to go too far."

"I hope that is the case, but Sara and Ray looked very happy and satisfied when they walked into the kitchen from doing the chores. I want to make sure Ray's moral compass is still centered on Jesus and his teachings. I will have to talk to him this afternoon."

"You will do no such thing, Bessie! It is none of our business!"

Bessie, taken aback by this sharp rebuke from her husband, said, "Why is it none of our business? We promised the Peabodys that we would take care of Sara as one of our own. If something like that happened before they are married, how will I ever be able to face Alma and Samuel? I would be simply mortified."

"We have to trust our son would do nothing to bring shame to himself or Sara. I am sure you are making a mountain out of a mole hill here. Ray has earned our trust, and we should not do or say anything that makes it appear that we question his behavior."

"All right, Raymond. I will not ask Ray anything about it only because I do not want him to think that we are questioning his character."

While Raymond and Bessie were conversing at home, Ray and Sara were carrying on a similar conversation on their walk to the church. They both knew that they had come very close to crossing the line this morning in their passion.

Ray said, "Sara, it was right that you stopped us from making the mistake of completely giving in to our passion this morning. I love you, and want to give our marriage the right foundation which means we wait until marriage before we consummate our love. I vow that I am willing to wait until that special night."

"Ray, that makes me feel so much better. I too want to wait until we are married, but I also found myself giving to the passion as well this morning. I vow that I too will wait until our wedding night for the wonderful consummation of our love. We must guard our hearts and our emotions to prevent putting ourselves in the position where it will be easy to give into our love."

"Thank you, Sara."

"You told me earlier that you saw men die during boot camp. What happened to cause their deaths?"

"Sara, boot camp is the practice of breaking down a recruit mentally and physically to the point that they can be molded to follow orders without question. During one drill, the recruits were required to crawl underneath a barbed wire enclosure with animal entrails lining the trench. The first few passes through the course are done without live fire and then we were ordered to complete the course under live fire. Our drill instructor gave us orders to keep our heads down because live ammunition is being fired about two feet over the top of the course. We must crawl as quickly as we can through the course while keeping our heads down in the blood and entrails. One guy could not take the blood and gore in his face and raised his head above the level of the course and was killed instantly. Our entire platoon was chewed out for not following orders, and we were required to repeat it several more times because of that guy's mistake."

Sara, visibly paling, replied, "How were you able to repeat the course after that happened? Did the drill instructor make you start the course immediately?"

Ray, with matter of fact tone, said, "The DI made us repeat the course immediately after the body had been removed, but he did give us the quick choice to quit the Marines or repeat the course. Three recruits quit immediately while the rest of us repeated the course until the drill instructor was satisfied that we had learned the lesson of keeping our heads down no matter how we felt. The entire boot camp process is designed to remove any vestige of self and replace it with the idea of accomplishing objectives through teamwork. I was never comfortable during boot camp because my instructor pushed me harder than most to excel even with my ankle injury."

Sara was now visibly shaken with this admission from Ray, and she grabbed his hand so that she did not collapse from the trauma of his boot camp story. He knew that he must keep the story as sanitized as possible for anyone who had not experienced the difficulty of Marine boot camp training. He figured out that Sara was unable to comprehend the difficulty and the pain of overcoming one's personal limitations to press the process forward to a successful completion. His success had come from the story his mother reminded him about the championship game where he contributed even after his arm was broken. Being able to push through mental limitations and persevere against overwhelming mental stress was the trait that Sergeant Garrett exploited in boot camp to help him succeed.

Sara, still shaking, said, "I now understand why you have not told me much about your training because it would make me worry more than I already do. I have missed you terribly and this weekend has really helped me overcome that sense of loss of not having you near me during these past three months."

"I have missed you terribly, too. The few times I wrote you from boot camp were some of my lowest points in training, and the thought that I could not make it through were resonating loudly in my mind. The letters to you helped me regain my focus and push through. Your love and my family's love have been my lifeline during boot camp, and you don't realize how much your letters meant to me."

"I did not realize that I had done anything to help you make it through your training. I thought you had forgotten all about me. I promise I will write you more regularly now that you have told me how much those letters mean to you." Sara choked back a tear.

With a renewal of their relationship through this conversation, the couple walked up the front steps of First Baptist Church. Ray was welcomed home by the ushers and the couple made their way to the family pew for the worship service.

• • • • • • • • • • • • • • • • • • • •

All too soon the weekend came to an end, and Ray and Sara told each other goodbye on the platform of the Charlotte Bus Station at nine o'clock that morning. He could have departed on a later bus, but after telling his dad that the court martial proceedings would start at nine o'clock Tuesday morning, his dad recommended that he leave on the earlier bus in order to get back in time to prepare. With a special bag lunch of Elva's fried chicken and potato salad in his hand, Ray kissed Sara goodbye, shook his father's hand, and boarded the bus to Wilmington for the long ride back to the New River Marine Base. Ray's thoughts were jumbled thinking about how wonderful the weekend had been and the understanding that this may be the last time he saw his family or Sara for a very long time, if ever again.

As the bus pulled out of the station, Raymond said to Sara, "I hope you have enjoyed your visit with Ray this weekend."

She replied, "Mr. Johnson, Ray and I were able to reconnect and now I know that I will be able to endure whatever separation is imposed on us. Ray firmly believes in what he is doing and I believe in him. That's all that matters for me."

Raymond said, "I am glad to hear you say that because I know how firm his convictions are about fighting. It is not about proving to himself that he can do it, but about knowing that he is contributing to the effort to overcome our enemies. I am proud of both of you and the way you both have rekindled your relationship this weekend."

She said, "That was the best part of the weekend, Mr. Johnson. Being able to finally talk to Ray about some of the things he saw during boot camp, and how hard it was for him to overcome the obstacles that were placed in his way. He told me on numerous occasions that my letters helped him get through some of the lowest points in his training with my words of encouragement. Is that how the letters from Bessie worked for you during the Great War?"

"Yes, Sara, every letter I received from Bessie while I was in Europe was a boost to my morale and my lifeline home. Without them, I do not know if I would have made it back home to her. She was very cognizant to tell me how much I mattered to her and how much she loved me. Those letters at some of my darkest moments gave me the strength and courage to believe and fight on. I would ask that you continue writing Ray even if he does not reply right away."

Sara stifled a sob, replying, "Thank you, Mr. Johnson. I will make sure that I write him very often and talk of all the wonderful things we will do once he gets home."

At ten, the bus to Raleigh pulled into the station and started boarding passengers. Raymond helped Sara load her luggage.

Sara said, "Tell Mrs. Johnson and the family how much I appreciated spending the weekend with them. I love you all very much. Thank you for inviting me to share this weekend with Ray and the rest of you. It meant a lot to me that you allowed me to share this time with all of you."

Raymond gave Sara a hug, saying, "We are always glad to see you. Bessie and I love you very much and we look forward to the day that we can call you our daughter as well. Have a safe trip back to Meredith College and give our regards to your parents."

With that, Sara boarded the bus, found her seat, and was immediately lost in thought about the uncertainty of the future, but safe in the knowledge that she has a larger family now that will help her overcome anything life and the war threw at her.

New River Marine Base ~ Jacksonville, North Carolina
Monday, March 30, 1942 - 6:00pm
● ●

Ray reported back to base twelve hours early in order to get a good night's sleep, and to make sure that he was ready for the resumption of his training. He reported to Sergeant Hoggren at the company headquarters and turned in his used seventy-two hour pass.

He walked in and said, "Private Johnson reporting in from furlough, Sir."

Sergeant Hoggren replied, "Welcome back, Private First Class Johnson. Lieutenant Mercer wants to see you before you stow your gear. Wait right here."

Sergeant Hoggren walked into Lieutenant Mercer's office and said, "Private First Class Johnson is back from furlough, Sir. He is twelve hours early."

Lieutenant Mercer replied, "Just as I expected he would be; send him in, Sergeant."

Sergeant Hoggren walked out to the orderly room and summoned Ray in to the lieutenant's office.

Ray walked into the office, stood at attention, and snapped the lieutenant a salute then said, "Private First Class Johnson, reporting as ordered, Sir."

Lieutenant Mercer responded, "At ease, Johnson. Are you back early because of tomorrow's court martial proceedings?"

"Sir! Yes, Sir! The affidavit I signed, stated the proceedings would start at 0900 tomorrow, Sir, and I wanted to get a good night's sleep before having to testify, Sir."

"Johnson, you will be the first witness called to testify when the proceedings open at 0900. Do you have anything you can add to the case?"

"Sir, I know that ten days ago most of second platoon was at the Slop Chute along with a few members of first platoon including Private Renton. There seemed to be some argument over which platoon was better, and Private Renton did most of the name calling. He was pretty drunk, Sir."

"Was there a fight, Johnson?"

"Yes, Sir. There was a full fledged fight between Private Jeffrey and Private Renton. Private Jeffrey beat the hell out of Private Renton who swore he would get even with the entire platoon. I did not realize he meant murder as a way to get his revenge, Sir. I thought it was just a fight to blow off some steam and it did not seem all that serious until seen in the light of what happened Friday."

"Thank you, Johnson. I will have this drawn up as evidence for the court martial. Tell Private Jeffrey that I might summon him later to discuss the incident. You are dismissed."

Ray came to attention, saluted the lieutenant, left the office, grabbed his sea bag, and returned to the barracks. There he found platoon members whose furloughs were revoked due to various infractions such as failed inspections or military code violations. Private Lawson Jeffrey was one of those who had lost his pass for his conduct during the training exercise on Onslow Beach. Private Jeffrey was sitting on his bunk reading his mail when Ray walked in, placed his sea bag on his bunk, and started unpacking.

Private Lawson Jeffrey said, "How was your three-day pass? Did you pass muster with your girl?"

"I had a great time at home and I passed muster. What's the scuttlebutt here, Lawson?"

"I believe Private Renton will be getting a dishonorable discharge after his court martial. He told me he was going to take some of us out after our fight a couple of weeks back, but I didn't think he would do it with a live grenade during an exercise."

"I told the lieutenant about your fight and he might summon you to answer some questions."

"That's just great, Johnson! I didn't want to get involved in this and now you've put me front and center, thanks for nothing."

Sergeant Hoggren walked into the barracks and overheard the conversation. He strode up to Private Jeffrey and told him the lieutenant wanted to see him immediately. As Lawson was leaving the barracks to report to the lieutenant, he glared menacingly at Ray as if to say, "I will get you for this."

Sergeant Hoggren said, "Private Johnson, now that you are a squad leader, you cannot take any backtalk and shit from the other members of your squad. You need to be firm and lead by example just like you've been doing since you were assigned to this platoon. The hardest part will be getting guys like Private Jeffrey to fall in line. He is nothing more than a foul-up that will get guys killed if he doesn't follow orders. You will have to ride his ass to make him do what you order him to do."

"Sergeant Hoggren, how much leeway do I have to make an order stick? Can I get on their ass and expect it to be done? And, if it does not get done, can I discipline them myself; or do I bring them to you? I'm hoping that the guys will follow my orders without me having to be a hard ass."

"You have the leeway of rank and as the squad leader, you can mete out whatever punishment you see fit. I know from the looks of your squad, you probably won't have too much trouble except from a guy like Private Jeffrey who is always looking for trouble and spoiling for a fight. You may even have to take him out behind the barn and kick his ass to make him fall in line. But make damn sure you do it someplace the brass and MP's won't get wind of it. I won't be able to help you then."

Ray replied, "Understood. I hope it does not come to that. Thank you, Sir."

Ray finished making up his bunk and prepared his sea bag and footlocker for an inspection he knew would surely come once everyone returned from their short furloughs. Ray was thankful that Elva cleaned and pressed his khaki uniform so that it would be ready for the court martial proceedings in the morning. After getting his bunk in order and footlocker prepared for inspection, he dashed off a quick letter to Sara telling her how wonderful it was to be able to spend the weekend with her in Montcross. After sticking the letter in an envelope, he took the letter to the mailbox and walked on to the mess hall for a dinner of spam and eggs. Spam and eggs after a weekend of Elva's wonderful cooking was an insult to his tastebuds, but what was a Marine to do other than eat what was served. He knew another furlough probably would not be in the offing very soon if at all, but he had his memories of this past weekend which would sustain and prepare him for what lay ahead. By listening and learning from the likes of Sergeant Hoggren and Lieutenant Mercer, Ray knew that he had been training with the best and would be able to meet the challenges he faced in the future on the battle field.

New River Marine Base ~ Jacksonville, North Carolina
Tuesday, March 31, 1942

• •

With the dawning of a new day, Ray was up as reveille sounded, dressed quickly, and had his machine gun squad out for a physical training run along with the rest of the platoon. Ray and the rest of the platoon completed the three mile run in less than a half-hour and route marched to the mess hall for breakfast. Sergeant Hoggren and the rest of the squad leaders sat together during breakfast to discuss the training exercises that would be taking place this week.

Sergeant Hoggren said to Ray, "Johnson, I know you will be tied up this week with the Private Renton court martial and may not make it to any of the exercises. Who is your second in command?"

Ray replied, "I have named Private Leonard Trantham as my second in command because he is studious and knows what is going on with the machine gun squad. His four-man crew always runs like a well-oiled machine. Is that acceptable, Sergeant Hoggren?"

Sergeant Hoggren replied, "That's a great choice and I'm sure he will do an excellent job until you can get back to the squad at the completion of the proceedings. At 0900, we are marching out to our bivouac area to set up a base of operations for the weeks' exercises and training problems. I will brief the squads once we get set up in the area of operation."

Ray left the group sitting at the table to hustle back to the barracks for a shower and shave. He dressed in his properly pressed khaki uniform for the court martial, and at 0830, he walked into the conference room where the proceedings were to be held. He reported his arrival to the sergeant in charge and the Marine prosecutor told him that the proceedings would start promptly at 0900. The prosecutor showed Ray his seat just behind the prosecutor's desk in the large sterile conference room.

The judges panel called the proceedings to order promptly at 0900 and read the charges which were twelve counts of attempted murder and dereliction of duty. Major Henry, the Marine prosecutor, called Ray to the witness stand to get his testimony about what happened on the dunes overlooking Onslow Beach at 0947 on the morning of Friday 27 March 1942. Major Henry swore Ray in and asked him to take his seat on the witness stand.

Major Henry said, "Private First Class Johnson, tell us what you witnessed at 0947 on the morning of 27 March 1942, please."

Ray answered, "Sir, on the morning of 27 March, my second platoon of G Company was taking part in a mock assault on a beachhead held by the first platoon of G company located at the south end of Onslow Beach. Second platoon came ashore under mock battle conditions with blank ammunition and dummy grenades in order to take first platoon's defensive position. My job is, once deployed, to set my machine gun squad in the most advantageous position to assist the riflemen in their attack. At the top of a flanking dune, I set up my machine gun squad and we were in a position to observe the action and assist where needed in the assault. The second platoon was just about to crest the defended dune when I saw Private Renton throw a grenade that briefly showed gray smoke then went out, I knew immediately that it was a live grenade and shouted as loudly as I could, 'LIVE GRENADE! SCATTER!' Luckily, Sergeant Hoggren and the rest of the assault rifle squad heard me and dove for cover. Thankfully, there were no casualties."

Major Henry asked, "Thank you, Private First Class Johnson. How did you know the grenade was live and not a dummy grenade that you had been issued?"

Ray responded, "On 27 March, the dummy grenades we were assigned either emitted green smoke for the attacking platoon or red smoke for the defending platoon. This grenade showed gray smoke then went out which meant it was a live pineapple. I knew unless I acted quickly a lot of good men were either going to die or be grievously injured."

Major Henry said, "Did you know the Marine before that incident on the beach?"

Ray responded, "Yes, Sir. He picked a fight with a member of our platoon at the Slop Chute about ten days ago. Private Renton was always trying to argue with anyone who would listen about which platoon was the best in G company. Private Jeffrey on this occasion obliged him in the fight and really mopped the floor with him. After the fight, Private Renton swore he would get even with the second platoon. I think the incident on the morning of 27 March was an attempt to get revenge for the beating he had taken at the Slop Chute."

Major Henry said, "Thank you, Private First Class Johnson. No further questions."

This completed the direct questioning of Ray by Major Henry and Captain Stanton was now allowed to cross-examine Ray.

Captain Stanton stood and said, "Private First Class Johnson, are you sure that Private Renton was the person you saw throw the grenade."

Ray replied, "Yes, Sir, I know who I saw. Private Renton admitted it to his platoon leader, Lieutenant Grantham. He tried to tell Lieutenant Grantham that the grenade was disarmed and intended as a joke. After close examination of the blast area by both platoons, it was determined that the grenade had not been disarmed and had functioned properly."

Captain Stanton said, "Thank you. No further questions at this time for this witness."

One of the judges told Ray to step down and take his seat. Other witnesses testified to what they saw on that fateful morning with Private Renton taking the stand as the defense's only witness.

Captain Stanton administered the oath to Private Renton who then took the stand.

Captain Stanton asked, "You have heard the testimony by these witnesses. Can you give us your account of what happened on the beach on 27 March 1942?"

Private Renton answered, "I had been issued the dummy grenades as prescribed in the training exercise and placed them in my combat pack. I also had a disarmed grenade that I was going to use to scare the members of the lousy second platoon. They don't know their ass from a hole in the ground when it comes to being good Marines, but they always seem to get the plum assignments. The disarmed grenade I threw was meant as a joke and payback for the beating I took from Private Jeffrey."

Captain Stanton stated, "How did you know for sure you had disarmed the grenade? Have you disarmed that many grenades to test and be able to verify that you had disarmed it properly?"

Private Renton replied, "I had poured out the powder of several grenades and tested to see whether they would explode. All those other grenades did was pop gray smoke; and after the standard fuse time just made a small popping sound without explosion and fragmentation. So, I felt certain the grenade I threw on the morning of 27 March would do the same."

Captain Stanton said, "Thank you, Private Renton. No further questions."

Major Henry started his cross-examination by saying, "Private Renton, if you thought the grenade would not explode, why did you run down the beach immediately after throwing it?"

Private Renton replied, "I did not run away. I was following the doctrine of changing positions after throwing ordnance in order to limit exposure to counterattack."

Major Henry asked, "If you were only changing positions, why were you found a half mile down the beach from your specified training area? Did you really think you needed to move that far to prevent a counterattack or were you running away? You knew you had thrown a live grenade and wanted to get away. Isn't that true?"

Private Renton answered truthfully for the first time, "Yes, Sir, I knew the grenade was live; and I ran because I was sure that the explosion would kill Private Jeffrey and several members of the second platoon who had laughed at me after the fight at the Slop Chute. They are lousy soldiers and don't deserve to be Marines."

Major Henry stated, "No further questions."

After a short deliberation, the judges reconvened and pronounced the judgement of guilty of dereliction of duty and attempted murder. The judges sentenced Private Renton to death by firing squad and remanded him to the brig. As Private Renton was led away by the Marine military policemen, he was visibly shaken and sobbing at the outcome of his trial. Ray was shocked, as well, by the outcome of the case and the sentence handed down by the judges. He exited the large conference room to return to the barracks, gather his gear, and meet the truck that would deliver him to second platoon's bivouac area.

On the drive out to the bivouac area, Ray considered everything he witnessed during the court martial of Private Renton; and while no one had been killed or wounded by Private Renton's actions, the private was still sentenced to death. He must put the court martial behind him before he entered the bivouac area and concentrate on getting his squad in the proper positions to accomplish each of the goals set forth in the week's exercises.

Jimmy Solos

• • • • • • • • • • • • • • • • • • • •

Over the past several weeks the training had been ramping up with every member of the company knowing that the time would soon come for them to leave for the front lines in either the European theater or the Pacific theater. The scuttlebutt around the camp had been that the company would be shipping out to the Pacific to fight the Japanese. Within the past two weeks, Sergeant Dick Hoggren had been promoted one grade to the full rank of Platoon Sergeant for his outstanding training and organization of the platoon in preparation for the upcoming deployment. Dick and Ray had become good friends since the episode on Onslow Beach where half the platoon could have been killed by the private bent on revenging the whipping he took at the hands of Private Jeffrey. Ray's work with his machine gun squad had been exemplary and everyone worked like a well oiled machine. During this week's exercises, Ray's squad had worked well in solving the tactical field problems designed to test the cohesiveness of the unit while pushing them to accomplish objectives. Only Private Lawson Jeffrey seemed to have a problem with following orders and working in concert with the rest of the squad. None of the men would have been able to solve the problems, individually, but as a team, they were able to achieve the goals set forth.

At the close of the latest exercise, Dick and Ray gathered with the other members of the platoon to discuss what may come soon and to debrief what happened during the last exercise which required the platoon to hopscotch towards an objective. The hopscotch maneuver required the machine gun and mortar squads to coordinate fire on a mock enemy positions while the rifle squad moved into position to take the strong point. Several problems occurred during the exercise because of Private Jeffrey. He was unwilling to follow the order given by Ray to grab the machine gun tripod, while Ray, as gunner, grabbed the rifle to move forward to the next position. Private Jeffrey had believed Ray was not worthy of his promotion and his calm demeanor grated on his nerves. During this exercise, Ray just moved Private Mason into Private Jeffrey's position in the gun squad and made Jeffrey the ammunition carrier. This did not sit well with Jeffrey at the time, and he tried his best to foul up the squad's performance in order to make Ray look bad to the platoon leader and platoon sergeant. Ray knew how to handle the situation with Jeffrey and that was to not get into an argument at the time. Ray calmly ordered the rest of the squad to carry the ammunition and Ray carried not only the gun but also a can of ammunition while continuing to lead by example. Private Jeffrey was left sputtering at the previous emplacement while the machine gun crew moved quickly to get in position for the next phase of the exercise. This move by Ray caught the eye of the lieutenant; and after the exercise, Lieutenant Mercer would confront Private Jeffrey about what happened during the exercise.

Lieutenant Mercer said to Platoon Sergeant Hoggren, "Get me Private Jeffrey and Private First Class Johnson, immediately!"

"Yes, Sir! On the double, Sir!"

Sergeant Hoggren jogged over to the machine gun squad's area and said, "Private First Class Johnson, get Private Jeffrey and report to the lieutenant on the double!"

"Yes, Sir, Sergeant! Private Jeffrey, front and center, NOW!"

Private Jeffrey responded, "What the hell for? You can't order me around."

With that, Ray jumped into the face of Private Jeffrey yelling, "You sorry piece of shit! That was a direct order private! Now get your ass in gear!"

Jeffrey, blustering, said, "I don't have to listen to you! You're nothing but an ass kisser who was gifted the rank of Private First Class."

At this point, Sergeant Hoggren said to Ray, "Go report to the lieutenant! Let him know that I will be there with Private Jeffrey momentarily."

Ray hustled to report to the lieutenant while Sergeant Hoggren handled the unruly Private Jeffrey.

"Private First Class Johnson, reporting as ordered, Sir!"

The lieutenant replied, "Where the hell is Private Jeffrey?"

Ray answered, "Sir, Sergeant Hoggren asked that I report that he and Private Jeffrey will be here momentarily."

"Ok, Johnson. Tell me what the hell happened during the exercise today. It looked like your entire squad went off and left Private Jeffrey behind when you moved to set up on the next objective."

"Insubordination, Sir. Private Jeffrey refused to grab the tripod when I gave the order to move out to our next position. Didn't have time to argue with him so I distributed the load between the rest of the men and moved up to our next position, Sir. I was not going to allow the actions of one jeopardize the rest of the platoon, so I made the decision to leave him behind and move forward."

"Excellent decision, Johnson, and you had your squad in perfect position for the next assault. Well done!"

Sergeant Hoggren walked up to the lieutenant pushing Private Jeffrey by the collar of his dungaree shirt. Private Jeffrey looked a little pale as he was pushed in front of the platoon leader.

Sergeant Hoggren stated flatly, "Reporting with Private Jeffrey as ordered, Sir."

Lieutenant Mercer asked, "What the hell took so long, Sergeant? Didn't Private Jeffrey know it was a DI-RECT order from Private FIRST CLASS Johnson to report to me?"

Sergeant Hoggren in his thick Illinois accent, replied, "Seems this piece of shit private refuses to take orders from PRIVATE FIRST CLASS Johnson. Seems to think that Johnson doesn't deserve the rank he earned. As a matter of fact, I heard him call Johnson an ass kisser, Sir."

Dumbfounded and now angry, Lieutenant Mercer said, "Is that the case, Maggot? Do you think Johnson kissed ass to get that Private First Class stripe?"

Private Jeffrey, blustering, responded, "Sir, yes, Sir! Johnson should not be leading our squad! I should be head gunner and squad leader because I know what it takes to lead men. My drill sergeant said so at Parris Island, and you passed me over in favor of Mr. Calm and Quiet. He doesn't know a damn thing about leadership and he doesn't have the respect of the other squad members!"

Lieutenant Mercer, yelled, "THAT'S ENOUGH, PRI-VATE! I saw the kind of respect the other squad members showed today during the exercise. Once your sorry ass committed insubordination, the rest of the squad pulled together and met the objective without you. That shows me that the rest of the squad has no problem following Private FIRST CLASS Johnson. Only you have that problem. What RANK are you, Maggot?"

Private Jeffrey responded, "I AM A PRIVATE, SIR!"

Lieutenant Mercer continued, "WHAT RANK IS JOHNSON?"

Private Jeffrey responded, "JOHNSON IS A PRIVATE FIRST CLASS, SIR!"

Lieutenant Mercer said, "What did you learn in boot camp about following orders? Don't you have to follow the orders of those superior in rank?"

"Sir, I must follow the orders of those Marines who are of a higher rank."

"Doesn't that also mean, following the orders of PRIVATE FIRST CLASS Johnson?"

"Yes, Sir! But, I will not follow the orders of a panty-waist ass kisser who came into the Corps the same time I did, and only got promoted because he is a brown-nosing piece of shit!"

"Private Jeffrey, you are now charged with insubordination in a time of war and will be dealt with by court martial. Is that understood?"

With all the wind knocked out of his sails, Private Jeffrey replied, "Sir, yes, Sir!"

Ray had watched the entire conversation unfold and he could see the possibility that Private Jeffrey would receive the same penalty as Private Renton since these charges were being brought in a time of war.

Ray asked, "Lieutenant Mercer, may I speak with you a moment in private, sir?"

Lieutenant Mercer answered, "Johnson, what would you like to speak to me about? Can't it be done in front of the Sergeant and this piece of shit, Private?"

Ray replied, "Sir, I believe that Private Jeffrey should not be brought up on the court martial charge of insubordination, although that is exactly what he did today. I think he should be put in the brig on bread and water and then allowed to return to the platoon. He's a good soldier when he doesn't fight the system as he has been doing ever since my promotion. Is that possible, Sir?"

Lieutenant Mercer, with a perplexed look on his face, asked, "Why, Johnson? You know he will probably pull something like this again once he is released from the brig. Would you be willing to take him back into your squad once a suitable punishment is meted out?"

"I think Private Jeffrey will be needed when we ship out and are in combat. He is a fine soldier who knows his business when it comes to being in the right place at the right time. I will take him back into the squad once his punishment for this infraction has been meted out. But, if anything like this happens again; I will not stand up to block whatever punishment is imposed."

Lieutenant Mercer glared at Private Jeffrey, saying, "After all your sorry ass has done, Private First Class Johnson is willing to give you another chance. Just so you get it through your thick skull, the promotion order came from Captain Hargrave because of Ray's quiet and calm leadership ability. That calm discipline stood out on the day he saved your life and the lives of all your platoon mates. What the hell do you have to say? If I agree to Johnson's proposal of punishment, would you follow his orders once you return?"

"Sir, yes, Sir! I will follow his orders to the letter, Sir. You will not have another problem out of me from here on, Sir."

"Good! Private Jeffrey, you are hereby sentenced to ten days in the brig with only bread and water and will be on probation until further notice with a reduction in pay by half for a period of ninety days. Understood?"

Private Jeffrey, knowing that Ray possibly saved him from the firing squad, replied, "Sir, YES, Sir!"

The lieutenant dismissed Ray to return to his squad and ordered Sergeant Hoggren to take Private Jeffrey to the brig back on the base. His orders for the prisoner were that he would only have bread and water for ten days. Lieutenant Mercer drew up the appropriate paperwork for the offense and walked it over to the company command post for approval by Captain Hargrave.

Once Ray left Lieutenant Mercer's tent, he started thinking about how harsh military justice could be. He hoped that Private Jeffrey learned his lesson and returned to the squad as a fully-functioning member who did his part without questioning or malingering.

MONTCROSS AIRPORT ~ MONTCROSS, NORTH CAROLINA
SATURDAY, MAY 23, 1942

• • • • • • • • • • • • • • • • • • •

Jimmy arrived at the Montcross Airport an hour before his scheduled check ride. If he passed his check ride today, he would earn his Airman's Certificate that would allow him to join the Army Air Corps Aviation Cadet Program after high school graduation in three weeks. Jimmy was understandably nervous about his check ride because he unfortunately got lost during his last cross-country flight a week ago. He had to land in a farmer's field and ask directions. The three hour flight from Montcross to Salisbury and back was the most trying flight of his young career because not only did he get lost on the return leg, but he also failed to make sure he had enough fuel.

On approach to the Montcross Airport, the engine suddenly quit from lack of fuel and he had to land the airplane without power. Mr. Rosen was at the airport waiting on Jimmy to finish his cross country flight when he saw the Piper Cub coming in for landing without power. Mr. Rosen was startled, but saw that Jimmy had the airplane under control with his approach angle and was keeping his speed up while descending to land. After landing, Jimmy was able to use the momentum to get the airplane off of the runway and almost to the ramp. During the debrief with Mr. Rosen, Jimmy admitted that he did not get fuel in Salisbury, because according to his calculation he had enough fuel to make it back to Montcross with a thirty minute cushion.

Mr. Rosen asked, "Did you measure how much fuel you had in the tank before you left?"

Jimmy replied, "I measured the fuel in the tank and it had nine gallons of fuel which equates to two hours of flying time and my trip from Salisbury was only forty-five minutes. But, I did have to land and ask directions because I got lost coming back."

"Let's check the tank to see if there is any fuel left. The other problem is that you did not take into account the takeoff and landing you performed to get directions. That maneuver definitely increased your fuel burn."

The two men checked the tank and found that there was about a gallon of fuel left in the tank. Jimmy definitely knew that he had been lucky to be so close to the airport when the engine stopped. With a gallon of fuel in the tank he should have had enough to make it to the airport easily.

Mr. Rosen said to Jimmy, "You did not run out of fuel; the amount left should have been enough to make it safely to the airport and land under power. Did you turn on the carburetor heat when you started the descent into the landing pattern and did you make sure to occasionally open the throttle to keep the engine warm?"

Jimmy replied, "I did not push the carburetor heat on in the descent to the landing pattern and I did not open the throttle occasionally either. Both of those probably contributed to my engine stoppage. When the engine stopped, I set up the best glide, kept my airspeed up, but did not try to restart the engine. I knew I had enough altitude and speed to make a safe landing. Was that the proper procedure for the issue I had?"

"That was absolutely the safest maneuver you could have chosen. You instinctively knew, based on your instruments, that you had enough altitude and airspeed to get the airplane safely on the ground. I do not know if the airplane would have restarted if the carburetor had ice in it and if you had made the attempt then you could have been too distracted to maintain altitude and airspeed which as you know are the two keys to safe flying."

———

After the debrief a week ago, Mr. Rosen scheduled Jimmy's Civilian Aeronautics Authority check ride for today because he was pleased with his decision-making skills; and Jimmy had finished the requisite instruction and flying time. While Jimmy waited on the CAA's designated examiner to arrive at the Montcross Airport, he contemplated what maneuvers the examiner might ask him to perform. He felt like he should pass the check ride fairly easily today as long as he did not allow himself to get flustered by any mistakes he made flying the maneuvers. After Truett put the finishing touches on some paperwork for the city, he started a conversation with Jimmy about his upcoming check ride.

Truett asked, "Jimmy, do you think you will pass your check ride today? I've heard this examiner is a stickler for stall and spin recovery along with making sure you follow all the checklist procedures."

Jimmy replied, "I sure think I am ready and Mr. Rosen had me do a lot of stall and spin recoveries until I could do them without having to think through the process. My last cross country flight taught me to follow my checklist religiously. I had to make a dead stick landing, as you well know, because I failed to turn the carburetor heat on during my descent to landing here. Scary as it was to have the engine cut off, I am pleased that I followed the landing procedures and safely landed. If I do not allow my nerves to get the best of me, I am sure I will do just fine. Do you know if Mr. Rosen is going to be here later?"

Truett answered, "I heard about your incident and I am glad everything turned out all right because we both know what can happen if you don't follow procedures. I think Mr. Rosen will be here in about an hour for a lesson."

A stranger walked into the office and said, "I am Civilian Aeronautics Authority flight examiner, Alexander McCloud. Do you know if James Johnson has arrived yet?"

Jimmy walked up to Mr. McCloud, stuck out his hand in greeting, and responded, "I am James Johnson. I am pleased to meet you, Sir."

The two shook hands and got down to the business of the written test and check ride. If Jimmy did not pass the written portion of the two-part examination, he would have to wait a week to try again. The examiner and Jimmy used Mr. Rosen's office for the written exam which took an hour. Jimmy completed the exam in forty-five minutes and handed it to the examiner. While he graded the test, Mr. McCloud sent Jimmy out to the main office.

Jimmy walked out and said to Truett, "Well, I think I passed the written exam with a pretty high grade. It seemed like I knew the answer to every question from my studying and flying experience. Hopefully, my grade will say the same thing."

"That's good, Jimmy. I hope you pass. Mr. Rosen told me you had the highest grade in the CPTP class and that your school grades were improving which might help you get the coveted first choice for the Army Air Corps Aviation Cadet program. Good luck."

"Thanks, Truett, I am hoping that I will get the first pick, but if not, I will be happy to serve wherever the Army Air Corps places me."

Mr. McCloud walked out of Mr. Rosen's office after about fifteen minutes and told Jimmy that he had passed the written exam with a score of 92. Jimmy and the examiner donned their parachutes and walked to the J-3 for the flying portion of the examination. Jimmy did a complete and thorough pre-flight check and verified that the fuel tank was completely full and free of water. Jimmy climbed into the cockpit of the airplane, set the parking brake, and turned the ignition key to on. He exited the airplane and started it by pulling the prop through until engine coughed to life. He clambered into the back seat, put on the Gosport Helmet, and allowed the engine to warm up. Mr. McCloud got seated in the front and started giving instructions about the maneuvers he wanted Jimmy to fly during the check ride. After checking the magnetos for proper spark, Jimmy completed the rest of the pre-takeoff checklist. Everything was in tip-top shape with the airplane and Jimmy followed the instructions given by Mr. McCloud for the takeoff. Once one thousand feet above the ground but still over the airport, Mr. McCloud shut off the engine and made Jimmy do a safe dead stick landing. Jimmy pushed the carburetor heat on even though the engine was not running and then made a wide spiraling descent to the runway to land safely. Mr. McCloud pushed the mixture nob to full rich and the engine restarted immediately. They took off again and this time Mr. McCloud had him do a series of maneuvers that Jimmy completed fairly easily. Mr. McCloud took control and made the airplane stall and spin. Mr. McCloud returned the controls to Jimmy, who while a little flustered and making mistakes, did regain control of the airplane within the fifteen hundred foot altitude loss window as required by the examiner. Once the recovery was completed, Mr. McCloud told Jimmy to fly back to the airport and land.

Back on the ground with the airplane parked, Mr. McCloud said, "Congratulations, Mr. Johnson, you have earned your private pilot's wings. Your instructor should be very proud of you. You have great control over the airplane and you do not panic when things are not what you expect. Keep up the good work. Where do you plan on using your piloting skills?"

"Thank you, Sir. Hopefully I will be allowed to fly fighters after I complete the Army Air Corps Aviation Cadet Program. I want to fly for the Army and help win the war."

Mr. McCloud said, "You should do just fine in the Air Corps because you have a calmness when you fly that I've only seen in a few pilots. That calm demeanor is what helped them become some of the best pilots I know. Good luck."

Jimmy replied, "Thank you. Good luck to you as well, Sir."

Jimmy was ecstatic about earning his wings and he could not wait to get home to tell his parents. Before leaving the airport for home, he stopped by the main office to let Truett know that he now had his private pilot's wings.

Johnson Family Home ~ Montcross, North Carolina
Saturday - 4:00pm

. . . .

Jimmy returned home from his check ride ecstatic that he was now a private pilot and would be able to continue his dream of flying for the Army Air Corps. He could not wait to tell his family and Ray about it. The first person Jimmy saw while pulling into the driveway was his father. He was walking Lillie's bike up the driveway. From the looks of the bike and the bent tires, Lillie had been in a pretty significant wreck and he began to worry about his baby sister. Jimmy parked his car and walked over to his father.

"Dad, is Lillie going to be ok? From the looks of that bike, she had a terrible wreck."

"Dr. Preslar is in the house now with her and your Mom. She was unconscious for a little while after the accident but seems to be coming around now. I think she will be all right but we will not know for sure until she has some x-rays at the hospital to verify Dr. Preslar's suspicions of a broken arm."

Jimmy asked, getting more concerned by the minute, "What happened?"

"Lillie was riding her bike up and down the driveway when she decided she wants to ride around the block. She took off down the driveway and failed to turn at the bottom of the hill onto the sidewalk and ended up in the street at the same time a car was coming. Alfred Mather and his family were going to lunch downtown and Lillie rode right out in front of them before they could stop. Alfred hit her and the bike going about fifteen miles per hour. She was thrown a few feet from the bike and hit her head on the road. His wife Bea came rushing up the driveway to tell us what happened. Elizabeth called Dr. Preslar while your Mom and I went down to check on Lillie. She was still unconscious when we got to her. Alfred and I placed a blanket underneath her so that we could carry her into the house as gently as possible."

Jimmy said, "When should the ambulance get here? Can I do anything to help?"

His dad replied, "You can help by keeping Myra calm while we are at the hospital. She is very upset about her sister's accident. Elva is coming to cook supper for Elizabeth, Myra, and you. We will probably stay at the hospital overnight with Lillie. She is a frightened young lady right now."

The ambulance arrived at the front of the house, parked behind Mr. Mather's car, and the attendants prepared the gurney for Lillie's transportation to the hospital. Jimmy walked into the house to check on his little sister and what he saw was startling. She has bruises about her head and her left arm looked pretty bad, but she was awake and crying a little from the pain.

Jimmy said, "How are you feeling?"

Lillie wanly responded, "I hurt all over and I want to go to sleep, but Mommy won't let me."

Jimmy replied, "I know. Mom, how is she?"

His mom replied, "Dr. Preslar thinks she has a concussion and a broken left arm. There may be other injuries that Dr. Preslar cannot diagnose, That is why we are taking her to the hospital."

"How long ago did this happen?"

"About thirty minutes ago. Dr. Preslar has been here for twenty minutes preparing Lillie for the trip to the hospital."

"That is scary, Mother. Do you think she will be all right?"

"Yes, Jimmy. I remember almost the same thing happening to you at her age except you wrapped your bicycle around the tree in the back yard after you decided you would try to ride it down the sliding board. That was scary as well, but after a night in the hospital and a cast on your leg, you were as good as new in a few weeks. Lillie will be, too."

Dr. Preslar and the ambulance attendants put Lillie on the gurney and moved her to the ambulance for the ride to Charlotte Mercy Hospital. Bessie entered the ambulance with Lillie while Raymond said he would follow shortly in the car. Dr. Preslar got in his car and followed the ambulance to the hospital. Raymond remembered that Jimmy had taken his check ride today and had not thought to ask him about it.

His dad asked, "Jimmy, I know we have been a little preoccupied with Lillie, but how did you do with your check ride?"

"I did fine, Dad. I earned my private pilot's wings but that accomplishment pales in comparison to what is happening to Lillie."

His dad beamed, saying, "Congratulations, Son, I am so proud of your accomplishment. Tell me all about it when I get back from the hospital. Tell Elizabeth and Myra that I will call as soon as we know something about Lillie."

"I will, Dad. Tell Lillie we all love her and that we cannot wait until she comes home."

Raymond backed the family car out of the driveway to go to the hospital. After his dad left, Jimmy's thoughts turned to his baby sister and hoped that she would heal quickly. Jimmy walked in the house and was bombarded with questions from Myra about her little sister.

Myra, crying, said, "Jimmy, is Lillie going to be all right? She wouldn't wake up after the crash. I'm scared."

Jimmy cradled the ten-year old, Myra, in his arms and said as soothingly as possibly, "Myra, I know Lillie did not look good after the accident and she did not wake up for a long time, but I am sure she will be just fine. Dad told me that he would call us and let us know how Lillie is doing as soon as he can. Elva is on her way to make us supper and I bet that she will make your favorite dessert if you ask her. Would that make you feel better?"

Myra, wiping the tears from her eyes, replied, "Yes. I hope Lillie comes home soon."

He continued hugging Myra and said, "I do too, Myra. Do you want to say a prayer for her? You know that God is taking care of Lillie right now and helping the doctors fix her broken pieces."

"I know God is taking care of Lillie, and I want to say a prayer. God please help Lillie feel better and a make all her broken pieces well. Amen."

Jimmy and Elizabeth had Myra come with them to the den to play games which would hopefully distract her from thinking about Lillie. The two older siblings talked about things around town that would not arouse any more fear from Myra about the well-being of her sister. A little past five o'clock, Elva arrived to fix supper for the three of them, and she also told Myra that Lillie would be just fine. At seven, the phone rang and it was their dad calling to give them an update on Lillie.

Jimmy said, "Hello."

His dad replied, "Hello, Jimmy, just wanted to tell you that Lillie will be just fine. The doctors want to keep her several days because even though the x-rays did not reveal a skull fracture, they are concerned about the concussion and possible swelling."

"That's good news. Myra has been scared since you left and I think she will feel better after I tell her the news. Did Lillie break anything?"

"Tell Myra that Lillie will be just fine. Yes, there are two breaks in her left arm that they have set; and Lillie has a broken tail-bone that will take a little while in healing. She is one lucky young lady."

"Yes, she is. I am glad that the prognosis is good. Will you be coming home tonight or are you and Mom staying at the hospital?"

"Your Mom is staying overnight in Lillie's room to keep her company, and I will come home once visiting hours are over. Don't let Myra stay up too late, please."

"Thanks, Dad. I will give the girls the news and let them know that you will be home later tonight."

Jimmy hung up the phone and gave Myra and Elizabeth the news about Lillie. Myra's mood immediately improved. The next few days would tell the story, but for Jimmy, today had given him two blessings. First, he earned his wings; and second, his baby sister survived her accident. Jimmy silently gave thanks, *"Dear God thank you for your many blessings today and for sparing the life of Lillie. Please watch over her and help her get well quickly. In Jesus Name, amen."*

ARMY AIR CORPS RECRUITMENT STATION ~ CHARLOTTE, NORTH CAROLINA
JUNE 9, 1942

• • • • • • • • • • • • • • • • • • • •

On June 5, 1942, Jimmy received his high school diploma signifying his graduation from Montcross High School and with his grades, attendance, and pilot certificate, he was ready to move on to the next phase in flight training in the Army Air Corps. Today he would take his diploma and pilot certificate to the Charlotte Army Air Corps Recruiting Station to be inducted into the United States Army Air Corps. When Jimmy arrived at the AAC recruiting station, he was greeted by a line of recent high school graduates, but only a few held the coveted private pilot's certificate that was required to move directly into flight training after a period of boot camp. Jimmy waited for about a half-hour before moving to the head of the line. He was greeted by Corporal Graves who was the recruiting officer.

Jimmy presented his paperwork, saying, "James Johnson, reporting for flight training per the requirements of my Civilian Pilot Training Program contract."

Corporal Graves looked over the paperwork, saw that everything with the paperwork was in order; and said, "Mr. Johnson, as you know, you are required to enlist for the duration of the war plus six months."

Jimmy responded, "Yes, Sir. I am prepared to enlist for the duration."

Cpl. Graves replied, "Good. Sign your contract and walk down the hall to the last door on the left and enter. There you will receive your Army Air Corps written examination along with your physical and mental screenings."

Jimmy signed his enlistment paperwork and followed the hallway to the designated room where twenty other men were preparing to take the exam. Jimmy was overwhelmed by the size of the room and the number of candidates; and he knew that he must score very high on this written examination if he wanted to continue in the program. The war had taken a toll lately on the Army Air Corps training schedules and the Air Corps required many more pilots than the training program could safely turn out. There had been numerous accidents and fatalities because of the short time allowed to either qualify a pilot or wash him out. This examination was a quicker way to wash a pilot candidate out than waiting until they are six weeks into the program to find out they had no chance of ever flying for the AAF. He took a seat for the exam which according to the time on the blackboard would start in fifteen minutes.

A captain walked in and passed out the written examination to everyone in the room and told them that they had one hour to complete it. Jimmy started his exam only to find that it looked very similar to the written exam he passed just two weeks earlier to obtain his pilot's license, but with additional questions in physics and mathematics. He was very thankful that he had taken advanced physics and calculus as a senior at Montcross High. Those two classes not only gave him the weight for his final grade point average but also gave him the added benefit of understanding the questions being asked on this exam. At the forty-five minute mark, Jimmy left his seat to turn in the exam and was one of the first candidates to complete it. That could be seen as either good or bad. The captain told Jimmy that he could wait in the hall until everyone else completed the exam. He walked into the hallway, got a sip water from the fountain, and found a chair in which to wait until the others were finished. One by one, the young men filed out of the large sterile classroom to find some of their buddies and ask how they thought they had done on the exam. Everyone awaited the results so they could find out if they qualified for the Army Air Forces Cadet Training program.

One of Jimmy's CPTP classmates, Timothy Leary, came up to him, saying, "You always seemed to do well on the tests that Mr. Rosen gave in our ground school. How do you think you did on this one?"

Jimmy replied, "Timothy, the airplane, instrumentation, and flight questions did not seem all that bad compared with the written exam I took two weeks ago to qualify for my private pilot's license. What worried me was all the math and physics that was on the exam. I am certainly glad I took advanced physics and calculus this year because that understanding really helped me. I think I did well enough to qualify. How do you think you did on the exam?"

Timothy replied, "I think I did all right on the flying portion of the exam, but the math and physics really got me good. I don't think I got any of those questions right and will probably not qualify for flight training unless I decide to try the exam again in a few weeks with more studying."

Jimmy said, "You might surprise yourself, because some of the physics questions seemed fairly straightforward. Since we have our private pilot's license and if we qualify, we will be assigned to the primary flight phase of Army Air Corps flight training instead of basic flight training after boot camp."

Timothy responded, "It looks like the captain is posting the grades now. Let's go take a look."

―――――――――――

The captain announced, "The grades are now posted and ranked. If you passed the exam, go to the last door on the right for your physical and induction."

Jimmy and Timothy walked over to the bulletin board to see out how they did. Jimmy's name was fifth on the list and Timothy was twenty-first which meant they both qualified to enter the Army Air Corps as pilot cadets. They walked into another large sterile room where a corporal instructed them to strip for their physicals. Just like the Marine induction for Ray, Jimmy must be poked, prodded, and questioned to determine fitness for flight training before receiving his induction into the United States Army Air Corps. The poking and prodding mercifully ended after an hour and a half and everyone was allowed to dress. Those who were deemed unfit had been asked to leave, and out of thirty who started, only twenty-three remain to complete the enlistment. Jimmy swore his oath of allegiance and was sworn into the Army.

The corporal said, "Congratulations, all of you are now in the Army Air Corps. You will need to report to Fort Jackson in Columbia, South Carolina on June 16, 1942 by nine o'clock in the morning."

Jimmy pulled out of the recruiting station and drove home knowing that he was leaving in a week to start his service in the war as a pilot training cadet. He understood that the training would be tough and that he would have to overcome a lot just like Ray did when he went through Marine boot camp. Now, he knew that he could accomplish anything in order to fulfill his dream. His only thought, *I have to tell Mom I am leaving next week to go fly for the Army. She will be worried about me just like she worries about Ray. I hope everything turns out all right for both of us and we come home in one piece when the war is over.*

JOHNSON FAMILY HOME ~ MONTCROSS, NORTH CAROLINA
JUNE 15, 1942

• •

Jimmy awakened at seven this morning in his own bed for the last time. Today, Jimmy would leave from the Charlotte Bus Station to go to Columbia, South Carolina and Fort Jackson. At nine o'clock tomorrow morning, Jimmy would be inducted into the Army Air Corps Cadet Flying Program and assigned his boot camp facility to begin his training. Right now though, he needed to get up and do his chores. Elva would be here soon to cook breakfast and help with Lillie who was still recovering from her horrific biking accident three weeks ago. As he passed his parent's room on the way out the kitchen door, he overheard his mom talking to his dad about what today meant to them.

He paused just long enough to hear his mom say, "Raymond, we have not heard from Ray in the last ten days; do you think he's being sent overseas? And today, Jimmy will leave us for boot camp and training in the Army Air Corps. I am beginning to worry about the war just like I did when you left to fight in the Great War."

Jimmy did not wait to hear his father's response, but he continued through the house to the kitchen where he grabbed the egg basket and milk pail before walking out to the hen house and cow shed. While gathering the eggs, he pondered his mom's comments about Ray and began to wonder how the family would handle the grief if one of the brothers were killed or wounded in combat or training. He knew he must put these thoughts out of his head if he wanted to succeed in fulfilling his dream of serving in the Air Corps as a fighter or bomber pilot. Just like he did regarding the

CPTP flight training and his final two quarters at Montcross High School, Jimmy made a vow to put his entire effort behind learning everything he could and giving only his best effort. With the eggs gathered and Gertrude milked, he walked back to the kitchen where he hoped Elva would be cooking his favorite breakfast of pancakes with plenty of molasses syrup, sausage, and scrambled eggs. As he walked into the kitchen, he saw that his mother had come from her room and was making the coffee.

"Good morning, Mom."

"Good morning, how many eggs did the hens give us today?"

"The hens were in a fairly giving mood. They gave us two dozen and Gertrude was even more giving; she almost filled the pail."

"They must know that today is special. Elva wants to know if you would like pancakes, sausage, and scrambled eggs this morning."

"That would be wonderful, Mom! After breakfast, I need to go downtown for a little while to pick up the stationery I ordered along with a couple of other things. Do you have any plans for the day?"

"I was hoping we could have a talk like I had with Ray before you leave. You have made me so proud with how much you have matured and everything you had to overcome to earn your pilot's wings. I just hope that the maturity and perseverance will carry over to your service in the Air Corps."

Jimmy, knowing that his mother was having difficulty with the fact that her second son was leaving, replied, "I could use some of the advice you gave Ray as well. I do not know what to expect in the Army and I am a little apprehensive about leaving. Was Ray apprehensive when he left? He never really showed any fear when we talked about it other than to say that he was worried how Sara was going to do with the separation. I think he approached it like it was just another problem to solve or obstacle to overcome."

His mom said, "Jimmy, Ray was definitely worried when he left for boot camp because he did not know if he had the mental fortitude to handle the constant berating and harassment of the boot camp drill instructors. At one point in his training, Ray told me that he almost believed that he was as worthless as his drill instructor made him feel until he remembered that he could overcome anything life threw at him because he knew the Lord was watching over him and would not allow him to receive any more than he could handle. When Ray told me that he gave his problems to Jesus, while according to his drill instructor his butt belonged to him, that helped me know that Ray would be just fine with whatever life, the Marine Corps, or the enemy threw at him. What about you, Jimmy? Are you going to be all right if you have a similar issue?"

Jimmy answered, "After everything that has happened over the last six months, I have gone from the lowest of lows when Mr. Mayerhofer died in the plane crash to the highest of highs when I earned my private pilot's wings and graduated from high school. But, there have been many times over that same period when I questioned whether I could go one more day with all the pain and turmoil in my life. Mr. Cameron's constant harassment really began to take a toll on me mentally and I came close to giving up on my dream. After the altercation with Mr. Cameron on the day I soloed, I knew that I would be fine once I made those three takeoffs and landings while Dad and Ray watched. The quiet way Ray handled that situation that morning really showed me what brotherly love was all about, and that if Ray could handle boot camp and fulfill his dream of serving in the same outfit as Dad, then I could handle anything life threw at me and I could fulfill my own dream. I know there will be setbacks and problems during my Army training, but I will approach them with the same ideals that you, Dad, and Ray have shown me."

His mom, hiding her face to wipe away a tear, replied, "Yes, Jimmy, you will be able to do all things because Christ will strengthen you just like He does all of us when we face any type of trial or tribulation. I love you very much and I want you to know how proud I am of you. I will miss you just like I miss Ray, but I know both of you are doing exactly what you feel you must in our country's current trial."

"Thanks, Mom. I love you, too. I know how hard it is going to be on the entire family having both Ray and me away in the service especially while Lillie is still recovering from her accident. She does seem to be healing pretty well. What has Dr. Preslar said about her long term prognosis with the head injury? I know her arm and tailbone will heal."

"Lillie's head injury has caused some problems with her balance; but Dr. Preslar and the specialists at Charlotte Mercy Hospital seem to think that in about a month or so, Lillie will be as good as new. I am not so sure. Ever since the accident, she has had slurred speech and blurred vision which worries me a great deal, but the doctors that have been treating Lillie say that is normal with someone who had as severe an accident as she did. Time will tell and I will continue to pray for her just like I pray for all my children."

Raymond, Elizabeth, and Myra walked into the kitchen just as Bessie told Jimmy that she must go wake up Lillie and get her downstairs for breakfast with the family. This accident had been a trial for Bessie and the loss of her two sons to the military for service had almost pushed her past her breaking point. He did not know how his mother had kept it all together with all of the upheaval. He promised himself that today he would help his mom with anything she needed until the time came for him to leave for Charlotte and the unknown world of Army boot camp.

Jimmy said, "Mom, can I help you with Lillie this morning? I need to tell her that I am leaving for a school trip."

His mom replied, "That would be nice Jimmy. And unlike Ray, with Lillie in this condition, we are going to tell her that you are going on a school trip so that she will not worry about you along with everything else that has happened to her."

Raymond broke in, saying, "Bessie, do you really think that is a good idea? What if something happens to Jimmy? How are we going to explain it Lillie? I think it is better if she knows the truth that Jimmy is going off to war like Ray did."

Bessie responded curtly, "Raymond, I think right now, my only hope is that Lillie will recover from her accident. Once she is a little farther along in her healing, then we can tell her that Jimmy is in the Army like Ray is in the Marines. Is that all right?"

"Bessie, while I think it is best that we not hide anything of this magnitude from any of the children, in this case it might be best. I will let you determine when it is safe to tell Lillie that Jimmy has joined the Army Air Corps."

Jimmy and Bessie climbed the stairs to Myra and Lillie's room to find Lillie working hard to get dressed by herself. This made Bessie very proud of the little girl because that showed determination on Lillie's part to get better. Lillie looked up from trying to pull on her overalls to see her mother and Jimmy in the doorway to her room.

Lillie exclaimed, "Mommy, Jimmy! Uh…What are you doing here?"

Jimmy replied, "Coming to help you get dressed, but it looks like we are just about too late for that. How's your arm feeling?"

Lillie replied, "An…uh…other little bit and I would have had it. Uh, uh, uh…I can't button them."

Jimmy laughed, saying, "I could not button my overalls either at your age. Looks like you did pretty well though."

Bessie asked Lillie, "How does your arm feel this morning?"

"Hurts Mommy. Wh…uh…en…will it stop?"

"After breakfast, you can have some medicine to make it feel better? How are your eyes?"

"Mommy, still fuzzy."

"Did you go to the bathroom this morning by yourself? Or, did Myra have to help you?"

"I…uh…did it."

Bessie knowing that Lillie had required help getting to and from the bathroom, said, "That's wonderful. Sounds like you are getting better. I think you will be well before you know it!"

Jimmy said, "Lillie, I have something to tell you."

"Uh….What?"

Jimmy says, "I am going a trip for school today and I will be gone for a pretty long time. I will write you as much as I can to check on you and to tell you how I am doing."

Lillie replied, "Like Ray? Did you join the Marines too?"

Jimmy, with his eyes asking his mom, who nodded yes, whether it was all right to tell Lillie the truth, answered, "Yes, like Ray. No, I did not join the Marines. Lillie, I am going into the Army Air Corps to fly airplanes like I have been doing since Christmas."

Lillie, with tears in her eyes and still stuttering, exclaimed, "Why is everyone leaving me? I don't want you to leave!"

Jimmy, holding back his own tears, said, "Lillie, you know about the war that we are fighting against Germany and Japan. I have to help our country win just like Ray is helping. I will be gone a little while this time and then I will get to come home and see you like Ray did. I am sorry you feel like everyone is leaving you but Mom, Dad, Elizabeth, and Myra will still be here with you. I am sure they will help you when you need something just like Ray and I do. I love you, Lillie."

"I love you, too. Please come home soon."

"I will come home just as soon as I can. Now, we need to get down to breakfast before all of the pancakes and sausage are gone."

"My favorite!", Lillie exclaimed.

Jimmy picked up Lillie and carried her down the stairs, then put her down. From the stairs, she walked unaided to the kitchen which was a wonderful step in the right direction for her recovery. Bessie was overcome with joy as Lillie slowly made her way to the kitchen by herself. Raymond took one look at Lillie walking unaided into the kitchen, gave a shout of joy himself, and told Lillie that she was definitely going to be as good as new very soon. He gave his youngest daughter a big hug for this momentous accomplishment, then helped her to her seat.

Once seated, Lillie said, "Daddy, Jimmy is leaving. He will help our country win just like Ray."

Raymond responded, "Yes he is, Lillie. "

"I don't want him to leave."

"Lillie, I will be here with Mom, Elizabeth, Myra, and you. I am sure they will both come home as soon as they can."

Elizabeth said, "Jimmy, are you going to be better than Ray at writing us letters while you are away? I have not seen a letter from Ray in a couple of weeks and it was a couple of weeks before that when the last letter came."

Jimmy replied, "I cannot tell you whether or not I will be any better than Ray at letter writing. It will depend on how much work I have to do during boot camp and then primary flight training. All I can say is that I will try."

"That is all I can ask. Good luck, Jimmy. Be careful and come home soon," Elizabeth replied.

"I will do my best, Elizabeth."

Elva served them breakfast and everyone enjoyed the pancakes, sausage, and scrambled eggs. Lillie seemed to enjoy her food more than usual and ate three big pancakes this morning and two sausage links. Jimmy ate more than his normal share of the outstanding breakfast knowing that this would the next to last meal prepared by Elva for him before he left this evening.

After breakfast, Jimmy got into the brothers' Model-A sedan to go pick up his stationery and go to the post office for stamps to mail his letters home. While he was at the post office, Jimmy picked up three one-dollar war stamps for his sisters to put in their war stamp booklets. After a few more errands, Jimmy went home to pack for his departure to Fort Jackson and boot camp later this afternoon. After packing, Jimmy found his dad in the study during his lunch hour going over some bills and other assorted paperwork. Jimmy wanted to talk with his dad about what to expect in Army boot camp.

"Dad, in about two hours, I leave for Army basic training and I do not know how well I will do. I am sure you probably had the same conversation with Ray before he left for Marine boot camp, but how do you think Army basic training will be?"

"I do not know about Army basic but I know that Marine basic pushes you to the limit both physically and mentally. If you keep the same attitude you had when having to face down Mr. Cameron every time you took a lesson, I think you will be just fine. Work hard on anything you are assigned and never tell anyone you cannot do something. If they are asking you do to something hard, they already know you will have trouble accomplishing it; but they want to make sure you will not quit. Learn everything you can as if your life depended on it because one day that lesson might just save your life. You have proven to me over the last six months that you have more fortitude and wherewithal than I thought. As you told me almost six months ago, you just coasted through life doing just enough to get by, but now you have had to work to achieve your pilot's wings and you have proven to yourself that you can accomplish anything. Continue with that attitude and I believe you will do just fine. I am proud of you, Son. Keep working hard and you will make it back here safe and sound."

Jimmy replied, "Thanks, Dad. I will do my best."

———

At three o'clock, Bessie, Elizabeth, Myra, and Lille said their goodbyes before Raymond took Jimmy to the Charlotte Bus Station. At the bus station, as Jimmy gathered his belongings from the trunk, his dad gave him ten dollars to pay for the hotel room and buy a meal since his induction would not occur until tomorrow morning at nine o'clock. Jimmy gave his father a hug and told him goodbye just before boarding the bus bound for Columbia. As with Ray, this was a bittersweet parting with their dad not knowing when and if either son would ever return home.

Ray Deploys to the Pacific

* *

On Saturday, June 13, 1942, the Marines of G Company, 2nd Battalion, 1st Marine Regiment of the First Marine Division boarded the train in New River, North Carolina with an unknown destination. This train was carrying the entire 2nd Battalion and Ray knew instinctively that his battalion must be preparing to leave the country. The entire 2nd platoon was berthed in one Pullman car with uniformed porters serving the needs of the travelers throughout the long train trip across the country. The platoon sergeant made sure that his men handled the trip well and did not cause any problems for the negro porters and conductors. The days on the train were spent playing cards, reading, and sleeping along with eating the delicious meals that were served in the luxurious dining car. During several stops, Ray was assigned by Platoon Sergeant Dick Hoggren to guard duty on the platforms where the trains stopped to prevent civilians from boarding the military only transports. Ray had many conversations with his machine gun squad during the trip and even got to know Private Lawson Jeffrey better. Since Private Jeffrey had returned from the brig, he was a lot better soldier and one of the men Ray had come to count on during the rigorous training of the past month.

During dinner one evening on the train, Ray sat down with Sergeant Hoggren to talk about what they might be into in the very near future.

Ray asked Sergeant Dick Hoggren, "What's the dope on this movement? Are we shipping out for good now?"

"I think we are heading out of the country for training, then possible deployment in an offensive action against the Japanese. I still think we are six months away from an actual engagement because we really need more amphibious training to be ready to face the formidable Japanese Army."

"That makes some sense. I certainly hope that we will have the chance to prepare before being thrust into combat, because I do not feel all that certain how I will react once the bullets start flying. My goal is not to let any of my squad down during our first combat experience."

"I have been watching you since you first arrived, Ray. You have nothing to worry about because I have tried, just like your drill instructor at Parris Island, everything that I could think of to push you to your breaking point. I know that I have pushed you close to reaching it, but you have always proved to me that you have some reserve that helped you persevere through even the toughest problems. I am more worried about our younger platoon members like Private George Mason who seems so young on occasion; especially when he must solve an overwhelming field problem. I've watched him come very close to cutting and running, but somehow he manages to squeak through the exercise after you give him encouragement. How you help your men and push them is the sign that you will be a fine combat leader."

"Thanks, Dick. I am just following the example set, not only by father when he manages the men at the rail yard, but also how you lead the men in our platoon as well. I will work hard to make sure that all the men in my squad come through safely."

"Ray, the only thing you can do is the best you can do and in war there is a rule that young men die. The other rule is that you can't change the rule about young men dying. You will do just fine because you lead your squad by an example that even Private Jeffrey seems willing to follow now."

Sergeant Hoggren and most of the squad leaders of second platoon had become pretty good friends and they all worked together to make it through specific field problems and other training exercises. This camaraderie would have to hold true if the 2nd Platoon men of G Company were going to make it through the war.

———

On Thursday, June 18, 1942, the 2nd Battalion's troop train arrived in Oakland, California; and the men were transferred to buses for the ride over the Oakland Bay Bridge to the San Francisco Wharf where the USS George F. Elliott was moored. The men were ordered aboard the ship, but the battalion commander, Lieutenant Colonel Pollack, made sure that the men were granted as much liberty as possible before the ship left the harbor. The men of 2nd Platoon were ordered by their platoon leader to supervise the loading of nine-thousand tons of ammunition, small arms, hand grenades, mortar shells and other explosives onto one of the attack cargo ships. The loading was not to combat load specification which gave the men the idea that there would be time for training and other exercises before they were expected to storm a hostile beach and attack the enemy.[1]

Ray and the rest of the men grumbled about the accommodations on the Elliott because they were cramped with the bunks strung five high in one of the holds where no air circulated. The head facilities were open trough urinals and open area toilets and as one of the 2nd Battalion members commented, "Forget privacy, forget odors, forget everything, sleep with your weapons, sleep with your pack, sleep with your life jacket, no sheets, just green USMC blankets, sleep in your clothing."[2] On Sunday, June 21st, the men of the 2nd Battalion were told that they should send their families postcards with their new Fleet Marine Forces

---

1 • Bartsch, William H., Victory Fever on Guadalcanal, p. 30

2 • Bartsch, William H., Victory Fever on Guadalcanal, p. 29.

mailing address because tomorrow they were sailing. Ray mailed the prescribed post cards to his family in Montcross and Sara in Edenton. He also made sure to send everyone a letter letting them know that he was fine and in San Francisco. That was all he could tell them because he knew any more information would be grounds for the censors to either cut out entire passages of his letter or not allow it through at all. These letters would be the last letters Ray would send for a long period of time.

On Monday, June 22, 1942, the USS George F. Elliott slowly sailed under the Golden Gate Bridge and past Alcatraz Island with Ray and his fellow Marines on board. The enlisted soldiers had no idea where they were going, but they all knew instinctively that this trip was the beginning of their combat tour and would last for the duration of the war or until they were sent home or buried. As the ship slowly churned out into the Pacific, Ray could not help but think, "I hope I do my duty well and lead my comrades in a manner that brings them all home safely. If I should fail at that, I hope no one will be disappointed in me." Ray said a silent prayer for safety and watched as the Golden Gate Bridge faded into the distance.

Epilogue

Jimmy had joined the Army Air Corps and was in boot camp at Keesler Field in Mississippi. He would be learning everything about being an Army Air Corps pilot. This was the first step on his road to deploying overseas to fight either in Europe or the Pacific. His journey would be a long one from basic through commissioning as an officer in the Army Air Corps. He had already seen a lot of tragedy in the last six months of his eighteenth year, but he would see much more over the next three years.

Ray and his comrades did not know it, but their current voyage would end in confrontation with the enemy on a previously unknown island, Guadalcanal. The squad under his command would demonstrate courage under fire, and Ray would distinguish himself as a fine leader during the four and a half months that the First Marine Division was deployed on the island. Ray's platoon would see action in other battles to retake Japanese Island fortresses and would distinguish itself among the best of the best fighting forces. The force would fight numerous engagements of merciless combat with a maniacal Japanese enemy driven by the code of Bushido.

The Johnson family of Montcross, North Carolina were typical of the small town families that grew up during the Great Depression and came of age during World War II. This story was just one of many that could be told about other families in other small towns through these great United States. It was because of the supreme sacrifices of these families that the country was able to overcome enemies on two completely different fronts. From the home front to the battlefront, the United States overcame its enemies because the home front worked in concert to provide, support, and deliver whatever the battlefront needed to win the conflict.

www.ingramcontent.com/pod-product-compliance
Lightning Source LLC
Chambersburg PA
CBHW020211260626
47156CB00002B/323